Marianna's Resolve

Stephanie Logan

No Part of this publication may be
reproduced, stored in a retrieval system, or
transmitted in any form or by any means
electronic, mechanical, photocopying,
recording, or otherwise, without written
permission of the publisher.

Published by Stephanie Logan Publications.

Dedication

For my husband Chris.   I love you.
Thank you for your patience, love, and
encouragement while I devoted
countless hours towards writing.   You
are the best.   You are my everything.

CHAPTER ONE

What's happening?

Marianna woke with a start. Someone was yelling. It scared her. She didn't like it when people were mad. She crept out of bed to listen by the door.

"No. No. You can't have her." Mama yelled.

Why was Mama so upset? Who was she talking to? Was it Papa? No that wasn't right, Mama and Papa never yelled like that to each other. Mama sounded scared.

She pulled her door open a crack to peek out trying to stay as silent as she could. There were soldiers in the house. Why were there soldiers in the house? They said something to Mama.

"No. Please," Mama said.

She was crying. Oh no. Something

really bad was happening.

"I don't give a damn what your orders are, you are not taking our daughter," Papa said.

He ran up to one of the soldiers and grabbed him around both arms and tried to push him back out the door. But the other soldier hit Papa in the head really hard. Papa fell onto the floor. He wasn't moving.

"Please. Please don't. Please." Mama begged. "I will give you anything that you want. Please don't take her."

"Orders." The soldier that Papa had grabbed said.

He pushed Mama out of the way. She tripped over Papa and fell to the floor. Both soldiers walked towards Marianna's room.

"Oh no. They're coming for me."

She backed away from the door.

The door slammed open. She backed up to the corner of her room holding her hands up in front of her.

The man who hit Papa stepped into her room. "You have to come with us child."

She shook her head over and over again. "No. I don't want to. I want to stay with Mama and Papa. Please, I don't want to." She cried. She was so scared.

Mama grabbed his ankle making him

stumble.   "Don't take her.   Please."

He kicked his leg making her let go of him. He looked at her with the scariest look on his face.   He was going to hurt her, Marianna could tell.   He lifted his foot to kick Mama.

"NO!   Please.   I will come with you.   Just don't hurt her.   Please."   Marianna said stepping towards the soldier hands clasped in front of her.

The man reached out and grabbed her by the wrist and pulled her towards him.

"No, no, you can't take her please," Mama begged.   She kneeled at the soldier's feet. She reached up and grabbed the man's arm that was holding Marianna.

"Get off me."   The man said as he kicked Mama in the head to get her away from him. She jumped back up, continuing to beg.
The man ignored her.   He pulled Marianna out of her room and out of her house.

She looked back as she was being pulled away from her home.

Mama was kneeling with her hands clasped in front of her, her face soaked with tears.   Papa was still laying on the floor unmoving blood leaking from his head.

There was a shriek.   She turned to look down the road.   A soldier was dragging somebody across the ground kicking and screaming. A bunch of wagons lined up the street filled with people. The soldier that had her wrist was leading her to one of those wagons.

He pulled open the back gate of the wagon.

"Get in." He ordered. She looked up into the dark wagon. There was movement of several more people inside. She hesitated. She didn't want to go. She wanted to go back to Mama and Papa. She wanted to know if Papa was alright. She wanted to hug Mama so that she would stop crying.

The soldier tugged on her arm really hard. She whimpered.

"Get in, or I will make you get in." He said.

She looked at him. His face was so angry. She didn't want him to hurt her. She climbed up and into the wagon.

The wagon was so dark that she couldn't see anything. She crawled until she felt the foot of somebody under her hand. She felt around her a little bit to find a bench to sit on. There was no bench. The person was sitting on the floor. She adjusted herself so that her back was against the wall of the wagon, sat, and wrapped her arms around her legs.   Then the tears started coming and she couldn't make them stop.

There were quiet cries of several more people in the wagon.   And there was still an occasional scream outside, but the sound was buffered by the walls and door of the wagon.

She looked up to try and see who else was in the wagon with her, but it was too dark for her eyes to make anything out.   She shook.   She had always been afraid of the dark, but this was so much worse.   She was terrified.   What could be happening? Where was she being taken?

The door opened again, and she saw Rayden being lifted into the wagon.   She was glad that she would know somebody who was with her.   But she felt bad that he was being taken away from his family too. When were they going to be allowed to come back home?

The door closed again blanketing the wagon in darkness.   A shiver of fear rattled through her.

"Rayden."   She whispered.

"Who's there?   What's going on?"   He

whispered back, the sound growing closer as he crawled towards her.

"It's me, Marianna." She said still whispering. She didn't want to get in trouble by being too loud.

"Anna I'm so glad that it's you. Well, I'm not glad that you are here too...Just..."

"It's ok. I understand. I'm glad you are here too." She interrupted. She knew how he felt because she felt the same way.

"Do you know what's happening? Why are they doing this?" He asked.

"I don't know. I was asleep when they came. I didn't hear why they were taking us or where we are supposed to be going. I'm scared." She said.

"Me too." He said.

He touched her on the shoulder as he was trying to find his way to her. She grabbed his hand, pulled it down and squeezed it. She snuggled up to him as he sat with his back against the wall next to her.

"Who else is in here?" Rayden asked.

"I don't know." She hadn't thought to find out who else was in the Wagon with her.

"I'm here, Citron. I was the first one in the wagon. I've counted twelve people since I got here." He said from the far corner all the way inside.

Citron was here too. Oh no. Would she ever be able to get away from him? He was so annoying. But what was she thinking? At least she was with people that she knew. Was that a good thing or a bad thing?

"Twelve. This cart could easily carry forty people." Somebody said just across from her.

"Who's there?" She whispered not recognizing the voice.

"Oaklee. I'm Councilman Raven's daughter." She said a little louder than Marianna was comfortable with.

She found herself scrunching down. Rayden pulled his hand away from hers and wrapped his arm around her pulling her in closer to him. She felt a little bit better.

"You're not a kid. How old are you? I thought they were only taking kids?" Somebody else said. "Oh yeah sorry, It's Ginger. I've only seen kids so far. I'm ten."

"I'm thirty-two. I'm not a child. In fact, I have two children who were put in a different wagon. I don't know why this is happening any more than any of you, but I did notice that they seem to be taking more children than adults.   Is there anyone else in here that is an adult?"   Oaklee asked.

"Me."   A deep man's voice said.

"Who are you?"   Marianna asked after a long silence.

"Daniel Pryor."   He said sounding annoyed.

"Wow.   Oh shit.   You're the son of the most powerful noble in the Kingdom.   I guess they're not discriminating by status. I'm Steven by the way.   I'm eighteen."   He said.

"No, I guess not," Daniel said.   "I offered a year's salary worth of money each to the soldiers that came to get me, but they refused.   All they would say about why they were taking me was that they had orders.   I didn't know that I wasn't the only one being taken until I was dragged outside. That's when I saw the wagons lined down the street.   I have never heard of something like this happening before.

"Maybe we can escape.   I'm Alex Cunningham, thirteen, hey Anna, Rayden.

"If we all rush the door the next time somebody opens it, then we can get out." He said.

Marianna found herself smiling a tiny bit.

Alex was her best friend. She would have Rayden and Alex with her. Things didn't seem as scary. She liked his idea of escaping. They could all attack at once.

"I think we should try. There are a lot of us. There were only two soldiers that came to get me, so we might only have to get away from a couple. And our parents and families can come out and fight with us. We can open the other wagons and let everyone out." Marianna said with excitement.

"We can't," Oaklee said.

"We should at least try," Marianna argued.

"We can't," Oaklee said with more intensity. "They will kill you. And anyone trying to help you escape will be killed as well."

"Maybe they won't," Alex said sounding defeated and sad.

"Uh-uh. We can't." A girl whispered so quietly that Marianna barely heard her.

"We can't. If we want to have any hope, we need to survive tonight.

"I had just put my children to bed. I was finishing up with some cleaning, and then I was going to bed myself. The soldiers broke down my door. By the time I could react one of the soldiers had already grabbed me and was dragging me toward the doorway. The other was already in my children's room when my husband tried to stop him. The soldier stabbed him through the chest before my husband could do or say anything. He was dead in moments.

"They did it without hesitation. These men have killed before, and they have no problem doing it again. But I guess anybody who is willing to break into people's homes and take their children in the night don't have a moral compass.

"They dragged me out to the streets. My children were screaming, begging me to help them. I tried to fight to get to them, I tried, but my attempts were pointless, the man who held me was too strong and I was too weak.

"The soldier pulled me towards this wagon, and my children were dragged to a separate wagon. As they were doing this, I watched as the group within the wagon they were being taken to, attempt an escape. They did it the same way you want to do it. They killed every person who attempted to escape. As far as I could tell only three people survived. By the Great Spirits

mercy, my children were not hurt.   The
survivors were separated into different
wagons.   One of the little girls was brought
to this wagon."   Oaklee explained.

"It was me."   The little girl who had also
rejected the idea of escaping cried.   "My
name is Annelese.   They killed my brother.
He was only ten.   He was just doing what
they told him to do.   He didn't want to."
She whimpered.

"At least ten people were killed during
that attempt.   I have never seen anything
like it.   I've only seen one person die in my
life before tonight, and she died sick in her
bed.   There was so much blood.   Ten
people, mostly children, in moments lost
their lives.

"I don't want to die.   I want to see my
children again.   I don't know if that is even
possible.   But I would much rather live long
enough to see where we are going, and if
there is a way for me to be reunited with
them.   If there is any chance to see my kids
again, I must take it.   Nothing else matters.
My husband is dead; my children are all I
have left to live for.   And I choose to live for
them."   Oaklee said.

Marianna sat back letting her head rest

back on the wall of the wagon. She didn't know what to do. She was too scared to actually do anything. She couldn't attack a soldier. She was only ten. She didn't want to die.

She sat there staring at the darkness. Everybody went quiet. After the possibility of escape was gone, there was nothing left to be said. The door opened a bunch more times to let people in. And just like Ginger had said it was mostly kids, young kids, littler than her by a lot.

The Wagon got filled so full that she was squished up against Rayden and the person sitting on the other side of her. She didn't think they would ever stop opening the door to push more people into the wagon. There was no more room, but they managed to somehow fit more people in.

Eventually, they did stop cramming people in. That's when the wagon started to move.

Another wave of fear swept through her. She cried again. What if she never saw Mama and Papa again. She wasn't even sure if her Papa was alive, he wasn't moving the last time she saw him. What if he was dead? What would Mama do if her husband and child were both gone?

There was crying throughout the wagon. Younger and older people, boys and girls, they were all crying. Not even the grownups could do anything; there was no chance that she could. Rayden rubbed her back with his hand. He was trying to make her feel better, but it wasn't working.

Because of the bumping from the movement of the wagon and because she was so tired Marianna fell asleep. When she woke up a little bit of light was beaming in through the cracks of the wood in the wagon.

Was it daytime? Had she slept the whole time? She looked around the cramped interior and saw that almost everyone was asleep. How long had they been moving?

Rayden's head was resting against her shoulder, so she tried to stay still so that she wouldn't wake him. Alex was just across from her with his head slumped forward bobbing with the bumps. He would be sore when he woke up. They would all be sore. She was sore. Her legs were still drawn up in front of her, and the space was so tiny that she couldn't stretch them out without kicking somebody. Her arms felt like they hadn't moved in hours, which she figured was probably true.

Some of the younger kids had crawled on top of older people and fallen asleep. Maybe it made them feel better to know that they weren't alone.

There were a bunch more people that she recognized from her town, but no more of her close friends.   She wasn't sure how she felt about that.   Did that mean that they had not been taken, if so why were they allowed to stay with their families while she was taken from hers?   Maybe they were in different wagons, and none of her friends had escaped.   She would possibly be able to see her friends again, but that would mean that they were also being taken away.   She leaned her head back and cried.

A while later the wagon came to a stop. Rayden lifted his head off her and looked towards the door, as did most of the wagons inhabitants.   They were not disappointed as the door was opened just a short time later. Nobody spoke.   If they were all like Marianna, they were all too scared to speak. She had never been around so many people who were so quiet.   That was scary by itself.

All the people within her wagon were

being ushered outside. When Marianna stepped out, the sun was so bright that it blinded her for a moment. Her eyes hurt, and she did everything she could to not close them. It wasn't long before her eyes adjusted.

They had stopped in some random clear patch of wilderness. Trees were all around her. Were they in a forest? There was a tiny almost unnoticeable trail that the wagons had made, but no other signs of people. They were alone. Well as alone as thousands of prisoners and hundreds of soldiers could be.

The soldiers were sorting the people from the wagons into groups as they exited. Boys and girls were moved to opposite sides of the clearing. They separated the boys and girls by age. Anybody under the age of seven was placed in one line, people under thirteen were placed in another line, and anybody over the age of thirteen was placed in the third line.

They made everybody over the age of thirteen get back into the wagons. Marianna had never felt so happy to not be thirteen yet. Were they going to be taken somewhere else? She didn't like that possibility. The older people were probably the only ones who could figure out a way to escape. There were a bunch of grownups in that group. What if the only grownups that she would be left with were the soldiers that had taken them all? She shivered at that thought.

The older people were kept separated by male and female as they were put back into the wagons. She didn't know what to think about that. Why were boys and girls being kept away from each other? Why was anybody being separated?

The soldiers made all the younger kids get back into the wagons with the older people. Boys were put with boys and girls with girls. The older groups were told to keep the young ones quiet while the middle-aged group including Marianna were put to work. The boys were taken out into the trees. She didn't know why or what they were doing.

The soldiers led Marianna's group to an open-topped wagon. The wagon was filled with different tools, dishes, toiletries, and other random supplies.

Marianna was given a shovel. "What am I supposed to do with this?" She asked fearing the worst. Shovels were used to dig graves.   The man who handed it to her didn't answer her or even acknowledge that she was speaking.   She was made to continue moving with the group.

The girls were all spread out into small groups of three and four.   Not everyone had shovels, so they were ordered to do other things.   Marianna's group included two other girls.   Both looked younger than her.

They were told to dig any areas that were elevated.   They had to fill in any depressions with the dirt that they had dug. She was already so sore from riding for so long in the wagon, but she didn't want to make the soldiers mad at her, so she dug. She and the other two girls in her tiny group dug all day long.   It was early in the fall, so the sun wasn't very hot, but that didn't stop her from being drenched in sweat by the end of the day.

She had only been given three small bathroom breaks where she was taken to an area in the woods to go, and then she was given some water and a piece of stale bread and dried meat to eat.   The other girls were each taken at different times to take the same short breaks.   They weren't allowed to speak with each other.   Anytime they tried the soldiers would separate them so that it wasn't even possible anymore. So, Marianna stopped trying to talk with them, and they stopped trying to talk with her.

The clearing was so quiet. Small groups worked at the different tasks assigned to them working as silent drones. The only sounds were shovels hitting dirt, axes hitting trees, and soldiers ordering people to do their random tasks.

Marianna learned in a short time that it was easier to work as a group. Without a need to discuss what they were doing; her group had created a system of working so that each of them had equal time at the required jobs to move the dirt. One person would break the hard dirt, another would shovel the soft broken dirt out away, and the third would move the dirt to a depression.

They would rotate jobs as needed to rest the different sets of muscles that each job required. The most difficult task by far for her was moving the heavy loads of dirt to fill in the depressions. She would have to scoop and lift the heavy dirt, place the handle end of the shovel against her body, and walking with care, without spilling it or tripping, walk to where a dip would be and empty her shovel.   Her arms would shake, and her back would scream in pain as she carried the heavy loads.   Once she dumped several heaps of dirt, she would have to pack the dirt down.   First, she would smash it with the shovel over and over until it was fairly flat, and then finally she would stomp on it until it no longer moved under her feet.

The entire process was exhausting, and within just a couple of trips, she would be so tired that her muscles shook almost refusing to keep working.   Thank the Great Spirits, by the time she got to that point she and her working partners were changing positions.

The youngest girl in her group had a harder time breaking up the dirt.   It was because she was so little, and her body weight was barely enough on top of the shovel to make any headway.   So instead of kicking the shovel with one leg like Marianna and the other girl was doing, she would have to jump with both feet to put her whole weight on the shovel.   This was very tiring, and before long she would be heaving with every breath.   Her technique also caused her to fall several times when she would miss the shovel, or the dirt would give way easier than she was expecting and she would tumble over the shovel.   She ended up with several cuts and scrapes on her knees, hands, and elbows.

The third girl was able to accomplish each job well.   It was as if she understood what she was doing better than both Marianna and the youngest girl.   Marianna guessed that she had spent a lot of time working outside in the fields around the outskirts of the town.

By the time night fell, she was so exhausted she could barely move. Everybody else working in the clearing was showing similar signs of weariness.   The soldiers finally let them stop working.   They led them back to the wagons.   Marianna didn't want to go back to the wagon, but she was desperate to sit.   As she was ushered back towards the wagon she was given a final bathroom break and another measly meal and drink of water.   She climbed up into the wagon without resistance.   She was too tired to struggle, and it would be pointless anyway.

Her wagon was filled with all girls in her age group, who looked just as tired and miserable as she felt.   She intended to ask for names and learn about her wagon-mates, but she was too tired.   She ate her tiny meal and immediately fell asleep with her head on the shoulder of another girl who didn't protest her using her as a makeshift pillow. Many of the girls used one another in a way to be more comfortable as they slept.

The next day they were all moved out of the wagons again first thing in the morning. They were lined up, given a bathroom break and small meal of meat and bread, and then her age group was given the task to keep the youngest children as quiet and happy as possible.   This job was even more tiresome mentally.   Any time the young ones would get rowdy, loud, or start crying, a soldier would pound on the side of the wagon causing everyone to jump, and some of the youngsters to cry more.   It was their job to quiet them as much as possible and keep them happy.

If they were unable to maintain the little ones' peace and near silence, a soldier would remove the loud child, publicly beat them until they fell quiet, and then return them to the wagon to be tended to.

The soldier would then remove the oldest girl who was sitting nearest to the loud child, publicly beat them, and return them to the wagon.   Every child that was beaten would make Marianna feel guilty.   But every time she was removed from the wagon to receive a beating she grew angry at the small children.   The guards seemed to grab her the most often.   She was one of the biggest in her group, and she should have somehow been able to stop the children from being loud, and therefore, prevented the beating.

She didn't get to see Alex, Rayden, or any of the other people she had originally traveled with.   She would cycle back and forth between manual labor that would leave her physically exhausted, and tending to the obnoxious little ones which would make her want to pull out her hair in frustration.

She never got to work with the same people.   Some dynamics worked well together, and they were able to get a lot accomplished within a day, while other groups barely made it through the day without starting an argument, which would lead to anybody involved in the argument being made an example of by the soldiers. She only needed that retribution once.

She had gotten into an argument with one of the other girls about how to handle a misbehaving child.   The girl was almost six years old and was being loud to draw attention to their wagon.   She knew what her actions would do, and yet she did it anyway.   Marianna wanted to hit her until she was obedient; the girl she was arguing with wanted to talk to her.   She said that the girl just missed her mummy and was acting up because of it.   They were all missing someone.   That didn't give the brat a reason to bring negative attention to everyone in their wagon.

She and the girl that she disagreed with, had an argument that grew loud enough to draw the guards' attention.   They were both pulled from the wagon.

Two soldiers held Marianna by her arms. They pulled her clothes off, leaving her exposed to everyone.   She was so embarrassed.   A third soldier whipped her over and over again until she was unable to hold herself up because of the pain.   She was thrown back into the wagon naked. The other girl followed shortly after, but she for some reason was allowed to keep her clothes on.   Marianna felt unclean and angry at the other girl for having it easier.

She was able to get her clothes back the next day at the beginning of her physical labor shift.   She resolved that she would not allow another incident to allow her to be in such a compromising situation in front of everyone.   She found her patience with the little ones growing shorter and shorter.   So, she would smack them as soon as they came close to acting up or getting loud.   She would not allow another one of their actions to cause her to be punished.

She preferred her days when she was working, as opposed to those when she was caring for the children.   When she was working, she was responsible for herself and nobody else.   Only her actions or inactions would lead to punishment.   When she was with the little children, that wasn't the case. More and more often caretakers were punished for the actions of the little ones. This included her, even if she had nothing to do with them making noise or not listening. It wasn't fair.   And she hated them for it. She couldn't do anything right when she was with them.

The next several weeks continued in such a manner.   Or what she guessed was several weeks.   After the first several days in captivity, she was unable to keep track of time, and all her days blended together.

Over time they built up a decent sized camp.

One day, months into their imprisonment, they were given a chance to sleep in the barracks that they had spent so much time building. They were still separated into gender and age groups. They were never left unguarded no matter what they were doing; there was always somebody watching them.

Once they were assigned their barracks, they were assigned their more permanent duties in the camp. Marianna didn't know what any other group was responsible for, and she didn't really care. She just wanted to do what she was responsible for. The Great Spirits had mercy on her and did not require her to tend to the unruly children any longer. Instead, she was given kitchen duty.

Some of the boys within her age group were required to hunt and bring back game, for her and her counterparts to clean and prepare. Other boys and girls were employed to gather plants, fruits, and vegetables. She was fine with these jobs. They left her dependent on herself, and so she was able to avoid almost all punishment.

She worked with the same ten girls for the next year. For the first several months she would still find herself crying at night. Or if she ever got a quiet moment she would long for her Mama and Papa to hold her again. But eventually, she stopped. Her prayers to the Great Spirits were not going to be answered. She was never going to see her Mama and Papa again. She was alone, even though she was surrounded by people.

Her next couple years she worked with a couple different groups of girls. She never learned any of their names, their ages, or anything else about them. Conversations between camp members were limited to work related information only, and they were always being monitored.

She wasn't going to give any reason to let one of the soldiers find a motive to punish her because it would take her days or even weeks sometimes to fully recover from their brutal punishments.

She kept to herself, and as long as she did that she was safe. She had no other concerns. She must protect herself because nobody else was going to.

CHAPTER TWO

Marianna's New Life

Marianna got out of her bed and got dressed in the gray shirt and skirts that she had been provided. The rags were so disgusting looking from constant wear, that she could never tell if they were clean or dirty. She ran her fingers through her hair, which was dirty. She knew that she had auburn hair, but the greasy, dirty appearance made it difficult to see the true color.

She was up before most of the other girls, as with every morning, in fact, she was up earlier than most of the camp. Her duty required her to be up to prepare breakfast before everyone else got going.

She liked her assigned duty, as much as anyone could like a job as an indentured servant.   She was good at it.   She was never late, never overwhelmed by the workload, and therefore never had to be punished; when she had the luxury of working with only middle-agers that was.

Some days she would be forced to work with young ones as helpers.   She hated them being around.   They were always causing trouble; they didn't listen, and they never did what they were supposed to be doing.   Every time they would come into her kitchen they would be more of a burden then anything.   And their constant disobedience would lead to her receive a beating for not getting the day's work done promptly.

She never knew whether her day would include the young ones until she got to her kitchen.   So, she never knew if she would have an easy day or not.   Fifteen other girls worked with her in the kitchen on a regular basis.   They were all decent at their duties also.   And they all worked pretty well as a team.   Marianna was responsible for washing, peeling, and prepping all the vegetables that were needed for a meal. Because her job would have to be completed before the other girls could cook and serve, she was required to wake up extra early to get to work.

She only had one soldier guarding her during the early morning hours. It was usually the same man. He was older, maybe in his fifties, judging by the gray hair and deep-set wrinkles on his face. He was one of the oldest looking soldiers that she saw around the camp, but his age didn't hinder his abilities to do his job. He was quick. Anybody who stepped out of line even a little, would not get past him and his swift hands. He was brutal when he was required to dish out a beating. She dreaded the days he was with her when the young ones were assigned to her kitchen.

She remembered one unforgettable beating that she received from him a couple of months back. She was confident that she had a few broken ribs afterward. She had trouble breathing, moving, or raising her arms above her head. And sleeping was nearly impossible because her rib injuries were on both sides, so there was no way for her to lay without being in pain. She still had pain on one side if she coughed or sneezed too hard.

She left the barracks. It was still dark out.

The moon and stars were still visible. It would be at least an hour before there were any signs of dawns approach. As she walked towards the kitchen, she passed by a group of soldiers lined up. Her heart began to race as she saw them. They had never gathered in such a way before. And most of the soldiers were still asleep at this hour. Why were they out this morning?

She slowed to try and hear what the commanding officer was saying to them, but her guard refused to let her stop. He pushed her forward making her stumble over her own feet almost falling to the ground. She was able to stop the fall, just barely, and regain her footing to keep moving towards the kitchen. It wouldn't matter if she knew what they were doing anyway. Knowing more would just make her worry more about things she had no control over.

She continued to the kitchen where even on days when she had the young ones working with her things made sense. She was lucky. The young ones would not be coming to work. She was content with that. She sat on her stool and began working.

As she prepared thousands of root and

vine vegetables that would be used to feed the thousands of people, she tried to not think of what the early morning assemblage of soldiers could mean. It wasn't long before she found herself lost in the monotony of her duties. The sun had already started creeping through the windows, and she didn't even notice when her prep partner had gotten there to prepare the meat.

People began shuffling into the dining area to eat before moving towards their prospective duties for the day. Her kitchen filled up with the morning chatter of people, dishes of food being served, and soldiers barking orders. It was comfortable because it was familiar, but she was not happy. She feared that she would never know true happiness again.

Meal times were the only respite that the camp members had, which also gave them the only opportunity throughout the day to speak to one another. Meal times were short, just enough time to get the food from the line, shovel it into their mouths and then get to work. But somehow people still managed to find time to talk to one another.

Meal times were also the only time that the

separated groups were able to co-mingle, men, women, and children.   Everybody needed to eat, and they only had one kitchen, so everybody was served in the same place, at the same time.   It was still done in a guarded and orderly fashion so that nobody got any ideas about escaping or plotting any sort of revolt, but it gave them all a chance to communicate with others.

Marianna rarely spoke to anybody else.   It was too difficult for her.   She didn't want to do anything that could allow her to become attached to anything or anyone again.   So, she refused to allow herself to get close to anybody, which was a pretty easy thing to keep up with when she only had a few minutes a day, and only sometimes, where she had access to others.

Her access was an even shorter amount of time than everyone else who came to eat. As a kitchen attendant, it was her job to make sure everybody was fed promptly, for each meal.   She didn't have time to socialize; because by the time one service time for a meal was complete it was time to start preparing for the next one.

But on a very rare occasion, she was actually able to talk to Alex or Rayden.

They were the only connection she had to her previous life; the only connection she had to anything really. Rayden was the same pleasant, happy person she had grown up with. Somehow, he was able to stay optimistic through all the dark times. But over the course of the few years, Alex had grown angry, cold, and distant. Marianna shared this sentiment. Her life had become a nightmare, and no matter what she did she couldn't wake up.

This happened to be one of those rare days. She had completed her prep work a little bit earlier than anticipated, and so she had a few extra minutes to spare. She stepped out of the kitchen and into the dining area. It was weird to do that while it was still full of people, she didn't usually get to enter the dining room until after the meal, and only to clean. She ate her own food in the kitchen between meals.

She found a seat near the corner. She had already eaten her breakfast while she was prepping. But she still wanted to sit for a moment and do nothing for a time. She closed her eyes and leaned her head back on her chair and took a deep relaxing breath. Before she even had time to let her mind begin wandering, Rayden plopped in a chair across from her slamming his tray on the table, making her jump.

"Hey Anna. It's been a while since you've been out here. How's life been treating you?" He said cheerfully.

She opened her eyes and glared at him. She hated how happy he could be. Life was bleak, but he didn't seem to notice.

"I'm a slave. How do you think life's been treating me?" She said keeping her tone cool. She kept her head resting on the back of the chair.

"Yeah." He said in an unconcerned air. "We've almost got the farmlands ready to start sowing. If we're lucky and get a good harvest, in a few months, we might be able to have fresh food instead of the near rotten stuff we've been getting."

She snickered. "Lucky. Only you would think that it was lucky to get the things that most civilized people have access to."

Secretly she did feel a little bit of excitement at the thought of fresh food. It would be so much easier to prepare food that didn't squish beneath her fingers as she peeled and cut it. She longed for a day when she didn't spend most of her time cutting out the rotten, moldy, bad spots in the food that she was preparing to serve to people. How much free time would she have then?

"Is that a smile I see?" He said grinning at her with a mouth full of food.

"What? No." She said realizing he was right. She was smiling. She couldn't let that happen. She couldn't allow herself to accept this new life. Looking forward to things, accepting that her future was in this place, was very dangerous.

He shrugged taking another large bite of food, but he still stared at her with his grinning cheerful expression. She wanted to get up and walk away from it and him, but if she got up her tiny moment of rest would be taken from her.

Alex sat between them in his usual gloomy mood. His emotions made more sense to her. He stared into space not acknowledging either of them. It was as if he only sat with them as an old habit, not because of any actual desire to connect with either of them. Marianna had a similar feeling. Only Rayden with his sunny disposition appeared to be openly content with their tiny moments of companionship.

And it was only due to his persistence that they all still came together at all.

Marianna only admitted to herself, that she actually enjoyed their time together, even if it was only minutes at a time sometimes weeks apart from each meetup.

"So, what have you been doing Alex?   I haven't seen you, in almost as much time as it's been since I saw Anna last.   Why is that? Have you been avoiding me?"   Rayden said with his mouth full of his last bite of food.

Alex's eyes had a defiant look to them that surprised Marianna.

Rayden smiled broadly at the look.   She frowned in confusion at the two of them. She was curious.   What was Rayden referring to?

"I've been doing my job.   Just like you." Alex muttered sounding annoyed.

"Yes well, all jobs have their importance. Anna and I are both responsible for feeding people, in one way or another, and you, well, you know what you do."   Rayden said putting his chin in his hand and resting his elbow on the table.   He had a knowing smile.

Alex glared at him but said nothing.

"Alright," Marianna said, her curiosity

getting the best of her.   "What do you do?
I know that Rayden has been clearing, and
preparing the fields to start planting, but I've
never known what you were assigned to."

Alex shook his head over and over again.

Rayden smiled even bigger if that was
possible.   "Yeah, Alex, why don't you tell
her?"

Alex looked up at her with some look, was
it sorrow, regret, shame?   She couldn't tell.
He looked back at Rayden at first glaring
again, but then not.   His eyes started
watering.

Rayden's smile disappeared in an instant,
and he frowned.

"I empty out the toilets.   He caught me
doing it one day."   He said gesturing to
Rayden who gave a half smile for a moment
but then let it drop as he saw how upset Alex
was.   Rayden was an optimist and a joker
who could find humor in anything, but he
wasn't cruel.   He wasn't one to intentionally
cause someone pain or sorrow.

"It's a disgusting job."   Alex continued.
"But you don't know why I do it."   He said
to Rayden as he wiped his face.

Rayden's normal carefree look was gone
as the seriousness of Alex's statement was

evident.   He scowled and shook his head. "No, I don't know."

"It was a punishment.   I refused to..." Marianna's guard grabbed him from his seat by his arm, before he could finish what he was saying, and dragged him out of the dining room.

Marianna watched as Alex was dragged away.   She didn't react.   She just watched and then turned to Rayden.   He was looking down at his empty plate with an obvious look of guilt.   He took a deep breath in looked up at Marianna and gave her a halfhearted smile.

"You think he's gonna finish that?"   He said gesturing to Alex's barely touched tray of food.

Marianna chuckled despite herself.   She looked toward the door where Alex had been taken and shook her head.   "No, I don't think he will be back for a while."

He nodded while grabbing Alex's plate of food taking a bite.   "Do you want some?" He said with his mouth full of food, holding the tray up to her.

"Not really, thanks."   She said pursing her lips.

He scowled at her.   "Are you sure?   I

never see you eat.   You've gotten so skinny. It worries me a little."

But he wasn't too worried because he took another large bite.

"Don't worry about me.   I ate already in the kitchen."

He shrugged and shoveled the rest of the food into his mouth.

"Do you think he'll be alright?"   Rayden asked looking towards the door.

Marianna didn't know, and even though his optimism sickened her, she couldn't be the one to shatter it.   He was actually able to find a way to not slip into the same state of depression that she, Alex, and many of the other camp inhabitants spent most of their time in.   And she needed his happiness to let her keep a slight feeling of hope.   So, she feigned her own optimism.

She smiled as genuinely as she could, hoping that he wouldn't see through her guise. "I'm sure he's fine.   If his punishment before was emptying the toilets, what do you think they will make him do now?   Lick them clean, it can't get much worse than that."

He broke out in laughter so loud that everyone in the room turned to look at him.

He smacked the table several times as his jovial nature alighted.   It was his usual warm, comforting spirit, which surprisingly made her truly smile.

Several other people smiled a little bit too, which made her smile even more.   His joy was contagious.   And it was stronger and more resilient than all the horrible depressing days that they had been forced to experience.

Her guard walked back into the dining room with sweat dripping from his brow and a dangerous look on his face.

Rayden stopped laughing but remained smiling.

"I've got to get back to the kitchen.   I've been out here too long."   Marianna said getting up and grabbing both empty trays.

Rayden nodded fervently as he watched the intimidating guard move into the room. Despite his happy demeanor, he was just as terrified of the man as she was.

"I'll see you soon, I hope."   He said moving around the perimeter of the room to avoid the guard's gaze and left the building.

She followed his example moving around the edge of the room collecting empty trays as she went to look like she had been keeping herself busy.

She moved back into the kitchen and deposited her collected trays in the sink to be washed, and then moved back to her usual spot to prepare the vegetables for the next meal.

The guard stepped into the prep area of the kitchen a little bit later with four more following behind. That wasn't normal. Her heart pounded as she watched them move into the room. She tried to look busy peeling the potato that was in her hand, but her hands were shaking so badly, and she was paying too little attention to what she was doing that she sliced through her finger.

Involuntarily she yelped out in pain, but then regretted it. The last thing she wanted to do was draw attention to herself. That was why she tried to keep to herself most of the time, to avoid any unwanted attention.

Amazingly her little outburst went unnoticed by the guards. She wiped her bleeding finger on her shirt and continued peeling. She was afraid to do anything else. What were they doing? She watched the guards walk up to three of the other kitchen workers and say something to them. One of the other girls was led out of the kitchen by a guard, and then the remaining guards moved towards her.

She breathed so hard that she was making herself dizzy. She didn't know what to do.

"How old are you?" Her regular guard asked. She sat staring in terror unable to think or make herself speak.

He grabbed her by the arm and pulled her to her feet. She started crying.

"How old are you?" He repeated sounding exasperated.

"I... I'm twelve, sir. I think. I might be thirteen now." She managed to say through terrified gasps.

"Take her." He said handing her off to one of the other guards.

She walked on trembling legs as he led her out of the kitchen and into the light of day. She never had access to the sun. She always got to her job before the sun came up and left after it went down. She didn't realize how much she missed it.

She was taken down the road in a direction she had never had a chance to go. She didn't know where anything was other than her barracks, the kitchen dining room, and the washhouse where she was occasionally given a chance to clean herself.

All the buildings looked the same. Which made sense, being that they were all built using the same trees that were harvested from the forest that surrounded them. She was amazed at how much it looked like a small city instead of a temporary camp that had only begun being built two years before.

After walking for about ten minutes, they finally stopped in an empty clearing. She looked around and saw a bunch of other people being led to the same place. The panic rose in her again as she considered the possibilities. Had the soldiers brought them all to be killed? She shook her head trying to dismiss the idea, but no matter what she did she couldn't shake it.

The soldiers had everybody line up. For the first time since getting to the camp, they didn't put them in separate lines for boys and girls. That scared her too. She had gotten to a point where she knew what to expect, and now that was gone.

She looked around as everybody was being gathered in one place. She was in the field that Rayden was talking about, the one that had been cleared to be used to grow food. Maybe they just needed more people to do the planting. That thought didn't comfort her as much as she would have liked, but it did give her a little bit of hope that she wasn't going to be killed.

After lining everyone up in rows, the soldiers moved up and down the lines. They pulled individuals from the ranks. Boys and girls alike were being grabbed, but not everyone. It was a strange thing. She didn't know which group she would want to be a part of. Not that she had any say in the matter or knowledge of what each group would be doing.

Two guards moved up her line growing closer to her. Her legs shook again, and her breathing hastened. What was happening?

A guard stepped in front of her; he looked at her inspecting her head to toe. He shook his head and moved past her. She sighed in relief. She wasn't sure why. There was no way for her to know which way was better, but she just felt that she was lucky.

After all the people in the lines had been picked through, her group was led away from the field and back into the camp. They were taken down an adjacent street to the one she had grown familiar with. It had a similar setup to the one she was accustomed to.

The boys and girls were separated again, which gave her a huge sense of relief. Things were starting to make sense again. There was an order to things in the camp, and when that order wasn't followed, it made her feel lost.

Slowly different girls were taken to different areas of this new part of camp. Finally, she got to a place where a set of guards directed her and three other girls into a large building.

As the door was opened, she heard chaos.

Her world was closing in on her as she stepped into the warehouse-style room filled with screaming, crying, maddening young ones.

CHAPTER THREE

Punishment

Marianna opened her eyes but just lay in her bed. She hated waking up because waking up meant that she would have to go to her duty of caring for and teaching the young ones. She had been at her new duty for over ten months.

The other girls working with her kept telling her that it would get better. That it would get easier once she got to know the children, and learned each of their unique personalities. They were wrong. She hated it more and more the longer she was with them.

They were annoying, selfish, inconsiderate brats that intentionally did things to make her get into trouble. They were monsters.

And she was in charge of teaching them to listen to the guards, to obey all orders given, and to do so without complaint.   It was impossible.   They weren't learning.   And it didn't matter how much the children were punished for misbehaving, they would still misbehave knowing that they would be punished.

She forced herself out of her bed.   She would have to gather the children and lead them to the dining room for breakfast.

Her bed was in the same building as the young ones.   This meant that most nights she was up with at least one of them sick, or crying, or scared about something, so she was always tired.   She had five other young women with her helping to tend to forty-eight children.   That meant eight young ones to every helper.   And their young ones were not separated by gender. They had boys and girls to tend to.

At first, they separated the young ones by age and had one helper with each age from three to eight years old.   They would rotate groups, every two days to prevent anyone getting burned out by caring for one group longest.   But that method wasn't very productive.   The number in each group wasn't even, meaning that the girls responsible for the four and six-year old's had several more children to tend to than the other age groups.

But that wasn't the biggest problem. The three and four-year-old groups needed the most attention, and so they were late for almost all their tasks, meaning that whoever the caregiver was would almost always get a beating. Every time the children would start to connect with one caretaker they would switch caretakers and cause unrest in the young ones.

After several weeks of trying this technique without success, they changed tactics. Each person got eight children. They tried to separate the different ages as evenly as they could, and then those eight children were assigned to one caretaker indefinitely.

This was how they had been doing things for the last several months, and it did appear to work better, for everyone except for Marianna. She had somehow gotten all the most defiant children in the bunch. And what was even more infuriating was that her assigned children had no problem listening to the other caretakers, they just refused to listen to her.

She stepped out into the great room to find one of her assigned brats screaming at another child. Marianna didn't care what she was screaming about; they were always screaming about something, she just wanted to make her stop.

She stomped over to the girl and grabbed her by the arm tugging her away from the other child.

"She wouldn't..."

"I don't care. You are supposed to be dressed and ready to go eat. I don't care what she did, or you did, or who did what first. Get dressed now!" Marianna demanded.

The seven-year-old Ava started crying. Why were they always crying?

"But..."

"Do you really want to start the day like this? I said get dressed. If you are not dressed and lined up at the door by the time I round up the others, I will leave you behind. You will not get any breakfast, and I will make sure that whatever we are assigned, you will get the hardest job." Marianna said through clenched teeth.

She was trying to stay calm with them.

She didn't like the angry shouting person that she was when she was around them.

She released the girl, who took off running towards the chest of clothes. Marianna rounded the large room gathering up the other seven children that she was assigned. She clothed the youngest ones while encouraging the older ones to dress themselves. Within minutes she had everyone lined up and ready to leave, including Ava.

She nodded contently at herself as she looked around the large room. Almost everyone else was ready also. Once again, her group of young ones was one of the last to be ready to leave. She huffed irritated and motioned for her group to leave the building.

They moved down the street in individual lines towards the dining hall. Before even reaching the adjacent street, Marianna's eight-year-old Giles took off running towards some middle-aged boy that was walking down the street.

"Gaaahh. Get back in line. You know that you are not allowed to separate from the group." Marianna yelled running after the boy.

"James? James is that you?" Giles said as he approached the middle-aged boy. He looked to be around ten.

The boy turned and squealed in a way that grated on Marianna's spine. It was shrill and annoying. "Giles! Oh, merciful spirits. Brother, you're here. You're here. I didn't know where you were. I didn't know if you were still alive. I'm so glad that you are alright." He said as he wrapped Giles up in a gratifying embrace. Apparently, it was James.

Marianna didn't know why it bothered her so much to watch the reunion. Maybe it was because she knew that she didn't have any family to be reunited with. Perhaps it was because she knew that two guards had witnessed the reunion and she was responsible for keeping her assigned young ones under control, and she had failed. She would be punished; again.

But it was more than her imminent beating that bothered her. It was that everybody around her was able to find trivial things to give them joy, and she had nothing. She at least had contentment in her kitchen duty, but that had been taken from her. Now she had these horrible, annoying brats to contend with and they made her even more miserable.

One of the guards got to the reminiscing pair before Marianna could. He didn't look angry, he looked disappointed.

"Come on boy. Get back where you belong." The Guard said grabbing Giles by the arm and pulling him away from James.

James looked devastated, and Giles started crying like a blubbering baby.

Marianna got to them at that point. "I'm sorry. I will take him." She said trying to sound respectful, but instead, she just sounded like she was snapping at the guard.

He looked at her dangerously. Why was he angrier at her, than at the person who had been disobedient?

"You. You are responsible for this? Again? Can you never keep your charges under control? How many times have you been punished this week alone? Nobody else seems so motivated to suffer beatings." He shouted at her.

"I'm sorry. They won't listen to me. I try, but they just won't." She whispered feeling defeated.

The guard huffed. He motioned for Giles to get back in line, which he did quickly and without complaint.

Marianna stared as Giles did as he was told by somebody else again. Why wouldn't the young ones ever do what she told them? Why did they always defy her? Did they enjoy watching her receive punishments for their disobedience?

The guard grabbed Marianna by the arm, and then grabbed James by the other and walked them over to one of the whipping posts that stood at the intersection between two streets. This put the post in the most visible spot.

It was meant to be public, even when nobody stopped to ogle the recipients of the whippings, it still instilled fear, and fear helped prevent rampant disobedience.

He instructed James to remove his shirt and then turned to Marianna to instruct her of the same, but she was already doing it. As he had already mentioned, this was not her first time. She already had gashes across her back and legs in multiple stages of healing.

She was creating a new record for herself. She had never been whipped before the assignment that was given to her group, or before breakfast for that matter. She hated her life.   When she was working in the kitchen, she rarely got in trouble, and when she did she never got whipped she only received beatings.   Yes, some of those beatings were brutal, but they weren't the same as the indescribable pain and embarrassment that a whipping caused. Since starting her new assignment, she received multiple beatings and whippings every month.   But the last two months had been particularly bad.

The guard lashed the rope around her wrists and then slid the rope through the ring at the top of the pole.   He pulled the rope which forced her arms up tight.   He stretched the rope so tightly that she was forced to stand on her toes.   It was still early, and the post was dripping with dew, and so the slimy mildew that grew on the post made it too slippery for her to lean against for balance.   So, she stood in place like a pendulum shifting her weight from one foot to the other.   She couldn't stand on both feet without it putting a painful strain on her wrists and shoulders.

He tied James to the post as well.   They were both forced to stand pressed against each other's sides.   He was already whimpering and trembling beside her. He looked at her with tears running down her face.

"What do I do?" He asked with a shaky voice.

She stared at him disbelievingly. Had he never been whipped before, or watched someone who had been? It was one of the more extreme forms of punishment because it could sometimes leave the punished unable to work for a couple of days, although she never got that luxury, but it was still common enough. Surely, he would have had it done at least once, or at least watched somebody at some time in the years since they arrived.

Pain was coming. There was nothing to do but bear it. There was no other thing that she experienced that was as real as pain. She could not rely on being able to eat, or a place to sleep, she certainly couldn't rely on which job she was assigned to, but she could always rely on pain to come to her.

She turned from his crying face and stared at a droplet of water that was hanging on the post ready to fall at any moment. Her face was stoic. The droplet of water fell.

The whip cracked, and a moment later, the

burning scream of pain sliced across her back.   Her vision went white, and her knees went weak and gave out beneath her.   She hung by her arms for several moments before the initial shock of the pain subsided. Her vision came back to her, and she was able to get her feet back under her to stand back up.

The whip snapped again followed by an agonized scream from James.

Another crack and another blinding shock of pain this time across her butt and right upper thigh.   She gasped.   Her whole body trembled as she tried to recover from the strike as much as she could.

Another scream from James followed by quiet sobs beside her, and moments later another crack and then instant darkness.

Sometime later, she couldn't know how long, her vision came back to her.   She was still tied to the post.   James cried beside her. She was dangling from her arms, and an excruciating ache ran through her left shoulder.

She shakily tried to move her feet back under her to stand up and take the pressure off her arms, but her mind moved sluggishly, and her legs wobbled like jelly.

She lifted her head up to look at James. She needed to know if he was also having trouble standing. A burning, aching pain radiated from her head and down her neck. Her vision was foggy, and her mind was still too slow to understand what was going on.

She dropped her head back down and tried again to hold her weight up with her legs, but they refused to move.

She closed her eyes. Her head swam. The whip hadn't made any more sounds. Perhaps it was over. She opened her eyes again as there was movement beside her. Again her notion of time was unclear, and she wasn't sure how long her eyes had been closed.

The guard untied James, who was still on his feet but was whimpering. She watched as he walked away. Thick red dripping lines streaked his back. He was given his shirt but would be foolish to put it on before the blood dried.

Marianna made that mistake the first time that she had been whipped. When she tried to remove her shirt later in the evening, she found that it was stuck on all her wounds and had to be torn back open to remove the shirt.

The guard moved back and untied the rope holding Marianna up. She fell in a heap on the ground unable to make herself move.

He reached down and grabbed her arm to pull her to her feet. She screamed as the pain in her shoulder exploded.

He dropped her arm in shock. He leaned over her and rolled her over to get a better look at her. He pressed on her shoulder, and she screeched.

"It's dislocated. Great Spirits damn you. You'll have to go to the Medica. Get up." He said with an exasperated tone.

Marianna lifted her head in an attempt to stand up, but her head swam with the movement and dropped back down. He leaned over her with a look of confusion. He wrapped his hand around her head to help her sit up, white star-bursts danced in her eyes. He said something that she couldn't understand and gently lowered her head back down to the ground. He looked at his hand, and it was covered in blood. Was that her blood?

She closed her eyes for what felt like moments, but when she opened them again, she was being carried somewhere. Pain shot through her back, through her shoulder, and through the back of her head and neck. She tried to move so that she could be in a less painful position, but she couldn't.

She closed her eyes again. When she opened them, she was being lowered onto something soft. People were talking around her, but everything was muffled. Somebody leaned over her, but she couldn't make out the face. They said some incoherent thing and poked at her. But all she felt was a dull unspecified pain.

But then whoever was standing over her grabbed her arm and pushed on it. A loud pop resounded in her ears, at the same time an overwhelming pain and an odd rush of relief moved through her shoulder. The sudden shock of pain brought her back into awareness.

"Wha...Where am I?" She managed to ask. But it was difficult to form the full thought needed to get the words out.

A young woman leaned over her and said something. She couldn't understand what the woman was saying. The woman said something else in a soft, comforting tone that reminded her of her Mama's voice. She smiled and closed her eyes again. A warm darkness enveloped her.

CHAPTER FOUR

The Medica

Marianna opened her eyes and looked around.   She was lying in a very comfortable bed and covered with a thick, soft, warm comforter.   She attempted to sit up on the bed, but her head pounded with every beat of her heart.   She groaned and set her head back on her bed.

The same young woman from before ran up to her.   "No, no.   Don't you try to get up?   You need your rest.   You should take the opportunity while you have it.   We don't get much time for rest around here, do we?"   She chirped as she pulled the blanket back up to cover Marianna.

"Where am I?   What's going on?" Marianna asked feeling grateful for the comfort in the caring act.   Her words were still sluggish, but her thoughts felt clearer.

"You are in the Medica.   You were unfortunately struck in the head during your lashing.   It jostled your mind a bit.   If you don't rest appropriately, you may never get all your faculties back.   So, stay down, and let me tend to you."   She said.

The memory of her being whipped came back to her.   The strike that knocked her unconscious must have been what she was referring to.   It all made sense now.

"Who are you?"   She asked.   She was actually enjoying the woman's company and didn't want her to leave.

She smiled.   She had a kind face.   "My name is Kania.   And what can I call you?"

"Marianna.   How old are you?   I'm sorry.   That's rude.   It's just that you look older than most of the people that I see, other than guards."   She blurted.

Kania smiled warmly.   "I'm thirty-five. And I take no offense to your question."

Marianna thought about that for a moment.   "Really?   I've never seen anyone older than twenty.   And I used to work in the kitchen.   I saw everyone."

"Well, there is a very good reason for that.

You are assigned to the child side of the camp.   I am a part of the adult side."

"Adult side?   There are more adults here?"   Marianna asked.

Kania chuckled.   It was the warmest most genuine sound.   It made Marianna smile at its comforting nature.   "Hmm... Yes, there are probably as many adults as there are children, I would guess, though I don't know that for sure.   But by the number of children that I have seen coming through here, it seems a plausible guess."

"You have helped other children after a whipping?"

Kania's smile faltered, but only for a moment.   "Well yes.   But I usually treat illnesses rather than injuries.   The guards are generally pretty good at keeping the punishments to a less ruthless nature.   It is rare for me to have to tend to somebody when a punishment gets out of hand.   Your life-threatening injury, I believe was unintentional.   The guard did not mean to strike you in the head."

"Life-threatening?"   She asked shocked by the possibility.

"Well yes.   You almost died quite a few times over the last several days.   But you are strong, and I believe that you will pull through this all very well." She said. Her words should have upset Marianna, but her sweet voice and the tone she used when she spoke made it difficult. But it was frightening to know that she had almost died more than once.

"Wait did you say several days. How long have I been here?"

"Hmm. Um...I think it will be a week tomorrow. It was touch and go there for a while. You kept falling into fits. We had to tie you down for a bit, to keep you from hurting yourself even more. I don't think your body could have handled any more shock." Kania explained.

Marianna pushed the blanket down to learn whether she was still tied down or not. The movement caused a searing pain in her shoulder that took her breath away. And when she inadvertently shuddered from the sudden pain, the familiar burning sting of her whipped back and leg struck her. She pulled in a sharp breath through her teeth.

"Now, hold still. You aren't ready to be getting up yet. Can I ask you something?" Kania said as she helped Marianna lay back into a position that didn't hurt as much.

"I guess.   What do you want to ask?"

"You had a lot of healed and healing lashes across your back, and other bruises from beatings I would guess.   What has gotten you into so much trouble?"   Her voice rang with true concern.   Marianna wasn't used to anybody caring about her in any way.

"I never used to get in trouble like that. When I worked in the kitchen, I would get in trouble maybe once every couple of weeks or even months sometimes.   But they moved me.   Now I must care for the young ones, and if they don't listen to me, then I get in trouble.   And they never listen to me. Ever.   So, I'm always in trouble now."   Her face grew hot as she talked about it.

Kania nodded.   "I see.   Hmm.   I thought it might be because you were deliberately disobedient."   She said.   She still smiled but sounded a little disappointed.

"No.   I want to be obedient, but the young ones refuse to be obedient to me." She said hoping to remove any disappointment that Kania would have towards her.   For some reason, it actually upset her a little.   She wasn't sure why she cared what Kania thought about her.

Kania nodded again. "Hmm. Well, that's good." She said. She sounded even more disappointed, and this time she completely lost her smile.

Marianna turned her eyes down. She couldn't stand to see the disappointment in the woman's eyes. There was no reason for it to bother her, but it did. A lump formed in her throat, and for the first time in almost a year, she could feel tears in her eyes. She didn't cry anymore, it never helped anything, and it just revealed weakness, but the tears came in spite of her.

"Shh shh shh... Why do you cry?" Kania said as she sat on the edge of Marianna's bed. She pushed Marianna's chin up with her finger and gazed into her eyes.

"I don't know. I'm sorry. I just...you seem so upset that I am disobedient enough to get so many beatings and whippings. And I don't mean to be. And I just...I don't know." She said. She openly cried.

Kania smiled warmly again easing Marianna's distress. "I am not upset with you. I thought when I saw all your scars; I thought that it meant that you still had a fight left in you. But, I guess that I just hoped, but no. I don't think anybody really has a fight left in them." She said looking down and losing her smile again.

Marianna frowned. She didn't understand.

"Don't worry about that now. You need your rest." Kania said smiling again. It was amazing how her smile made Marianna feel a little bit better. It was also amazing how tired she felt. She had only just woken up and barely moved at all, but she felt exhausted.

She nodded her head and smiled back at Kania, who was wiping the tears off her face like her Mama used to do when she was upset. That's when she recognized why she cared so much about what Kania thought about her. That was why she gained so much comfort by the woman's smile; because she made Marianna think about her Mama.

Marianna closed her eyes while Kania gently rubbed her cheek and sang a lullaby. She drifted off to sleep before the song was over.

When she opened her eyes again, there was a bright light shining through a window near her bed. She hadn't even noticed that she was near a window when she had woken up before.

There were several other beds around her, but only two had people in them. One was a young boy who was shivering violently, even though he was covered in several blankets, and it was a comfortable temperature in the room. He must be having fever chills. It took her a moment to recognize him. He was one of the children that her group was assigned to care for. She couldn't remember his name, but she could remember that he was always sickly. She never knew why.

The other person looked like a man in his late twenty's. He had several thick bandages wrapped around his arm and stomach. Red blood soaked through the bandage around his stomach. What had caused such a wound?

She tried to push herself up into a sitting position, but the pain in her shoulder kept her from being able to do it. She groaned and laid back and stared at the sun streaming in through the window. She watched the dust dance in the light, and the curtains rustle in the wind. It was nice, relaxing. She lay there for several minutes before anybody entered the room. It was

Kania again which made Marianna smile
broadly. It was odd to smile so often,
especially when she was hurting so badly.

Kania smiled back at her, but stopped at
the bed with the bandaged man and spoke to
him in whispered tones. He didn't appear
to be conscious, but he groaned as she
removed the blood-soaked bandage around
his stomach. Marianna strained her neck as
she tried to hold her head up to get a better
look at his wounds. He had a clean straight
line sliced across his midsection. It had
been stitched back together beautifully.

Kania wiped his wound with some strange
yellow colored liquid, which caused him to
gasp. But he still appeared to be
unconscious. She wrapped a clean bandage
back around him. She lifted the edges of
the wrap around his arm dabbed it a couple
of times with the yellow liquid and
readjusted the bandage. She said
something else to him in a whispered hush
that was too quiet for Marianna to
comprehend. She moved over to the sick
boy's bed.

She poured clean water over her hands as
she rubbed them together and shook them
several times removing excess water. She

poured some of the pure water over a cloth and squeezed the water into the sick boy's mouth.   The water just dribbled out of the edges of his mouth.   Kania looked down and shook her head.   She looked sad, really sad.   Did she know the boy?   She took the moist cloth and draped it over the boy's forehead and eyes.   She caressed his cheek with the back of her hand.   She must know him.   Was he her son or her brother?

She walked away from the sick child and rinsed her hands off again with clean water and moved over to Marianna's bed her warm, sweet smile returning to her face.

"How are you feeling?"

"My shoulder hurts.   But I think I am feeling a little bit better.   My head is clearer than before."   Marianna said.   Her thoughts sluggish but not as much as before.

"Good, I'm glad to hear it.   Your shoulder was dislocated, and I believe that the weight of your body pulling down on your dislocated shoulder injured your muscles. It will take time to heal.   I must change the bandages on your back.   I need you to roll over."   She explained.

Marianna wanted to protest because of how bad she knew rolling would hurt her shoulder, but she knew what happened if a wound was left to fester under dirty bandages.   So, she took in a deep breath and attempted to roll over quickly to get the pain over with, but she failed.   The jerking movement sent searing pains through her back and shoulder.   She gasped in pain and fell back onto her back.

"Shhhh... shh... shh... shhhh.   Now don't be so hasty.   Let me help you."   Kania said moving to Marianna's injured shoulder side of the bed.   She tugged on the bed linens that were under Marianna forcing her to roll without much effort.   It was much more comfortable with help.

Once Marianna was on her stomach she became more aware of how painful the wounds on her back felt.   They had been such a familiar pain over the last several months that she found that she was able to almost forget about the burning ache.

Kania went to work.   She could feel that she had individual pieces of bandage on the lashed wounds across her neck, back, and legs.   Kania pulled each of the bandages up careful not to pull at the wounds, exposing her wounds to open air.   It stung so much that Marianna couldn't think of anything else.   Kania wiped her wounds down with something that made them sting and burn even more, and placed fresh bandages, which was oddly comforting.   She helped Marianna roll back onto her back, and helped set her up with soft pillows behind her back.   It was luxurious.   Marianna couldn't remember ever being pampered so much.

"Watch my hand," Kania said as she moved her hand around in front of Marianna's face.   Marianna frowned but did as she was asked.

After several strange sweeping motions with her hand, Kania smiled and said, "much better."

Marinna tilted her head in confusion. "Were you casting a spell on me?"

Kania chuckled shaking her head.   "No. I was just checking to see if your head is getting better.   It's medicine that I do, not magic."

"Oh.   Alright.   Well, what was that yellow stuff that you put on us?   It burned really bad."   Marianna asked.   She had never been to a Medica or healer before, not even before she had been taken, so she didn't know what was happening.

"It was a salve.   It helps to keep it from festering as wounds tend to do.   And the more wounds a person has, the more likely one will fester.   And you have more than your share of wounds.   I'm sorry that it hurt, but it is for the best that it stays on there."   Kania explained.   She was sweet and understanding with her response, which Marianna was not used to.   She was the only adult that Marianna had spoken with since being taken that didn't talk down to her like a stupid child.   It was refreshing.

"How do you know him?"   Marianna asked nodding over to the still shaking sick boy.

Kania frowned for a moment.   "I do not know him.   Not any more than I know you. He was here one other time several months ago for a few days.   I was able to nurse him back to health then, but I fear this time, he may not pull through."

"But you care about him.   I saw you. You stroked his cheek like a mother.   And you look sad when you talk about how sick he is."   Marianna argued.

"Of course I care.   I could not do this job if I didn't care.   I don't like losing my patients.   I am sad anytime one doesn't pull through. You should understand this more than most. You tend to the young ones. Don't you care about them?" Kania asked.

Marianna leaned her head back on the stacked pillows behind her and thought hard about what Kania asked. How could somebody care about people that they barely even knew? How could she care about people she was forced to tend to? She found herself shaking her head as she thought to herself. She didn't care about the young ones. It did not matter to her what happened to them. If every one of them were to fall sick and die tomorrow, she would feel nothing, except relief for no longer needing to tend to them.

"I see," Kania said with a sound of deep hurt in her voice. Marianna lifted her head and looked at the once lively woman, all evidence of warmth, happiness, and hope had left her face and composure.

Marianna felt bad. She had somehow upset the only person to show her true compassion in years.

"I'm sorry I made you mad," Marianna said looking at her blanket. The sun's beams had moved to shine on her. She watched the dust play in the light.

"I am not mad at you. I'm just disappointed about what this place has done to you. You are too young to be so bleak. But don't worry about that now. You need to rest." Kania said as she pulled Marianna's blanket up onto her legs and stood up.

Marianna grabbed her hand. "Please don't go. I've rested enough. I'm not tired at all; please can't we just talk for a while?" She pleaded.

She didn't even realize how badly she missed casual conversation. She was never able to speak freely, and it was refreshing to have a conversation with someone without being watched by the guards and punished for saying the wrong thing.

Kania took in a deep breath and smiled halfway. "What would you like to talk about?"

Marianna leaned back and thought about it. What would she want to talk about?

"You were upset before when you found out that I was obedient, but I don't understand why. You're a grown-up, wouldn't you want me to do what is expected of me?" Marianna asked. It was a question that had bothered her.

Kania smiled even more. "You are a clever one and very observant. I am here against my will just like you, and it gave me hope when I thought that there still might be someone out there fighting against their bonds of servitude. It was a pointless hope because I know that there is nothing that any of us can really do, we can't fight, not really, but I don't know, I was just hoping." She revealed.

"Really? Wow. I didn't know anybody felt that way, especially not a grown up. But you are the only grown up I've seen; except for the guards. I didn't even know there were any here."

Kania frowned. "They keep us that separated, do they? I guess I have been more fortunate working here in the Medica. I have seen all different ages, injuries, and illnesses. Hmm. I wonder, how much do you know about why we are all here? Do you know what our purpose is?"

Marianna frowned shaking her head. "I have no idea. I always wondered, but nobody is allowed to talk about anything. We are always kept so busy that there is no time to figure anything out, and even if there was, we are always being guarded."

Kania nodded. "Yes, that makes sense. I knew some were kept in the dark, but I guess since I have known for so long, I just assumed everybody had found out by now. We have all been conscripted into the service of the Atheran Kingdom to build an army." Kania explained.

Marianna leaned her head back against the wall. An army. Of all reasons that Marianna had come up with about why they were all there, building and army had never crossed her mind.

"Wow. Really? An army. Well, why didn't they just tell us all? No, I think you are wrong." She decided.

"No, I am not wrong. I do not know why they kept the truth from some. I don't know much about their reasons for doing anything that they do. I just know what they do, not why they do it."

Marianna thought about it and shrugged her uninjured shoulder. "I guess it makes sense. A little bit. They could have just told us what we were all here for. They wouldn't have to keep us here against our will. I'm sure that if they had just asked for people to sign up for an army, people would have volunteered."

"They probably have their reasons, but I agree with you.   I wish I knew more." Kania said.

"At least you know something.   All I know is what they allow me to know." Marianna grumbled.

"Yes, well from what I have gathered from you, you haven't exactly sought out information.   You seem content being told what to do, and knowing as little as needed to get your given job done."   Kania said raising her eyebrows.

Marianna looked down and wrung her hands together.   She didn't know what to say.   It was true.   She hadn't tried, she just wanted to be left alone to do her work, and that was it.   She sat for several minutes, not knowing what to say.   Kania sat wordlessly as well.

"Why do they need children to be here anyway?"   She asked looking back up to look at Kania.

The kind young woman's face looked to age several decades.   She shook her head. "I don't know for sure, but if I had to guess I would say it is because as you all grow up in this life, you will be more obedient, and follow any orders given to you.   Yes, the grown adults that were taken are being trained to be soldiers, but they will never be completely obedient. But that is just a guess as I said. I honestly do not know." She mused.

"It is time for me to tend to the other patients. And I think it is time for you to move around a bit more. I want you to get up out of this bed and help me. Can you do that?" Kania asked.

Marianna nodded and swung her legs over the edge of the bed. Her back ached, but not as bad as it had before. What was in the salve? She moved her back around a bit. It was amazing.

"I wish I had this stuff before. It works great against the lashings." She said as she climbed to her feet with careful motions.

Kania's eyebrows drew together as she stared back at Marianna. "Yes well, go get some water and wash up, we have work to do."

CHAPTER FIVE

Snapped

Marianna spent several more days in the Medica. Over time she spent more and more time out of her bed helping Kania tend to the other patients. She must have said or done something to Kania because she never had an open conversation with Marianna again. She spoke with her, but never anything of importance. Marianna didn't know why.

Before she felt ready her time was over in the Medica. The slashes on her back were nearly healed, but her back was tight from the scars. Her shoulder still ached on a regular basis, but she was able to move it and carry out daily tasks without much problem. Her head stopped feeling heavy all the time, but if she were up and moving around for too long, it would pound so badly that it was hard for her to keep her eyes open. But none of that mattered. If she could perform her duties without passing out or hurting somebody, she was fit to go back to her assignment.

The moment that she dreaded over the last couple of weeks came. She was sent back to the boarding house where she was forced to care for the young ones again. Kania had asked her something that reverberated in her mind. She asked Marianna if she cared about the children she was charged with. She honestly did not. If every one of her charges were to die, she would feel relief rather than sorrow.

So, she made a conscious choice to try to form a bond with and care about the well-being of the children. They were children after all, and their actions were no more than the normal actions of children.

But even with all her best efforts to show the children more kindness and tolerance, her patience with them waned after a couple of weeks.

For several weeks she managed to not receive any beatings and stay off the whipping post. She wasn't sure if her lack of punishments was because the children were more well behaved, or if the guards were just going easy on her because of her recent stint at the Medica.

Her reprieve from punishment ended spectacularly. Over the next seven months, she had been whipped and beaten so many times that she was never fully healed from a wound. She was always in pain, always bleeding, always bruised, nothing she ever did was good enough to keep her safe from the wrath of the guards.

In a matter of three days, she had managed to be whipped five times. By the end of the fifth whipping her back, legs, and arms were so torn up that she couldn't move without tearing one of her lashing open.

The end of the third day she finally got all her assigned children to sleep, and she was able to retire herself to her own tiny room. She tried to remove her shirt slowly, but it was stuck to her back in several places where it had broken open and bled. She attempted to gingerly remove it, but it was too excruciating to keep doing. So finally, she took a deep breath, and in one swift move she tugged her shirt up and off her body. She screamed out and fell to her knees gasping in excruciating pain.

She laid her head on the floor and wept from pain, frustration, and an overwhelming feeling of helplessness. She was trapped in her indentured life, and there was nothing that she could do to escape. An army was being built, and the children were being conditioned to be more obedient with their orders, which meant that they were there for the long run. She couldn't just live day to day anymore in hopes that somehow tomorrow would be just a little bit better. Especially when the tomorrows that came only got worse as the days went on.

As she lay on the ground wallowing in her pain and predicament, she heard a young one whimpering.

She gritted her teeth and sat up. If the other children were woken up due to the noise, she was going to be furious. The guards were hostile during the day with good sleep, but if they didn't get a full night's sleep and it was because of Marianna's young ones she would pay for it twice. She couldn't handle being beaten or whipped again. She didn't know if she could survive another time if she weren't able to heal a bit.

She opened the door to her room just as a second child began crying.

"Be quiet. Shhhh.... Both of you. Please be quiet." She begged as she moved to the crying children.

It was one of her four-year-old girls Omiah and a Six-year-old boy Clive. Omiah looked like she had just woken up, so Marianna moved as quickly and quietly as she could over to her. She sat on the edge of the girl's bed shushing her and laying her back down.

"It's ok. Shhhh. Just go back to sleep. Shhhh." She whispered. She ran her fingers through the little girl's hair shushing her. In moments Omiah had stopped crying and was curling up in her thin blanket.

Marianna stood back up trying not to shake the bed too much to upset Omiah and was surprisingly successful in her first attempt. Omiah stayed still and silent as Marianna moved away. She made her way over to Clive who was still whimpering but not as loudly as he had been to start with.

She leaned over to shush Clive but as soon as he saw her he whined even louder.

"Shhhh! You're going to wake the others." She said in a stern whisper.

He started completely crying. "Shhh... Please. Be quiet." Marianna begged in hushed tones but louder than she had intended it to be.

Several of the young ones began to stir. Before they could be disturbed enough to wake up, she covered Clive's mouth with her hand, lifted him up awkwardly and rushed into her room and shut the door.

He whimpered through her hand, but the sound was muffled and barely audible. "Would you be quiet? What is wrong with you? Just be quiet and go to sleep."

She sat on her bed. Slowly and painfully she leaned her back against the wall she suppressed a scream as she rested all her weight against the wall. She moved him up into the bed on top of her continuing to hold her hand over his mouth.

"Please stop. Please. Just go back to sleep. Please." She cried; first just silent, tear-free whimpers, but then uncontrollable sobs. She remained quiet as she cried, but she cried unrelentingly. She cried for so long that tears stopped flowing, but the sobs continued.

She wasn't sure how long she had cried or when Clive had fallen asleep in her arms, but her head nodded, which stretched the skin on her back enough to cause searing pain to move down her back. She hissed through gritted teeth. Luckily the noise and her sudden jump didn't wake Clive. She tried to move him off her and onto his bed, but she couldn't lift him in a way that didn't hurt so badly that she bit her lips to keep from crying out.

She leaned her head back against the wall and closed her eyes. She fell asleep just long enough for her head to drop to the side and wake her again with excruciating pain. The pattern of nodding off only to wake in pain continued the rest of the night until the sun lit up the horizon.

By that time, she was in constant agonizing pain. She was so frustrated by lack of sleep and inability to move without waking Clive that she wanted to scream. She was stiff, aching from her wounds, and sleep deprived for the fourth night in a row. She wanted to cry again but didn't have the will.

A few minutes after the sun rose, one of the children made a moaning noise, and then moments later another child, and then another. She shook Clive awake. Bleary eyed he stood up wobbling some and then left her room without saying anything.

She leaned forward pealing her back away from the wall.   She shrieked as several scabs tore off her back.   As the overwhelming pain made her vision go completely white, she fell to the floor onto her hands and knees.

It took several panting breaths for her vision to go back to normal.   She crawled over to where her clothes were.   Every one of her shirts was stained with blood.   She grabbed a clean shirt and put it on, whimpering with each movement.   Outside her room, several of the children were laughing.

They were laughing while she was in agonizing pain.   They didn't care about her at all.   They had to have heard her scream out, but not one of them was concerned enough to come to her.   She hated them all so much.

She could feel hot tears of anger welling up in her eyes.   She took in a deep breath trying to stop them from turning into the constant crying like the night before.   Her eyes and face were already puffy, tired, and sore from crying so much.

She pushed herself up onto her feet and stepped out to get the children ready.

"What are you doing?   What makes you think this is alright?   Why do you all have to be such terrible children?"   She shrieked as she saw what they had been doing.

Four mattresses had been pulled off their frames and were stacked up in the middle of the room, while the children took turns jumping from the empty frames onto the mattress causing straw to puff out of the ends of the mattresses and cover the children, floor, and other beds.   It was a mess, they were a mess, and it was almost time for them to leave for breakfast.   If she didn't get to eat breakfast again from the selfish, awful children, she was going to lose it.

"Stop now!   Put these back on the frames! You and you pick up this straw, and the rest of you get ready NOW!!!"   She shrieked. They saw how angry she was, because none of them argued, or hesitated.   She got the youngest children dressed and ready to go. In a surprisingly short amount of time, the room looked close to the way it usually looked.

She led the children out and to the

cafeteria where, amazingly, they all ate without much trouble.   After shoveling down her food as quickly as she could and then finishing off a few of the other children's leftovers, she lined her children up and led them out to receive their assignment for the day. As her guard told her where they were assigned she had to fight down a cry in frustration.   She was going to get another beating.   There was no way to avoid it.

Their assigned job for the day was to clean and organize the food storehouse.   More guards were posted to monitor assignments at the storehouse than any other place she was allowed to go.   It was the guard's job to ensure no food was stolen, eaten, or destroyed.

But the littlest of the young ones didn't understand or didn't care that they were not supposed to just eat the food that they were working with.   Someone was going to eat something, destroy some kind of edible, or cause some kind of trouble that would lead Marianna to get another whipping.

Just the thought of another lashing across her already mauled back made her feel like she was going to be sick.   Her overstuffed stomach twisted. She swallowed several mouthfuls of saliva and tried to force the feeling away.

She was able to keep herself from getting sick, but she could not breathe. Her chest was tight. She forced in a breath, and then another, and another. She couldn't get enough air. She breathed faster and deeper trying to catch her breath, but it just made her feel dizzy. She panicked, breathing in and out even faster. She couldn't fall; her body couldn't handle that kind of pain. She was spinning, and she still couldn't catch her breath. Her vision narrowed. She could feel herself about to pass out. She leaned down putting her hands on her knees and tried to calm herself.

Somebody grabbed her shoulder which burned across the lashing that was being touched. She gasped and stood back up, as tears poured from her eyes. It was the guard who had given her the assignment. He looked concerned and was saying something, but she couldn't hear him over the loud ringing in her ears. As she looked at him trying to speak with her, she was able to slow her breathing, and slowly the ringing quieted enough to hear again.

"What's wrong with you?   Are you sick? Why won't you say anything?"

She stared at him not sure what to say. She was still dizzy, and still nauseous.

"Listen, if there is something I can do to help you, you have to tell me."   He said.

She didn't know how to respond.   There wasn't anything that he could do.   Unless he could get her away from the children, get her somewhere where she could rest pain-free, or let her go home, there was nothing that could be done to help her.

"I don't know what's wrong with you girl, but I need you to take the rest of the children here and get to your assignment.   I've got work to do, and I don't have time to take care of you and your children."

She chuckled in exasperation.   Nodded her head and just thoughtlessly walked towards the storeroom.   She didn't know or care if all her charges were following her. She just moved.   She got to the storeroom just minutes later.   When she opened the door and looked back, she saw that all the children were still with her, following as quietly as she had been.

For the first couple of hours, every person kept to their assigned jobs, without incident.

But then the inevitable event that she dreaded came.

Two of the girls played with some of the bagged vegetables, pretending they were babies and carrying them around. Marianna tried to ignore them and continue working. Clive saw them playing and wanted to join them, but the girls did not want him to play. They started arguing. Marianna ran over to them shouting for them all to stop. Clive grabbed a bag and tugged on it causing the frayed edge to begin to unravel. He dropped the unraveling bag causing the vegetables to shift forward and spill out of the opening that had been formed and roll all over the floor. The girl dropped the bag, but not before half of the bag had spilled.

"I didn't mean to. I'm sorry. I didn't mean to." Clive said over and over.

One of the guards had overheard the commotion and came for them. Marianna couldn't get another whipping. She just couldn't.

"PICK THEM UP NOW!!!!" She shouted as she knelt and frantically picked them up.

The girl dropped to her hands and knees gathering vegetables in her arms. The other girl, dropped the bag of vegetables that she had been holding to help pick up, which caused it to break open and spill out.

Marianna screamed.

Clive just stood there staring at everything and did nothing.

She growled jumping up and grabbing Clive by the hair and tugging him to the floor. He screamed and began crying.

"CLEAN UP YOUR MESS." She screeched.

"What have you done?" The guard said as he rounded the corner around one of the counters. He stood over all them looking at the mess of strewn vegetables. An overwhelming panic filled Marianna as she thought about what he would do to her, because of the mess. She gathered as many vegetables as she could in her arms and shoved them in the bag.

"You kids are ruining our food." He said as he kicked a carrot towards Marianna.

She looked up as she was about to apologize when she saw Clive sitting and crying and still not cleaning up the mess that he made. She squeezed the turnip that was in her hand trying to keep herself from shouting. She knew from experience that if she shouted at one of the guards, her beatings were even worse.

"Who is responsible for this mess?"   The guard asked.

The guard, both girls, and Clive all looked at Marianna.   They were blaming her again. When it was Clive and the girls who were playing, arguing, and destroying things, and all she did was try to stop them, and she was being blamed.

"It was you."   She squealed.

She swung the turnip that was in her hand and smashed it across Clive's head.   He shouted out and grabbed his head.   She swung again with her other hand in a fist and hit him in the neck.

"It is always you."   She charged at him and pushed him onto his back.

She climbed on top of him, wrapping both hands around the turnip and slamming it into his chest over and over again.

"It's always all of you.   And I am always the one being punished."   She cried.

The guard was shouting at her, she heard Clive crying beneath her, but she couldn't stop herself.   She just kept striking the young boy over and over again.   His blood covered her hands, but she couldn't stop.

The guard grabbed her shoulder to pull her off.   She threw the turnip at him hitting him in the eye.   Clive had made her hurt a guard.   She was going to be punished so much worse than she ever had been before. She shrieked.

She wrapped her hands around Clive's throat and squeezed as hard as she could while she pulled him towards her and then slammed his head and body back against the floor.   She couldn't stop squeezing and slamming.

"Let him go!"   She heard.

She couldn't.   Even when his throat crushed in her hands, she squeezed harder. Even when his skull crunched against the ground, she continued slamming his head into the floor.   The crunching turned to squishing and still she continued.

Two sets of hands wrapped around each of her arms and lifted her from the floor; the overwhelming pain that shot through her back caused her to scream out.   But she still held onto the young boy.   His body was limp as she was lifted and lifted him up in the process.   He didn't look like a boy anymore.   He looked like fresh slaughtered game, blood and bone and brain mashed together like a meal made from leftovers.

"Let him go." One of the guards that held her said.

He tried to pry her hands off his neck, but her grip held. They shook her causing more pain to shoot through her back forcing her to let the boy go. His body crumbled to the floor limp and lifeless.

"What is wrong with you girl?" One of the guards asked.

"I think she has snapped. She's gone completely mad. Look at her." Somebody else said.

Marianna heaved huge breaths, her heart pounding in her chest. She couldn't calm herself. She wanted the guards to put her down so that she could keep on hammering the boy into the ground. But as she stared at the lump of the boy that was Clive's body, she knew what she was looking at.

He was dead. She had killed him. She wanted to feel sorry for it, but she couldn't help but feel like it was still his fault. If he wouldn't have been misbehaving, if he wouldn't have been just sitting there and not helping clean up the mess that he had made, if he wouldn't have tried to blame his actions on her, then she wouldn't have lost control.

He deserved what he got.

The guards that were holding her dragged her out of the storeroom. The bright sun was a harsh contrast to the dimly lit storeroom, and it made her eyes hurt.

"What do we do with her?" The broad-shouldered guard holding her left arm asked.

He sounded scared, not angry. She didn't know that the guards could feel scared. She only ever saw them angry or emotionless. But fear was an odd emotion to experience from one of them. His fear scared her even more than his anger would have. How badly would he make her pay for making him feel afraid?

"I don't know. We can't take her back in there." The other guard responded sounding just as scared as the other.

"We need to take her to the Captain. If he hears about this from somebody else, it will be our hides. I don't fancy a stint with the border guard." The guard on the left said.

"I don't know if we will be able to avoid it. You remember what happened to Jarvin. His charge went crazy and slammed his own head against the ground so many times that it rendered him dumb. Jarvin was immediately sent to the border. I don't know exactly what happens in that guard, but the men who are sent there are never the same, they're savage. I can't be sent there. I just can't." The other guard said.

Marianna had never heard the guards talk so openly. They weren't withholding information from her, they weren't hiding their thoughts on what they believed about things. It was a scary thing. What did that mean for her? They didn't feel the need to hide the truth from her anymore; it couldn't be a good sign.

"I know. I don't want to go there either, that's why we need to be proactive and take her straight to the Captain. Jarvin tried to hide what really happened. I think he would have been in less trouble if he would have just gone forward with the boy and what happened from the beginning. He would have just been reprimanded, put on the stocks, or whipped, but since he tried hiding it, he got the full punishment." The other guard said.

Marianna never knew the guards got punishments just like everybody else. She thought they were in charge and they were only the ones dishing out the beatings and

whippings.   But from what she gathered
from their conversation, they were just as
likely to be punished when those they
oversaw acted up; just like she got in trouble
when her children acted up.   It was odd
paralleling the guard's lives with her own.

"Yes, but this time is worse.   This crazy
girl actually killed a boy.   And I mean she
really killed him.   She was brutal.   How do
we explain that we didn't see it was coming?
I mean honestly, if I had to go through the
same number of punishments as this girl, I
would have snapped a long time ago."   The
guard to her left said.

"She never kept her charges in line.   They
were always acting up and causing trouble,
she deserved what she got."   The guard
said.

Marianna's jaw dropped as she realized
what was just said.   Just as she was blaming
Clive for the vicious beating and
strangulation that was brought to him at her
own hands, the guards blamed her for the
beatings and whippings that they punished
her with.

"I don't know.   I mean we have been
merciless with this one.   Isn't she the one
who ended up in the Medica because of one

of the beatings?"   The guard on her left said.

"It's her own fault.   She knows what her job is.   She has been with that group of children for years.   She should be able to keep them under control by now.   Have you seen her?   She is either screaming at them like a mad woman but still not keeping them under control, or she is sulking around half dazed, barely aware of what is going on around her."   The guard on her right said.

"She's barely older than a child herself, and she is expected to keep a group of younger children contained.   I've seen this girl lose more and more of her sanity; I've seen all her hope being crushed.   I've been there to crush it.   I've seen her getting to this point, and I have done nothing to help her. Nobody has.   We are responsible for that boy's death, and just as responsible for this girl snapping."   The guard on her left said.

He looked like he was battling with his own guilt.   He honestly believed that he was responsible for her killing Clive.   She didn't understand how he could feel that way.   The guards did not care about anybody.   All they did was give out the orders or the punishments.

"Don't you go talking like that to the

Captain or we are sure to be sent to the border guard. She made her choice, and she is responsible for her own actions. I have been a good soldier. I have done everything that was asked of me. And I am not going to let you or her take everything that I have worked for, away. We will take her to the Captain, and she will be given whatever fate it is that he sees fit." The guard on the right said.

Neither of them spoke again as they carried her deeper and deeper into the rows of buildings far beyond anywhere she had been allowed to go before.

CHAPTER SIX

Murderer

Marianna was carried for hours. Why did the guards never attempt to put her down? She was fully capable of walking. It was strange being taken so far away from her part of the camp. The buildings were larger and fancier the farther they got. By the time they stopped, she could not recognize where she was. Except for the buildings strategic placement, the place barely looked like it was a part of the camp at all.

The building that she was carried into was huge. It was as tall as three or four barracks stacked on top of each other and was a bright blue color. The door that they entered was bright white and cleaner than anything she had ever seen.

When they entered the building, the inside

was even prettier than the outside. The floors were polished stone that reflected everything as clear as a looking glass.

Marianna stared at the reflection of herself and saw that her hands, arms, clothes, and even her face were soaked and splattered with blood. She was used to seeing blood. Her own blood was a frequent sight, but to see someone else's blood covering her made her feel sick. She pulled her hands up to look at it more closely. None of her skin was visible below the caked-on blood. And she had a mess of hair wrapped around one of her fingers and attached to the hair was a chunk of flesh and bone.

She unwound it from around her finger and studied the strange thing that she had unknowingly carried with her. It was dark reddish brown, instead of the light sandy blond that Clive's hair had been. But because of her, his hair would forever be blood-soaked. She had killed the boy. She had taken a life with her own hands. She should feel bad, or sad, or disgusted, but she didn't. She was numb.

She looked back up to marvel at the inside of the building, when she saw the guard that was carrying her on the left side staring at her frowning. She just stared blankly back at him. He was displaying some kind of emotion towards her. Was it concern? She wasn't sure.

They stopped at a large heavy looking carved door. There were flowers and birds carved into it in amazing detail. Marianna gazed at the ornate door as the guards holding her knocked. They stood still after knocking, waiting for a reply. They didn't have to wait long.

"Who's there?" A deep burly voice bellowed from the other side of the door.

"We have a prisoner sir." The guard on her left said.

A prisoner? Was she a prisoner? It never occurred to her that she would be considered a prisoner.

"Come in. You better not be wasting my time." The man said sounding irritated.

The men opened the large door which looked to take some effort to move and stepped into the massive room.

A large desk with thick pillars sat in the center of the room. And behind the desk sitting in a large thick cushioned chair sat a somewhat overweight but muscular looking man. He wore a fancy coat that was decorated with fancy carved stones that shimmered in the light as he moved. He had papers spread across his desk in disarray with strange tools and sticks all around.

He looked back and forth between Marianna and her two guards with an uninterested air.

"Well. Why are you here?" The man said hastily. "Is this your prisoner? It looks like she has already been disciplined, what more do you think she needs?" He said.

"Sir. This isn't her blood. She killed a young boy in her charge. She went crazy. She beat and strangled the child. She wouldn't stop. We had to pull her away from the boy kicking and screaming. She just snapped. We couldn't leave her around the other children in case she was still in the murdering mood. Her assigned duty is caring for and teaching a group of young ones, the boy was one of those she was assigned."

The burly man looked at Marianna, studying her up and down. His eyes stopped on one of her blood-caked hands. His expression morphed from surprise and confusion to concern and recognition as he watched her hand.

She looked at where he was staring. She had been rolling the piece of Clive's scalp between her thumb and forefinger. She lifted it up to examine it again. Her own finger was bleeding. She had not even recognized that there had been pain. There was a chunk of bone that was attached to the skin and hair, which she had used to carve a deep circular groove into her finger.

She watched as she moved the piece of bone around across the injury, but even with her being aware that she was doing it, and that it should be painful. There was only a dull awareness of the contact but no pain at all. In fact, for the first time, she recognized that she didn't feel any pain at all. She smiled. No pain. She giggled to herself. No pain.

She looked back up to the Captain. The frown that he wore as he looked at her was so deep that a trickle of sweat from his forehead, moved towards the deep valley between his brows, and fell into the man's eye. She giggled again as she watched another drop of sweat moving towards the groove.

The Captain turned away from her gaze and looked back and forth between the guards at each side of her.

"You're right. She's insane." He chewed on some of his beard hair at the bottom of his lip as he looked back and forth between her guards. He was doing everything that he could to not look at her again.

"What happened? I mean how did she get like this? Never mind. I know how she got like this. Has she been punished yet?"

The guard on her left answered. "Sir. I don't think she could survive another punishment."

The Captain looked at the guard with a raised eyebrow. "What does that mean?"

"She has had years to get her charges under control. We have given her so many chances to figure it out. But she just doesn't seem to care. We've tried everything. She can never keep them out of trouble." The guard on her right babbled.

"What makes you think she wouldn't survive another punishment? Because her crime cannot go unpunished." The Captain said chewing on his beard hair again. He looked just as uncomfortable about everything as the guards that had carried her to him did.

The guards looked at one another over her head, nodded to each other and then simultaneously set her down. Her feet were unsteady beneath her. She wobbled a bit before getting her balance.

"Take off your shirt child." The guard on her right ordered.

She stared at him. She had recognized that he spoke. She had understood what he said. She knew that she should listen. She had been given an order. She knew the consequences of disobeying an order. But she couldn't make herself make the decision to do anything. She couldn't decide on obeying her order. She couldn't decide on being willfully defiant. She just couldn't decide to do anything. So, she just stood and stared at the guard.

"Did you hear me girl?" He said exasperatedly. He snapped his fingers in front of her face several times. "Girl. Take it off." The guard huffed shaking his head with a scowl on his face.

He looked back at the Captain for a moment and then grabbed Marianna by the arm and turned her back to the Captain. He lifted the back of her shirt up.

The pain came back to her in an instant, as an excruciating searing burn cascaded across her body. An uncontrolled scream escaped her as she fell to her hands and knees. Her entire body trembled, and her arms barely held her up.

"Great spirits." The Captain exclaimed.

The two guards wrapped their hands around her arms again and lifted her off the ground. They turned her around to face the Captain again and set her back on the ground. Neither of the guards had taken their hands off her arms.

Marianna whimpered as the burning pain continued.

The Captain just stared at her shaking his head ever so slightly, chewing on his beard.

"I've got to do something with her. Your right. She won't survive another lashing. I don't know how she withstood all of those. She can't be returned to where the young ones are. No. No that won't work. She could, but no. Not that either." The captain rambled more to himself as he rubbed his chin with his hand. He paced back and forth in front of his desk as he continued mumbling to himself.

She glanced at her two guards who both

looked as confused as she was about the Captains mutterings.

The Captain stopped in place and looked back at her. The deep valley between his eyebrows somehow deeper than it had been before. He shook his head several times and then nodded.

He sat down at his desk and started writing something.

Oh. They were pens and pencils on his desk.

After filling up two full sheets of paper with what he was writing, he rolled up the pages together.

He looked between the two guards, seeming to avoid looking at her directly.

"It's the only place I can think of. She is too dangerous for anywhere else. Most women last a good year before breaking down, dying, or finding a way to kill themselves. She is just crazy enough, that maybe she will do it sooner. I hate to send someone so young. But there's nowhere else. Take her to the row houses. She will be a Vassal Lady. Keep her away from the breeders. She's not suited to become one of them. Take her to Faisal directly, he'll know how to handle and prepare her. And she still needs to be punished for her crime, he has a unique expertise in that area."

CHAPTER SEVEN

Marianna's New Home

Marianna's guards carried her out of the Captain's office, out of the ornate building, and deeper into the camp than she even knew existed. The buildings were bigger than they had been on her side of the camp, but they weren't as pretty or grand as the buildings around the part of the camp as the captain's building.

She didn't understand where she was being taken. The Captain said that she would not be going back to tending to the young ones, which was good news to her, but he did say that she was going to be taken to be a Vassal Lady, whatever that meant. But he also said that she was still going to be punished for what she did to Clive. So, she knew that where ever the guards were taking her, it would not be good for her. But just as everything in her life for the last four years or so, she had no control over what was going to happen to her, so she just let the guards carry her away without a fight.

They had taken so many turns down streets that were covered with stones that Marianna had lost track of which direction she could be.   It was disorienting being carried for so long.   But they rounded a large wood and stone building that she couldn't guess the use of, and stepped out into a stretch of decorated buildings with music, and loud conversations, and something she barely even recognized anymore, laughter.   It was a bustling street with grown men and women inside and outside socializing like friends, instead of slaves.   They were all enjoying themselves. She didn't even know that was possible anymore.

The buildings all lined one side of the street, and on the other, there was a massive lake.   There were offshoots from the street which led out onto the shoreline, and some straight out to the water.   Some of them were wood planked and actually sat over the water.   Floating carriages were sitting on the water next to those spots.

People, all adults, were getting on and off the water carriages or playing in the water. Most of them looked happy like they were having fun.   Some of the adults around the water carriages looked busy, or grumpy like she usually felt.   They were dragging big bags full of holes, filled with fish.

"Oh.   They're boats."   She mused out loud.

Both guards who were carrying her stopped and looked at her.

"She speaks."   The guard on her right said.   "Now is not the time for you to regain your sanity."   He said chuckling to himself.

"Really?   She's just a child."   The guard on her left said with a sad look on his face.

"She's a murderer.   You saw what she did to that boy.   How old was he, like three?" The guard on her right said exasperatedly.

"Four," Marianna said emotionless.

The two guards stared at her with confused expressions on their faces.   The one on her right just shook his head in disbelief.

"You should have stayed crazy little girl." The guard on her right said.   "You're not going to like what's about to happen to you."

Marianna frowned at him. "I don't like anything that happens to me." She said in a cool tone.

Her life since being taken from her home so many years before had been progressively getting worse. Every day had been some form of torture for her. So, hearing that she wouldn't like what was going to happen to her was not a surprise.

The guard on her left just nodded in a way that said that he understood and agreed with her.

"You brought it on yourself little girl." The guard on her right said sounding irritated.

She looked at him confused. "I don't have any control over anything that I do. I'm a slave."

A look of distress moved across his face for a moment but was then replaced by a look of anger.

"None of us wants to be here. But you don't see any of us losing our minds and beating an innocent child to death." He said sounding defensive.

"I was beaten or whipped almost every day." Marianna reflected, more to herself than the guards.

"You only got what you deserved. You were being punished for disobedience. And now you're going to be punished for murder." He said while gesturing to the other guard to pick her back up.

She stared in the direction that she was being taken. The sun was starting to kiss the horizon. The purples and reds in the sky reflected off the water. It was pretty.

Before the sun dipped below the water, the guards stopped in front of a large multistory building. There was a large balcony wrapping each floor around the entire building. There were guards at each corner of the building, as well as two posted at the door. There were guards at each of the doorways that exited out onto the balconies. She had never seen a building so guarded before.

The part of the street that they were at was extra crowded. Marianna had not seen such a large crowd since she had stopped working in the kitchens. Except there were no children at all, excluding herself of course?

Her guards approached the guards at the front door. They were huge and muscular.

They looked like they were looming over her two guards, even though they were close to the same height. There was a foreboding look about them that screamed that these men were not to be trifled with.

The door guards looked back and forth between the two carrying her and then one of them locked eyes on her. His wide burly face was stoic, but his stance said that he was a barely contained animal ready to strike at any moment. Marianna shivered at his stare. His eyes dug into her, making her pull back as much as she could while being held in place. She wanted to look away, but at the same time, her instincts told her that turning away while being in his sights was as dangerous as tensing her muscles just before the whip was snapped across her back.

The man had darker hair that came down to his shoulder, and he had a thick raised scar that stretched from his right ear, down his neck, and down below his shirt. She idly wondered how he got it, and how far down it stretched. As she studied his scar, her uneasiness towards him relaxed a bit. She wasn't sure why. Surviving whatever wound would have caused such an extensive scar only proved to her how dangerous the man really could be. It should have made her more uncomfortable, but it didn't.

"What is this?" The guard who was not looking at her asked. He was just as large as the other man, but his presence was less threatening. Not that he wasn't also dangerous because she was sure that he was, but he didn't feel as primal to her.

"We were ordered by the Captain to bring this one to be a Vassal Lady." The guard on her right said. He sounded like he was trying to sound more confident than he was. Even he appeared nervous to be before the two foreboding men.

That guard had a look of confusion move across his face. He too looked at Marianna; his eyes scanning her up and down several times before stopping on her hands. She lifted her hands up to look at them as well. In the dim light, they looked red again, instead of the dark brown of dried blood. Goosebumps moved across her skin as she looked at her blood covered hands.

Her own blood was a common sight to her from her countless beatings and whippings over the years, but she had never had so much blood on her hands that was not her own.

Marianna dropped her hands back down and looked back up. Both door guards were looking at her with revulsion.

"You must be mistaken. She's too young. She's not healthy enough to be a Breeder. Look at her she has no meat on her at all. She wouldn't survive, and even if she did, she would only produce weak or sick offspring. She is no good for us in this state." The man with the scar proclaimed.

It was true. Marianna was skin and bone. Every one of her ribs was visible. Her hips too jutted out sharply underneath her skin. She was never hungry, and the few times when she felt hunger one of her charges would act out, making her lose her appetite. Or they would do something while she was eating that would make her not be able to continue. So, she rarely ate as much as she should.

"No, she's to be a Vassal lady, not a Breeder; orders from the Captain." The guard on her left said quickly.

"That is not how it is done." The man without a scar said shaking his head.

"Vassal ladies are only used if a Breeder is determined to be barren or unsuitable.

Nobody just starts out as one. It destroys the women. None of them would last if it were done that way. If anything, she would be a Breeder, but she looks too young, and as I said before, too unhealthy." The scarred man explained.

"She is to be punished for her crime." The guard on her right said still sounding like he was trying to appear more confident than he was.

"Punished for what crime?" The man without a scar asked. He and the scarred man looked back at her, their eyes falling on her hands.

"She murdered a young child that was in her care. She beat him and strangled him. She can't be put back on the children's side of the camp. She's too volatile. For that reason, she can't be put in any other service job either. She's crazy.

"So, the Captain determined that this would be the best place for her. He said she is to be dealt with by Faisal himself. And that she is to be punished. She must also be locked up until Faisal deems her safe enough to be let out, if he ever does." The guard on her right explained as he handed over the rolled-up papers that the Captain had given to him.

The scarred man furrowed his brows and just nodded.

"Very well, follow me."   The guard without the scar said as he opened the door.

The guard with the scar looked straight at Marianna like he could see straight through her.   His eyes stayed locked on hers as she was carried inside.   As if she too had the look of a wild animal ready to strike.

CHAPTER EIGHT

Dangerous Child

Marianna was carried into the building.
It was so well lit that it was as bright as day.
Lanterns burned in each of the corners of the
grand room, and a fire burned in a large
fireplace. Huge plush chairs and couches
were sitting in a half circle. It was not
winter cold outside yet, but there was a deep
chill in the air when the sun went down, and
it was a fantastic feeling to be in a room and
feel the warmth of a fire on a cool night.

She was carried up a wide staircase, two
long hallways split by the staircase with
eaves wrapping around viewing the great
room below. The guards carried her down
one of the hallways which were lined with
multiple doors. She was taken to the
second to the last door. The room was

larger than the tiny room that she had when she tended to the children. There was an enormous bed in the center of the room three times the size of her usual bed. Marianna imagined how comfortable it would be.

There was a small table with two wooden chairs on each side sitting against the wall on one side of the room, and on the other side of the room attached to the floor were thick chains and shackles.

Marianna nodded to herself as she was taken to the chains. That made more sense. That was where she belonged, not on the big luxurious bed, but chained to the floor.

Her guards shackled her wrists and ankles. The two guards each took their final looks at her, both with a look of remorse on their faces before leaving the room and closing the door behind them. There were no fires in the room, and the window had a heavy thick drape hanging in it. The room was dark except for a strip of light flickering from under her door, and a tiny strip along the edges of the drapes which was dimming as the sun went down.

The chains were much heavier than they looked; it was difficult for her to lift her arms up. She sat on the wood floor and adjusted the chains and shackles in a way so that she wouldn't be sitting on them. She was fortunate that they were long enough to allow her to move around a little bit.

It was more than what she expected. She had come to know that comfort was never a consideration for the indentured. But true comfort was not possible for her with her torn up back. The weeping and scabbed wounds cracked and burned with every movement that she made. It was agonizing and almost unbearable.

She sat in the dark for countless hours. Eventually, she fell asleep leaning her head against the wall. When she woke up, sunlight was breaking through the edges of the curtains.

She was surprised to see the sunlight. Despite her pain and predicament of being chained up with an unknown fate before her, she slept better than she had in as long as she could remember. She was unsure why. Perhaps it was the craziness of the previous day. Perhaps it was the pain. Or perhaps it was because there was no whining, arguing, or crying children to keep her awake. She was free from them finally. No matter what horrors her future held, she was finally free from the children.

She should have been scared about what may be in store for her, but she wasn't. She was resolute in whatever was to come. What felt like a couple of hours after waking, activity sounded outside her door. The sounds were all muffled, so she couldn't tell what was going on. But she did recognize that there were multiple voices.

There was rattling at her door. It must have been locked. That was very strange to her. She was never locked in before. Locks were put on places like the food storeroom building, the guards' weapons stations, and the guards' barracks. They were to keep people out, not in.

She was a slave. Guards were everywhere. She was never alone no matter what she did or where she went; there were always guards. And with those guards came brutal punishment for small or sometimes even imagined indiscretions.

She had heard of people who tried to avoid their duties and the punishments that would last days. She had never heard of anyone trying to escape, although she was sure there must have been some. She couldn't even imagine what kind of punishments they would experience.

As she thought of that, the first pang of fear hit her. What kind of punishment was in store for her? She had killed somebody. She had killed one of her charges. She had murdered a child. The type of punishment that she would receive was worse than anything she had ever received before, and she had received more than her share of disciplines.

She remembered the dread, fear, and regret on the faces of the Captain and the guards who had carried her to her imprisonment. But none of that bothered her at the time or even as she thought about them. But the looks on the faces of the two foreboding guards at the door of her current building were the most concerning. They knew what was in store for her. They enforced it. And even they seemed hesitant and remorseful.

It took several minutes after the noise at her door before voices were outside it again. She figured that they knew that she couldn't try to escape even if the door wasn't locked and there weren't guards everywhere. She was chained up to the wall. She really was a prisoner. How much worse would her life be as a prisoner instead of a slave? Could it be any worse?

Two deep-voiced men spoke outside the door. She still couldn't hear what was being said. Her door must be very thick solid wood to muffle voices that were just outside. She heard one of them laugh, and then both. The sound of laughter was strange to her. Except voiced by young ones that she was forced to care for, she rarely heard the sound.

The door opened pouring in the bright light from the hallway. There was a door across the landing from where her room was. How could she get to the other side? Then she remembered the staircase that she was carried up. It split the upstairs into two landings. She had never seen a building with an upstairs that was not a single room.

A thin man stepped into the room and shut the door behind him. The sudden darkness shadowed his form so much that she wasn't sure where he was in the room. Suddenly the shades were pulled to the side revealing the bright light of late morning. It was painfully bright for a moment, and she squinted against the intensity of it. The man tied the shades to the side of the window with a sash that was attached to the wall.

The man turned to look at her.   He frowned as he inspected her.   His eyes moved across every bit of her several times with scrutiny.

"Hmm."   He grumbled.

He was a tall man.   She was sitting on the floor, but she could tell that it was not from the angle of her position that made him look so tall.   He had a thin frame but still had visible muscles on his arms.   She couldn't tell what age he was.   But she couldn't tell how old any of the adults were.   The only adults she saw were guards, and they never spoke to her beyond giving her orders, yelling at her to get control of her charges, or gloating over the punishments that they had issued upon her.

The man walked over to her, gesturing for her to stand up.   She pulled her back away from the wall and hissed as pain from her more recent lashings made it difficult to breathe.   She took several deep, intentional breaths to regain her ability to move and pushed herself off the ground.   The chains were so heavy that her balance was thrown off making her stumble into the wall which sent a new wave of searing pain through her wounds. She groaned as she pushed away from it to stand as steadily as she could before the man.

He watched her with an unexpected expression; concern. It was strange to see so many adults concerned about her. It was strange that anybody was concerned for her, but especially adults. They were the ones in charge, and everything that had happened to her was because of them. So, it didn't make sense why they would care.

"Here let me get those." The man said as he approached her with keys. She stared at him in confusion.

"Come on. Don't you want those off?" He asked.

She stared at him dumbfounded. She nodded, and then with significant effort lifted one of her hands. He grabbed it and helped her hold it up as he unlocked the manacle.

"I thought that once they were on, they would never come off again." She said as he unlocked her other hand. He dropped the manacles, and they clanged against the floor.

"Hmm." The man said as he leaned down

and unlocked her ankles.

She had not recognized how uncomfortable they had been until they were gone. She rubbed her wrists.

"Why are you here?" The man asked with genuine confusion in his voice.

She frowned at him. How did he not know?

"I killed Clive. So, I was brought here to be punished." She said straightforwardly.

He nodded, looking up and down at her again. "Hmm." He said again.

"You'll make a lousy breeder." He mused.

She shook her head at his statement. "No. They said I'm supposed to be something else. I can't remember what they called it, but they said I'm supposed to be punished. Not a breeder, something else." She corrected.

"A Vassal Lady? You are to be a Vassal Lady?" He said a deep frown forming between his eyebrows. "That doesn't make any sense. How old are you?" He asked.

"I don't know." She said shrugging her shoulders and then groaned in pain as the movement tugged at the lashes on her back.

"I think fourteen or fifteen." She answered through gasps. She wasn't sure how long she had been in the camp. She

132

thought four years, but she wasn't sure of any specifics.

"You're barely even old enough to be a breeder and at your age you would have years of that before you would become a Vassal Lady.   This is not how it works." The man said again looking at her up and down.

"That's what the guards at the door said," Marianna said.   She had no idea what was going on.

"Hmm."   He said again.   "What did this Clide do to you?"   He asked as he circled her grabbing a lock of her wiry auburn hair, lifting it up and then dropping it like it was something foul.

"It's Clive.   And he was playing again like he always did."

"Wait he was a child?   Not a guard?"   He interrupted.   He looked confused.

She narrowed her eyes at him in confusion.   "Yes, he was one of the young ones that I was in charge of.   Well, anyways he broke the bag of vegetables.   And he wasn't listening, and he wasn't helping.   He was just crying, and then the guards came, and I couldn't be whipped again, I just couldn't.

"So, I hit him, once, then twice, then over and over again. I couldn't stop. They pulled on me, trying to get me to stop, and then I wrapped my hands around his throat, and I slammed him against the floor again and again. I knew he was dying, but I couldn't stop. I didn't want to stop."

The man listened to her explanation and with every word his frown towards her deepened. The look caused the angles of his face to sharpen.

"I see." He stared into her eyes and remained silent for several minutes. The whole time he continued gazing into her eyes like he was searching for something in them. It made her uncomfortable, but she didn't dare look away.

"You have no remorse for what you did, do you." He said. It was a statement, not a question. She looked at him with confusion. Why would she have remorse? She didn't do anything wrong. Nothing would have happened if Clive had just listened.

She found herself shaking her head. It was an obvious answer to her. His frown sunk even deeper into his face. She didn't think that possible.

"Hmm." He said pulling his eyes away from her with noticeable effort. He said that a lot.

"Well let's see you then. Take off your clothes." He said sitting on the bed and crossing his legs. He placed his hands on his knees and watched with keenness.

She wasn't sure what he was looking for, but it didn't matter. So, she did as he asked.

She slowly pulled her shirt, knowing that it would be stuck. She wheezed as she tugged at it. Her back crackled as she peeled her scabs away with the shirt. Once it was away from her back, she gingerly lifted it over her head. It hurt to raise her arms up. She dropped the bloody shirt onto the ground and without much effort took off her skirts and dropped them to the ground as well.

She was uncomfortable under his scrutinizing eyes for some reason. He looked at her like she used to look at her vegetables to determine which ones were good enough to use, and which would have to be thrown out. What would be his criteria to throw her out?

After gazing at her for a long time, he stood up to circle around her. He gathered her hair up and lifted it up to look at her back.   He sucked his breath in between his teeth.   He dropped her hair and moved back around to her front.

He poked at her hips, and then at her ribs with a look of disgust.   He pushed on her chest sighing.

"I don't know what I'm going to do with you.   You're too thin, too mutilated, too wounded, and too crazy to be of any beneficial use.   You have no breasts, no hair, no appeal, and you look like a little boy. You haven't even started your blood phase yet have you?"   He said poking at her some more.

She shook her head answering his question.   She looked at herself feeling ashamed of the way she looked.

"Before I can even try doing anything with you, you will need to be cleaned up.   Even the most desperate or lustful of youths won't get stiff looking at you like this.   Come on." He said as he grabbed her by the arm and led her out the door.

He walked her down the hall and down the stairs.   There were so many windows letting in light from all around.   He walked her through two more large rooms; each had men and women talking to each other. They were casual conversations, which was something she was not used to. A few of them looked at her as she was led past them. They all had looks ranging from disgust, to sadness, to shock.

He walked her into a washroom with several large wash tubs. There were two other women in the room, one in a tub, and the other standing in front of a wash basin scrubbing clean a dress.

Marianna stepped into the tub that he led her to and sat. She made sure she didn't touch her back to any part of the metal.

"Get some water in this thing and clean her up." He instructed the woman at the basin in a calm but firm tone.

"Yes sir. Right away." The woman said hurriedly.

The man left the room leaving Marianna alone with the two women.

The woman at the basin filled a large bucket with water, walked over to Marianna and poured it on top of her. Marianna gasped as the cold water covered her. She wrapped her arms around her body and shivered. The woman filled the bucket again and poured it over her. It was even colder than the first one.

"Where'd they get you? They must be getting desperate if they are using an ugly wisp of a thing like you as a breeder." The woman said as she poured the third bucket of freezing water over her.

"No," Marianna said through chattering teeth. "Nnn...not a breeder. Th...th...they said not a breeder."

The woman stopped and turned to look at Marianna with the same look of shock that everybody else had when they heard the same news. "What?"

"I'm here ff...o... oor punishment. I would...wouldn't survive another lashing, and I couldn't stay with children. So, the captain made the guards bring me here to be a Vassal lady." Marianna explained, shivering less as she spoke. The woman's eyes widened as she stared at her.

She didn't know what it meant to be a Vassal lady or a Breeder for that matter. But she knew from everybody's reaction, that something terrible was in store for her. She still couldn't bring herself to be very afraid. In her mind, she knew that the fear should be there. But feelings, any feelings, good, bad, scared, they were distant and un-graspable.   She felt nothing at all.

The woman stared into Marianna's eyes for a long time; she too was searching for something in her.   She pulled her eyes away from Marianna with an effort and walked back to the basin.   She came back to her with a wet cloth.   Her eyes scanned Marianna's partially submerged body.   She moved over to Marianna's back to start washing her and gasped.

"Great Spirits child, what have they done to you?"   She exclaimed as she dropped the cloth into the tub.

The woman washing in the other tub next to her stood up and walked over to look at what the woman was talking about.

She was beautiful.   She looked quite a bit older than Marianna, and she looked like a woman should look.   Marianna looked at herself; the man was right when he said that Marianna looked like a boy.

The young woman had straight golden hair that fell perfectly even though it was wet.   Her naked body made Marianna envious.   She had full round breasts, opposite of the flat boy like chest that Marianna owned.

The younger blond woman touched her

back.   Marianna jerked away and winced. "Oh, wow.   What did you do?"   The woman asked with a hint of amusement.

She rounded on Marianna prodding her in the same way that the man had done, poking her hips and chest.   She had a condescending smile on her face.

"Leave her be Evadnie."   The other woman said.   She looked much older than the blond-haired woman, but not old.   She too was a gorgeous woman.   She had thick curly brown hair that fell to the middle of her back.   The clothes she wore were plain, but they fell on her in a way that accentuated every curve which were all a bit thicker than the younger woman but still very womanly. She pushed the younger woman she called Evadnie away.

"Don't mind Evadnie.   She can be a little difficult to get along with sometimes."   The older woman said as she grabbed the cloth and scrubbed Marianna's legs.   Evadnie stuck her tongue out at the older woman.   It reminded Marianna of the young ones.

"I'm sorry," Evadnie said not sounding sorry at all.   "I have never seen someone that looks like a naked rat that lost a fight with a cat."   She said.

"Please Evadnie. If you are not going to help me, just leave. I can't handle you right now." The older woman said sounding exasperated.

"I'll help you Sarafina," Evadnie said grabbing a bar of soap from the tub that she had been in. She rubbed the soap on Marianna's hair until a thick lather was formed.

"You are filthy." The older woman Sarafina said as she moved her scrubbing cloth to Marianna's arms.

"I haven't been to the bathhouse in a few weeks," Marianna said defensively.

"Weeks! Weeks? Well, no wonder. No, you will go two, three days at most between baths here. Do you understand? The men will not want you if you are this disgusting. And Faisal will not allow that kind of filth in his house." Sarafina said while Evadnie poured another bucket of cold water over her head, sending a new round of shivers through Marianna.

"So, seriously, what did you do?" Evadnie asked.

"I'm curious too. I know people get punished, but this is on a level I have never seen. Even some of the soldiers who deliberately disobey orders have never looked like this.   This looks like layers and layers of lashes and bruises.   Some look older than the others."   Sarafina asked.

All the attention on her back was making her awareness of the pain amplify.   She wished that they would just stop talking about it so that she could put her mind on something else.   She had never had so much interest directed at her.   It was unusual, and she didn't know how to react to it.

"How often do you get in trouble?" Evadnie asked with an obvious tone of condescension.

"All the time," Marianna grumbled more to herself.

"Why are you so disobedient?   Do you just like the attention of being in trouble? Are you refusing your duties?   Or were you trying to escape?"   Evadnie asked; her voice climbing in pitch and excitement with every question.

"No.   Why does everybody think that I want to get in trouble?   I don't want to be disobedient.   I do as I am told.   I do.   It was my stupid charges.   Those inconsiderate little brats never listen to me. I try to make them do as we are told, and they deliberately disobey me, and then I get punished for it.

"I do what I am told.   I don't like being beaten like this.   I don't like being in pain every moment of my life.   I don't like waking up every day not knowing if today I will receive a beating or whipping.   Because there will always be one.   I do as I am told." Marianna screeched defending herself.

It took everything she had to not scream at the women.   The first true emotion that she had felt since beating Clive to death was an overwhelming anger that made her vision tunnel.   She felt like she had in the moments that she was striking Clive.

"Calm down child.   Calm down.   We understand.   It was out of your control." Sarafina said nervously.

"I was only wondering because punishments for not obeying here are different than those you have suffered.   And you don't seem to have weathered your previous punishments very well.   I'm not sure how you will handle the punishments here if you are as disobedient.

"I still don't understand why you are here though.   You said you are not to be a Breeder, which makes sense.   I mean look at

143

you.   But I have never heard of someone being brought in directly to be a Vassal lady. It just doesn't happen that way.   They want to use up the Breeders for as long as they can before turning them into Vassal ladies, but they bring you straight in as one.

"What could you have possibly done to make them do that?   I mean, I guess the other forms of punishment weren't working on you. Otherwise, you wouldn't have so many scars, but this seems extreme.   Even for them, this seems overly harsh."   Evadnie said.   She still had a haughty air about her but was puzzled.

Both women stopped scrubbing her and looked at her expectantly, waiting for her answer.   She had no reason to not tell them, and she didn't care if they knew.

"I killed someone.   He got me in trouble again yesterday.   It made me so angry that I beat him into the ground until his head crushed, and his brain spilled out into my hands."   She said indifferently.

Evadnie scoffed smiling broadly, but as she looked at Marianna, the smile left her face.   Sarafina took a step away from Marianna as if she was poisonous.

"You're not joking, are you?"   Evadnie

said losing all hints of amusement.

Marianna shook her head.   Her anger was beginning to subside being replaced by her feeling of nothingness again.

"You're clean.   Go get Faisal.   Tell him she is ready for him."   Sarafina said. Evadnie looked at the woman with a look of concern but then left the room in a hurry.

"You're dangerous child.   Not because you killed someone, and not because you obviously feel no guilt about it.   You are dangerous because you are like broken glass. You are nothing but sharp edges that will slice anybody who holds you.   You are like a wild animal that has been beaten into submission.   But you will never be tame.

"And now they bring you here to be broken further.   I do not want to be near you when your wild nature comes out.   I should feel fear for you, for I know what is to come.   But instead I fear you, and what will come from you.   I do not like it." Sarafina said.

Evadnie stepped into the room with Faisal close behind her.   She stepped to the side with her head down as the man passed her. As soon as he was beyond her, she lifted her head back up and watched with a small smile on her face.

Sarafina also averted her gaze as the man entered. They each showed a level of fear towards the man. Why? He had been kind to her. Compared to her usual contact with adults, he wasn't that bad. Not yet at least.

Faisal gestured for Marianna to stand up. She did as he instructed, feeling much colder as the air hit her wet skin. She wrapped her arms around herself and fought off shivers as goosebumps formed.

The man circled her inspecting her body. He shook his head as he looked at her.

"I fear that you will be more trouble than you are worth. I don't know what to do with you." He said.

Marianna was ashamed again. She was no good anywhere that she went. She watched as Faisal circled her several more times. He was looking at every bit of her and looking for each and every flaw. He poked at her in several places again sighing as he did so. He finished circling and stood in front of her looking up and down her body. He stepped forward as close as he could without stepping into the wash tub with her. He reached out and grabbed both of her hips and pulled her up against him.

She gasped in surprise by the movement. It happened so quickly.

She looked up at him as he looked down at her. He put his hand on her face cupping her cheek and without saying a thing pulled her into a kiss. She tried to pull away from the unexpected shock of it, but he held her close gripping her face and hip tighter. She stared at him as he moved his mouth around, sucking at her lip, and then pushing his tongue into her mouth and moving it around. It was strange.

After a while, he pulled away and looked down at her. She stared back at him and wavered a bit as he moved away from her.

"Hmm." He said as he stared at her.

"That was creepy. She just stared at you the entire time." Evadnie said as she intentionally shuddered.

"I have a lot of work to do on you before you will be ready. But you seem obedient, so there is a possibility that you have potential." Faisal said skeptically.

"Well, that's good," Sarafina said looking visibly relieved. Despite her claims of being afraid of Marianna, she still was concerned about her. Her care towards Marianna confused her.

"When was the last time you ate?" Faisal asked.

Marianna considered his question and tried to remember the last time that she had eaten. "I had breakfast yesterday." She said.

He huffed and then nodded. "Eat first, and then we will get started." He said.

She stared at him, not sure how to respond. He poked at her hip again and then looked at Sarafina. "Make sure she eats enough. We need to get some meat on her if we ever want to start using her. Nobody will want her like this." He said grimacing.

Sarafina nodded.

He looked back at Marianna as she just stared at him. Nobody ever cared whether she ate or not. Well except for Alex and Rayden, but they were the only ones. Would she ever see them again? She rarely saw them anymore anyway, but they were the closest things to friends she had.

Faisal shook his head with a deep frown on his face. "So much work. You are going to take so much work." He squeezed the bridge of his nose and then turned and walked out of the room still shaking his head.

"Well, let's get some clothes on you and then get you something to eat, shall we," Sarafina said with a light tone in her voice.

Marianna looked down at herself. She had forgotten entirely that she was naked still.

"What do you think we have that will fit her?" Evadnie asked as she gestured towards Marianna to step out of the tub.

"Nothing without some finagling. But we can find something and make it work." Sarafina said.

They led her into an adjacent room which was full of tall wardrobes. There were such distinct types of clothes inside them Marianna was amazed. She did not know that clothing could have so many colors.

Sarafina stepped up to one of the wardrobes and pushed aside several pieces before settling on a light green dress. Marianna couldn't remember the last time she wore a dress. She only ever wore her children's camp skirts and shirts; nothing with color, and no dresses. Dresses weren't practical for growing children. They would have to be sized too often. Skirts and shirts had more give to fit assorted sizes as children grew.

Sarafina handed her the dress.   She carefully pulled it over her back and then let it drop down.   It hung to her ankles.   It was very loose on her.   The woman stepped around to tie a bow, pulling the dress much tighter around her.   Marianna hissed and pulled away as the pain from the hugging dress pressed against her back.

"Oh, sorry dear," Sarafina said as she loosened the tie a bit.

Again, Marianna was shocked by the unexpected care she was being shown.

"Well turn around.   Let us see you." Evadnie said.

Marianna spun slowly around only to find herself facing a full-length mirror.   The dress was stunning.   It still looked way too big on her, but she liked it.

Evadnie studied her with her mouth cocked to the side.   She moved around her and gathered Marianna's wet hair up, moved it around some, and then attached it to the top of her head with something.   Marianna watched as the woman did so, but she couldn't figure out how she got her hair to look like she did.   Half of her auburn hair still fell down her back, while the other half sat curled on the top of her head. A couple of locks fell next to her face.

"Eh. It'll work." Evadnie said as she moved back around to look at Marianna from the front.

"Well come on, let's get some food in you," Sarafina said as she carefully pulled the dress in a way that made it hug Marianna's front more but put no additional pressure on her back.

Evadnie and Sarafina led Marianna into a room with a large table surrounded by two dozen chairs. How many people were in the building?

"The kitchen is preparing for dinner right now, so you are going to have to eat your food cold," Sarafina said with an apologetic air.

Marianna didn't care what temperature her food was. As long as it was not going sour, she would eat anything that she was given.

A large plate of food was set in front of her. It had three times the amount of food from what she was usually given. There was a large piece of bread, several pieces of fruit, a large chunk of pork, some potatoes, and some kind of mashed green vegetable.

It looked amazing. Much better than anything she had ever been served or made while she was in the children's camp.

As she ate, she became aware of just how hungry she was. She finished every piece of food. She would have never been able to eat so much before. Even if she had been given so much food while in the children's camp, she would have had to stop eating before finishing due to one of her charges doing something that would either make her stop eating, or make her stop wanting to eat.

"Well, it looks like we may not have too much trouble fattening you up," Evadnie said with a hint of disgust in her tone.

"It was really good," Marianna said.

"I see that," Evadnie said. Both women were keeping their distance from her still. What was it that she did that made them so hesitant around her?

"Well, it's time.

"Do everything that he says. Do not fight him. He always gets what he wants.

"Don't give him a reason to get angry. With the state you are in, I don't think you could survive it if he did." Sarafina said.

She looked solemn as she spoke, which somehow made her look even older. She wasn't old.   Marianna knew that.   She was just older than what she was used to seeing a person.

Marianna didn't know what to think about the woman's advice.   She didn't want to do anything that would get her beaten again.   She didn't know if she could survive more abuse either, but the thought of it possibly killing her didn't bother her either.   She didn't care if she lived or died, she just didn't want to be in any more pain.   No matter what she did or didn't do, being punished was inevitable.   So, there was no point to dwell on it.

"Well, are you ready?"   Sarafina asked.   All previous signs of distance were gone.   She looked genuinely concerned.

"Would it matter if I wasn't?"   Marianna said as she shrugged.

"No, it wouldn't.   But it is good that you know that already."   Sarafina said as she shook her head.

"So, let's see what my life has in store for me now."

Marianna walked back to the room where she had been chained up.   Faisal was sitting on the bed reading a book.   He closed the book and stood up as she entered.   Again, he scanned her calculatingly. He circled her lifting the hem of her dress and then dropping it again. He faced her; scrutinizing every bit of her like she was a hog being selected for the slaughter. He licked his lips as he looked up and down her body.

He looked dangerous. She didn't know what about him looked dangerous, but she knew on some unknown level, that she should be terrified of him. She wasn't. She should have been for so many reasons, but being afraid didn't stop the terrors from happening. She would still be hurt, enslaved, and in a hopeless situation. She had no control over what would or wouldn't happen to her. So why be afraid? Instead, she just felt nothing at all. Maybe she was broken like Sarafina had said.

Faisal lifted her chin so that she would look at him. He grabbed one of the locks of hair that was hanging in her face and twirled it in his fingers, and then pushed it behind her ear, stroking her cheek as he did.

"How far have you gone with a boy?" Faisal asked.

Marianna scowled in confusion. "I don't understand."

Faisal stepped back and studied her more intently.

"When you screw around with your boyfriend, what have you done?   Have you kissed?   Has he fiddled you under your skirts?   Have you touched him, sucked him, fucked him?   How far have you gone?"

Marianna could feel her cheeks grow red as he so blatantly asked her.   She fervently shook her head.   "I don't have a boyfriend. I've never.   I mean, I'm a slave, I don't really have any time to myself.   I don't really have any friends, not ones that I can talk to or, well what you were talking about."   She stammered as she spoke.

"They brought me an emaciated, crazy, inexperienced child, to be a Vassal Lady; what do they expect me to do with you? Am I supposed to just throw you to these animals until you are so spent you are debilitated, die of exhaustion, or just kill yourself?"

"The guards did say something like that I think.   I don't remember for sure.   It's all a little bit fuzzy."   Marianna mused.

Faisal scowled and stepped away from her another step.   He too was wary of her.   She should be the one afraid, but instead, he was.

She didn't understand why.

He scratched his brow and stared at her for a long time without saying anything.

"Hmm..." He mumbled as he paced the floor a bit chewing on his bottom lip.

"Well, I guess I don't have to break you of any unpleasant habits. I can teach you everything myself. I might enjoy that. Maybe with enough training, some hefty portions of food, and time I can actually get some beneficial use out of you." He stopped pacing and approached her.

The lock of hair that he had pushed behind her ear had fallen back in front of her face. He twirled it around his finger several times and then let it drop back down to dangle.

He ran a finger down the side of her body, it tickled a bit until he got to one of the lashings that had wrapped around the flesh of her back to her side. His touching it made her gasp and pull away in pain.

"Oh. Sorry about that. I forgot how battered you are." He said.

She stared at him in shock with her mouth gaping open.

"What is that look about?" He asked as he moved closer to her again.

"You apologized for hurting me. Nobody

ever does that.

"You don't want to hurt me?"   She asked and then regretted it.   What if she made him angry?   It wasn't her place to question those in charge.

"Hmm..."   He stared at her as he twirled her lock of hair again.

"You've only ever been hurt.   You don't know anything else, do you?"

She shook her head.   She started to cry. She didn't know why, and she couldn't stop herself.

Faisal scowled and wiped her cheek with his thumb.   "I don't want to hurt you."

Tears poured from her eyes.

"What I need to do today may hurt a little bit.   But I don't do it because I want to hurt you.   It just sometimes hurts the first time. But it is nothing like the beatings and lashings that you have received.   I will be as gentle as I can, and I will try not to put any strain on any of the places where you are already hurt.   If you cooperate, it shouldn't be that bad.   It's only if you don't cooperate that things will get unpleasant."   He explained with care.

She didn't know how to respond.   He seemed genuine, but how could he be?

"I'm going to take off your dress.   Guide me however you need to so that it doesn't stick to any of your wounds."

She nodded her head.   He untied her dress and began pulling it slowly over her head.   She wiggled so that it wouldn't catch her lashes.   Other than the movement, it didn't hurt.

He dropped her dress on the ground.

He circled her again, lifting her hair off her back to look at it.

"You can't lie on the bed with these."   He dropped her hair, just the light touch of her hair sweeping across her back made her hiss and jerk.

He moved back to stand in front of her. His eyes scrutinized her exposed body.   For a moment she saw a look of disgust as he looked at her emaciated frame.   She couldn't help but feel self-conscious.

"Take my clothes off."   He said.   She scowled in confusion but did as she was told.   She untied the back of the neck of his shirt and pulled it up over his head.

"Not so fast."   He said.

She nodded.   She slowly unbuttoned each of the buttons on his pants.   She pulled them down as he stepped out of each leg.

She had never seen a grown man naked before, only the little boys she was charged with.

She stood back up.

"Touch me." He gently grabbed her hand and directed her to softly run her hand down his chest.

He grabbed her other hand and placed it on his penis. "Touch it. Slow and gentle."

She crouched and lightly touched him. As she touched him, his penis grew longer and angled up. It was hot and very hard. She ran her fingers up and down feeling little bumps and ridges. It bounced some while she touched it. The top felt different from the rest of it. It was kind of spongy, and it was a little wet and sticky. His breathing sped up as she investigated it with her fingers. He grabbed her arms and pulled her to stand.

"I'm sorry. Did I do something wrong." She asked shakily. Even though he said he didn't want to hurt her, she didn't want to be punished.

"Shh..." He said as he put his finger on top of her lips. He leaned towards her and kissed her, gently at first and then more forcefully. Her heart raced.

He pulled away a little. "Close your eyes." She had been staring at him as he kissed her, not sure what else to do.

She closed her eyes, and he kissed her again. "Kiss me back." He said through the side of his mouth and then continued kissing her. She wasn't sure how to kiss, but she tried to mimic what he was doing. He pushed his tongue into her mouth, she attempted to do the same.

He ran his hand down her side. He stopped at her nipple and rubbed his finger around.

He pulled his mouth away from hers and kissed her on the cheek and then on the neck. She could feel his breath on her neck. It felt really good. She liked it. He kissed and sucked on her neck, she tilted her head to give him more access. He bit down gently making her gasp. She was breathing heavy, and her heart was racing.

He moved up to her ear breathing a hot, heavy breath and then sucking on her earlobe. Goosebumps covered her skin. She giggled. He pulled away from her. She opened her eyes and found that surprisingly he was smiling. She smiled back.

He cocked his head to the side.   He crouched, lightly running his fingers down the front of her.   He kissed her belly button, and then licked around it.   It tickled, and she giggled a little again.   He smiled, and then kissed her again.   He moved over to her hip and kissed it and then sucked on it, causing a shocking tingle to go up her spine. Her whole body wiggled, and she sighed and then laughed as the tingle turned into a tickle.

His smile grew, and he chuckled.

He lightly ran both of his hands down her thighs.   He kissed her moving from her hip down to her thigh, opening his mouth between each kiss, so that he was half kissing, half sucking.   He ran his hand between her legs and gently touched her as he continued to kiss her thigh.   She shuddered and closed her eyes.   He pushed her leg over a little making her step to spread her legs out more.   He gently touched her again and then rubbed her several times and then pushed a finger up inside her.

"Wow.   You are so moist.   You are enjoying this."   He said.

She smiled giggling a little.   She loved it.

He smiled broadly and then continued kissing her inner thigh.

He moved his finger around inside her while rubbing her on the outside with his other hand. She could feel herself getting warmer. Her body undulated as the intensity that she felt increased. Her breath became heavier.

He pulled his hands away. She groaned a little, not wanting him to stop. He stood back up and led her over to the bed.

"Lean over here." He told her as he gently pushed her forward so that she was bending over the side of the bed.

Standing behind her he leaned down breathing into her ear. Her eyes rolled as goosebumps moved across her skin again. "I will try to be gentle. Don't move, let me do everything." He whispered.

He stood up and grabbed the front of her hips. He managed to avoid touching any of her lashings.

She could feel something rubbing up between her legs and then pushing up inside her. He slowly moved back and forth, she could feel every one of his ridges rubbing inside of her making her warmer and wetter. He moved his hand from her hip down between her legs and rubbed her, her toes curled. She moaned every time he moved in, and even though he had told her not to move, she found herself moving her body towards him every time he moved away.

He moved his other hand up from her hip running it up her stomach and then to her chest. He grabbed her forcefully, but not painfully, and rubbed at her breast. He let go of her breast and let his fingers caress her nipple. His hand moved away from her nipple, and he reached around her back, she was afraid he was going to touch her back, but instead, he grabbed a handful of her hair and tugged gently, while at the same time speeding up and becoming more forceful in his thrusting. She cried out in surprise by the intensity of it. The pleasure was almost too much, but she didn't want him to stop.

He unexpectedly pulled himself out of her, leaning over her without touching her back, and grabbed the bed's comforter with both hands, his whole body shook, as he made a noise that sounded like a mix between a groan and a cry. He was breathing heavily. He moved away from her laying on the bed next to her and sprawled out on his back. His whole body was relaxed and glistened with sweat, and he had a smile on his face.

She turned onto her side and watched him.   She too felt relaxed, and she smiled widely.   Her whole body tingled.   She had lost track of all time and thoughts of pain, fear, or suffering.   She had never been so distanced from the reality of her life.

He rolled up onto his side to look at her. "I couldn't have been more wrong about you."   He said.

She frowned, not sure what he meant.

"You were stupendous, so much fun.   I haven't felt this amazing in a long time. You were enjoying it all, you really wanted it.   I don't think I have ever experienced that when I am breaking a woman in.   You didn't need any coercion, just direction.   It was wonderful.   Did I hurt you?"   He asked with real concern in his tone.

"That was the first time for as long as I can remember where I didn't feel any pain anywhere."   She said realizing that she still wasn't feeling any pain.   She smiled.

He pushed her hair out of her face and tucked it behind her ear, and then leaned in and kissed her.   She closed her eyes and melted into the kiss.

"I'm going to enjoy training you."   He

said lightheartedly.

"Was that part of my training?"   She asked.

He nodded.

"I liked it."   She said laying her head on his arm.

He smirked and looked at her with a puzzled expression.

"What do you know about Breeders or Vassal ladies?"   He asked.

Marianna shrugged.   "I never heard of them before."

"Where were you again before you came here?   Oh yeah, you were on the other side of town with most of the children.

"So, you probably didn't hear about it. Well, let me explain.   We have a camp here with about twenty thousand soldiers, around the same number of women, and only about five thousand children."   He explained.

"So, is this really an army?"   She asked, remembering back to when she was in the Medica being cared for by Kania.   She had been such a nice woman.

"Of course it is.   What do they teach you on the children's side?   What did you think this was?"   Faisal asked in awe.

"The grownups only ever talk to us when they are telling us what to do."

Faisal shook his head in disbelief. "How are we ever expected to function, if we don't properly train the most flexible members? Well, none of that matters now. We are an army. This army has been established to fight a future war. We don't know when, and we don't know who we will be fighting. I'm sure the higher officers know those things, but most of us do not, so we just keep training and growing our numbers. Breeders are meant to reproduce with the strongest, smartest, and bravest men to build an even better army in the future.

"It is important that the women who are used as Breeders are kept in peak physical shape. We make sure they are cared for in every way to produce the best offspring. They continue to bear children and then care for them until weaned. That is when the children are sent over to your side of town to be raised until they are old enough to start training for whatever duty they will be assigned.

"Some of the women die in childbirth. Some don't handle their responsibilities very well and find ways to end their lives. But many of the women endure until they are no longer bearing children, or until the children that are bore become inferior quality, at which point they become Vassal Ladies.

"To keep the soldiers performing the best that they can, they need all their physical needs met. They need food and lodging, they need clothing and washing, and they need women for companionship and to satisfy them. If the men are deprived of any of these things for too long, their ability to train, fight, and follow commands diminishes. Only a select type of men are chosen to be paired with a Breeder. The rest of the men still have needs. So, Vassal Ladies are there to be the men's physical companions.

"Usually the Vassal Ladies have already been broken into some degree as a Breeder. It is my job to break in Breeders and to teach the Vassal Ladies to be the best companion they can be. I instruct them, by showing them how to pleasure the men in whatever way is needed. I also discipline any woman who refuses to do their duty, or if she intentionally harms any of the soldiers.

"I will train you to do whatever the men want and to know what the men want, even if they themselves don't completely know. Do you understand anything that I just told you?" He asked.

Marianna thought about what he said for a while. "I think so. I was never assigned to the growing part of food, but I know somebody who is. He used to talk about separating the pigs and chickens in a way so that the right ones would mate. That way they got better animals from the babies. So, the Breeders are for that."

"You don't seem to have a problem with it. Does it bother you to know how some of the women are used?" He asked raising one of his eyebrows.

"Not really. It makes sense. You want to have the strongest army, you put together the best people to make it better." She said.

"Hmm." He mused as he stared at her for a long time.

"You are a strange girl." He said.

She looked down in shame.

"But I think you might be very useful." He said as he lifted her chin up to look at him.

She stared back, not sure what else to do or say. From what he explained, being a Vassal Lady didn't sound like a dreadful thing. It would be her job to be a soldier's companion. It had to be worse than what she was being told. But then Faisal did tell her that he would try to not hurt her, and he had kept his word on that.

"Why don't you want to hurt me?" She asked. It was an alien concept to her.

He raised his eyebrow and tilted his head. He sat up and gestured for her to do the same. He wrapped his hands gently around her arms.

"Listen to me. It is my job to keep you from being hurt. The guards posted make sure nobody hurts the Ladies. Any man attempting to hurt any of the Breeders or Vassal Ladies is severely punished. You may not understand this yet, but your job is vital for the sanity of the soldiers. It is not taken lightly for anyone to cause problems with the ladies that could cause them to lose their usefulness.

"The only time I hurt a lady is when they fight back or when I am punishing them for not doing their job.

"You do your job, and I promise you, nobody will ever hurt you again."

CHAPTER NINE

Settling In

Faisal spent hours training Marianna, and she loved every bit of it. Her body took over allowing her to lose herself in what they were doing, letting everything else fade into the back of her mind. It was wonderful.

She sat at the foot of the bed as he lay sprawled on his back smiling yet again.

"I am exhausted." He said still out of breath. She smiled. It was the third time he had said it, but it didn't stop him.

"You are so much fun. I didn't realize how much I missed being with somebody who enjoyed fucking me." He said as he climbed out of bed.

"What are you doing?" Marianna asked as he grabbed his pants.

He chuckled and then grabbed her face

and kissed her. "I have to eat. And so do you."

"Oh, wow, I'm actually really hungry," Marianna said.

She wasn't used to feeling so much hunger. She was usually so aggravated by the young children that she used to oversee, that she barely wanted to eat anything. It was why she was so skinny. She had access to food. All the slaves did. It wasn't the best quality food, but it was enough to fill a working stomach. But she just lost all desire to eat most days.

Faisal tilted his head and studied her again shaking his head. He seemed to be continually trying to figure her out, but couldn't.

"I would think so. You should be. You definitely worked up an appetite." He said licking his lips and raised his eyebrows.

He grabbed her hands and pulled so that she would stand up. He leaned and grabbed her dress and handed it to her, while he grabbed his shirt. As she put the dress on and it dropped against her back, she became aware of the pain for the first time in hours. She cried out.

He looked at her with concern and then

nodded in realization about what had hurt her. He wrapped his arms around her and loosely tied her dress, careful to not touch her back.

"I cannot wait to be able to wrap my arms around you. And there are some wonderful things I can show you, while you are on your back." He whispered in her ear. She giggled.

He grabbed her face again and kissed her forcefully, making her heart race. "Let's go eat."

She followed him out the door. As she descended the staircase, the smell of food wafted up. It smelled delicious and made her stomach growl.

They rounded the corner, moved through the great room, and then entered the dining room with the large table. There were people gathered all around the table eating food. A few that Marianna recognized, Sarafina, and both guards from the front door. But all the others she didn't recognize. One other guard, and four women, one of which was big and pregnant. She must be a Breeder.

Were the other three women, Breeders or Vassal Ladies?

Everyone was having a conversation with someone else at the table. It was odd that, so many people were having casual conversations. All conversations stopped when she and Faisal entered the room. One of the women jumped up to pull a chair out for Faisal. He nodded at her, but Marianna doubted that the woman saw it because she was looking down the entire time.

Faisal gestured for Marianna to take a seat across the table from him. She sat taking care not to put her back against the chair. Now that she was no longer lost in her physical deeds with Faisal she was becoming more and more aware of the pain from her lashings.

All eyes were on her. She was uncomfortable under everyone's gaze. Sarafina and some of the other women looked remorseful. Two of guards looked ashamed. The guard with the large scar looked curious.

"Well, I guess introductions are due. What is your name?" Faisal said looking at Marianna. She was taken aback. He didn't know her name.

"Marianna. My name is Marianna." She said. She had not even had a reason to say her own name in years. It felt odd.

"Hmm. Pretty name. I think I'll let you keep it." Faisal said.

She looked at him, not sure what he meant. Was it possible for even that to be taken away from her?

One of the women scoffed. Sarafina gasped looking towards the woman.

Faisal licked his lip and looked at the woman. Even though he didn't look angry, he looked terrifying.

"Do you have something to say about that Evonne?" His tone was calm, but it had an edge to it that made everyone nervous.

"No sir," Evonne said shaking her head. The panic in her voice was startling. "I'm sorry." The woman looked down at the table the entire time.

Marianna looked around. There was a palpable anxiety resonating from everyone in the room.

Faisal looked away from the woman and back to Marianna. The unease lessoned but nobody was truly relaxed.

"So, Marianna and I need some food." He said.

Barely a moment passed before one of the women, and one of the guards stood up and headed towards the kitchen. Everyone was terrified of Faisal. Marianna's heart sped up as she thought about it. What about him made him so foreboding. She hoped she wouldn't find out. He told her that he didn't want to hurt her. He promised her that if she did what she was told, she wouldn't be hurt again. She had no intention of not doing what she was told.

In no time at all the guard and woman came back into the room each with a large plate of food and a cup. Everybody had been having conversations before she and Faisal had come into the room, but now the room was silent. Marianna ate everything on her plate again. The food was much better than anything she ever had on the children's side of the camp.

Everyone kept looking at her with questions on their faces. She wanted to ask why but she didn't want to speak. If everyone was silent, there must have been a reason for it.

She finished eating before almost everyone at the table. She actually felt full. She wanted to sit back in her chair and relax, but she couldn't. So, she just sat quietly with her hands in her lap.

Faisal was the last to finish his food. Nobody left the table while he was eating. He did sit back and sigh as he finished.

"Marianna, I'm done with you for tonight. Marte, why don't you show her around, and teach her the house rules." He said looking at the guard that had gotten her food. The man nodded, without making eye contact.

"Evonne, you're with me." He said standing up.

Evonne looked down, even more, her lip quivering as her eyes welled up. She stood up and followed Faisal out of the room her head lowered the entire way.

Marianna frowned as she watched them leave. What was she so upset about. He was going to punish her. Marianna shook her head. She would never be free from punishment.

Marte approached her with an apologetic smile on his face. She stood up not sure what to expect.

"Hi. I'm Marte. Marianna, right? That is a pretty name. Follow me, I'll show you around."

"You're a guard, right?" Marianna asked as she followed him into the kitchen.

He laughed. "No. Definitely not. Jon

and Trevino. He's the one with the scar, I'm sure you noticed?" He asked looking back at her.

She nodded.

"They are guards. There is nobody that can get past those two. We have other guards too. They each have their shifts. You'll get to know who's where and when. We have at least ten guards on duty at all times. Sometimes it's more, depending on how many soldiers are here.

"Most of them are pretty decent. But don't ever make the mistake of underestimating them. They all have the right job, and they will do everything that they must to make sure the rules are being followed. No, I'm not a guard, I'm a special kind of Vassal Lady." He said laughing a little, but there was no humor in it.

Marianna frowned. "But you're a man."

He smiled at her. "You noticed that did you?"

"How can you be a Vassal Lady if you are not a lady?" She asked.

"That's what makes me special." He said smiling, but his eyes looked pained. "Sometimes a soldier needs companionship but doesn't find any interest in women. So, they have me." He said.

"Oh," Marianna said nodding her head. But she had no idea what he was talking about.

"So, this is the kitchen, as I'm sure you can tell. This would be where, you guessed it, the cooking is done. We each have an assigned duty to maintain the house. You'll get yours once you're...um...put to work. Nobody is assigned any house duties while they are in training. Faisal insists on having all your energy and attention." He said.

She nodded along. It was a big kitchen, not as large as the one she had worked in, but still sizable. Evadnie was at a sink washing a large pot. She was no longer wearing her pretty dress, but instead, she wore a plainer looking shift that still managed to hug her curves in a very flattering way.

Marianna waved at her as she looked up, but she just rolled her eyes and went back to scrubbing.

They left the kitchen and entered the washroom. Marianna frowned in confusion. When she had been brought into the room earlier, she had come in through a different door. It must have been a circle.

"So, this is where you wash up. Where we bathe." He said as he walked through to the room with all the wardrobes full of clothes.

"It is our job to stay presentable at all times. You never know when your services will be required. So, we have to be dressed for the occasion even when we are taking care of our house duties or sleeping.

"If we are called to satisfy a soldier, we are to drop everything else. We can always get back to something, or if ordered, somebody else can take over and finish the chore. Our job is always to be here for the men. Everything else will work itself out."

Marianna nodded as she thought back to Evadnie cleaning in the kitchen. Even though the clothes were plainer, they still accentuated her body.

They walked back through the washroom to the great room and then up the stairs.

"Every Lady has a room. There are more Breeders than Vassal Ladies. Currently, we have thirty-four Breeders, and with you now seventeen Vassal Ladies. That side is all Breeders, and this side is a mix. Your room is down here. Mine is two doors down from yours." He said walking down the hall pointing at his door.   She nodded.

"But you are not allowed in anybody else's
room.   It doesn't matter if they are in there
or not.   It doesn't matter if they ask you to
go in, you are not allowed."   He said.

Marianna nodded.

He walked back downstairs back into the
great room.   Three other people were in the
room.   One guard standing at the front
door, and two women.   One of the women
was sitting in a big chair reading a book,
which was amazing to Marianna, who didn't
know how to read, and the other woman
was knitting something.

"This is where we all get together when
we are home and aren't working."   He said.

"When you're home?   People leave here?
I thought everyone would have to stay here,
especially with you having your own
kitchen.   Isn't that what the guards are for?"
Marianna mused as she looked around the
large room.

"Yes, the guards are there to keep us in
and to keep others out.   Officers don't come
here.   When they need someone, the Ladies
go to them, with an escort of course.

"Also, if you perform well, then you can
get certain privileges.   Not right away, of

course, you have to work up to it, but still, if you do things right, you can leave for a couple of hours a few times a week. But just know if you get that privilege and you do anything to take advantage of it, you lose it for good." He said.

He walked over to a soft looking couch and sat. He patted the cushion next to him smiling. She sat, careful not to touch her back to the couch.

"So, house rules. The ones I already told you of course. Number one rule; be submissive and obedient to Faisal. Above all else do this. He controls this place. Do what he tells you. Do not rebel against him. You will always lose. Always. Do you understand." He asked her gravely.

She nodded.

"I'm serious. You never want to cross him. If he tells you to do something, do it. If he asks you to do something, do it. If he jokingly mentions in passing you do something, do it." He insisted.

"Alright," Marianna said.

"Good. Rule number two; never disrespect Faisal. He doesn't take kindly to any criticism towards him. You saw how he reacted when he thought Evonne was obstinate. He was careful about how he reacted tonight. He restrained himself around you. He can be that way when a new lady comes into the house. It won't last for long. He has a temper. You don't want to experience what he is capable of when he gets angry."

"How often do new ladies come here?" Marianna asked.

"Not that often. Maybe one every six or eight months. Sometimes longer. When one of the Breeders leaves to birth and care for her babies, and they need to replace her, or when they transfer a lady from one of the other houses if she just isn't working well in her previous one, or when someone is sent here to be punished." He said gesturing to her.

She looked down in shame. "How many other houses are like this one?" She asked after considering what he said.

He shrugged. "This whole strip of houses that I know of for sure. There's probably fifteen along the water, and the same amount on the street behind us."

"Oh," Marianna said.

"Okay, back to the rules. The guards are the next in line for who you must listen to.

They don't usually give orders because they must listen to Faisal too, and he doesn't like anyone else telling us what to do, but if they tell you to do something you listen.
Assume that they are working on Faisal's orders.   Because they probably are.

"Don't fight with them.   They know ways to punish you without leaving any marks that would make you less appealing to men. And as long as Faisal doesn't see proof of the punishments, he won't do anything to the guards for dishing one out."

Marianna shivered at the thought of being hurt again.   He looked at her curiously.

"So, I'm sorry, I have to ask.   Is it true that you were brought here to be a Vassal Lady?" Marte asked with eagerness.

Marianna just nodded.

"Wow.   You must have done something seriously bad to go straight to that.   I've never heard of anyone coming straight in for that, except me of course, can't exactly be a Breeder."   He said lifting his eyebrows in anticipation.   She could tell that he wanted her to tell him about it, but she didn't want to keep talking about it.

"She killed someone," Evadnie said walking into the room drying her hands on the front of her dress.

Marte's eyes widened.   "Really?"

Marianna huffed in annoyance and nodded.

"You should have seen her earlier.   She was still covered in the person's blood." Evadnie said sitting on one of the couches and putting her feet up.   "That was blood, wasn't it?"   She said looking just as arrogant as she had earlier in the day.   "Because I've seen some dirty people, but what was all over you, it was all caked on and, well it looked like dried blood.   And you should see her back.   I've never seen someone with so many lashings."

Marianna looked down at her hands remembering the chunk of the scalp that had been caught under her fingernail.   She could almost see the blood again.   She could feel the squishiness of Clive's head as she slammed it into the ground over and over again.

She looked back up.   Marte and Evadnie were looking at her like she was crazy, and they were in danger from her.

"Wait, was that really blood?"   Evadnie asked smiling.

Marte looked over at her in annoyance and

then looked back at Marianna who was nodding. He took several steps away from her. "Whoa."

The other people in the room were looking at her as well. Just as the stares were getting uncomfortable, Sarafina walked into the room.

"Oh, thank the Great Spirits child, come over here and let me look at you." She said.

Marianna looked at her in confusion. The last time they had spoken, the woman had told her that she was dangerous, and now she wanted to take care of her.

Sarafina smiled and walked over to Marianna instead. "How are you?" She asked.

Marianna shrugged her shoulders and then hissed as the movement hurt her back.

"No really, how are you? The first day here can be very tough. We've all been there." She said gesturing to Marte and Evadnie who were both nodding with looks of sadness.

Marianna shrugged again, but more carefully. Except for all the attention she was getting making her uncomfortable, she was fine. "I'm alright." She said.

Sarafina gave her a half-smile. "You will

be.   You may never like what your life has become, but there are benefits.   When you have free time, as long as you aren't causing trouble, like Evonne tonight, you are free to do whatever you want in here.   We have great food, and if you behave, the beds are very comfortable.   You may not get to sleep in one yet, but you will, I'm sure of it.   We are all here for each other, so if you have a problem, or you need anything, you just let someone know.   If we can help, we will."

Marte was nodding, while Evadnie rolled her eyes.

"Are you hurt.   I mean, obviously you are hurt, what with your back being as bad as it is, but are you hurt anymore?"   Sarafina asked looking down Marianna's body.

She shook her head.

"Good.   Good."   She said frowning a bit.

"How are you even walking?"   Evadnie asked.   "My first week here, I could barely move.   Food had to be brought to me one of the days because I was hurt so badly.   So why aren't you?   Is it because you are already hurt so bad that you are just numb to the pain?"

Marianna shrugged again while shaking her head.   She was a little sore, but not that bad.

"How often were you whipped? Seriously look at her back."   Evadnie said to Marte as she stood up and grabbed the back of Marianna's dress tugging it up over her head.   Marianna yelped in pain and pulled away.   Her dress stayed draped over her head, and she heard several gasps.

"Oh, Great Spirits.   What happened to you?   Who did you kill?"   Marte asked with a pained sound in his voice.

Marianna pushed her dress off her head letting it drop back down.   Nobody had ever cared about her being hurt before, and now everybody seemed to.   It made her uncomfortable.   She was ashamed of her lashings in a way she never had been before.

Two more women had walked into the room and stood to stare in shock.   Marte, the woman reading, the woman knitting, and even the door guard had remorseful looks on their faces.

"My back was like this before I killed him," Marianna said feeling annoyed.

"Did he do that?   Is that why you killed him?"   Evadnie asked excitedly.

Marianna shook her head.   Why was everybody so interested in what she did?

"No. The guard did this. Clive was one of my charges." She said.

Sarafina scowled. "One of your charges. You are not old enough to be in charge of anyone. How old are you?"

Marianna shrugged. She had done this already with Faisal. "I think I'm fourteen or fifteen. I'm not sure."

"And you were brought to be a Vassal Lady?" The woman knitting asked in disbelief.

"You're not the first woman to be brought here as a punishment. But at your age, you should have been assigned as a Breeder. They don't like to waste a chance to use somebody as much as possible." Marte said.

"Wait, if you are so young, how old was your charge that you killed?" Sarafina asked. She looked terrified. She appeared to be afraid of the answer.

Marianna huffed. "Four. Clive was four." She said feeling her agitation increase. Why did it matter how old he was, or she was?

One of the women at the door fell to her knees and wailed. Sarafina and two of the other women ran over to her.

"Oh Celene, I'm so sorry," Sarafina said as she knelt and wrapped the woman in an embrace as Celene cried.

The woman knitting dropped her needles and started crying as she wrapped her arm around her stomach.   Marte looked devastated as he stared at Marianna.   Even Evadnie looked defeated.

Marianna stood confused by the change in mood throughout the room.   Everyone stood in silent except for Celene crying and Sarafina shushing her softly.

"Why?"   Celene cried.   She looked up at Marianna her face was red and puffy. "Why did you kill my boy?"

Her boy?   It was her son.   Celene stood up and stepped towards Marianna. Sarafina grabbed hold of her arm, but she pushed her away.   She took several steps towards Marianna and then rushed towards her tackling her to the floor.

Marianna screamed out in pain as her back struck the ground and then slid against it. The distraught woman grabbed the collar of her dress and shook her violently. "You killed my boy."   She screamed

The guard at the door rushed over to them and with no effort pulled the woman off her.

189

As she released her dress, Marianna dropped back hard onto the floor making her cry out again.

The guard held onto Celene as she dropped limply in his arms and dropped back to her knees crying.

Marianna pushed herself off the ground. "It was his fault. He made me. He spilled the vegetables. I was going to get in trouble again because he was playing. And he didn't care. None of them cared. Ever. I couldn't let them beat me again. I couldn't. They never listened to me. And I always got punished for it. Always. I couldn't be beaten again. I just couldn't." She shrieked. She could hear the frenzy in her voice which just made her feel more agitated.

She looked back at her hands. They still felt like they were covered in blood.

"It was his fault. If he would have just listened to me. It was his fault. Why wouldn't they ever listen to me? I did everything for them, and they did nothing for me." She whispered balling her hands up into fists. The overwhelming anger that she had felt when she had killed him was back.

"I wish I could have killed more of them. I wish I could kill all of them. None of them helped me. None of them cared about me. They just used me and laughed behind my back every time I got beat or whipped, because of them. They just laughed. I hate them all. I hate them." She growled.

Her vision went red. She pounded at her head to try and knock the red from her sight.

Her hands squished. She looked at them again. She thought she could see the blood. She could feel it squishing in her hands as she opened and closed them. She smiled at the thought. But her wavering awareness told her that she was really seeing blood. It was her own blood. Her nails had dug so deep into the palms of her hands that she had pierced them. The squishing feeling was her own blood.

She hadn't even felt the pain from it. The pain in her back was distant in her mind as well.

All she could think about was how angry she felt. She was breathing so heavy it was making her dizzy. She shook her head several times to try and make the dizziness go away.

"Why couldn't I have killed them all?

The children, the guards, all of them. Then everything would have been better."

She looked back up. Marte had moved far away from her. Evadnie was looking around like she was trying to find a way to escape. Even the guard looked unnerved and ready to act if he needed to.

"What the hell is going on in here?" Jon, the guard with the scar, growled, as he stepped into the room. He scanned the room looking more and more confused as he looked at each person and his eyes stopped on Marianna. He visibly tensed up like a predator prepared to strike.

"I understand now why they don't want her to be a Breeder," Evadnie said. She had managed to make her way to the other side of the couch, further away from Marianna. "She's completely insane."

The guard who had grabbed Celene was nodding. Everyone was terrified of her.

"Jon, get her out of here. She's dangerous." The guard barked. "You're going to be more trouble than you're worth." He said to her shaking his head.

Jon grabbed her arm and led her up the stairs to her room. He chained her to the floor and left her in the dark where she belonged.

CHAPTER TEN

What to do with you

Marianna woke up with her back leaning against the wall. The room was still dark, but a tiny bit of light shone through under the thick shades and door. It must be daytime. Even though she was chained to the wall and sitting on the floor, she had managed to sleep fairly well again.

Was it because she was finally away from the nightmare children that she had been charged with before? She no longer had to worry about them waking up in the middle of the night and risking waking a guard, who would inevitably take his sleepless rage out on her.

The thought of her endless punishments from the guards made her aware of her still sore back that she was leaning on while she slept.   She groaned just thinking about how much it would hurt to pull her back away from the wall.   The pain was too much. She had to stay still, unless she had no other choice but to move.

   She drifted in and out of sleep for the next several hours.   She didn't have anything else to do, and the dark, quiet room was indicative of sleep.   A few times there were some soft rustling noises outside her door or muffled distant voices talking, but that was it.

   After waiting as long as she physically could without peeing all over herself, she finally moved her back away from the wall. The pain that she imagined didn't even compare to the actual pain that coursed through her body.   It took her breath away, and then made her pass out for several seconds before she woke back up with her face on the floor, and her back throbbing incessantly.   She crawled as best as she could to a bucket in the corner and relieved herself.

   She crawled back to the spot where she had been.   She couldn't bring herself to lean her back against the wall again, so she just stayed on her knees while leaning and placing her face on the floor.   The position was not comfortable.   Her knees hurt with so much of her weight pressing them against the floor, and her neck ached.   So, she would lay with her face looking to one side for several minutes, and then she would shift it to face the other direction for several minutes.   She also tried to intermittently move most of her weight from one knee to the other.   Her shoulders ached as they pressed against the floor, and so did her elbows.

She couldn't stay in the position for much longer, she would have to sit with her back against the wall again.   She pushed herself off the floor and stood up for several minutes trying to work herself up to sitting back against the wall.   Just as she had convinced herself to sit back down, a voice just outside her door resounded.   She waited sitting on the floor without pressing her back against the wall for several minutes, trying to catch what was being said, but she couldn't hear enough to understand.   She couldn't even tell who was speaking.

Several minutes passed while she listened to the inaudible conversation before her door handle rattled.   It was locked again.   She was puzzled.   Why did they feel a need to lock her door when they had her chained to the floor?

Her heart sped up.   She didn't know what to expect.

The door swung open, and it was a guard she had never seen before.   He approached her like someone would approach a dangerous animal.   He had a tray of food and drink on it.   He carefully placed the tray on the ground and then slid it towards her with his foot.   She stared at him in wonderment.   Did he really think that she was that dangerous?   She was a tiny girl chained to a floor.

"Eat it."

He left the room.   He re-locked the door.

She looked at the food.   The room was dark, but with the small amount of light that filtered into the room, she was able to make out shapes.   She could see where her drink was, and some of the food.   She had to eat it all with her hands because there were no utensils.   What did they think she would do with a spoon?

The food was cold but tasted great.   Even cold it was so much better than anything that she had on the children's side of the camp, so she was happy about that.

She slid the tray away from herself towards the door and rotated her body as much as she could so that she was facing the wall. She leaned forward, letting her face and chest rest against the wall. It was not comfortable, but it was so much better than letting her back set against the wall, and it was a little bit better than when her face was on the floor. She found that it was a position that she was able to hold for a long time without needing to shift.

Time dragged on forever. It got dark beyond her curtain, and then eventually got dark underneath her door. She drifted in and out of sleep until daylight.

She spent the next couple of weeks exactly the same. She stayed chained to the floor in the dark of her silent room. The only interaction she had was with a guard, who would cautiously bring her food while removing her old tray, and every couple of days change out the bucket that she used for a bathroom.

She lost track of how many days had gone by. The only difference that she noticed was the pain in her back changing in severity, until one day she recognized that it barely even hurt anymore. It had been years, and she had never gone far enough between beatings and lashings, that she had wholly healed wounds without sustaining more.

She spent hours that day moving her back on and off the wall, marveling at the lack of intense pain. Instead, it just felt tender.

She barely knew the difference between day and night, she slept in spurts, never for long stretches any longer. She talked to herself for a few days, or weeks, or possibly months, she didn't know, but eventually, she just cycled between sleeping and being awake.

She would spend hours imagining what the shadowed shapes in the dark were, sometimes imagining that they were moving. Sometimes when there were muffled conversations outside her door she would imagine that the shadowed shapes were people. She would pretend to have conversations with them, or she would pretend that they were having conversations with each other.

Because she could never hear enough of what was being said outside her door, she would make up what was being said between her shadowed characters. She had started to imagine one of the short stocky shadows to be a man and one of the thin shadows to be a woman. Sometimes they would talk to each other, sometimes they would talk to her. She knew that none of it was real, but it did not matter, she started to grow attached to the shadowed figures. She couldn't remember what the room looked like in full light.

The door opened and closed again. But there was no guard there to deliver food. The change in routine scared her. Marianna stared at the door. Had they decided to stop bringing her food? She didn't really care if they had. She didn't have enough energy to care. It was strange to feel so exhausted all the time when she barely ever moved and slept too much.

The shades got pulled back revealing light that was so bright it was painful. She covered her eyes with her hand and squinted to try and see who had opened the shades, but it hurt too much. So, she closed them again.

After a couple of minutes of squinting, and closing her eyes over and over again, she was finally able to keep her eyes open. It still hurt and was difficult for her to make anything out, but she could keep them open. She could tell that someone was standing at the window, but she couldn't know who.

She blinked for several more minutes before she could tell that it was Faisal who was standing at the window. She still couldn't see him clearly, but she recognized his stature. He gazed out the window only occasionally looking in her direction. She didn't know what to say to him, so she just remained quiet. It was pretty easy to do since it was all that she had done for however long it was, since the last time she spoke to herself.

After a while, he stopped staring out the window and instead stared at her. She just stared back, not sure what else to do.

"I have a decision to make about you. I have learned all the details of your crime. You killed a child, Celene's son. Poor boy." He shook his head in disgust.

"You didn't just kill him. You made him unrecognizable. I saw the boy. We slaughter pigs with more care than you had for that child." He searched her face with his eyes. It was like he was looking for something. He huffed, shaking his head in disappointment. He turned his body away from the window and leaned against it with his arms crossed in front of his chest.

"Nobody here feels safe having you around. You can't go back to the children's side of the camp, you can't be trusted to go free on this side either." Marianna's whole body tensed at the mention of being sent back to the children's side. She shuddered and tried to relax. He frowned at her.

"The other ladies are terrified of you. Even my guards don't feel safe knowing how unstable you are. They don't like the idea having to worry about another threat if you are ever loose. And I can't risk the possibility of you snapping and killing everybody in your path until you are stopped."

Marianna looked down at her hands. Was she really so dangerous? She killed somebody. But he deserved it. If he would have just listened to her. She grasped her hands together in an attempt to calm herself. She didn't want to prove his point by growing so angry that she saw red again. She took several deep calming breaths and looked back up at him.

He watched her intently without

expression.   He continued.

"The idea of sending you out with the soldiers on training missions has been tossed around.   You would be the soldiers' plaything until you are used up or killed. They wouldn't have to be careful with you because nobody wants you around anyways, so if you don't come back from a mission, it would be no great loss.   But that could be a bad precedent to start."

She scowled at the thought.   Even though she didn't know exactly what he meant when he said that she would be used up or killed, it sounded terrifying.

"We can't just keep you chained up in here forever.   This room could be used by somebody useful, it's being wasted on you as it is now.   We don't have a prison in this camp.   There is no need for one.   We are very good at finding a use for every individual.   And if that person becomes more of a problem than they are worth, even though we don't like wasting resources, we will get rid of them."

He searched her face again.   What was he looking for?

"The Captain has given me the choice of what to do with you.   It would be easiest to just put you down right here and now. Then you would be no more trouble to anyone. But I didn't lie when I said before that I thought you had potential. And I really did have a lot of fun with you. It would be a shame to give that up.

"I don't like wasting my time and resources on a lost cause, but I also don't think that someone as young as you, should be a lost cause. You are so pliable. You could be so useful, or you could end up being my worst mistake. So, what to do with you?" He said. He stared at her chewing on his lip. He looked torn. He really didn't know what to do with her.

They stared at each other wordlessly for several long minutes. He was more and more disappointed as he stared. He turned to stare out the window again.

She didn't know if he wanted her to say something or not. She didn't know what to say. She was dangerous. Nobody wanted to have to deal with her. Nobody wanted her.

"I don't want to die." She finally whispered. Her voice rasping as she spoke for the first time in such a long time.

She had spent so much time in pain,

misery, and imprisonment, it would have been easier for her to cease to be, and she had tried to convince herself so many times that everybody would be better off if she were gone forever.   But it didn't matter. Despite everything that had happened to her.   She still wanted to live.

He turned to look at her.   He studied her face with his eyes.

He walked over to her and reached down for her to take his hand.   He helped her to her feet.   She wobbled from the weight of the chains and the lack of energy she had.   It had been weeks since she stood.   She just didn't have the energy or desire anymore.

He scowled and looked down at her shackles.   He looked back at her and then down at her shackles several more times, moving his mouth around like he was chewing on something that wasn't there.

He licked his lips several times and then nodded.   He stepped away and knocked on the door three times.   The door opened instantly, and in moments two guards stepped into the room.

"Get me the keys to the shackles," Faisal said.

Both guards frowned, but each nodded,

and one stepped out of the room. Faisal turned back to look at her. He was nervous, but not nearly as much as the guard who had stayed in the room.

The second guard stepped back into the room with a key ring and handed them to Faisal. Both guards stood ready to act as Faisal unlocked the shackles first on Marianna's wrists, and then on her ankles. The lack of weight threw off her balance making her stumble towards Faisal.

Both guards acted so quickly that Marianna didn't even know what happened. Before she knew it, she had been lifted off the ground, one guard with a hand around her throat and under one arm, and the other guard with her hands held behind her back. She screeched in surprise.

"Put her down, please. I'm fine." Faisal said standing back up from unshackling her ankles.

The guards cautiously set her back on her feet but didn't release her from their hold.

"Leave us," Faisal said calmly.

"Sir?" One of them protested.

Faisal put both hands up as if to show that he was uninjured.

"I'm fine. I can handle her. Leave us."

He said.

They reluctantly released her. "We will be just outside the door if you need anything."

He nodded, and they stepped out the door and shut it. They locked it again.

She looked at her wrists, which were aching from the guard's embrace and the shackles. They were ringed with thick dark bruises.

She looked back up to Faisal who was watching her intently.

He walked over to the bed and sat. He patted his hand on a spot next to him for her to sit. As she did the softness of the bed felt unbelievable. She ran her hands across the comforter. She didn't know how much she missed having a bed. Even the small hard bed that she had on the children's side of the camp was better than the stone floor and wall.

She looked back up to Faisal. He watched her hand as she touched the soft blanket. He looked sad. He reached down and placed his hand on hers.

"You have known nothing but suffering. You have been tortured, starved, driven to insanity, and chained to a floor in the dark

for months.   But you still want to live.   And
you still seek out comfort."   He said with an
awed smile.

She just nodded.   She didn't know what
else to do.

"I have done a lot of things, to a lot of
women.   It's my job to break you.   And I
am very good at my job.   Either the women
break and do everything I tell them, and get
put to work, or they break and disintegrate
into nothing.   They lose their sanity or take
their own life.   But they always break,
always.   As I said, I am very good at my job.
But how do I break someone so strong, yet
already broken into so many pieces?   You
are an enigma.   A puzzle that I long to put
together, but fear to let loose on the world."

She stared at him wordlessly.   What did
he want her to say?   Did he even want her
to speak?

He huffed and turned away.

"I don't know what's wrong with me."
She rasped.   He turned back to look at her,
studying her as she spoke.

"I try to do what I am told.   I'm obedient,
I am.   But it never matters.   I get in trouble.
I get beat, I get whipped, I get chained up.
Everyone is afraid of me.   Nobody wants

me.   Nobody.   Not anywhere.   They all
hate me.   I should want to give up.   I
should want to just die.   I've tried
convincing myself that I do, because at least
if I'm dead, I don't hurt anymore.   At least if
I'm dead, nobody has to deal with me.   But I
don't want to die.   I want to do what I am
told.   I want to not hurt all the time.   I just
want to live."   She rambled.

He watched her with growing interest as
she spoke.

"Stand up."   He said.

She nodded and stood.

"Take off that disgusting dress."   He said
looking nauseated as he looked at it.

She looked down.   She was still wearing
the too big dress that she had put on when
she first arrived.   It had no discernable color
left to it at all.   She pulled the dress up over
her head and dropped it on the floor.   It felt
great to get it off.   She wasn't sure why.

Faisal cocked an eyebrow as he looked at
her.   "You've started developing."

She looked down at herself and saw that
she had breasts and hair.   She had also put
on some weight.   Even though she only ate
once a day, she didn't move most of the day,
so she was no longer emaciated.

Faisal stood up and walked to the door. He knocked on it three times again. The door was unlocked from the other side. The guards stepped in.

"Get me a wash basin and cloth." He said to one of the guards. The man nodded and quickly left the room. "And soap." He shouted after him.

The other guard eyed Marianna and smirked. Faisal watched the man and grinned. He looked at her again taking in every bit of her slowly with his eyes. His smile widened.

The other guard stepped back into the room with the basin. The soap and cloth both inside it. He offered it to Faisal who shook his head. "You. I want you to wash her down."

"Sir?" The guard asked confused.

"She's filthy. You know I don't like filth. I want you to wash her." Faisal said with an intrigued expression on his face.

The guard nodded and approached her with the basin wetting the cloth and then soaping it up. He scrubbed her face. He moved down to her neck and shoulders. She glanced at him but was more interested in Faisal who was intently watching the other guard, with a sly smile on his face.

The other guard never took his eyes off her.   He watched every spot where she was wet with growing interest.   He looked hungry as he watched her, and the more attentively he watched, the bigger the smile grew on Faisal's face.

The guard finished scrubbing her body and placed the dirty cloth back into the basin.

"I won't be able to clean her hair with this, not without soaking the floor."   He said as he looked back up.

Faisal's smile fell to a serious expression. "No.   That will do for now.   You two can go."

Both guards nodded and walked back out of the room, but not before each of them turned back to eye Marianna's body one last time.   They shut the door and locked it again.

Faisal looked up and down her wet body licking his lips.   "Potential.   So much potential."

He stepped to the door and knocked on it three times before the guards had a chance to re-lock it.   He pulled the door open and nodded at the guards.

"I'll get some food brought up here. And I'll have one of the ladies up to get your filthy hair washed. You can't leave this room. You know that, right?"

She nodded.

"I still haven't decided what I want to do with you yet. But I don't have to choose right now. I won't chain you back up unless you give me a reason. You can move around freely in this room.

"I'll make sure you have a knife to cut your food tonight. In case you change your mind about killing yourself. You could take this decision away from me, make my job easier. Just know, that the knife will only be provided this one time, you won't be given another opportunity. Otherwise, I will see you tomorrow. Perhaps you will have a good night's rest." He said nodding at the bed and then leaving the room.

Faisal left Marianna alone in her room. She stood naked and dripping wet after being scrubbed clean by the guard. She crossed her arms over her chest shivering. She looked down at the dress that she had taken off. It was disgusting. She didn't want to put it back on. It was a symbol of her time being chained up.

She looked at the heavy chains and shackles that were sitting empty on the floor and broke down crying. She knelt on the floor looking at the thick bruises that encircled her wrists and cried. She was free from the shackles. Finally, she could move away from the wall.

She stood back up, determined to not spend any more time on the floor. She walked over to the window. Her eyes were still sensitive to the light, after being in the dark for so long. The sun shone through the window and felt hot on her skin as she looked out.

When she had been brought to the house that had become her new prison, it was the beginning of autumn. The leaves had just begun falling from the trees, and the weather was cool. But now the trees were covered in bright green leaves. Wildflowers had bloomed across the ground. And the sun felt hot. It was summertime. She had spent at least six months in the dark chained up.

She leaned against the hot window, feeling the warmth seep into her skin, she closed her eyes. It was amazing. She stood there for several minutes shifting her body to let different spots touch the hot glass, warming her up.

She looked back out the window. The street in front of the large house was bustling with activity. Men and women traveling quickly from place to place, each looking like they were moving with purpose. The waterway was just as busy. Boats were being loaded and unloaded with varying things. Fish were being traded, and picked up in large quantities, and taken away in carts drawn by mules and horses.

People looked content. Nobody looked particularly happy or sad, but they were content. Marianna yearned to find that kind of contentment in life. She didn't think she could ever find happiness. But she wished that she could just get to a point in her life, where she didn't dread each new day, afraid of what new horror was in store for her.

The sound of her door being unlocked shook her from her daydreaming. Sarafina and the two door guards entered her room. Sarafina was carrying a fresh basin of water that she set on the floor just inside the door. She looked uncomfortable and nervous. The guards closed the door behind them and stood at the ready not taking their eyes off her.

They were all terrified of her. Was she really so frightening?

Sarafina beckoned her to come closer. She moved away from the warmth of the sun and towards the basin of water that she knew was going to make her cold again. But she already felt so much better with her body being cleaned, she was sure if she got her hair washed as well, she would feel even better.

She stopped just in front of the older woman. Sarafina scanned Marianna up and down nodding.

"Well let's do this. Crouch here, and dangle your hair over the basin. I want to keep as much water in the tub as I can." Sarafina said as she grabbed a small cup from inside the basin.

Marianna knelt and did as she was told. Her hair fell forward in a knotted clump. It was so dirty that the auburn color of it was impossible to distinguish.

Sarafina poured several cups of surprisingly warm water over her head. She grabbed the soap and scrubbed it up into a thick lather. It felt so nice having the

woman's hands move through her hair.
Marianna closed her eyes trying to enjoy it as
much as she could.   Depending on what
Faisal decided to do with her, she may be
experiencing the last bit of gentle human
contact before being killed or sent away with
the soldiers.

The woman poured several more cups of
water over her hair rinsing the soap from it
and wringing it in her hands.   Marianna
opened her eyes and stood back up.   The
basin of water was unbelievably dirty.
How had it gotten so filthy when she had
spent so much time in just a single corner of
one room?

Sarafina set a brush on the floor, gathered
up the basin and the dirty dress that was still
on the floor and moved away waiting for the
door to be opened.   She didn't want to be
near Marianna any longer than she had to.
Both guards were looking at her even more
hungrily.   Sarafina nodded at them, and
they opened the door without hesitation to
let her out and quickly follow her out.

One of them stepped back in moments
later with a tray of food and set it on the
ground, and left the room again locking the
door behind him.

Marianna stared down at the tray of food. Faisal didn't lie about providing her with a knife. She had a fork too, which she hadn't had access to in months.

She leaned and picked up the tray and sat on the side of the bed. She smiled at how soft it was. She ate every bit of her food. Picking up each piece with her fork.

The meal didn't actually have anything in it that required the use of a knife, which meant that it had been provided solely for her to use on herself. She picked it up and twirled it in her hands. She didn't want to die, but if she were going to be killed, or used up until she died, then maybe it would be a better option.

She stared at the knife. If she was to kill herself with it, how would she do it? She could try to stab herself, but she doubted she could penetrate deep enough to cause a killing wound, so she would just end up hurting. She could try to cut her own throat. That was the way they slaughtered the livestock because it was easy, and the animals would just bleed out until they died.

She sighed and put the knife back on the tray and set the tray on the floor. She didn't want to die. Even if she was going to be killed anyways, she wanted to live for as long she could.

She picked up the brush to run it through her hair, but it got stuck in the tangled mess of it.   It took over an hour for her to be able to smoothly run the brush through it.   It felt nice, and made her feel even more clean than her sponge bath had.

She climbed into the bed and pulled the comforter back.   She smiled as she pressed on the soft pillow. She nestled into the bed and curled up in the comforter.   It was so cozy.   She wasn't even cold, but she bundled up in the blanket like she would if it was freezing outside.   Before she knew it, she had fallen asleep.

She woke to the sound of her door being unlocked.   She opened her eyes.   The sun was still up.   She wrapped herself in the blanket as the door opened not wanting to get up.

A guard, a different one from before, peeked his head in, first locating Marianna in the bed, and then looking down at the tray with the knife.   He turned his head and said something that she couldn't hear enough to understand and then stepped into the room grabbing the tray and handing it to someone outside the door.

Another guard stepped into the room as the first approached her.   He grabbed at the comforter and pulled it off her.   He looked at her in surprise.

"You're alive?"   He said as his eyes scanned her still naked body.   She nodded.

"Well, we owe Faisal.   He said she wouldn't use the knife."   The first guard said to the second.

"He's the only one who thought you wouldn't."   The guard said to her shaking his head.   "Personally, I think you should have.   And it's not because I'd win a few coins from him if you did.   He won't give you another chance.   Is it because you were afraid?   We can help you if you need it. This is your last chance."   He explained.

Marianna shook her head fervently.   "I don't want to die."   She whispered.

Both guards' eyes widened in surprise. Was it really so hard to believe that she wanted to live?

The first guard shrugged his shoulders and dropped the blanket back down on her. They both left her room locking the door.

She curled back up in the blanket, enjoying its warmth and softness against her skin.

She was just nodding back off to sleep when she heard her door again.

Faisal stepped into her room smiling as he looked at her. "I see you like the bed."

She nodded pulling the covers up under her chin more.

"So, I gave you a decision to make yesterday, and you decided you truly wanted to live." He said as he sat on the edge of the bed looking at her.

"That was yesterday? I didn't know I slept that long." She said amazed.

He smirked and looked at her curiously.

"So now it is time for me to make my decision." He said looking away from her.

She sat up on the bed, letting the blanket drop as she did. She didn't want to die. What would she do if he decided that she needed to? She pulled her legs up to her chest and hugged them tightly. She breathed heavier, terrified of what his decision might be.

He looked at her and placed his hand on her knee. She was shaking. He studied her. He considered her as tears welled up and then began falling. He tilted his head and smiled at her mournfully. He cupped her face with his hand, wiping away her trail of tears gently with his thumb.

"You're scared." He said in amazement.

She nodded.

He moved the hand that was on her knee to cup the other side of her face.

"I forget how young you really are. You've been through so much. You know this is the first time I have seen you afraid. You've had plenty of reasons before, and you probably were at times, but you are so difficult to read." He said studying every inch of her face.

She took several deep breaths trying to stop herself from crying.

"You have two levels. You either show no emotion at all, or you are consumed by them. That's what makes you so intriguing. But it's also what makes you so dangerous." He said shaking his head as he continued looking at every bit of her face.

"If I could harness that, you could be magnificent. Not a day has gone by where I haven't thought about the intense passion I got out of you the day I broke you in." He said closing his eyes and biting his lower lip. "Mmm." He grunted.

She smiled a little remembering herself. He smiled and licked his lips.

"Mmm." He said again. "But I've also seen the crazy sizzling behind your eyes, barely staying contained. And I have seen the result of that passion being unleashed." He just shook his head over and over again losing all sense of his momentary joviality.

What could she say? She couldn't control how she felt, or how intensely she felt things. She couldn't take back anything that she had done. She had killed Clive in a heated rage. And if she got that angry again, she was sure that she could kill again. So, she was dangerous. She couldn't help it. She couldn't stop it. And she couldn't control it.

"There you go again. No emotion. You just shut down." He said.

He was right. She didn't really feel anything anymore. Her breathing slowed back to normal. And she had stopped crying. Just like that.

"What were you thinking about just then? What made you do that?" He asked fervently. He was trying so hard to understand her.

She shrugged.

"No, tell me. Now!" He demanded.

"I just realized why everyone thinks I'm so dangerous." She said trying to look away, but he held her face in place so that she had to look at him.

"Because you killed a child with no remorse?"   He asked.

She nodded.   He raised his eyebrows.

"And I could do it again.   I would do it again, if I got that angry."   She said honestly.

He scowled and nodded.

"So, what do I do with you?   You're so volatile."   He asked.

She shrugged again.

He stared into her eyes for a long time. He shook his head.   "Nothing. There is nothing there."

He took his hands away from her face. His eyes moved from her face and then slowly down her body.   He reached up and lightly touched her shoulder and traced down her arm with one finger. Goosebumps erupted following his finger.

His finger continued lightly touching her, moving from her hip up the side of her body, barely brushing against her breast, and then up her neck.   She tipped her head to the side.   Her heart sped up.

He leaned over and barely brushed his lips on her neck.   She gasped as her eyes rolled.

He backed away from her looking into her eyes.   He smiled.

"There you are."

He crawled onto the bed and grabbed her calves with both hands running his hands up and down and then pulling her legs down and apart.   He slowly kissed her starting on her knee and moving up her inner thigh. She closed her eyes and leaned her head against the wall.   Every kiss made her breathing speed up.

He grabbed her hips and in one swift motion pulled her down the bed so that she was laying down completely.   The sudden motion made her yelp giggling.

He straddled her as he looked into her eyes.   She yearned for him to continue.

He ran both of his hands down her chest. She grabbed the bottom of his shirt and pulled it off over his head.   He smiled broadly.

She ran her hands down his bare chest. When her fingers reached his pants, she unbuttoned each of the buttons.   She could feel how hard and ready he was as she did.

He leaned and kissed her forcefully.   She passionately kissed him back.   He wiggled around kicking his legs out of his pants.   As

he kissed down her neck.   She giggled and
then kissed his neck.

"I told you we would have some fun when
you're back healed."   He whispered in her
ear.   His hot breath made her moan.   He sat
up and looked at her hungrily.   She smiled
and grabbed him pulling him back in to kiss
her.

CHAPTER ELEVEN

Decision

Marianna lay on Faisal's chest running her fingers across some bruises and scratches that he had. He was propped up on a pillow with one hand behind his head watching her with a smile on his face. His other arm wrapped around her back lightly running his nails across her skin.

"How did you get these?" She asked kissing each spot.

"Hmm?" He lifted his head from his arm to see what she was talking about. "Oh, those. I've been breaking in a new lady. She's less eager about our meetings than you have been. It's an expected consequence of my job." He said setting his head back down as he took in a deep relaxing breath.

Marianna scowled, lifting her head off his

chest and looking at him in confusion.   "I don't understand.   She did this to you?   Why?"

He lifted his eyebrows.   "A lot of the encounters I have when breaking a lady in, get confrontational.   Not many are as willing of a participant as you are. Honestly, none have been as enthusiastic as you."   He said grabbing her between her legs and rubbing.   Her eyes rolled as she moaned.   He stopped just as suddenly, causing her whole body to shudder, as she caught her breath.   He laughed.

"Some fight back to try and stop me."   He said as he resumed lightly scratching her back.

"They try to stop you?   What do you do?" She asked putting her head back down on his chest and twirling his chest hair in her fingers.

"I don't let them.   I've been doing this for long enough to know how to use any attempted attack to my advantage.   She bit me," he said nodding to the bruise that she had been talking about, "so I gave her something else to use her mouth for."

Marianna's scowl deepened.   She sat up to look at him.   He put his other hand behind his head and watched her with curiosity.

"Why would she bite you?"

"I was doing something she didn't like." He said with growing interest.

"What were you doing?"

"I was fucking her."

"She didn't want you to?"

He shook his head. "That doesn't matter. I do what needs to be done. It's my job to break the ladies in. And it is their job to be fucked. What they want or don't want isn't my concern."

She chewed on her lip as she considered what he told her.

"What's going through that head of yours?" He asked sitting up more.

She looked at him. "I've spent a lot of time as a slave. I've had to do a lot of things that I didn't want to do. But I've never not wanted something so badly, that I tried to fight. Except with Clive, and I was desperate, I just lost it. I was just wondering what would make the lady that you are breaking in so desperate that she would try to fight you?" She shook her head and shrugged. "It just seems like forcing somebody who is that desperate, to do something that she doesn't want, is wrong.   I don't know why.   It just feels so wrong."

He lifted one eyebrow.   "So, a murderer, is lecturing me on morality?"

She looked down in shame shaking her head.   "No, I wasn't...You asked what I was thinking.   That's what I was thinking."

"You were in charge of how many children before?"

"Eight."   She said looking at him, wondering why he asked.

"If it was time for them to say, need a bath. It was your job to ensure that they got one. Right?"

She nodded.

"Did they ever refuse?"

"All the time."   She said getting aggravated just thinking about it.

He smirked.   "Did they ever fight you? Hit, kick, bite, scream?"

She nodded.

"Did you stop?"

She shook her head.

"Was it wrong for you to force them even if they didn't want it?   Even with them fighting you?"

She frowned.   "No.   The guards didn't

like being stuck with stinky dirty children. I would get in trouble if they didn't bathe."

She could feel her skin grow hot as she recalled a particularly brutal beating that resulted from one of the little girls soiling herself, just after bathing and refusing to bathe again. Marianna had gotten so frustrated and tired of struggling with her, that she made the girl sleep in her own filth. The guards didn't appreciate the smell when they came in the next day, and she paid for it.

Faisal touched her leg causing her to jump in surprise. "Don't lose yourself. Come back to me." Her heart raced as her mind became aware of her surroundings again.

He shook his head as he studied her. "So volatile. What am I going to do with you?" He said to himself.

She stared at him as she tried to get her breathing back to normal.

"Are you with me?" He asked grabbing her face. She nodded.

"Good." He said looking paranoid. He was afraid of her again.

He leaned in and kissed her softly at first and then more forcefully. Her anger shifted back to passion, as he climbed back on top of her, and she got caught up in everything he was doing to her body again. Everything else melted away from her as they found new ways to pleasure each other.

He climbed back out of the bed as she hung onto him, kissing his back. He pushed her arms off him and turned to look at her smiling. He leaned down and kissed her. "I could lose myself with you for days. But I do have a house to run."

She crawled to the side of the bed and sat as he got dressed. She didn't want him to go.

He looked at her and smiled sadly. Stepping in front of her he wrapped his arm around her and pulled her against him as he kissed her.

"I'll get them to bring you some food." He said as he walked to the door and knocked twice.

He left her sitting on the bed.

A while later her door unlocked. A guard entered the room with a tray of hot food. Steam was coming off it. She could barely remember the last time she had hot food. He handed it to her and left her alone to eat it. It was delicious. She ate every last morsel.

She spent the next couple hours looking out the window, watching the busy lives of the strangers below her.

Just as the sun started to set, her door unlocked.   She looked up expecting it to be a guard there to get her tray, but it was Faisal again.

He smiled as he looked at her standing in the window.   He bit his lip and stared at her.   He looked like he was trying to decide something.   Her heart pounded in fear that he had decided to have her killed, ridding himself of her for good.

He stepped into the room, saying something to the guard and then shutting the door.   He placed a candelabra on the small table near the window.   Three candles flickered with the movement.

"I want you to see what I do."   He said.

She frowned in confusion.

"Come here."   He said gesturing for her to approach.   She walked over to him.   He grabbed her by the hand and led her to the wall with the chains.

Terrified she looked at him.   What had she done wrong?

He grabbed a shackle as he gently ran his finger over the still dark bruise on her wrist from being chained up before. "This is just precautionary. I'll let you out of them when I'm done. Unless you give me a reason not to." He said as he clasped each shackle around her wrists and ankles.

She stared at him feeling scared and baffled.

The door opened again. A guard pushed a young woman into the room and shut the door as he followed her inside. The guard made his way to the corner of the room parallel to where Marianna was chained up.

The woman was crying and wrapping her arms around herself. She looked at Faisal and cried out. "No. Please, don't do this to me. Please, not again." She begged.

She looked over at Marianna chained naked to the floor. She fell to her knees crying even harder.

Marianna watched the girl curiously. She was terrified of Faisal. Just as everybody in the house was.

He stepped up to the young woman grabbed her by her arm and effortlessly lifted her up off the floor to stand. Marianna knew the man was strong, she had experienced his strength and endurance several times, but watching how little effort he used when he lifted the woman with one hand, made it more real to her.

He guided her to the opposite side of the bed from where Marianna was chained up.

The woman was visibly trembling. She shook her head no, over and over again, as he leaned towards her still holding onto her arm, and whispered something in her ear. She whimpered, shrugging her shoulders as far as she could and tilting her head to keep him away from her ear.

He pulled away from her to look her in the face. He grabbed her chin tilting her head back so that she would look at him. She cried pitifully.

He licked his lips, "do I need to convince you again?"

She just barely shook her head no as he continued to hold her chin.

She unwrapped her arms from around her body. Whimpering she unbuttoned the front of the beautiful gold colored dress that she wore.

He released his grasp from around her arm. He ran his hands under the unbuttoned dress, and pushed it over both of her shoulders, pushing it down her back, and then over her hips, making it drop to the floor.

She wrapped her arms around herself again, as he leaned and kissed her shoulder. She shuddered and shrugged her shoulders trying to crouch away from him, but he had his arms around her back, he held her close to him.

He kissed her shoulder again. As he kissed up her neck, Marianna felt a pang of jealousy. She wanted to be the one whose neck he was kissing. The woman pushed at him, but he wasn't even fazed by it.

He leaned away from the woman looking down at her. He grabbed her hips rotating her so that her back was facing the side of the bed and Marianna. He squeezed digging his nails into her flesh. She screeched. He pushed her causing her to stumble back hitting her legs on the bed, she fell back onto the bed.

In a flash of movement, Faisal pulled his shirt off and climbed on top of the young woman straddling her so that she couldn't sit up. She cried out and pushed at his chest. She kicked her legs that were dangling from the other side of the bed and thrashed about, but it had no effect.

She grabbed his chest, digging her nails in

and scratching down to his stomach. He growled, grabbing her hand and twisting it in a way that made her scream out.

He looked down at the blood trickling from the scratches in his chest and twisted her hand and arm even further. She arched her back and screamed until no more sound came out.

He unbuttoned his pants with his free hand. He released her twisted hand and guided it to touch him. She whimpered and tried pulling away, but he held tight making her hand move back and forth to stroke him. With his free hand, he ran his finger slowly up her body starting at her hip up to her breast. He cupped her breast and then squeezed it before releasing it to continue drawing his finger up to her neck and then her lips.

He continued to move her hand against himself as he leaned down to kiss her lips. She curled them inside her mouth so that no part of her lips was exposed and turned her head away to keep him from kissing them. He just kissed down her neck instead. She tried to turn her head to stop him, but he held her in place.

He let go of her hand, shifting his weight

from her, he grabbed her under the arms and slid her up on the bed more. She yelped as he pushed her legs apart and settled his body between them. She kicked frantically without making contact with him making the kicks pointless.

She pushed at his bloody chest screaming. He grabbed both of her wrists with only one of his and forced them onto the bed over her head. He leaned down and kissed her on the breast moving around her nipple before wrapping his lips around it and sucking.

He glanced at Marianna as he sucked on the woman. He smiled at her. She frowned, tilting her head, not sure what he was smiling at. He smiled broader.

He sat up to look back at the woman who was watching him with terrified eyes. He pulled himself out of his pants and pushed himself up inside her. She screamed and cried as he moved inside her. He was not gentle with her, and she never ceased trying to stop him.

It was plain as Marianna watched that he was thoroughly enjoying himself, but in a different way than he did when he was with her. For the first time, she saw the predator in him. He was there to conquer and control, and he was a master at it. She finally understood what he meant when he said that he broke the ladies.

He forced himself on them, retaliated if they ever fought back, and put them in positions in which they had no hope of actually escaping.

That was what was done to her from the moment she was taken from her home all those years before. She understood how she was already so broken. She was forced into slavery, forced into caring for the young ones when she was clearly no good at it. If she ever made a mistake or refused to do something, she was beaten or whipped into submission. And there were guards everywhere making it impossible to escape. She had been thoroughly broken. She had lost all hope that her life could be any different. And so, she lost all her will to try to control any aspect of her own life.

Faisal's subjugation continued for hours. He was relentless, never letting up, never giving the young woman any form of reprieve. Marianna watched with fascination as the woman crumbled into a blubbering mess. He occasionally watched Marianna, studying her expressions.

Perhaps he was searching for a reaction, or he was getting some other kind of pleasure from her presence, she didn't know.

After one final act to defile the woman, in retribution to her kneeing him, he forced himself into her mouth and down her throat so far that he gagged her to the point of throwing up.   He pushed her away from him disgusted.   She fell onto her hands and knees and continued throwing up on the floor.

"I'm done with her.   Get her out of here." He said to the guard in the corner.   He leaned and pulled his pants back on while throwing the woman's dress at her.   She grabbed the dress and hugged it against her body like a shield.

The guard knocked on the door five times. Another guard entered the room and the two of them grabbed the woman by the arms and led her whimpering, out of the room.

Faisal wordlessly finished dressing.   He sat on the edge of the bed and looked at Marianna expectantly.   She stared back at him for a long time.   He said nothing to her as he watched her.

"You do that to every lady that comes here?"   She asked.   How many women had he broken?

He nodded slowly. "It's not always like that. I've found that usually there are two types of women. Ones like her." He said nodding to the door. "Fighters. They are strong, resilient, and difficult to break. It can sometimes take months before they are obedient enough to be trusted to be used as a Breeder, but that fire in them keeps them interesting. If they ever last long enough to become Vassal Ladies, they are more valuable.

"And then there are the ladies who start off submissive. They don't fight, they just lay there, distant from what is happening to them. They bring with them their own set of challenges. They can be used as Breeders right away because I don't worry about them attacking a soldier, but if they ever end up as Vassal Ladies, they are less desirable. Nobody wants to fuck a lifeless doll. And despite my efforts to prevent it, they are also more likely to find a way to kill themselves."

Marianna frowned. "You gave me a knife so that I could kill myself if I wanted to. You don't do that with the others?"

"I don't like wasting my resources. I told you that before. It's my job to take the ladies that are given to me and transform them into assets.   It would ruin my business if I just gave them all the opportunity to remove themselves from this life.   But there are many ways to take ones life, and I cannot stop them all.

"You are a complicated case.   You're not the first to be sent to me as a punishment. You're not even the first murderer that I have had to deal with.   But you are insane, unsafe, and no longer an asset.   I figured if you just killed yourself, you would have saved me the trouble.   But you didn't."   He said walking over to her.   He unlocked her shackles and dropped them to clatter against the floor.

He grabbed her hand.   "You are unlike any other."

"Why did you want me to see?"   She asked.

He smirked.   "I wanted to see your reaction.   And it was just as I had hoped it would be."

"What did you hope it would be?"

"Curiosity.   Fascination.   You are so far from normal.   I think that you can recognize other people's emotions, but you can't understand them.

"I share that sentiment with you. I can read anybody. I'm even beginning to read you. But I can't relate to them. And neither can you. You understand what should be right and wrong, but you don't understand why. You are either an empty observer of what's going on around you, or you are so driven by your passion that you lose sight of anything else. You are psychotic, dangerous, but I think, useful."

She looked at him in surprise as he smiled at her.

"I've decided what to do with you." He said.

Her heart sped up as well as her breathing. She tried to keep herself from panicking.

He shook his head. "No. I'm not going to kill you. I have a special job for you."

She raised her eyebrows in question.

"Not all soldiers are as willing to be with a Vassal Lady. Some are just inexperienced and need guidance. Others just need extra coaxing. It is important that they release their physical passions so that they can remain dutiful and keep their concentrations where they need to be. I want you to be the one to persuade them." He said watching her closely.

"I'll be doing what you do?"   She asked.

He nodded.   "Essentially, yes."

"I don't know how."   She said.

He smiled broadly and kissed her.   "I'll teach you."

CHAPTER TWELVE

A New Start

Marianna woke up just as the sun was rising. It was a big day. After months of training with Faisal, it was time for her to use everything that she was taught. His method of teaching was unique.

She spent countless days, watching as Faisal continued to break in his new Breeder which he named Crystal. Marianna couldn't remember what the woman's name used to be. It didn't matter, once a lady was named, she would be referred to as nothing else. He explained that it was sometimes necessary to make the ladies more compliant with a new identity.

He used different methods to break the woman. He visited her at various times, so she never knew when she would be at his mercy. Sometimes he would go a couple of days between, and other times he would require her multiple times in one day.

Crystal hated him. She told him all the time. He would laugh at her every time she said it. Until one time when she was especially frustrated with him she screamed out that she hated him, his response stopped her from ever repeating it. He said, 'It's not my job to get you to like me, it's my job to get you to fuck me.' Marianna saw how the comment affected the woman's psyche. It tempered some of the fire that drove her to fight.

He had imaginary ways to punish Crystal. He was always very quick to provide retribution if she ever physically hurt him. But his abuses towards her didn't end there. She refused to undress for him one day, so he forced her to go through the house without clothes for the next week. If there were any soldiers there to be serviced by one of the other ladies, he would make her stay in their presence to be gawked at, until they were taken to a bedroom to be otherwise engaged. He said that she needed to be comfortable being naked in front of men.

He would also chain Crystal to her wall

while he brought some of the other ladies in to show her what to do to please a man. The other ladies did everything that he asked, and many things that he didn't ask for. They had been well trained to know what he wanted from them. When she tried to close her eyes or turn away to not watch the show, he had a solution to prevent her from doing so.

He would bolt a strip of metal around her throat holding her against the wall. The metal contraption had spikes pointing up toward her head in such a way that if she turned her head in either direction, they would stab into her. He also put a barbed wire across her eyes that would bite into her eyelids when she closed them.

At one point she had a couple of days in a row where she was especially combative, and so he punished her in a genuinely barbaric way. He and the guards placed her naked on what Faisal referred to as the Horse. It was a four-legged contraption that had a wooden rod that sat in the center of its back.

The guards lowered her to sit on the Horse so that the rod was up inside her. Her ankles were restrained to the front legs of the contraption in such a way that it was impossible for her to push herself up enough to free herself.   They chained the Horse to a spot on the floor.   They left her hands unshackled.   Faisal told Marianna later that it was to give Crystal hope of escape, but escape was impossible.   It helped to prove just how pointless fighting was.

When they entered Crystals room the next morning, the Horse was laying on its side. She was still connected to it.   It was evident that she had tried to escape but only managed to hurt herself even more.   She was out of service for two weeks while she healed from the ordeal.   Faisal said he didn't mind hurting them when punishment was due, but they still needed to be able to be put to work when he was done with them.

Marianna watched in fascination as the once lively, combative, feisty woman crumbled into a timid, lethargic, obedient shred of what she once was. Crystal lost all her fight, but she persevered. She ate, slept, and lived as close to normal an existence as she could outside of her meetings with Faisal. The other Ladies in the house took her in like they shared an alliance. She belonged, and they cared for her when she needed it.

And when Faisal decided that Crystal was ready to be put to work, she cooperated just as he said she would. He was a master of control. He took all sense of power away from her. He knew when she lost her will to fight, and then he pushed her even further. She was broken, and he was triumphant.

He made a point to, what he called 'check in' on the ladies that he had already broken, on a regular basis. He had to make sure they weren't regaining any of their original spirit. The meetings with the working ladies were usually brief, except when he was using them as a teaching tool for Crystal. He did just enough to remind them of the control he still had on their lives. And they never forgot.

His individual meetings with Marianna were completely different. She found that he was more sensual with her than he was with any of the other ladies. He enjoyed taking control of the other ladies, but his meetings with her weren't about control. She was a willing party in every way, so he never had to force her. He got a different type of satisfaction from his times with just her. He wasn't trying to conquer her. He was instead losing himself to her passion.

He taught her every conceivable way to pleasure a man. He also taught her how to take control of the encounter and drive him to pleasure her, which was her favorite lesson. He was a very good teacher.

It was ideal for her to take control of the situation so that she could stop the men when it was necessary. He taught her how to know when a man was on the verge of finishing. As a Vassal Lady as opposed to a Breeder, it was her job to not let the men finish inside her so that she didn't get pregnant. Faisal was an expert at stopping himself before coming to fruition, but he explained that many men would not be. Especially if they were inexperienced or being coerced by her. She would need to recognize his physical cues and remove him from within her to finish him off another way.

When they weren't otherwise engaged, he spent a lot of their time trying to find the triggers to her craziness. He said if she could get a handle on what caused her crazy moments, he would give her full access to the house. As it was the only access she had was during meal times, where she always ate at the same time as him, and bath times, because he couldn't stand filth.

One way that caused her to lose herself was bringing up her past. Talking about the murder was another big one. But she had other triggers, unusual ones. When she began her first blood phase, and Faisal didn't want anything to do with her for a couple of days, she lost her mind. After attacking one of the guards and breaking his nose, when he had come to her get her out to get food. She was chained back up for a week and kept confined to the room for nearly two months. Even after he revisited her, she was on the edge of collapse for several weeks. She handled her next blood phases much better, most of the time.

One especially dangerous trigger was when he mentioned the possibility of her being reassigned somewhere else if he found that there were too many conflicts between her and the mother of the boy she killed, Celene. Marianna began panicking immediately. The idea of someone else taking control of her, the prospect of somebody other than Faisal deciding her fate, terrified her. Faisal saw something in her that nobody else did. The other members of the household were nearly as scared of her as they were of Faisal. He said that he had never seen that before. Even his guards were wary of her.

But Faisal saw something. He compared her to himself. He told her if circumstances were different and either of them was unleashed on a world that wasn't under the structure of building a force of merciless warriors, they would both be cast outs at best and executed at worst.

He laughed about his time before coming to the camp, when nobody wanted him near their families. He was shunned by the entire community. They compared him to a dangerous animal. He told her that his sexual appetite was just as intense, but it was an undesirable trait in normal society. In an unexpected turn of events, the Atheran Kingdom enslaved thousands of people to be used as an eventual army. He watched from the outskirts of his hometown on the day when everybody was rounded up. After intense searching, he found out where everybody had been taken and why. It intrigued him. He traveled to the camp on his own and offered to join.

As he was so good at reading people, he was able to locate other men like himself. One of them just happened to be a high-ranking officer from the Atheran kingdom. Faisal and the other men convinced the officer to create the Breeding houses to grow numbers and produce an obedient generation of soldiers. It didn't take much convincing according to him. Even some of the naysayers were swayed once he recommended the Vassal Ladies as well so that everybody had a chance at using the services. And so, the Breeders and Vassal Ladies were created.

In time, he was able to convince the others to let him take command of the first of the houses. He explained the importance of breaking in the women so that they would perform as necessary. They agreed, and in turn, assigned him as Head of House. In very little time it was clear that his idea was favorable. He knew how to take control and keep control. He trained other Heads of House to do the same. Because many of the other Heads of House becoming lax in their methods of control, his house was the most successful at breaking in quality women, with the lowest number of suicides and revolts.

It was the first time that Marianna had learned that not everybody who was there was a slave. Some were assigned, like many of the officers, some volunteered to be there like Faisal, and some were sent there as temporary punishment. In the years since the camp was first built, some of the officers and volunteered members actually started to call the place home. Faisal explained that many families had settled around the outskirts of the adult side of the camp. The growing camp had started to become a functioning community with its own system of commerce and governing force, which Faisal had a powerful role in.

Money and trade were abundant. And the Vassal Lady business was booming. It wasn't just pent up soldiers that used them. Businessmen, traders, nobleman, and officers frequently requested their services. Some even employed a lady to be used indefinitely by a single individual, and not always for breeding alone. And they paid well for the services.

He told her that if she played the game right, she could have the men eating out of the palm of her hands. Physically desperate men were willing to give and pay excessively if she learned how to coax them in the right way. She could be living in luxury, as long as she followed the rules. He said he didn't understand why more of the ladies that came to the house refused to recognize that.

It was her time to use everything that he taught her. The day that she would be put to work had finally come. She was nervous that she might do something wrong. But she was also a bit excited to find out if she would be as good at the job as Faisal thought she would be.

Her door unlocked, and Faisal stepped into her room with one of her customarily assigned door guards Geoff. Faisal hungrily eyed her up and down. She smiled as her body instantly hungered for him. He stepped over to her running his fingers slowly up her body. He stopped so that he was standing pressed against her back. He pushed her hair off of her neck and kissed it lightly. She melted as her eyes rolled. He moved up to her ear and whispered, "are you ready?"

She opened her eyes despite the goosebumps moving across her skin from his hot breath. Geoff licked his lips as he watched the provocative exchange between them. She smiled more. Faisal had been making a point to do things in front of witnesses. He said he wanted to prove how desirable she was to a man. And it proved accurate every time. She was no longer the emaciated, inexperienced, child who looked like a little boy. She was a maturing, developing, sexual young woman who easily aroused men.

"Yes." She said as she ran her hand up her body and stopping at touching her breast, just to watch the guards' reaction. The man's breath caught, as he adjusted himself. Marianna smiled broader. "I'm ready."

He spun her around and kissed her passionately as he ran his fingers through her auburn hair. She lost herself in him. He released her way sooner than she wanted. Her body was on fire. She was ready to fall into full ecstasy with him.

"Let's get you washed and dressed. I've picked the perfect man for you to start with." He said grabbing her by the hand and leading her out the door.

After cleaning up, she found a skin-tight, knee-length green dress that fit her perfectly.

When she arrived over a year before, she couldn't fit any of the dresses, it was amazing to her that she could now fit almost all of them. They may not all be perfect fits, but they would work if she dressed them up with the right accessories.

She emerged into the great room. Faisal was sitting on one of the couches reading a newer looking book. He read often. When he wasn't otherwise engaged in the ladies of the house, he was reading. He looked up from her book nodding as he saw her.

He stood up to inspect her more closely. He circled behind her and pulled her dress even tighter than she had it and tied it to stay. She had bound all her long auburn hair to sit on top of her head, he released it. Spinning it around he did something so that only half of it was bound. He circled back to face her. He grabbed one of her locks of hair and twirled it in his finger as he loved to do, and then dropped it so that it hung in her face. He nodded again this time smiling as he looked at her.

"I've lined up a nobleman as your first. It has been requested that you be brought to him." Faisal said as he opened the front door.

"I get to leave the house?" Marianna asked in surprise.

Nobody left the house for their first. The only time a Breeder left the house was if she was assigned somewhere else. The first couple of months after being put to work, the Breeder's would be passed between different guards, who like Faisal were able to stop themselves from finishing in the Breeder. This was another way of breaking the lady. As a rule, to keep the control in Faisal's hands, the Breeders would only bed with a guard from another house. It was forbidden for any of the guards to be with any of the ladies at the house that he was assigned to.

Once the Breeder lost all sense of fighting or refusal, she would be assigned to an individual man. If that man happened to be an officer, then that woman would be sent to stay with him exclusively until it was sure she was pregnant. It would then be the officer's prerogative on what to do next. Either the Breeder could stay with him, or he could send her back to her original house until she was near birth, at which point she would be sent to a birthing house to have her baby and care for it until weaning age.

A Vassal lady had a more extensive variety of men to work with. There was no need to break in any further with the guards because she would have already spent years as a breeder, and the first couple of months of meetings would still be chaperoned by Faisal or a guard. Faisal liked to be there for the first several encounters so that he could ensure the Vassal Lady was performing adequately. If she wasn't then he would take her back to continue training with him. If they were doing their job sufficiently then, he would make sure a guard was still present, just in case she got any violent ideas.

It took at least a year before a Vassal Lady was deemed worthy enough to leave the house for meetings. So, it was very surprising that Marianna's first assignment would be outside the house.

"I don't get to go out that much myself lately, what with me breaking in two ladies for over six months. You're different than any of the other ladies. I know what to expect out of you." He said as he led her to a horse-drawn carriage that was parked in front of the house.

CHAPTER THIRTEEN

Nobility

The guards each nodded at Faisal as he left
the house.   As they saw Marianna, they
looked at each other with a look of shock.
They were just as surprised as she was that
she was allowed to leave the house.

Faisal took Marianna's hand and helped
her into the carriage and then climbed up
into it himself. She smiled. She felt so special.

As the carriage moved through the town,
Marianna watched out the window. It had
been over a year since she had even been
allowed outside, and she had never been
anywhere else on the adult side of the camp.
It was spectacular. Nothing at all like the
children's side.

On the children's side of camp, there were
guards posted everywhere. All the buildings

looked the same, built on a grid-like street design. There was no color on any of the buildings, the streets were just flattened dirt. Nobody was on the streets unless they were moving from one building to another, and other than the young ones the general emotion was morose. But on the adult side, it was so different. Guards were still present, but not as high in numbers. The cobblestone streets were bustling with people. Some were even laughing and smiling. The streets and buildings were built in less strategic pattern. And the further they went, the more colorful and elaborate the buildings became.

Marianna looked back at Faisal after an hour of traveling. He was reading his book again. He looked at her over the book and smiled at her.

"I see you are enjoying the trip." He said.

"It's amazing. I've never seen anything like it. All these buildings are so pretty." She said looking back out the window.

"This is where the high-ranking officers and some of the nobility call home."

"Wow. It looks so nice." She said looking back at him.

He was reading his book again. She watched him for a while before he looked back up at her. He raised one eyebrow.

"What's that look about?" He said sounding a tiny bit concerned.

She shook her head.

He tilted his head as he leaned in and grabbed her chin to look at him. "What?" He commanded.

"I just wish that I could do that." She said.

He frowned in confusion. "Do what?"

She shrugged her shoulders. "Read. You are always reading, it looks so interesting. You are the smartest person that I've ever met. And all you do is read. I just wish I was smart enough to do that." She said.

He smirked. He released her chin from his grasp and stared at her. "Hmm."

He watched her for a long silent time. "Impress me. If you impress me, I'll teach you." He said.

She stared at him in awe. "Really? You think I could learn. I mean I'll do everything you tell me to, but really?"

He nodded. "Impress me."

She sat back trying to think of how she could impress him enough. Neither of them spoke for the rest of the ride.

When they arrived at the gates of a sizeable opulent mansion, Marianna was dumbfounded. She did not know something so grand existed. Even the Captain's house was plain in comparison.

"Wow," Marianna said as she looked at Faisal.

Even he was impressed as he looked at the mansion. He looked back at her and smiled kindly. "Well, it's time."

She nodded her head nervously.

He grabbed her face and looked into her eyes. "You'll do great."

She smiled at him.

"Do not disappoint me." He said in his serious tone. It said, 'if you disobey, you will regret it.' And she didn't doubt it. She had not experienced his wrath directed towards herself; because she was always obedient. But she had seen it directed towards others, and it was not something she wanted to experience for herself.

She nodded at him. He smiled broadly and kissed her intensely.

"You are the hardest for me to let go of. You are so much fun. I wish I could keep you to myself. But you just have too much potential for me to selfishly hold on to you." He said.

Tears welled up in her eyes. She felt so

special when she was with him.

He wiped at her cheek with his thumbs, as her tears fell.

"Now, now. None of that. We don't want to give the wrong impression here." He said.

She took several deep breaths to stop herself from crying. He pulled out the lock of hair that she had pushed behind her ear and twirled it around a few times before letting it drop in front of her face. He kissed her again and opened the door to the carriage. He offered his hand and helped her out.

They approached the gate. The guard looked at Faisal and nodded. He looked at Marianna and looked shocked. Marianna saw a guard that she hadn't seen since she first arrived at the house. He was the one who pulled Celene off her. He called her crazy and caused her to be chained to the floor in the dark for over six months. Marianna could feel it happening, but she couldn't stop it. The rage was overpowering. She wanted to wrap her hands around his throat and squeeze until his head popped like a berry.

Her grip on Faisal's hand tightened. He turned to look at her and instantly recognized that she was gone. He excused the two of them back towards the carriage. He held tightly onto her hand and wrapped his other hand around her arm to keep her from turning back.

"What happened?" He asked.

She wiggled her arm trying to free herself from his grip. She pulled her hand trying to get him to release it. He squeezed her arm, digging his nails into her. She barely felt the pain of it. Instead, she just grew even angrier.

"Where did you go?" He asked shaking her.

He leaned in to kiss her. She tried to pull away. He let go of her hand and ran his hand through her hair gathering a handful and pulling. He kissed her heatedly. Her anger diminished, being replaced by her passion. She intensely kissed him back, losing all sense of awareness and emotion.

He pulled away from the kiss as he grabbed both of her arms tightly and pushed her so that she was looking at him. He looked into her eyes. "Do I have you back?"

She nodded.

"What was that? What just happened there?"

"It was him. Because of him, I got chained

up in that room. Because of him." She said breathing heavily as she desperately tried to not lose control again.

He turned to look at the guard who was watching with a look of intrigued confusion.

He looked back at Marianna shaking his head. "I did that. I made the decision to lock you up. And it was because of me, that you stayed in there. He had nothing to do with it."

She looked at him wanting to cry but terrified that if she started, she wouldn't be able to stop herself.

"I'm sorry." She said shaking her head and opening and closing her fists.

"You need to let me know if you feel like you are falling. I can bring you back if I know soon enough, but if you do something irreversible, there is nothing I can do to help you. Do you understand?" He said.

He was genuinely concerned about her, which was strange because he had told her before how he found it difficult to really care about anybody.

"Do you understand me?" He said shaking her.

She nodded.

"Say it. Say that you understand me." He

commanded.

"I understand. If I feel like I'm losing myself, I'll let you know." She said feeling more relaxed just saying the words out loud.

"Good. Good." He said looking at her for several long moments. He kissed her again and then released her. He grabbed her hand and interlaced his fingers with hers holding her tightly.

She closed her eyes for a moment as he walked her back to the gate guard.

"What the hell was that?" The guard asked exasperatedly.

"It's her first time out. She's still a little overwhelmed." Faisal said smoothly.

The guard eyed Marianna up and down. He studied her face with a look of confusion that morphed into a look of recognition. "This is the crazy girl. Do you really think she should be out among the living?"

Faisal's glare made the guard take a step back. Even though he no longer worked under Faisal, he still openly feared the man. The guard refused to look at him in eyes.

"Are you questioning my judgment?" Faisal asked calmly but with a sharp undertone.

The guard shook his head. "No Sir."

Faisal nodded. "Good. Now let us in." He ordered.

The guard nodded, still careful to not make any eye contact. He unlocked and pulled open the large ornate iron gate.

Faisal led Marianna up the cobblestone walkway up to the door. A guard stood there as well. He too knew who Faisal was and had a fearful respect towards him. He opened the door without the need for a command.

When they stepped in, the immense entryway took Marianna's breath away. Faisal moved through the house, too quickly for Marianna to truly appreciate the grand interior. He knew his way around.

They stepped into a massive sitting room where a graying older man sat lounging as he looked through a stack of papers. He looked up as they entered.

"Faisal. I can't tell you how happy I am to see you." The man said standing up to shake Faisal's hand jovially.

The man looked at Marianna smiling as he looked at every aspect of her body. "So's this the girl then?"

Faisal nodded. He lifted his hand rotating it in a way that made Marianna twirl in place.

"Very nice, very nice." The man said rubbing his hands together. He looked up and down Marianna one more time. "Well let's not waste any time, shall we?" The man said gesturing towards the other door.

Marianna looked up at Faisal nervously. He looked at her and smiled nodding. They followed the man through several more rooms before stepping out into a grand courtyard. Flowers were everywhere. She smiled as she looked at all the colors. The floral scents mixed together amazingly. They walked through intricately grown bushes that acted as a pathway. They emerged in what she could only guess was the center of the path, since four individual paths shot off at the four compass points. A young man was laying back on a bench with his hands under his head and his feet crossed.

"Danny, my boy. Look what I got you for your birthday." The older man said excitedly.

Danny opened one eye looked at Faisal and then at Marianna, rolled his eyes and closed them again shaking his head.

"Come now." The man said happily. "Daniel." He said more sternly.

Danny huffed as he sat up to look more extensively at her. He looked unimpressed.

"I told you I didn't want that." He said gesturing at her.

"Where's your gratitude. I'm spending a great deal for this. Do not disrespect me." The older man said.

Danny huffed looking down and shaking his head. "Only you could see the disrespect in that way. What about my disrespect for Emily? What about my disrespect towards this poor girl? But no, you don't want me to disrespect your money."

"Excuse my son, he's got some fanciful ideas about how the world should work." The man said to Faisal, who just nodded his head in understanding.

"Your little girlfriend will never be accepted in any serious circles. You want to mess around with her, fine. You're a young man, you should be adventurous. But if you think that I will allow it to go any further than that, you are mistaken. Let me prove to you that what you get from her, you can get anywhere. You don't need to settle for the first little thing willing to show you an enjoyable time." The man said.

"That is not what she is to me. We love

each other. But you can never understand that can you?" Danny argued.

"Pfff. Love. You are too young to understand what love is. Now you do as I tell you, and enjoy your gift. Now. Time is money, and I will not waste either of them anymore with this pointless argument." His father said.

Danny shook his head.

"NOW!" His father shouted as he raised his hand and struck his son.   The young man cringed, cowering from the blow.

"Fine," Danny said jumping to his feet. He stormed off.

"Well, there you go. He'll take you to his room." The man said smiling at Marianna.

Faisal nodded and led her to follow.

CHAPTER FOURTEEN

First Assignment

They rounded through the shrubbery until they reached a door that Danny walked through without looking back, but he left the door open for them to follow.

They entered a majestic looking bedroom. A large four post bed stood in the center of the room encircled by sheer drapes that were pulled back. It was the fanciest bed she had ever seen.

Danny sat on the edge of the bed with his arms crossed over his chest. He looked at Marianna and then looked at Faisal and scowled.

"You're only being paid for your time, right? So, we don't have to do anything?"

Marianna looked at Faisal not sure how to answer. He was shaking his head.

"Normally that would be fine. You are being hired to do what the man wants. But I chose you for this job for a reason. His father and I have an arrangement. Do what you must to convince him. He's a young man, he shouldn't need much coaxing." Faisal whispered.

She nodded.

She walked over to Danny as Faisal kept his distance staying close to the door. She sat next to him on the side of the bed. He looked at her embarrassed. "I'm sorry about my father. He can be overzealous."

"Shhh. It's alright." She said putting her finger across his lips. He turned his head away.

"I can't. I mean you are beautiful. Really you are. But Emily. I just can't." He said.

He thought she was beautiful. Marianna smiled. "Emily never needs to know. How would she? I don't stay anywhere near here. Who's going to tell her? You?"

He looked at her shaking his head. "But I would know. I just can't. I'm sorry." He said looking away from her again.

Marianna looked up at Faisal for a moment. He was watching with interest. How could she convince the young man?

Perhaps the same way that Faisal convinced her. Physically.

She climbed over so that she was straddling his lap. He gasped in shock and reflexively pushed her away. She fell hard on the floor, hitting first her back, and then her head. Faisal took a step towards her immediately, but then stopped. He watched with curiosity.

"I'm so sorry. I didn't mean to. I mean you just surprised me is all. Are you alright? Did I hurt you?" Danny said jumping up to help her to her feet. She rubbed her head.

"I am so sorry." He said again.

"It's fine. I'm alright." She said wiping her dress off.

"Are you sure?" He asked looking at her head.

She nodded.

"Arguing with my father gets me so wound up sometimes. I shouldn't have done that." He said looking down in shame.

"I'm alright really. That was nothing. I've had much worse."

He looked at her sadly and then glanced at Faisal, before looking back to her. She leaned up and kissed him softly. He tried to pull away, but she wrapped her arms around him. He grabbed her around her hips and pushed back at her with very little force. But he kissed her back and then pulled her hips closer towards him.

The passion with kissing intensified and she was able to convince him to do more. Once she was in the heat of the moment, everything else faded away, just as it had for her with Faisal. She lost herself in the physical acts, and nothing else existed. She was able to persuade him multiple times. He was much more enthusiastic and needed shorter recovery time than Faisal did, but compared to Faisal in any other way, he was an amateur.   But it was fun for her to be the one to conquer. She understood why Faisal liked it so much.

Once she thought she had tired him out, they lay on the bed together. His face looked pained. She leaned over and kissed him again. He smiled at her sadly.

"Your back? What happened to it?" He asked.

She was caught off guard by his question. She thought that he was feeling guilty about Emily again as he had been several times before.

"I told you that I'd had worse." She said

referring to him pushing her.

He looked ashamed. And then looked over to Faisal with the question in his eyes.

"Not by him. This happened before I was sent to him." She said trying to ease his mind.

He nodded looking unconvinced. "So, do you like doing this? I mean you seemed to. And I know that it's your job to, but do you?"

She looked up at Faisal who was just as interested in her answer. "I do. You were my first actual assignment. But I did enjoy it." She answered honestly.

"I was your first. Wow. You were amazing. I mean I don't have a lot to compare you to, just, well, Emily, but wow." He said looking torn in his emotions again.

They found the encouragement to go one more time before she and Faisal left Danny conflicted in his bed.

"So how was my Danny boy?   A stallion I'm sure."   Danny's father asked Marianna enthusiastically.

She scowled at him unsure what he meant. "He was very fast, and he had a lot of energy."   She said hoping that was what the man meant when comparing his son to a horse.

The man beamed.   As Faisal chuckled, nodding at her in approval.

"I knew it.   I knew it.   He gets it from me you know."   The man bragged.

"So, I can trust that you completed the task that I paid you for?"   He said looking at Marianna, and then to Faisal.

Faisal nodded.   "She was very persuasive. His hesitancy was no match for her.   Just as I told you."

The man smiled ruefully.   "Good.   Very good.   Let's see how his little girlfriend handles the news.   I will not stand for that insolent brat to keep her claws in my son.   I will get rid of her one way or another.   At least this way he will blame himself, instead of me for the breakup.   He was the one who committed the act after all.   I just got him a birthday present, it was his choice how he used it."

She and Faisal both stood there as the man ranted about his dislike of the girl his son was in love with.   He didn't like that the family that she was from was part of the officer class instead of the nobility.   He said the officers liked to pretend to be on the same level, but his family's status couldn't be taken away from him due to a simple job loss, but the officers could.   So, his family name was more valuable.

He didn't like how the girl was causing his son to argue with him over everything.   But most of all he didn't like that the girl put fanciful ideas in Danny's head about how the world should be.   She thought that what was happening within the camp was wrong, and she wanted Danny to join others and rise up against those in charge.   He said that it was juvenile folly of course.   But it could start a bad precedent, and he refused to let his son sully the family name all because of some insignificant girl.

Marianna realized as she listened to the man's rant that even when people weren't slaves, there was still a drive to control others.   Danny wanted to take control of his own life, his father wanted to keep the hold he had on his son.   Emily wanted to break the control that Danny's father had and take control of him herself.   It was all about control.   She was understanding more and more what Faisal had been teaching her.

After Danny's father finally finished rambling, Faisal was able to respectfully excuse the two of them.   He said something about not wanting to travel too much after dark, which the man agreed with and escorted them to the door talking the entire way.

Marianna laughed as she and Faisal stepped out of the house and the door closed.   Faisal looked down at her with a knowing smile.   He took her hand and helped her step up into the carriage, and in moments they were off.   Neither spoke for a long time. She watched out the window as the sun was displaying magnificent colors as it set.   It made the entire world change colors.

"I felt something I don't think I have ever felt before when I was watching you today," Faisal said breaking the silence.

"Huh?"   She asked.

"Jealousy," Faisal said.

She looked at him not sure what to say. He wasn't looking at her.

"I feel possessive of you. I don't like somebody else playing with my favorite toy." He said as he looked up at her.

She smiled.   She was his favorite.

"You were magnificent by the way. You took control perfectly. You may not be able to empathize with others, but you are an expert at manipulating them to get what you want. I should know. You did it to me." He said chuckling.

"What do you mean?" She asked.

"You convinced me to keep you alive. I had already made my decision. I was just trying to figure out the easiest way to do it. Starving you would have caused a mess that somebody would have had to clean up, and it would have been slow. Executing you would have destroyed morale within the house, which is precarious at best. So, I decided that poisoning you and disposing of you myself would suffice.   It would have been easy. I came to explain to you why you would be disposed of.

"You see I've never been completely responsible for somebody else's life before. Not like that.   When the Captain turned your life over to me, well, it was invigorating.   I wanted to be the one to do it.   And I wanted to see your reaction as I did.

"But your spirit came through. It captivated me again. You did the same thing the first day that I met you. You made me reconsider my decision, and then eventually change my mind. You manipulated me to survive.

"I know you didn't do it intentionally. If you had tried, you would have only convinced me more quickly to get rid of you. But just knowing that you were able to do it, made me want you even more." He explained. He was always so open and honest with her. He told her things not caring about how she reacted or felt about it.

She sat thinking about what he told her. He was going to kill her. And she had somehow unintentionally convinced him not to.

"What are you thinking over there?" He asked expectantly.

"I'm glad that you didn't kill me." She said.

He smiled broadly. "So am I." He grabbed her head and pulled her into a kiss. Their passions took over until they got back to the house, where they each went off to their separate rooms.

CHAPTER FIFTEEN

Storm

It was raining when Marianna woke up. As she climbed out of bed to look out her window she saw that it was more than a simple rain. It was a huge storm. The wind was blowing so hard that two of the boats that had been tied to the moors had broken loose. People were moving about hastily trying to gather all tradeable goods and finding cover.

That could not be a good sign. She got herself dressed and left her room.

It had been two years since she was given full access to leave her room again, but she still felt nervous every time she opened the door, afraid that the guards would decide to lock the door on her.

When she got downstairs, she saw several

of the Ladies and guards all looking out the windows with fascination or nervousness.

"It's really bad out there.   I don't think I've ever seen a storm that big."   Marianna said standing on her tip toes to look beyond Geoff.

"It really is."   One of the Ladies said.

It caught Marianna off guard.   Somebody responded to her comment.   None of the ladies liked her.   They made a point to avoid talking to her whenever they could. The only time any of them would ever speak to her more than a few simple responses, was when Faisal was in the room with her. They didn't openly ignore her when he was around, but they were still very good at singling her out.

Faisal, of course, noticed it, because he could recognize when people were acting genuine or not.   He offered to punish each of them anytime they so blatantly ignored her, when he noticed her getting upset about it one night.   She considered it.   It would be nice to know that she could get retribution, but it wouldn't stop them from hating her, it would only make things worse.   She told him that she didn't want to cause more tension.   He agreed.   He said that it was hard enough to get so many people who were forced to live under the same roof to get along.

For a while, it bothered Marianna that they didn't like her. But then she found it empowering. They showed her nearly the same type of fear and respect as they did towards Faisal. At first, she thought it was because she was his favorite. It was obvious that she was. He openly played with her in front of others, in ways that he never did with anybody else. But after watching them she thought that it wasn't because of how much Faisal liked her over them, but it was because she was so much like him.

Faisal was right about her. She was excellent at manipulating, and she was getting better all the time. She also didn't really care what happened to anybody else. She should, so she tried to pretend like she did. But he told her that she was still too obvious. He said that unless she played the part flawlessly, other people would be able to sense the inauthenticity. She was working on it. She was still learning from him. He was very good at displaying the person that people wanted him to be and playing the part perfectly.

She had watched him through countless meetings with clients and marveled at how effortlessly he could slip into his character. And his clients were never the wiser. They accepted him easily, and he manipulated them to do exactly what he wanted. She watched every encounter eagerly trying to learn every method he used.

He told her that she was the first person that he had met that he could be completely open and honest with. She didn't judge him or fear him, the way others used to when he was a younger man and as inexperienced as she was at hiding his true face. She accepted him and even sought his company. He felt protective of her; he didn't like her to suffer. He told her that she was the only person he had ever felt that way for. That was one of the reasons he wanted to teach her. It took him a decade before he was adept as he was at creating his falsehoods. He wanted her to learn more quickly.

"Get away from the windows you fools!" Faisal ordered as he entered the great room.

Everybody jumped, including Marianna. They immediately listened to him and moved far away from the windows.

He was shaking his head. "Have none of you ever seen a storm before?"

"Not like this one, Sir." One of the guards said.

Faisal crooked his eyebrow and stepped towards one of the windows to look out. "Oh."

His entire demeanor changed as he gazed upon the ferocity of the storm outside. He morphed from a demanding tyrant into a concerned leader. He made everyone close all windows and doors throughout the house. He ordered his charges to gather candles, wood, food, and water to be moved into the great room. He called for the door guards that were posted outside to come inside. He was very proficient at preparing in a quick and orderly fashion.

Everybody gathered in the great room after collecting all the things that he ordered. There was an uncomfortable silence throughout the room. Everybody stood awkwardly unsure what to do. It was the first time that Marianna knew of, that everybody had ever been in the same room together.

Even though she lived and worked with all the people in the room, the number of people was overwhelming. The others must have felt the same way. It was also uncomfortable just having so many bodies in the same space.

Eventually, people sat on the couches and chairs that were intermittently spaced throughout the room, and when they were all taken, the remainder of the people sat on the floor. Faisal found a cushy chair near the fireplace.

Marianna was about to find a spot on the floor against the back of a couch so that she had something to prop her back on, but Faisal called her over to sit with him. She got plenty of nasty looks from everybody that she passed as she went to sit with him, but she didn't care. She was thrilled to be sitting with him.

He moved over so that she could squeeze in to sit next to him. She laid her head back on his chest just as a loud crack and flash of lightning struck. She jumped. Several of the ladies cried out in surprise. An uneasy quiet laugh moved through the room.

The sounds of things striking the outside of the building and windows veiled the howling wind at times. The room grew very dark. It was way darker than it should have been so early in the morning. It made Marianna nervous.

Faisal grabbed her arm and held it for several seconds. "You're shaking." He said as he wrapped his arm around her to pull her tight against him.

She giggled. "I'm scared." She admitted.

"Hmm." He said as he lightly ran his nails up and down her arm making her relax a little.

"I've never seen a storm like this." She said.

"Neither have I." He said.

"I have," Geoff said from his spot on the floor a couple of feet away from them.

Everybody looked at him expectantly. He looked around at everyone as if he was surprised to have so many people paying attention to him.

"Right. Well, you know I not originally from Athera." The guard said.

Marianna was not aware of that. But Faisal nodded as if he knew; as did several of the other ladies and guards. It had obviously been something that had been openly discussed within the house. But because Marianna was so isolated from her house mates she was clueless. She should have known.   He had an unusual accent.

"My family and I travel to Athera on grand ship.   In second month of voyage we were caught in storm like this one.   It toss our boat around like child's toy.   Boat almost tip.   The gods were watching that day. Kept boat floating.   It was most terrifying day of life.   Many lives lost that day.   Crew, passenger, son.   Sail break.   Water fill lower deck.   Crew very good at job.   Get us sailing again.   It take two more month to make dock.   More lives lost, from sickness, and starving.   Not enough food for longer voyage.   It unbelievable that I make it alive." He explained.

"That's awful," Sarafina said.

"It was a storm like this one."   One of the ladies asked him in a barely contained shrill.

Faisal stiffened and shook his head.

"Yes.   But we on land.   Much better." Geoff said smiling.

Nervous giggles spattered through the group.   Faisal relaxed.

"How long do you think it will last?"   A different lady asked.

"One from boat last all day and night. Rain last days more."   Geoff said.

Faisal shook his head playing with his

chin.   She recognized that he was nervous.
To see any true emotion from him was
strange.   Even though it was a subtle
change in expression for him.   She doubted
anyone else would even notice it.   She ran
her hand up his chest.   He looked down at
her and smirked.   He kissed her on the top
of her head.

"What will we do if it lasts that long?
Will we all stay in here?   Sleep in here?"
Evadnie asked.

"Yes.   If the storm remains as powerful as
it is currently, we will all remain in this
room."   Faisal answered.

"Great," Evadnie said sarcastically.

The room went quiet for a long time.
After a while, Faisal pulled out the latest
book that he was reading.   Marianna looked
at the words as he read.   She couldn't read
as fast as him, so she wasn't able to read
along with him, but she could read most of
the words without effort now.   He was a
very good teacher in that respect as well.

"I remember a storm, not this bad, but
pretty nasty.   I was eighteen.   And it was
my wedding day."   Jewel said.   She was a
round faced woman with mahogany hair
and the most stunning blue eyes.

Faisal put his book down to look at her with interest.   Everybody else looked as well.

"We'd planned it for months.   It was a union meant to strengthen our two houses. I was once nobility."   She said.

Several whispered comments moved through the room.   Marianna remembered back to the day when she was first taken from her home.   When she was forced into the wagon, one of the people she had spoken to said that he was nobility.   So, she knew that they were at the camp.   But she had always assumed they were moved to better jobs.

"We saw the clouds move in."   She continued.   "But we hoped that we could get through the ceremony before it got nasty. Just as I was walking towards him, the sky opened and poured down on us.   It was so bad that I could barely see him.   My father stood up from his spot and ushered me forward.

"The bishop was gathering his things to leave.   My father said he wasn't going to let a little thing like rain stops the union, so he threatened to withhold a year's worth of contributions if the bishop left without marrying us.   The bishop reluctantly stayed and rushed through the ceremony, so much that my husband's vows were skipped completely.   He blessed the union and then ran as quickly as he could to his carriage. He was gone before we could even say thank you.

"It was a running joke that I was married to him, but my husband wasn't married to me; because he never said the vows.   But he didn't mean it, of course.   We loved each other very much.   I wonder if he's remarried by now."   She lamented.

The room went quiet again.

"I was married also," Sarafina said.

"Me too."   Another lady said.

"So was I."   One of the guards said.

Several more made remarks about their past relationships before their time at the camp.

"My husband had died the night before, that day," Sarafina said glancing at Faisal. He nodded at her giving her permission to continue.   She didn't have to say anymore. Everybody knew what day she was referring to.

"He had been sick with fever for days.   He couldn't eat or drink anything without getting sick, and nothing I did was helping. He got so weak; I had never seen him in such a state. I wish I could say that he told me how much he loved me beforehand, or that we said goodbye to each other, but it wouldn't be true. He was delirious that final day, shouting ramblingly every time I tried to help him. The last hours he just kept crying out in pain. Until he wasn't making any sound at all. And he was just gone. Just like that.

"I spent part of the next day, mourning his death. I hadn't even let my neighbor know that he had died. I just couldn't speak about it yet.

"When the soldiers came into my town and broke down my door, they told me that they had come for him. They saw his lifeless body lying there on the bed. So, they took me instead. They said at least nobody would miss me when I was gone. Somehow, they didn't know about my two children sleeping in the other room. They were so young.

"When my two precious babies woke up, they would find their father dead and their mother missing. What kind of nightmare would that have been for them?" Sarafina said with tears streaming down her face. One of the other ladies rubbed her back to comfort her.

Over the next several hours each of the guards and ladies told stories of their time before the camp. Some spoke of the horrors of the day they were taken, others spoke of their families and friends, but each had something to say. So many of them had children, many of those children had also been taken. A few of the ladies were still young enough to live with their parents. Some tended to their houses, while others maintained extensive businesses. It was strange to know that each of them had once led such different lives before they were indentured.

Everybody stayed respectfully silent as each reminisced.

When the final person spoke, small conversations started up around the room.

"What's your story from before you were here?" Evadnie daringly asked Faisal.

The room fell silent as all eyes fell on him. He shook his head plainly, making it clear that he would not speak about himself. Nobody was brazened enough to push the issue with him. Was Marianna the only one who knew anything about his past?

"And what about you?" Faisal asked Marianna directly.

The room quieted as it always did whenever Faisal spoke. She sat uncomfortably, as all eyes turned to her. She didn't really want to talk about anything. She shrugged and shook her head.

"Speak. I want to know." Faisal said. His tone said, 'do not disobey.'

"I don't remember my family that much. It was just my Mama, Papa, and me. I think we were happy before, but I don't know.

"I woke to the sound of arguing. I thought that it was Mama and Papa fighting, but then my door was opened, and I was dragged out of by bed. My Papa tried to fight, and the guards stabbed him. My Mama didn't try fighting, but she begged for them to take her instead. They kicked her in the head. She fell over. I don't know if she's alive or not. I don't know if my Papa is alive or not. The only thing I really remember about my family was the day I was taken." She said, doing her best to feel very little emotion as she reminisced.

She didn't want to lose herself in front of everyone. It was difficult for her to avoid.

She could feel her heart racing, so she took slow, steady breaths to try and calm it down. Her vision grew red, so she closed her eyes trying to not think about it.

"So, this life is all you remember?" Evadnie asked sounding more sympathetic than Marianna had heard from the woman.

Marianna nodded. She was amazed at herself, that she was able to understand the question that was asked and respond to it. She had managed to stop herself from losing control. It was the first time she had accomplished such a feat. Nobody in the room perceived that she was on the verge of snapping either. Knowing that, allowed her to relax, even more, making it easier for her to keep her eyes open, and slow her breathing.

"How old were you when you came here?" Sarafina asked.

Marianna shrugged. "I think ten. I'm not sure." She was calm as she answered; almost emotionless. But not in the way that she used to be. She could feel which emotions she should feel, but she was able to keep them under control in a way that she had never done before. Faisal's time spent with her trying to find her triggers and then defuse her before she completely lost it, was working. She didn't want to explode. She didn't want to hurt anybody because of her show of venerability. She was at peace with what had happened to her and was able to let it go.

"So young," Sarafina said sorrowfully.

"And you don't remember your family?" One of the ladies asked.

She shook her head.

"My children might not even remember me." The lady said.

The room went silent again. After a while, Faisal began rereading his book. Over time little conversations from different groups filled the room. Marianna tried again to read Faisal's book, but he turned the pages way too fast for her to keep up with it. So, she tried to strain her ears to pick up on different conversations, but she couldn't separate the different groups with just her ears, and so she had difficulty following what was being spoken about.

The storm raged outside, but everybody seemed to have forgotten about it. Before long people had spread out apart from each other and laid down. Some fell asleep immediately, others continued whispering late into the night.   Faisal's book started dropping and then his head nodding, near the same time that Marianna felt tired.   His slow rhythmic breathing lulled her to sleep curled up against his chest.

#

Marianna woke up to a loud rumbling sound that she could feel as much as hear. In very little time everybody was awake and nervously talking about the ominous sound. Her ears were popping as the noise grew louder and louder.   Things were smashing against the outside of the house, making her jump every couple of seconds.

She was terrified.   She had never heard something so loud.   And it was eerily dark, even with the candlelight and fireplace. Faisal hugged her tightly, which gave her little comfort.

The house shook as the deep sound grew painfully loud.   She covered her ears.   She could feel the sound of it in her chest.   Loud creaking sounds came from the walls of the house.   What could make the house make those noises?   A window crashed followed by several screams including Marianna's. She had never been so scared.

Faisal squeezed her tighter; she could feel

that he was shaking too.   He was just as scared as she was.   There were a lot of things that he could control, but not this. He was just as helpless as everybody else.

The wind blew through the broken window tearing the curtains off and whipping them across the room just beside where Marianna sat.   Even so far away from the window, the wind was strong enough to push the thick curtains across the ground towards the fireplace.   Marianna pushed Faisal's hands away from around her and jumped up to grab the curtains.   If they caught fire the whole house would follow.

They were wet and heavy, too heavy for her to lift, so she sat on top of them to keep them from moving any closer to the fire, which was raging wildly from the wind.

Being off the chair Marianna could feel the intensity of the wind as it whipped her hair and dress all around.   Outside the window was blacker than night had ever looked before.   Her ears hurt so badly.   There was a heaviness pressing in on them over and over again.

Another window shattered as something long and thin shot through it and moved past her.   Several shards of glass sliced across her arms and face.   She screamed out in both pain and terror.   Faisal jumped up from his seat and circled her so quickly that she didn't have time to see what he was doing.   He wrapped his arms around her as he shoved her onto the floor, putting his back to the windows and blocking her from the flying debris coming in through them.

A huge startling crash came from the second floor louder than any other sound which was terrifying on its own.   The loud crash caused another wave of screams in the group.   The roar of wind somehow grew even louder.   And the creaking in the walls increased so much that she feared they would break apart.   Clattering sounds grew louder and more numerous and continued on the floor above them.

Another loud shattering sound pierced the other noises as a window broke into the bathing room next to them.   Moments later the door that connected the rooms exploded in towards them.

Every person screamed and scattered as far away as each could without getting too close to the windows.   Faisal lifted Marianna off the floor and pushed her away from the door and windows.   He forced her back down and again covered her with his body. Everybody was huddled up in the corner of the room, some held on to one another, some had faces pressed against the floor and their arms covering their heads, and others were curled up in balls.

The roaring outside quieted and the feeling that her ears were going to burst lessened. The sound of things hitting the building continued and the wind coming in through the windows still whistled loudly tossing debris around the room. After a terrifying amount of time the loud roaring became a distant sound and the rain poured down and blowing in through the broken windows.

Faisal sat up letting Marianna up as they both looked around the room. The fire in the fireplace was still going but just barely and all the candles had gone out and had been thrown around the room. Faisal stood up to grab the nearest candlestick and light it at the fireplace. He came back over shining it over Marianna to look at her.

"Are you alright?" He asked touching a spot of her face that made her jerk back.

"I think so." She said.

He used the candlelight to illuminate her

arm revealing a thick piece of glass protruding from it.   She barely even felt it.

He turned towards the rest of the group.

"Is anyone else hurt?"   He asked as he moved the candle around to look at everyone.

They helped each other up, looking at themselves and each other.

Marianna climbed to her feet to search for another candle.   The room was still so dark. She shuffled slowly scanning the floor for a candle.   She found a broken candlestick sitting on one of the couches.   It was a good thing that it had gone out before falling on the couch.

As she was heading to the fireplace to light her candle, she found several more.   She lit each of them and handed them to a few of the others who had followed her, to look for candles as well.

She moved around the room to gather more candles to place ones that could go into holders and to hand out ones that were too broken.   As she was rounding the chair that she and Faisal had been sitting in, she tripped over something.   She reached her hand out to brace for the fall, and as the weight of her body fell full force on her arm, she felt and heard her arm snap.   She screamed out in pain.

Faisal and two of the guards came running to her.   But they each stopped to stare at what she had tripped over.   She grabbed the candle with her uninjured hand and lifted it up to see what they were looking at.   Geoff was sprawled across the floor impaled by part of a tree.   The thick piece of wood was protruding from the man's chest, making it clear that he was dead.

"Look around.   Everybody.   See if anybody is hurt but unable to speak.   Now!" Faisal ordered.

Quickly the group in the corner of the room dispersed searching the dark room. The wind was still blowing through the windows making it difficult for the candles to stay lit near them.   Marianna cradled her arm and stood up to help with the search. In very little time it was determined that other than a few minor scrapes and cuts from flying debris, everybody else was fine.

"Alright.   The storm's not over.   I still think this is the safest room for us to all be in.   Everybody move close to the fireplace to keep warm and dry.   We will wait this out." Faisal said sounding confident.

All signs of fear were gone, and he was back to being in control. He was trying to keep everybody safe and calm, and he was doing an excellent job. Nobody would dare defy him anyways, but they all trusted his leadership in the crisis. They did as he asked, quickly and orderly.

Faisal was the last to come to the fireplace. He circled the room one final time with his candle looking all over the floor. He stopped at where Geoff lay and grabbed the curtain that Marianna had stopped, and draped it over the man's body. Marianna realized as he did, just how close the dead man was to where she had been sitting on the curtain.

CHAPTER SIXTEEN

Aftermath

Everybody sat huddled around the fire silently listening to the storm rage all around them. The rain was so much louder than it had been earlier in the night. Was it because the windows were open? But it was even louder than that would have explained.

It wasn't long before the light began showing through the windows. It was still dark from the storm, but the sunlight managed to lighten the inside of the house a bit. Marianna looked around the once dark room and saw pieces of broken glass, wood shards, tree branches and leaves, and water throughout the room. Four windows had been broken; one had been removed from the wall leaving a gaping hole. The rain was pouring so hard outside, that all she could see was gray beyond the windows. In the spot where the bathing room door was, only a tiny piece of wood still hung on to the hinges, and the other side of the door frame had broken away from the wall.

"Wow." She said as she saw how wrecked the place was.

"Yeah." One of the ladies said looking around also.

"Do you think the worst of it is over?" She asked Faisal who was sitting on the ground several people away from her.

He looked at her shaking his head and shrugging. "It's hard to say."

"What was that?" She asked referring to the terrifying time in the storm. She didn't have to elaborate. Everybody knew what she was referring to.

"I don't know," Faisal answered as well as several of the others in the group.

Marianna tried to stand up. She just barely moved her arm which sent an incredible pain from her wrist to her elbow. She had forgotten about her arm. She shouted out grabbing it and cradling it against her chest.

Faisal jumped up, clearing the people that

separated him from her.

"Let me see that," Faisal said.

She shook her head not wanting him to touch it, but at the same time, she moved her other arm away from guarding it so that he could look.

He knelt in front of her and grimaced as he looked over the arm.   He reached out towards her.   She jumped back sending a fresh wave of pain.

"Shh."   He comforted raising his hands up to show her that he intended her no harm.

He reached back towards her arm and grabbed it lightly with both hands, supporting it at her wrist and elbow.   He carefully guided it away from her body to look at it more which allowed her to get the first good look at it.   It was unnaturally bent and was swollen and bruised.

"You're not going to like this.   I must see how badly it's broken.   Don't pull away from me, or you will just hurt yourself more."   He warned.

She nodded frowning.

He pressed on her swollen arm pushing his fingers into the break.   She screamed out as tears immediately welled up in her eyes. It took all her willpower to not pull away despite what he said about it hurting her more.

When he released her arm, tears had soaked her face. Her arm throbbed and ached more than ever before. He moved it slowly pressing it lightly against her chest. She immediately reached up and supported it with her other hand trying her best not to move it.

"Normally I would send you to the Medica for that kind of break, but it's not safe out there, and there's no way to know how long this storm is going to be. It needs to be straightened out."

Marianna shook her head. "No. Please no. It hurts so bad. Please don't."

"If it heals wrong you may lose the ability to use it at all. I'll give you something to drink to dull the pain." He explained.

She cried but didn't argue. She didn't want to not be able to use her arm ever again. So, she would trust him.

"You, take a guard with you and get me some alcohol from the kitchen. Get me some towels as well. Be careful. Watch where you step." He said to Evadnie.

She nodded and headed to the kitchen. One of the guards followed after her without needing to be told.

"You clear this couch of any debris so that she can lie down." He ordered another of the ladies.

By the time the couch was clear, and he was leading Marianna to sit, Evadnie and the guard re-entered the room with what he had asked for.

"Drink. Quickly. You want it to hit you all at once." He said setting the cup off to the side and handing the full bottle to her.

She hated the taste of alcohol, and she hated, even more, the way it made her feel. She hadn't gotten very many chances to drink. It was only ever when she was working outside the house with a nobleman or officer.

Even though Faisal said he hated knowing that other men were enjoying her passions, he put her to work immediately after her first job. He said that she was too much of an asset to not use. And he was true to his word about pairing her with more hesitant partners, but she was very good at getting what she wanted, especially if she added alcohol.

But she had never had enough to be drunk. It was her job to take control of all encounters she had with the men she was assigned to, and it was too easy to lose control if she was drunk.

She tipped the bottle back and chugged as much as she could before her mouth registered that she was drinking. She gagged as soon as it did, and she had to take several deep breaths to prevent herself from bringing it back up. When the wave of nausea eased, she took several more, large swallows.

It didn't take long at all for her to feel the effects. Because she didn't drink that much, it didn't take much to hit her hard. In a matter of minutes, she was unable to see straight.

Faisal noticed when the alcohol took hold as he got her ready. He took one of the towels and wrapped it around her mouth and tied it behind her head. She frowned nervously.

"To bite down on, so you don't bite your tongue off." He explained as he her worry must have become evident on her face.

He lay her down and called two of the guards over. He ordered one to hold her legs down and the other to hold her shoulders. They were so strong that she couldn't move at all.   He called over another guard to grab above her elbow and hold her arm tightly.   He wrapped one of the towels around her wrist and hand and pulled.

Marianna shrieked as the pain overwhelmed all her senses.   Her vision became nothing, but bright star-bursts and her ears rang loudly.   She continued to scream as her vision came back to her.

He was wrapping the towel around her arm with a piece of the broken door holding it in place.   She stopped screaming and began whimpering, as he wrapped another towel around her arm.   She hadn't even noticed that the guards were no longer holding her down until he put his hand behind her back to help her sit up.   He tied the second towel around her back and shoulder securing her arm against her chest.

"You did better than most would. How's it feel?"   He said as he untied the gag from her mouth.

"Not bad."   She said.   Even though it was still throbbing horribly, it did feel a little bit better.

"Keep drinking."   He said handing her the bottle of alcohol again.   All feelings of intoxication were gone.

She tipped the bottle back and took several large swallows.

He took the towel that had been wrapped around her mouth and placed it on her other arm. Without warning, he pulled out the large piece of glass that was stuck in. She jumped and squealed. Blood poured from the wound. The sight of the blood, mixed with the pain in both arms, mixed with the effects of the alcohol hitting her all at once, caused her to pass out.

\#

Marianna woke up to busy sounds all around her. She opened her eyes to find that she was still on the couch that she had passed out on. Her broken arm was throbbing, and her other arm had a towel wrapped around it with blood seeping through.

She looked around. Several of the ladies were sweeping up debris from the floor, while others were gathering pieces from off the furniture and placing it in their skirts to discard in a corner where everything that was broken was being moved to.

People were working busily in the bathing room and others in the kitchen. Several people were working upstairs just in front of the hallway that led to the Vassal ladies' rooms, where her room was. A large section of the roof had fallen in and was blocking the hallway.

Looking around at all the devastation was intense. She had never experienced such a destructive storm; especially on the inside of a building.

Faisal stepped out of the kitchen and instructed everybody to temporarily stop the cleanup, and get something to eat. At the mention of food Marianna's stomach growled. All the Ladies and guards left their work areas and headed into the kitchen.

As Faisal scanned the room, he saw her sitting up. He hurried over to her. He sat down next to her pulling down the bandage that was wrapped around her arm where the glass had been in her. He frowned.

He got up and walked back into the kitchen. He came back out a couple of moments later with a towel in his hands and sat back down with her. He pulled the blood drenched bandage off her arm and replaced it with the new one. It stung as soon as it was exposed to the air and felt slightly better when he wrapped it back up.

"How's that feel?   Is it too tight?"   He asked as he tied it several times.

She shook her head.

"Good.   How's your other arm?"   He asked nodding at the arm that he had bound to her chest.

"It hurts."   She said.

He nodded.   "It will for a while."

"How did you know what to do?"   She asked.

He was very adept at treating to her wounds in a way that most of the people in the camp would not have been.

"Before I came here I was a shepherd.   I wasn't wanted in the town, as I told you before, so I had to do something for work. As a shepherd, my only concern was keeping the animals alive until they were eventually ready for slaughter.

"I had to learn how to keep the animals alive.   If one broke a leg, I had to tend to it in a way that would allow the animal to keep moving.   It's been a useful skill.   There have been a few times when I was breaking a Lady in, and I got a little too carried away. So, I've had to tend to some of the ladies as well."   He explained.

She smiled.   She loved learning new

313

things about him.   Every time he told her more about his past she understood him a little bit more about who he was.

"Do you remember how you broke it?" Faisal asked looking anxious.

She nodded.   "I tripped when I was gathering candles.   I think I tripped over Geoff."   She said.

"Hmm."   He said looking at her like he had been expecting something more.   "So that's why you screamed then?   Not because you found his body?"

She shook her head.   "I didn't even know he was there until you and the guards saw him."

"Why did you jump away from me after the first window broke?"

"The curtain was blowing towards the fireplace.   If it caught fire, the whole house could have followed.   So, I jumped on it to stop it from moving."   She explained.

"Oh."   He said in insight.   "Oh.   Yes. That makes sense."   His whole body relaxed.

She frowned at him in confusion.

"The others think that you were trying to save Geoff.   But I saw the branch that struck him, come through the window after you jumped away from me. So, I knew that wasn't what you did. I just wasn't sure what you were doing.

"They also think that your arm broke from trying to catch him as he fell, which is ridiculous, because he was sitting on the floor when he got struck, so there was nothing to catch, even if you had tried." He said.

They thought she was trying to save Geoff. How would she have even known that he was going to get hit by something? It was ridiculous.

"Don't correct their assumptions. Let them think that you were trying to save him. It may help them accept you." He ordered.

She nodded. He was right. She should use their ignorance to gain some advantage over them.

"You seemed relieved when I told you what really happened. Why?" She said recognizing just how much more relaxed he was since sitting with her.

He smirked. "Jealousy."

"What do you mean?" She asked confused by his response.

"Even though I thought I knew that they were wrong, the possibility that they weren't was disturbing to me.   If you would have told me that you jumped out of my arms, to save another man, even one as useful as Geoff, I don't think I would have handled that very well."   He said squeezing her thigh tightly.

"How do you think you would have handled it?"   She asked wondering what he would have done.

"I don't know.   I don't know.   It wouldn't have been good."   He said releasing her leg as he became aware of what he was doing. He gripped her dress tight in his hand instead.

"Oh."   She said not sure what else to say.

"I've never been this way about anyone before.   I know that I should get you sent to another of the houses because you've corrupted my judgment."

Her whole body tensed at the mention of him sending her away.   He thought she was corrupting him?   He thought that she needed to be sent away?

He ran his fingers through her auburn hair the way he did when he was trying to calm her down.

"When I heard you scream last night after you jumped away from me, a panic hit me in a way that I have never felt before. I was terrified that I was going to lose you, and with no regard for my own life, I protected you. Above anyone else. It could have just as easily have been me with that branch through my chest, but at that moment, I didn't care. As long as it meant that you were safe."

She relaxed a bit and smiled as she leaned into him to lay her head on his chest careful not to move her arm.

"You are my property. I should care no more about you as I do about the windows or the furniture. And with the other ladies, that is how I feel. But with you, I feel protective, possessive, and scared of the possibility of losing you. It frustrates me and fascinates me. But mostly it just makes me want to keep you even more close to me."

His words made her feel so special. She also wanted to be closer to him. She didn't want to lose him. The thought of being sent away from him scared her worse than the thought of dying. She never wanted to be separated from him.

"Let's get something to eat." He said standing up.

She nodded and took the hand that he

offered to help her up. She was still a bit woozy from the alcohol but managed to walk in a mostly straight line. But she held tight to his hand to help keep her balance.

The kitchen looked relatively untouched by the storm, but the dining room was trashed. Several of the windows had shattered. And strewn across the floor, was so much random debris that Marianna had to step over glass, large pieces of wood, and even a tree limb to get to the table.

As they walked in a couple of the guards jumped up so that they could sit. Many of the members of the household stood around the table as they ate. A couple of the Ladies looked up as she sat down and smiled at her. She didn't know what to do. They usually blatantly ignored her even with Faisal around. She smiled uneasily.

The food that was available was not cooked. It was raw carrots, apples, nuts, and some already baked bread. It didn't matter to her, it was all delicious. It had been more than a day since the last time she ate, so she ate every morsel that she had. By the time she was done eating most of the people had finished.

Even in the craziness of the day and with

so many people in the room, everybody waited for Faisal.   It was so ingrained in them that they didn't know what else to do. He didn't show it on his face, but Marianna could tell by his posture, how satisfied he was by their obedience.

He stood up nodding at all of them to release them from the table.   In no time, the room was empty of everybody except her and Faisal.   He helped her up and helped her across the obstacles in the room.   She appreciated the help because she did not want to fall on her broken arm.

As they entered the great room again, she looked around.   Geoff had been placed on one of the couches.   Part of the tree that had impaled him had been cut away.   He was placed in such a way that he looked like he was peacefully sleeping.   Faisal was looking at the man as well he looked over at her frowning.

"That could have just as easily been you. You were right next to where he fell.   If I'd have lost you..."   He trailed off looking back at the dead man.   He was scared.

"Sir.   You have to come see this."   The guard Jon said as he stepped in through the front door with a distraught look on his face.

CHAPTER SEVENTEEN

Destruction

Faisal scowled and walked out the front
door following Jon.   Marianna wasn't sure if
he had forgotten that he was still holding her
hand.

As they stepped outside into the rain, Jon
walked out into the street and looked back
towards the house.   The street wasn't even
recognizable.   Cobblestones had been torn
up and thrown all over the place, trees were
down everywhere.   The entire dock had
been torn up.   There was a boat broken in
half and sitting on the ground just in front of
where she was standing.

Faisal turned around and gasped.   She
turned to look at what he was reacting to,
and her mouth fell open in shock.   One
whole side of the second floor was gone.

There was no evidence that her room had ever even been there. But apparently, they were lucky. Because the house that was on the street behind theirs was gone. Nothing but broken wood and random pieces of furniture were left in the place where a once huge house stood.

Faisal walked around their house carefully helping Marianna to step over pieces of roof, and walls, and furniture that were strewn across the ground everywhere. Apparently, he had not forgotten that she was still with him.

As they rounded the edge of their broken house, the realization of just how lucky they really were, struck her.

Two entire streets of houses had been flattened. Not a single house or building remained standing as far as she could see in both directions.

"What could have done this?" She asked her voice cracking.

He looked down at her squeezing her hand. His face was all worry and shock. He shook his head. He had not been so venerable before.

"I've never seen anything like this. Ever. I've never heard of a storm being powerful

enough to do this.   I don't know.   This is...
just...I don't know."   He rambled.

She just nodded at him and looked back at
the wreckage.

She heard something.   "What's that?"

He looked down at her shaking his head
not sure what she was talking about.

"I think somebody is crying."   She said.

"I'm sure a lot of people are crying."   He
said looking around, trying to listen what
she was talking about.

"No, I mean from over there."   She said
pointing at the flattened house just ahead of
them.

"Oh."   He said.   "Oh!"   He said more
loudly and with comprehension.   "Wait
here, I'll be right back.   Don't move."   He
demanded.

She nodded, as he ran back into their
house.   Moments later he came back out
with several of the guards following behind.

Every one of the guards stopped in shock
for a moment as they took in the sight of the
decimated houses.   It only took moments
before they were all heading towards the
debris calling out for survivors.

Marianna watched as the guards pulled
people out of the rubble.   People trickled

out of the surrounding houses and buildings and before long; the decimated street was crawling with helpers.

Marianna tried to help too, but Faisal wouldn't let her. He said that with her injuries she wouldn't be able to help anyways, but she was pretty sure it was just because he didn't want her to get hurt anymore.

Eventually, she and a few of the other ladies from her house and some other nearby houses began taking in the survivors and helping them by tending to their wounds as best as they could and getting them food and water.

Faisal had sent two of his guards to find a carriage with an uninjured horse to take some of the more seriously injured people to the Medica. After delivering their first load of patients to the Medica, they came back with a few healers to help with the ones in the houses.

They spent weeks digging through the rubble pulling out survivors and then just bodies. Eventually, it was determined that too much time had gone by for anybody to be alive any longer. After the search for survivors ended, the time for cleanup began.

Their house became one of the many shelters for survivors.   They kept the collapsed second-floor roof in place inside the house.   It was sufficiently keeping the elements out, and seemed relatively stable. The temporary residents found extra couches and beds in the rubble and moved them inside, to be used as beds.   There were people everywhere on furniture and on the floors.   Some of them slept in shifts just to have a place to lie down.

Since Marianna's room had been wiped away, she had to find a place to sleep. Faisal insisted that she sleep with him.   His room was the only room in the entire house that wasn't full of people.   Nobody questioned his order to stay out of his room.

When it was time to go to bed the first night, she was thrilled to be able to go into his room.   Not only was it the quietest room in the house, but it was also his.

It amazed her when she first entered the room.   It was so elegant.   The walls were covered with beautiful paintings in all different shapes and sizes.   The pictures depicted ranged from flowers to landscapes, to sunsets.

Only one of the paintings had been

damaged in the storm. His room just had one window, and only a small corner of the window had been broken in the storm. He had a large floor to ceiling bookshelf full of books, and a second shelf that was half filled.

His bed was luxurious, and it was surrounded by thick curtains that hung from the ceiling all the way to the floor. And when she climbed into it for the first time she found that it was the softest thing she had ever felt.

He enjoyed her presence in his room as much as she enjoyed being there. Every night when he joined her, he melted into her. Most nights they would find the energy to lose each other in their passions. Sometimes they would talk for hour's afterword. Other times they would immediately drift off to sleep holding each other.

It took her arm a couple of months to heal enough for her to be able to use it, and he babied it and her, in a way that she had never seen from the man. He was usually the one delving out pain and punishments, not to her because she was always obedient, but he would have if she ever did disobey. But he did everything that he could to avoid causing her pain or even discomfort.

One night she was lying with him after a long day of relocating half of the residents of the house to a more permanent shelter that had been built in one of cleared out spots where a building used to be. She was exhausted, and he looked just as beat as she felt. They undressed each other and climbed into the bed. He surprisingly was content with just lying with her and holding her.

"I almost lost you." He whispered as he ran his nails lightly up and down her back. The scars on her back never seemed to bother him.

"Hmm." She said snuggling her head into his chest.

She traced her fingers along each of his muscles. The muscles in his chest and arms had become so much more pronounced in the months following the storm, from all the heavy lifting he had to do digging through rubble and then helping to clear it.

"I don't ever want to feel that way again. Don't ever let me lose you." He said lifting his head up to kiss her on the top of hers.

She smiled.

"I promise you. I'm never going to let

anything happen to you.   Ever again."   He
said setting his head back and wrapping his
arm around her hip and hugging her tight.

   She kissed him on the chest and then laid
her head back down to trace his muscles
more.

   "I mean it.   I can't lose you.   I love you
too much.   I just can't lose you."   He said
wrapping his other arm around her and
holding her.

   She smiled even bigger.   "So, you're not
going to send me to one of the other houses,
for corrupting you?"   She asked playfully,
but desperately wanting to know his answer.

   "Never.   You're not going anywhere.   I
promise.   You're mine."   He said leaning up
and kissing her head again.

   She lifted her head to look at him.   Tears
filling her eyes as the strength of his promise
hit her.   She leaned up to kiss him.

   He wasn't going to send her away.   He
wasn't going to get rid of her.   He wanted
her to be with him.   He really wanted her.
She kissed him again her passion taking
over.   Before long they lost each other to
their passions ignoring their tired bodies'
rebellions.

   She went to sleep for the first time that she

could remember, knowing that she was finally safe.

CHAPTER EIGHTEEN

Discovery

Marianna had been awake for several hours, but Faisal was still sleeping soundly, so she stayed in bed. He began moving around more as he woke up himself. It was barely dawn. He opened his eyes to look at her. When he saw that she was awake, he smiled at her. She smiled back.

"What are you doing awake?" He asked groggily, stretching his arms and then wrapping them around her.

Her smile grew. "I couldn't sleep." She said moving closer to him.

"Hmm. Are you worried?" He asked as he lightly ran his nails down her arm.

She shrugged. "A little."

"Everything will be fine. You have planned this move perfectly. I have no doubt that you have thought of every possible scenario that could make something go wrong, and come up with a solution." He said playfully.

She shook her head. "I'm sure that I've forgotten something." She said.

"You do realize that there are over forty of us moving. You do not have to take this all on by yourself. They will all listen to you. All you have to do is give them direction." He said.

It had been a year since the massive storm that destroyed so much and killed hundreds of people. So much had changed since that fateful night. She was no longer the target of ridicule and disdain from everybody in the household. In the aftermath of the disaster, Marianna had managed to step up into a leadership role within the house. Everybody listened and respected her as much as they did Faisal. There was still an air of fear in how they viewed her, but it wasn't the deciding factor for their respect towards her. Instead, it was her ability to bring everybody together to work towards a common goal. Her effectiveness in the planning towards recovery and clean up after the storm was matched by none.

She had first led the other ladies with the help of the Medica's to tend to the wounded. Her quick thinking had managed to save hundreds of people that would have been lost in those first devastating days. Because of her broken arm, she couldn't physically help, so instead, she helped by directing people. She came up with a system to get everybody treatment from the most injured to the least, which saved many lives. She also found a way for each person needing care to receive it in shifts so that everyone would be able to eat, rest, and sleep while still providing the necessary aid, which saved the minds and bodies of those who were helping.

She also helped plan the search for survivors. The first couple of days were chaotic, and though survivors were found, some of the people doing the searching ended up being just as hurt or sometimes even more so, than the survivors that they found. Some were injured from falling debris. While others were injured because rubble was being moved in one spot, while somebody was searching for another; causing loose spots and making the searchers fall into, and sometimes become buried by the rubble.

Marianna created a grid type system so that everybody knew where others were while searching. She also suggested that everybody search in teams. With one person digging, while the other watched for potential dangers and maintained safety. She also suggested a way that would ensure that the same places were not searched twice, which would have wasted time and resources, and risked more people staying trapped.

After the search for survivors ended, Marianna helped keep order within the house with all the people coming and going at all hours. She recognized the strengths of each person and found a job for each of them to help in the best way to utilize everybody's assets. Everybody was satisfied with the arrangement.

The other ladies, guards, and survivors all went to her for advice and plans to solve problems that arose over the year. Even Faisal came to her to bounce ideas off of. They all trusted her judgment and wisdom, but she still felt strange being the one telling others what to do. After being a slave for so long, all she knew was to follow orders, not give them.

He watched her lazily as the sun rose up filling the room with light. She looked around the room that she had grown to love. It was the first place that she had ever felt comfortable. The only thing left in the room was the bed and the emptied shelves. The walls were bare, all the paintings had been moved downstairs in preparation.

"This is the last time I get to wake up next to you in this room." She said reminiscently.

He chuckled and kissed her on the top of the head.

"You amaze me." He said.

She looked at him in confusion.

"I have watched you grow from a crazy child who terrified everybody who met you, into a respected, trustworthy, young woman. And you've done it without even trying. You take in everything that you experience or learn and use them in ways that nobody else could. You are one of a kind."

She smiled, yawned, and stretched. "Does it bother you to leave? I mean this has been your home for years." She asked sitting up and stretching some more.

He shook his head. "It was never a home

to me. It's only ever been the place that I work and sleep. And it's been broken for a year. It's time to move on. You were the one who suggested we leave this place. It will just be easier to demolish this place and rebuild. And we need to relocate to a place away from so much destruction. It's bad for business." He said without a care.

"I know. I just thought maybe you would miss this place." She said.

He shook his head climbing out of bed and grabbing his clothes at the foot of the bed. "As long as you are with me, I've got all that I need."

She stood up next to him and kissed him.

He pulled away from her with a silly grin on his face. He raised his eyebrows at her and looked back at the bed out of the corner of his eye. "How about we work on one last good memory of this place."

She giggled and kissed him again, giving into his suggestion.

Faisal left the room before she did heading down to get something to eat before starting the busy moving day. She stepped out of the room and stared at the collapsed roof that hid the missing section of the second floor, where her room once was. It was strange that she missed even that. It had been the first place that she had met Faisal. It was the place where she had somehow convinced him not to kill her. That room had changed her life.

She shook her head. The room had nothing to do with it. It was just a place. Nothing to get sentimental about. It was Faisal that had changed her life.

She stood at the top of the staircase watching all the busy activity as the entire household worked to empty the house. Several large carts lined the street outside the house, being loaded up with furniture and belongings.

She joined Faisal in the dining room.

"Make sure you eat well. We may not get a chance again today." He said.

She nodded and finished off her large plate of food.

After eating she rinsed her plate and put it in one of the wooden boxes filled with dishes, and then being the last to finish eating, she carried it to the cart.

Moving day went smoothly. By the time everything had been removed from the house it was beginning to grow dark. Several people rode in tiny spaces on the beds of the carts where ever they could fit. The rest of the group got to walk. Faisal jokingly mentioned taking a romantic carriage ride just the two of them, but too many Ladies were walking with too few guards for him to comfortably leave them to find their way. He liked keeping an eye on everyone. And they were less likely to act out or attempt escaping if he was around for fear of his retribution if they got caught.

But nobody tried anything. They were all too tired and sore. When they got to the place that would be their new house, everybody just found a place on the floor to sleep.

The next several days went by in a blur of exhaustive unloading and unpacking. Marianna directed most of the work with an efficient and steady pace, so within the week the place was finished and ready to be lived in.

Marianna sprawled out on one of the couches reading a book. She suggested to Faisal that it would be good for morale to let everybody have a couple days of rest after such a big move. He agreed, and so everybody found their own space within the large house to spend a lazy afternoon.

The new house had a different layout than the previous one.   First, it was about twice the size.   The kitchen had two parts to it.   A room for food storage and dishes, and a separate room for cooking and washing.

Instead of one large great room for the house members to spend their downtime and social time, the new house had four large rooms to make more intimate meetings outside of the bedrooms possible.   Faisal had requested the house to have that feature specifically so that it would be easier to entertain men, but still maintain a bit of privacy.   He also made sure that there were enough bedrooms to add numbers to his house.

He wanted to increase the Vassal lady side of the business.   He said that it was his original idea to have more Vassal ladies than Breeders, but the officers wanted to grow the numbers in the camp while establishing a relationship with one woman at a time.   So, everybody who came to the houses were put to work as Breeders until their usefulness in that duty ran out and they would be put to work as Vassal ladies.   He said that business would pick up and be more profitable if their focus moved off the Breeder aspect of the house and onto the Vassal lady aspect.

Faisal didn't get a house built to his specifications. It would have taken way too long with the cleanup efforts to get enough people to build a new house. So, he bartered with a few nobleman and officers and got what once was a barracks for a group of soldiers turned into the new Vassal house.

Marianna was with him when he spoke with the men. As she listened to and watched the exchanges occur between the haggling men, she learned so many unexpected things about Faisal. He was a very powerful man in the camp.

Six men; four noble, and two officers, haggled with Faisal for several days. It was easy to understand what the men asked for in trade, but it was amazing that Faisal was able to provide all the things requested. Firstly, the men wanted money. A lot of money. Each of the men demanded it. But Faisal easily agreed to the outrageous amount of money. He was not concerned with the amount.

How wealthy was he?

Another thing that was to be part of the exchange were political favors from him.

She discovered that he had grown to be a very influential person in society with a lot of pull in important decisions. He was in a position where nobody told him what to do within the house. He did what he wanted. But he also was able to do whatever he wanted outside the house as well. Nobody questioned or stopped him or anybody working for him, regardless of how illicit the activity was.

Marianna learned that he clandestinely ran many other business ventures in the camp. He was in charge of all of the houses. He also employed more guards than any other part of the camp, including the children's side. He had found other useful ways to use the guards' services. His influence in the camp was from more than just prestige and money. He was able to shape the political policies with muscle. His hold on so much of the purchasable strength within the camp gave him more authority than almost anybody else.

The individuals with the highest standing did not recognize just how much leverage Faisal had over all of them. But he knew. And it was clear to Marianna, just how influential he was.

The final request made by the men was ladies.   They wanted possession of a trained lady for each of them.   Faisal offered the men, the choice of any lady that they wanted, except for Marianna whom he claimed as his own.   None of them argued that point.

It was agreed that Faisal would give them any lady that they desired.   They didn't have to be one living in his house.   They didn't even have to be working as a Breeder or Vassal lady.   Faisal assured the men that he could break anyone to be exploited for their personal use, from a lowly slave to a high-class noblewoman.   He even promised to train them to do anything that the men requested, no matter how odd or undesirable it may seem.

And so, the agreement was made.   And even though it appeared like Faisal was getting less out of the deal than the six men, Marianna recognized that he wasn't.   When he agreed to pay such a significant amount of money without hesitation, he showed the men that money was of little consequence to him and how wealthy he was.   When he agreed to use his resources to sway political changes that the men wanted, he showed the men how influential he was. And when he agreed to break any woman to be used as a Vassal Lady, he revealed that anybody could be broken by him, no matter their status. The entire arrangement was used to his advantage. And the other men had no idea.

Discovering all the veiled ways that Faisal controlled everything, and everyone around him was disheartening. He was a master of manipulation, and everything that he did, was to gain his advantage, even over her.

When he claimed possession of her with the six men, ensuring that the other men knew that she was his, he was knowingly showing her that she could never get away from him. By letting her see what kind of control he had over everyone else, ensuring that she knew his ever-growing influence throughout the camp, he was showing her that he could do anything that he wanted without consequence. By letting her witness how easily and thoroughly he manipulated the entire situation he was showing her that she would never match him.

She may be good at manipulation, but she would never be as good as he was. All the meetings that he let her witness were not only about manipulating the six high-class men.   They were his way of reinforcing his total control over her life.

It didn't matter.   She was his, in all senses of the word.   She was his property, his slave, his lover, and his companion.   And if at any moment he decided that he was tired of her, he could get rid of her with no questions asked of him.   Her life belonged to him.   Nobody cared if she lived or died. She was only an asset because Faisal said that she was.   And he made certain that she knew it.

CHAPTER NINETEEN

Old Friends

After a couple of days of reprieve, the house members were put back to work. For some of the ladies, it had been months. So, Faisal required all encounters to have a guard chaperoning. If the guards reported any signs of disobedience, the ladies would be forced into some intensive training with Faisal, to re-solidify his hold over them. But his hold was still strong. All reports from the guards were favorable.

Marianna   had gone longer than any of the other ladies since the last time she had to work. First, her injury after the storm prevented her. Then her efforts were better spent directing the cleanup after the storm. Faisal was more reluctant about her being put back to work than any of the other ladies. But she was too valuable of an asset for him to keep her to himself. He told her that she was the only lady that he trusted with certain jobs.

She dressed in a body-hugging red dress that showed off the curves of her breasts just enough to show her most desirable features without being scantily clad. Faisal always said that it was sexier to show off just enough to get the imagination ignited, without revealing everything that was available. She left her auburn hair down and tucked it behind her ears, making sure to leave a curled lock to fall down the side of her face.

She had been told that her assignment would be with a younger soldier who had a problem with intentional insubordination. He had been punished more than any other soldier in his group. And he was on the verge of a permanent solution to deal with his disobedience. So, his friends had hired Marianna to break him of his rebelliousness. They were convinced that if he had the companion of a lady, he would start to behave like a proper soldier. According to Faisal, the young man had no desire to use her services, and so she would have to be extra persuasive. She had mastered her art of persuasion and looked forward to the endeavor. It had been a while since she was able to use her skills.

Because of the reluctance with many of the men that she was paired with, she never had the opportunity to spend social time outside of the bedroom. Even though she shared a bed to sleep in with Faisal, she was still given a room for work. So, she waited with the guard that was assigned to ensure her obedience.

The door opened, and four soldiers stepped into the room. Two had their arms around a third whom they carried in. His head drooped without control. She couldn't tell if the man was awake, or even alive. The fourth soldier walked behind the unconscious looking man, with his hand on the hilt of his sword. It seemed like the man being dragged in was dangerous even in the state that he was in.

The scene was unexpected. Nobody had ever been brought to her in such a state.

Marianna's guard Philip looked extremely uncomfortable about it all. His body tensed, and he drew his weapon, which was very rarely drawn. It wasn't usually necessary, as the guards were well trained in dealing with disobedient ladies and men without resorting to the use of a weapon.

The guards would utilize their weapons to protect the ladies from especially violent men, or men who tried to outstay their welcome, but weapons were not usually the first line of defense for the guards. Marianna thought that it was to keep the men more at ease during their recreations.

Who would win in a fight? Philip who was trained to dominate an attacker in a way that incapacitated but left no marks, or the soldiers who were trained to kill without regard.

The soldiers dropped the man onto the floor. His body fell limp. He groaned, proving that he was still conscious, but just barely, since he didn't move, even though he was laying on top of the shackles that were on the floor.

The two soldiers who had carried the man, stretched as if they had been uncomfortably carrying him for a long distance, while the third soldier moved his hand away from his sword. Philip visibly relaxed but kept his weapon drawn.

He was really nervous which made her

feel the same. She trusted the instincts of the guards. They knew how to recognize when somebody was dangerous and when to be extra cautious.   If her guard was uncomfortable, it was a good idea to pay extra attention to keep herself safe.

She had never been alone in a room with so many armed men. Usually, the encounters that the guards were present for, were with willing individual soldiers. And although she never saw a soldier without his weapon, those soldiers were usually too distractedly engaged in physical acts to be a true threat to the guards.

Marianna was one of the few ladies who usually worked alone with her more hesitant participants. It was only because it was her first day back to work that Faisal, unwilling to take any chances even with her, had her under guard. But even with her history working with men who needed more coaxing, she also had never been in a room with so many soldiers.

One of the soldiers who had carried the man pulled out a canteen and took a long swallow from it. He passed it to the man with the sword, who did the same and then passed it to the third man. They each looked up at Marianna and smiled as they looked at her body in her body-hugging red dress.

The man with the canteen dropped it on the floor, causing it to clatter. Before she even had time to react to the sound her guard Philip had taken a step towards the soldiers with his sword raised. At the same time, two of the soldiers drew their swords in reaction looking at the guard as if he was the threat. Everybody was hyper reactive, except for the one who dropped the canteen. He was staring wide-eyed at Marianna his mouth gaping open.

"Anna?"

She frowned taken aback by the shortened use of her name which she had not heard in years.

"Anna, oh shit it's really you, isn't it? You're alive. Shit. You're alive." The man said enthusiastically.

He knelt to the man on the floor. He grabbed the man's head and lifted it up to look at Marianna.

"Alex. Look who I found. Anna's not dead after all. Look buddy. It's your lucky day, twice." The man said.

"Alex?" She whispered, looking at the pitiful man on the floor as his eyes focused on her face. A look of recognition crossed his expression.

She looked at the speaking man studying his face. How did he know her?

"Rayden?" She said as recognition struck her.

He looked so different that if he had not made the connection between them known, she would have never guessed it was him. He was a man. The last time she had seen him, he was a wiry growing boy in the awkward stage where his feet and arms were longer than the rest of his body. His ears protruded from the sides of his head, and his teeth looked too big for his mouth.

But as an adult, he had completely changed. He had grown into all his features magnificently. He was a tall man. Even taller than Faisal, who was one of the tallest men that she saw regularly. His muscles were menacing. She had no doubts about how strong he was. His hair was still the same sandy yellow color cut short and close to his head.

He beamed as she called him by his name. And she saw that it was definitely Rayden. His smile showed that he was the same happy, optimistic Rayden that she used to know. She smiled back, which just made him smile broader.

He ran up to her lifting her off the bed and squeezing her in a tight hug while spinning her around. She giggled at the unexpected embrace.

He put her back down and looked up and down at her, joy radiating from him. The other soldiers and her guard stood staring at the two of them stupefied from the unexpected connection.

"I can't believe that you are alive. I mean, we heard what you did... Damn, that was brutal. And I've seen some crazy shit." He said with a disgusted look on his face.

She looked at him feeling ashamed that he knew what she had done. She didn't know why it mattered to her, she hadn't seen him in years, but it bothered her still. But not so much that she lost herself. It had been a long time since she had a true test of her control over her bouts of insanity, but she surprised herself by staying utterly calm at his mention of the murder.

"But here you are. Alive. And you look great." He said biting the side of his lip as he eyed her up and down.

She was used to men looking at her like he

was, but she suddenly felt self-conscious under his gaze. She didn't know how to react to the feeling.

"No, I mean it. I mean the last time I saw you, you were practically starving to death. You were all bones. But not anymore." He said with a hungry smile as he continued looking at her body.

She crossed her arms over herself which made him look back to her face which she could feel blush. She never blushed. What was happening?

"So, are you going to introduce us?" One of the soldiers said stepping up and putting his arm around her shoulder and looking up and down her body, while the other man circled her running his hand through her long auburn hair and then down her back before stopping to face her, licking his lips.

Rayden beamed. "Of course. Guys this is an old friend of ours, Marianna. Marianna these are the guys. Dale," he said pointing at the man who had circled her, "and Gerardo." He said putting his arm around the other side of the man who had his arm around her shoulder.

"You don't have friends who look like this. Tell me the truth. You previewed the girl, right?   Before we got here to make sure Alex will get what we paid for." Dale said laughing.

"What does a preview cost?" Gerardo asked looking over at Marianna's guard who was no longer wielding his sword but still stood ready to fight with his hand sitting on top of the hilt ready to draw. He said nothing in response to Gerardo's question. Instead he just rolled his eyes looking back at the man with annoyance. The man didn't even notice.

"Alex can't even appreciate her in the state that he's in right now," Dale said.

She looked down at Alex who had weakly pushed himself up so that he was sitting. His head bobbed around like he was dizzy, but he looked at her with sadness in his eyes. She frowned. She remembered that sorrow. It used to be all she knew in her own life.

"Let's have a little dress rehearsal with your supposed friend here," Dale said.

"She is our friend," Rayden reassured. "Both Alex and mine. Our homes were all near each other. We even rode to the camp together the night we were taken. It's been forever since I saw her, but we've known each other since we were both kids." Rayden said.

The two other soldiers each lost their playful attitudes for a moment at the mention of that night. It was a painful memory for everyone who was old enough to remember.

"Anna?" Alex whispered frailly.

Rayden smiled.

"How? How are you here?" Alex said.

He closed one eye to look at her, his head still bobbing.

"What happened to him?" She asked Rayden.

"Oh that. That's nothing." Rayden said cheerfully.

Dale and Gerardo both laughed.

She cocked her eyebrow at them and looked back down at Alex.

"We knew that he wouldn't come without a fight, so we slipped something into his food," Rayden said chuckling.

"You poisoned him?" She asked.

"What? No. We just gave him something that would make him more compliant." He explained.

"Is he drunk then?" She asked looking back at Alex who was still unable to stop wavering.

"Sorta. We gave him some Veruska." He said.

She shrugged shaking her head in confusion. He stared at her dumbfounded, and her guard was suddenly very interested in the conversation.

"Seriously? You don't know what Veruska is?" He said.

She shook her head again. Everybody else in the room was as shocked by her ignorance.

"It's a powder that comes from a flower. It makes you stop feeling pain, or worry, or regret. You just don't give a fuck about anything after taking it.   It doesn't last long though." Rayden said sounding disappointed by the last part.

"I think I might have been given something like that years ago when I was sent to the Medica after one of the whippings almost killed me. It didn't take away all of my pain, but it did take away most of it." Marianna mused as she remembered her short stint recovering.

"Probably the same shit. It's not supposed to be available outside of the Medica, but with enough money." He said shrugging, leaving the last bit for her to infer. She had been learning just how much money was flowing into the camp and what influences that money bought.

"So, why'd you give it to him?" She asked.

"We needed to get him here without fighting. If it was even suspected that he was being combative, he'd be screwed. You see our buddy over there has a reputation for insubordination. And he's on his last fucking warning. If he acts out again, he's done for. He doesn't give a shit, but I do. He thinks he's some noble hero fighting for our justice. But he's just the bastard intent on fighting a losing battle." He explained.

She nodded. She understood what Alex was experiencing. Was he actually being intentionally insubordinate, or was it like she used to be, was he just given the wrong job? When she was responsible for the young ones she too had the reputation of disobedience, and the punishments that went along with it. But once she was moved to a job that was more suited for her, she was seen completely opposite.

"So, I convinced these shits to chip in some of their bounties. I thought maybe he just needs to screw a lady and break him out of his rut. And if it doesn't work, then at least he gets to have a good fuck before he's put in the ground." He said.

She nodded again. It made sense. When she was with a man who had gone an extended period of time without the companionship of a lady, that man was much more likely to not follow orders. And once she was done with them, their satisfaction was apparent in their duties.

Gerardo took his arm from around her shoulder and spun her around to face him. "We paid your boss man extra so that he got a lady who could get him going even if he's not up for it. I thought the lady that we were going to get would be a little bit older, more experienced and all, you know? Not that I think you can't do it for him, I mean look at you, very fuck-able, but I didn't know there was anybody your age that wasn't in the popping out babies' business. Do you know what you are doing? I mean, no disrespect or anything, but you have done this before, right?" Gerardo asked.

"I know how to do my job." She said narrowing her eyes.

She didn't like the man. There was something about him just rubbed her the wrong way.   But she couldn't pinpoint it.

"Ooo. You're feisty. But I might need you to prove it to me. I mean we are paying a lot of money. We need to be sure that we're going to get what we paid for." He said, pulling her over to him by her hips and grinding against her.

She pushed him away making him trip over the foot of the bed and fall to the floor.

He jumped up with fury in his eyes and rushed at her. He picked her up and slammed her body against the wall knocking her breath out of her.

In moments her guard had grabbed the man. He twisted his arm around in a way that made him drop her, and then drop to his knees. Dale had drawn his sword and was holding it to her guard's throat. And Rayden was trying to put himself between her guard and Gerardo.

"Whoa. Everybody needs to calm the fuck down. Dale put that thing away." Rayden said calmly with his hands up.

Dale hesitated for a moment and then took the sword away from the guard's neck, but kept it drawn.   And his posture showed that he was ready to do whatever needed to be done.

"Good. Do you think you can let my friend

up?" Rayden said kneeling down to look at the guard.

"I know that he can be an asshole sometimes, and that was totally an asshole thing you did." He said looking at Gerardo, who was glaring at him.   "But if you don't let him up, then Dale here isn't going to like that too much, and a fight will ensue. It's three of us and only one of you. I don't think you want to test our abilities in a fight." Rayden said lightheartedly, but there was a certainty to his words.

Her guard looked nervous. He didn't want to fight them, but he didn't want to look weak either.

"I'm alright. You can let him up." Marianna said to Philip, smiling.

Her guard nodded and released Gerardo, who stood up pulling his arm away heatedly. He looked at her, rage bubbling within him. He was furious and dangerous.

Marianna had to diffuse the situation before something irreversible was done. "I'm sure if you take him to speak to Faisal they can make arrangements for him to enjoy the company of another lady; while I work with his friend here. I think he just needs a little companionship himself."

Marianna said trying to sound unconcerned.

At the mention of Faisal's name Gerardo's jaw clenched. So, Faisal's influence was known by the man. She had made the right call to bring him up.

"I think that is a great idea. Dale why don't you go with them. See if you can get yourself a lady as well. I'll pay for the two of you. It's the least I can do for you helping me with Alex. You two go have some fun." Rayden said optimistically.

Dale nodded and grabbed hold of Gerardo's arm. The man snatched his arm away.

"Come on you bastard. Let's go get our knobs polished. Rayden's got this handled. Why should Alex get all the fun, when we're the ones who always have to put up with his shit?" Dale said pushing on Gerardo's back urging him towards the door.

Marianna's guard looked torn. He was supposed to stay in the room with Marianna in case she refused to do her job, but if he let Gerardo hurt Marianna, Faisal would not be happy. He looked between her and the two soldiers at the door for several moments and then nodded and followed the men out of the bedroom.

She relaxed the moment they left the room. She hadn't even recognized how on edge she had felt until she was able to release the tension. Rayden also relaxed. While Alex was still in such a state that if he relaxed anymore, he would have been unconscious.

Rayden looked at her smiling broadly. She smiled back. His upbeat attitude was contagious.

"Did the asshole hurt you?" He asked looking at her arm where she had been grabbed while being slammed against the wall.

She shook her head. "I'm fine."

It had hurt. Her head had hit the stone wall, her back felt like it had been slapped, and both of her arms she was sure were going to bruise.   But she didn't want him to know about that.

He accepted her denial.

He looked around the room. "So, this is where you stay?"

She glanced around. She hadn't gotten a chance to look around her new assigned room. It was just like the one she used to have back at the other house, except it didn't have a window. Chains were attached to one wall, a bed against another, and a small table with two chairs around it sat in the corner.

"This is just where I work. I sleep somewhere else." She said rotating her shoulders in an attempt to stop the stinging pain in her back.

He looked at her in surprise. "Really? I thought you girls lived in these houses."

"We do. Most of the ladies' sleep in the same room that they work in, just not me." She said.

He cocked his head to the side. "Why not?" He looked at the chains hanging on the wall. "Do you stay in the basement or something?"

She scowled in confusion. "What? Why would I be in the basement?"

He shrugged. "You know. Because you murdered that kid. Wait. Did you murder a kid? Or was that just a story?"

"Oh. Yeah. I mean, yes, I killed him. And I was taken here for punishment, but I don't sleep in a basement."

He nodded. "So, why'd you do it? I know you hated your life over there. But I was talking to one of the girls that said she was there, and she said that you were a lunatic. She said that you beat the kid to death, but you didn't stop there. You just kept on smashing his head long after he was gone. And that when you were done with him, he was unrecognizable. Just brains and blood everywhere." He said enthusiastically.

She could feel it happening. Her heart sped up as her breathing became erratic. Her vision wavered. Her jaw clenched and all the muscles in her body tensed.

She closed her eyes intentionally taking deep breaths, to try and calm herself down. If she snapped with Rayden and Alex, what would she do? Could she kill the only two people that she had ever called friends? She had to calm herself down. She pumped her hands, trying to avoid letting her nails dig into her palms. She shook her head trying to stop the thoughts from overwhelming her. She opened her eyes to find Rayden staring at her nervously.

"You alright there, Anna?" He asked, backing away from her.

"I'm fine." She said taking several more deep breaths.

"Sure you are." He placed his hand on the hilt of his sword seemingly unconscious of the motion, as he took another step away from her.

She sat down on the bed grabbing her head and shaking it while she took several more deep breaths.

"I snapped." She whispered.

"I can see that." He said still watching her warily.

"Not now. The day that I killed Clive." She said pulling her legs up to hug them. He frowned.

"I sometimes get so overwhelmed, so angry that I just lose myself. I'm getting better at controlling it now."

"So, it's all true then? That you went crazy? That you murdered the kid? How you killed him?" He said with increasing curiosity, but still keeping his guard up.

She tightly closed her eyes, took in a deep breath, and looked at him. "Yes."

"Shit. And they let you live?"

"They let Faisal decide that."

His eyes opened wide. "And he let you live. Wow. How'd you manage that?"

She frowned at him and shrugged. "He saw something in me that nobody else did."

"That's great. You must have shown him something incredible. That man. He scares the shit out of me, and I've seen some shit. I don't know what you did to convince him.   Wow." He said enthusiastically, eying her up and down.

She watched as he shifted himself in the same way many other men did when they looked at her hungrily.   "You must be something special."

"Anna?"   Alex asked weakly from the floor.

She looked down at him.   He studied her face as if he was just realizing again that she was there.   She nodded at him.   He closed his eyes tightly rubbed them both several times with the palms of his hands, and then looked at her again.

"What are you doing here?   You were executed."   He said with a look of confusion.

"No.   I wasn't."   She assured him as she climbed off the bed to move closer to him.

He had changed even more than Rayden had.   His face was scruffy as if it had been several days since he had shaved last.   His mahogany brown hair was cut short and close in the same style as Rayden.   He looked like he had aged twenty years as opposed to the four or five since the last time that she had seen him.   His skin was weathered, thin, and wrinkling across his forehead and around his eyes.   He was thinner than she thought he should be.   But she could still see long sinewy muscles in his exposed arms.   His eyes were the most changed.   They looked like they had aged a hundred years.   They showed how weary, taxed, and beaten he was.

He reached out towards her to poke her shoulder, and then seemed surprised that he had touched her.

"But you're dead.   What'd you give me this time?"   He said wobbly looking at Rayden.

"It's just Veruska again," Rayden said defensively.

"I think you gave me too much this time. You've got me seeing dead people."   He stammered.

Rayden laughed out loudly.   His heartfelt laugh made her smile.   He always had a way of making her smile.

"I'm here.   I'm really here.   Well, actually you're here.   I live here."   She said gesturing around the room.

He pushed himself up off the ground. Rayden stepped over to help, but he pushed him away.   "Get off me."   He said groggily.

Rayden was not fazed by it.

Alex stood awkwardly wavering. He placed a hand against the wall behind him to stabilize himself as he grabbed his head with the other hand. He kept his eyes closed for several long moments as he tried to gain his bearings.

"Fuck. How much of that shit did you give me?" He griped.

Rayden smiled again. "A bit more than before. We had to get you adequately fucked up, to keep you from getting us all in deep shit with the commander. We put our asses on the line for you."

Alex scowled but kept his head down with his eyes shut. "I didn't ask any of you for a damn thing."

"What are friends for?" Rayden said shrugging.

Alex lifted his head slightly then stumbled and fell back against the wall, barely staying on his feet.

"Is he alright?" She asked.

"The strongest of it has worn off already. The sedative delirium part of it only lasts for about twenty minutes. Just long enough for us to get him here without him flipping out on us. Now he's feeling like a mix between being really drunk and really hungover at the same time." Rayden explained.

"How the fuck do you know how I feel? You and those other two assholes drugged me. Again! You all think this shit is funny. You force me into shit that I don't want to do, by drugging me. And what was it for this time?" He growled slightly incoherently.

He opened his eyes but looked pained as he did so. He looked around the room, stopping to look at Marianna again still looking stunned by her presence. He looked at the bed and scowled sharply, making his face look even gaunter than it did before. He shook his head and looked away from the bed, his eyes stopping at the shackles on the floor. His eyes widened, and he looked back up at her with a mournful look.

He looked back up at Rayden, who was running his hand through his sandy hair looking troubled.

"I didn't know man. I thought she was dead, just like you." Rayden said glancing at her for a moment before looking back at Alex.

"What exactly was your plan for me?" Alex asked intentionally avoiding looking at

Marianna.

"I don't know.   We just thought that maybe if you got a little action...um..." Rayden looked uncomfortably at her.   "Well that you would stop trying to get yourself killed."

Alex leaned his head and back against the wall.   "I'm not trying to get myself killed."

"You're not trying to keep yourself alive either," Rayden said bitterly.

Alex lifted his head off the wall to look at him.   "I just can't blindly follow orders.   I just can't."

"But you are a soldier.   That is your job. If you hesitate at the wrong moment, because what is asked might be immoral, you could get yourself killed.   Or you could get one of your brothers who is relying on you killed."

"You sound just like the officers want you to.   It's all bullshit.   It's just their way of trying to convince you that what you do doesn't matter.   That it doesn't matter if it's wrong, or if somebody innocent gets hurt or killed, as long as you and your brothers are safe."   Alex said sounding more and more coherent as he spoke.

"If you'd just stop worrying about what's

right or wrong, and just do as you are told, your life would be so much easier," Rayden argued.

"So, you're telling me that you felt that there was nothing wrong with what we were ordered to do in that village?"   Alex said sounding disgusted by whatever he was referring to.

Rayden looked at Marianna.   He seemed hesitant to talk freely in front of her.   He looked uncomfortable about what Alex was talking about as well.

"Is that what you are telling me?   You thought there was nothing wrong with that?"   Alex continued, seemingly unfazed by Marianna's presence for the conversation.

Rayden looked at his feet and kicked aimlessly.   He looked plagued by his thoughts on the subject.   "We thought they were combative.   We were just protecting ourselves."   He said sounding like he wasn't convinced by his own words.

"Bullshit.   We were told that they were dangerous.   We were told that they were combative.   But it was all bullshit.

"We were the dangerous, combative ones. How the hell should they have responded to an army entering their homes?   They were defending themselves.   And they had every reason to do so.   Everything about that day was wrong, and you know it.   Why am I the only one willing to admit that?"   Alex said lightly hitting his head against the wall.

"It was messed up.   The whole thing just got messed up.   But we can't dwell on it. We need to stay focused on the ultimate goal, to become the strongest army in the world.

"We are soldiers.   Sometimes we have to do things we don't want to do.   We can't get caught up in the morality of it all, while we are in the moment.   Sometimes some fucked up shit will happen.   And what happened was fucked up, but our main objective hasn't changed.   We try to only do what needs to be done.   And it's all for a good reason, in the long run."   Rayden defended.   He continued looking down at the ground aimlessly kicking his toes against the floor.

"As soon as you are willing to do what is wrong, for what you consider to be the right reasons, you become willing to do them for the wrong reasons too.   What order would be too far for you?"   Alex asked lifting his head from the wall to look at his friend.

Rayden looked up.   "I don't know."

"That's the problem.   They've turned you into the perfect obedient soldier.   You and all the other guys.   But I can't do it anymore Ray.   I just can't."   He said setting his head back against the wall and staring at the ceiling.

They both remained quiet for a long time. Neither of them looked at each other or Marianna.   She wasn't sure what to do or say.   She didn't know them anymore, but they were still her friends.   And she could tell that they were still good friends with each other.   And that felt good to know.

"What happened in the village?"   She asked; her curiosity about that part of the conversation getting the best of her.

They both looked at her with sorrowful expressions.

Alex glanced down at the shackles on the floor and then looked into her eyes.   He looked over to Rayden who shook his head as if he didn't want to talk about it and then looked back down at the floor.

"We all killed a lot of people.   We were told that they were armed and dangerous. We were told that they were building a combative force to come against us because they found our camp and saw what we were building.   But it was all lies.

"There were no enemy soldiers in that village, just farmers, and merchants, and families.   We told the officers what we found. They said that we were wrong, and we just hadn't found anything yet.   They ordered us to break into the villager's houses to find the hidden army.   We were told that if they fought back, it proved that they were really hostile, and so we were to take them out without regard.

"We broke through doors, windows, and walls to enter people's homes.   And they did fight back.   Of course they did, they were under attack, and they were terrified. But we did as ordered.   Home after home we did as ordered, massacring the villagers. When we finished ransacking the village it was discovered, that there never was any real threat.

"The few survivors we rounded up and brought them back here to be integrated into the camp.   We were told to take anything that we wanted as restitution for what we had to do.   We plundered everything of value and brought it back here as our own individual bounties."   Alex explained sounding angrier and angrier as he spoke.

Rayden stared blankly at the floor the entire time.

"Oh." She responded not sure what else to say. They both were upset by the event.

Alex looked back at her with a disturbed look. He studied her face. Glancing back at the chains and then back at her. He shook his head.

"What happened to you? We really thought that you had been executed. You just disappeared. We heard that you had done something to someone." Alex said asking the question without saying the words. He wasn't as blunt as Rayden had been.

She closed her eyes tightly, hating how quickly just the thought of that day would make her heart race.

"It's all true. What she did. She told me already." Rayden said with a little bit of his previous energy returning.

"Yes, it's all true. I lost my mind, and I killed a child. I didn't just kill him, I beat him into the floor until he squished between my fingers. And the only reason that I stopped was that the guards pulled me off him." She said through gritted teeth still with her eyes closed.

She could feel her whole body trembling with anger.   She needed to stop.   She couldn't lose herself.

She opened her eyes to find Alex watching her warily and Rayden's demeanor return to one of careful alertness, his hand resting on the hilt of his sword again.   He was all soldier.   Her familiarity with him and who he used to be, made her more complacent than she should be towards him.   He was a dangerous, well trained, armed soldier. And she knew that Alex was just as dangerous.   If she lost her mind and attacked either of them, they would strike her down in moments.   They weren't like the guards she was used to encountering. They weren't trained to defuse a violent situation in a nonlethal way, they were trained to kill.

She took several deep breaths to calm herself down.

"I'm sorry.   I get worked up when I talk about that day."   She explained.

Alex nodded in understanding, while Rayden continued to watch her cautiously.

"After the guards pulled me off Clive they took me to a Captain in this huge house.   He told them to bring me here as a punishment.

The idea was that I would be broken by Faisal, and then put to work as a Vassal lady and get used up until I eventually found a way to kill myself." She explained.

Alex closed his eyes and shook his head. He looked sad and disgusted at the same time. While Rayden looked away looking ashamed. He covered his face with his hand.

The door opened and two guards, different from the one in the room before, stepped into the room. In the time they had to step in and close the door behind them, Rayden had his sword drawn, and Alex had a small knife in his hand that Marianna wasn't even sure where he had gotten it. The guards both looked stunned. One pulled his own sword while the other put his hands up in surrender to show that he wasn't a threat.

"You two are just as jumpy as your buddies out there." The guard with his hands up said. He looked over at Marianna sitting on the bed and frowned. "You haven't even gotten started yet?" He asked.

Alex and Rayden each looked at her with sorrowful expressions. She shook her head to answer the guard.

"Right, well you need to leave too."   The guard with the drawn sword said nodding to Rayden.   "Only he's been paid for.   If you want a lady for yourself too, take it up with Faisal like your friends did."   He said pulling the door open and gesturing for Rayden to leave.

He stood there looking torn.   He looked back and forth between Alex and Marianna several times.

"Did you hear me?   You've got to get out of here."   The guard said more sternly.

Rayden looked up at the guard setting his jaw.   The guard tightened his grip on his sword and stood up taller.   The other guard reached down for his own sword.   Rayden looked back mournfully between Alex and Marianna and then looked back to the guards nodding his head.   He re-sheathed his sword causing both guards to visibly relax and walked out the door with one of the guards following behind him and shutting the door.

CHAPTER TWENTY

Mistake

Marianna looked at Alex who was incredibly uncomfortable being alone in the room with her and a guard. His wavering from being drugged with Veruska was lessening. She smiled at him not sure what else to do. He frowned, smiled back half-heartedly and then looked away with a look of revulsion.

Marianna looked over at the guard who had moved to stand against the opposite wall from where the bed was. He nodded at her and then turned his gaze to Alex.

She had already taken too long to get things started. Even though it was her first day back to work in a while, she was still expected to be efficient in her duties.

If the guard told Faisal that she was not

complying, what would he do?   Normally he would take a couple of weeks reestablishing his dominance and punishing for disobedience.   But she had never been disobedient with him, and she enjoyed her time with him, so she didn't know what he would do to punish her.   She was certain that he would punish her, despite his favoritism towards her.   Would he keep himself from her?   Or send her away, even though he had promised her that he never would?   That would be the worst thing he could do to her.   Just thinking about the possibility took her breath away.

She looked back at Alex and stood up moving towards him.   She smiled at him and moved her hand up her body slowly and softly brushing her breast, as she approached him.   He looked at her shaking his head with a troubled look in his eyes.

"No.   Anna.   No.   You don't have to." He said continuing to shake his head.

"Shh.   It's alright."   She whispered as she pressed her body against him.

She grabbed his arm and guided it to wrap around her back.   He continued shaking his head and moved his arm away.   She grabbed it again.

He pulled his arm away from her.   He grabbed her around both of her arms and pushed her away holding her tightly at arm's length.

"Anna.   No.   I don't want to do this." He said severely.

"I can convince you."   She said.

He closed his eyes shaking his head more fervently and squeezing her arms.   "I don't want you to.   Really, I'm fine.   You don't have to do anything."

"I do."   She said earnestly.

He closed his eyes tighter and then looked at her sorrowfully.   "Not with me."   He shook his head again.

She looked down ashamed.   Sometimes when she couldn't coax a man physically, she could do so emotionally.

"You don't want me."   She whimpered, trying to sound as hurt as she could by the possibility.

"No.   No, it's not that."   He said quickly. She looked back up at him innocently.

"Is it because you know me?   Does it make you uncomfortable?"   She asked with sincere suspicion.

He shook his head.   "A little, but no." He said releasing his tight grip on her arms as if he had just noticed how hard he was holding her.

"You don't think I'm sexy?" She asked trying to look ashamed again.

"Gah! No. I mean yes, I do. I mean, it's not that. You're beautiful, you are. Stunning really." He said looking her up and down.

She had to hold back a smile and instead tried for the innocent look again.

He seemed ashamed that he had even looked at her in such a way. "But I just can't with you. It's not right. With everything..." He looked down at the shackles and then at the guard. "It's just not right."

She chewed on her lip. How could she convince him? She could ask him what he liked about her body, but she thought that it might make him even more uncomfortable. She could keep playing innocent, but she thought that would make him resist even more.

"We can make it right." She said looking at him with a sultry look. He nervously shook his head again.

She stepped up to him again, and he backed up until he was against the wall.

Normally she would have kissed his mouth, but he was too tall to reach his lips without him leaning down. As it was the top of her head only reached the height of his shoulder. So, she ran her hands down his chest instead, slowly and softly at first and then faster while running her nails down.

He continued to shake his head in protest. She crouched while she moved her hands up under his shirt touching his skin lightly as she moved back up to his chest. She kissed his stomach lightly. His breath caught, and she smiled.

"Stop. Please stop. Marianna, please." He begged.

She continued kissing up his stomach while lifting his shirt up. His stomach muscles were so defined she could see each individual muscle. She was wrong about assuming his thinness was unhealthy. He was thin, but he was all muscle. It was impressive. She ran her tongue between two of his stomach muscles while kissing the two muscles themselves.

He shuddered. And grabbed her by both arms and lifted her up again causing his shirt to fall back down.

"Stop. I don't want to do this." He said.

She reached down and cupped him in her hand, causing him to gasp. He was as hard as a stone under his pants. She smiled. "That's not true."

He pushed her away covering himself with his hands. "I have no control over that."

She frowned for a moment but refused to get discouraged. "It's my job to take control." She said biting her lip and stepping back over to him.

A look of revulsion took over his expression. He looked into her eyes like he was looking for something, but the longer he looked, the more uncomfortable he grew.

She grabbed the wrist of one of his arms and moved it so that he was touching her breast. He pulled it away. She pressed her body against his trying to move her hands around his back, but he was so firmly pressed against the wall that she couldn't. So instead she brought her hand back around and rubbed him through his pants as she kissed his chest again. He tried to step sideways away from her.

"Why are you fighting me?" She asked trying to mute the irritation that she felt about it.

"I don't want to do this. You don't have to do this. Just stop." He said sounding desperate.

He managed to move away from her completely, while moving himself away from the wall as well. She pursued him. She didn't want to just make him because it was her job anymore. He was her conquest, and she would prevail.

"Please tell your boss, that I don't want to do this. He can keep whatever money was paid to him, but I'm done here." He requested looking at her guard Philip.

Philip shook his head slowly. "Doesn't work that way. Not with her." He said nodding at Marianna.

Alex looked at her his expression changing from confused, to understanding, to a sudden look of panic. "Please. I'll pay twice as much." He said backing away looking around frantically as he saw that he was backing himself into the corner.

"Sorry. That wasn't the arrangement." The guard said.

"I'll give you the money. Both of you. Just say that we did whatever. Nobody else has to know." He said scanning every bit of the room.

Marianna looked back at Philip who was considering the offer. He looked back at Marianna and then glanced at the door, and then hesitantly shook his head. "We can't. If Faisal found out..." He shook his head more vigorously. "No, sorry we can't."

Alex jumped at her, so quickly and unexpectedly that she had no way to react. He grabbed her by the throat spun her around and slammed her against the wall. In moments he grabbed two of the shackles and snapped them onto each of her wrists.

Philip grabbed him by the shoulder and pulled him, but the gesture barely budged Alex. Instead, it just turned his attention onto the guard. The guard had his sword drawn and held it out defensively. Alex charged the guard crouching low. He wrapped his arms around the guard's legs and tackled him to the floor. Philip yelled out as his back slammed hard against the stone and then he gasped as if his breath had been knocked out of him.

At some point in the attack Alex had managed to take control of the guard's sword, she didn't even see him grab it. He pressed the blade against the guard's throat while frantically looking around the room. The guard was still gasping for air and then started coughing.   The movement of the cough caused the blade to slip and slice under Philip's chin.

Philip yelped with a look of panic.

"Shit," Alex growled.

He leaned down, pushed Philip's head back to examine the wound, and then frowned.   "Hold that."   He said shortly as he grabbed the man's arm and guided him to put his hand over his throat.

"Don't move."   He said standing up but keeping the sword pointed down at the guard.   The guard nodded slightly with his eyes wide open.

"How many are there outside this door?" He asked moving closer to the door and leaning his head towards it as if he was trying to listen for something.

"I don't know.   Maybe five or six upstairs in the hallway, and twice as many down. But I can't be sure."   Philip rambled.

He pulled his hand away to look at how much blood there was, stared wide-eyed at it for a moment, and then wrapped both hands around his neck looking at Alex with a terrified look.   He had bled a lot.   More than Marianna thought he should from the size of the cut that she could see.

Alex nodded as his eyes darted around the room. He watched the guard for several long moments with a look of concern, and then looked back up to Marianna. He closed his eyes tightly and pursed his lips.

"Shit." He said quietly as he opened his eyes to look at Marianna again.

He grabbed the door handle and slowly moved it, scrunching his face as it clicked. He took in a deep breath and slowly moved the door open just enough for him to look out.

"Help! Everybody get in here!" The guard shouted as he moved along the floor away from Alex smearing blood as he moved.

Alex's eyes widened as the guard shouted. He pushed the door closed and backed away with the sword raised up in front of him.

The door burst open moments later. Three guards moved into the room all with swords ready. They each took in the sights of the room: Alex with sword drawn, a guard bleeding from the throat on the floor dragging a trail of blood, and Marianna chained to the wall. Cautiously they stepped further into the room circling Alex who spun around trying to keep them all in his sight.

Two more guards entered the room and joined the circle around Alex whose eyes were darting to look at each of them. He looked like a wild animal in a cage.

One of the guards who had circled around to Alex's back jumped on him wrapping his arm around his neck, just as he did that another guard struck Alex's arm with the hilt of his sword causing Alex to drop the sword in his hand.

He ducked his body rolling the guard that had grabbed around his throat and tossed him so that he fell on top of the guard who knocked his sword from his hand. They both tumbled to the floor.

He charged at a third guard keeping his body low to the ground. The guard twisted out of the way just before he was tackled and threw himself on top of Alex wrapping both of his arms around his neck, throwing off his center of balance and causing him to topple onto his face. With the momentum of his fall, Alex managed to tumble around again causing him to lay on top of the guard that was wrapped around his back.

He head-butted the man in the nose.   The
guard released his grip on Alex and grabbed
hold of his nose.   Alex got back to his feet.
As he was standing the two guards that he
had knocked over before charged at him.
One wrapped his arms around Alex's torso
while the other wrapped his arms around his
legs.

With the two guards working in tandem
they threw his balance off, he stumbled but
kept his footing, he flailed his arms out and
as he did one of the other guards grabbed
hold of his hand and twisted it around
awkwardly.   The man wrenched at Alex's
hand twisting it in a way that caused him to
contort his body while yelling out.   He fell
to his knees, and then with the momentum
of the fall and the uneven weight of the two
guards who were still wrapped around his
legs and torso, he fell sideways onto his
twisted arm, causing a loud crack, and then
another excruciating shout from him.

Two of the guards held their swords close
to Alex, one with his sword pointed at his
chest, the other at his stomach while the two
guards who were entangled with him
released him from their holds and stood
back up.

The guard who still had his arm in its twisted state climbed on top of Alex forcing both of his arms behind his back and then rolling him onto his stomach holding tightly onto both of his arms while pushing them up his back in a way that made it impossible for him to move them.   One of the guards that had stood up moved back over to him and then knelt on Alex's head placing most of his weight on his bent leg pressing the side of Alex's face into the floor.

Faisal stepped into the room looking around, the dangerous look on his face grew more and more terrifying as he took in the events in the room.   When he saw Marianna chained up, he snapped.   He charged at Alex, kicking him over and over again in the side.   Alex yelled out and then groaned as he gasped for breath.

Faisal crouched down motioning to the guard kneeling on his head to move.   He grabbed Alex by the hair and turned his head back farther to look into his eyes.

"If you hurt her, I will destroy you."

Alex looked over to Marianna for a second and then turned his gaze back over to Faisal. His eyes were defiant.

Faisal twisted his hand pulling his hair

even more.   "There are a thousand unique ways to torment someone, and I know them all.   If you think that you are safe because you're a soldier, know this, you fucked with the wrong man.   My authority here is limitless, as is my resolve."   He said coldly.

He slammed Alex's head against the floor and then stood back up.

He gestured to his guards, and they each moved around in a way to allow them to lift Alex to his feet.   His head and body drooped down forcing them to carry him out the door.   He looked like he had when he was carried into the room, except his face was covered in blood.

Another guard had entered the room during the commotion.   Faisal directed him to check on the bleeding guard, and then he moved over to her.

"Are you alright?"   He asked softly as he grabbed a key from one of the guards and unlocked her shackles dropping them to the floor.

She nodded her head, but the motion made her aware of the pain in the back of her head.   She reached around to touch it.   A warm wetness covered her hand.   She pulled her hand back around and saw it

dripping with blood.   When Alex slammed
her against the wall, her head must have hit
the wall harder than she had thought.   It
had all happened so fast she had no time to
think about it.

The look on Faisal's face when he saw the
blood scared her.   He was beyond anger.
He was murderous.   The thought of Faisal
killing Alex terrified her.   She didn't want
Alex to die.   Even with everything that had
just happened, he was her friend.   And she
didn't think that Alex was trying to hurt her,
he wasn't trying to hurt the guard, he was
just trying to get away.

"I'm fine.   Really, I am.   It hurts a little,
but I think it looks worse than it is."   She
tried to reassure him in an attempt to calm
him down.

He didn't look convinced.   He glared
menacingly back towards the door where
Alex had been carried away.

She grabbed his hand with her clean hand
and wove her fingers around his.   He
turned back with a tender look.

"I'm alright."   She said smiling.

He nodded, but his stern look never
changed.   She had never witnessed him so
angry.   He was always dangerous, she

knew that, and so did everybody else. But it took a lot to make him truly angry. What Alex had done made him furious.

"Sir!" The guard tending to the injured one said drawing both of their attention.

He squeezed her hand and pulled her to walk over to the guards with him.

"It doesn't look good sir. I can't stop the bleeding." The guard said.

He was covered in blood as was the floor. The injured guard didn't look conscious anymore, and he was gray.

"I'll send for a Medica. Stay with him and do what you can to keep him alive." Faisal said.

The guard nodded and pushed both of his hands against the man's wound.

They walked out of the room, Faisal pulling her along with him.

"How many other soldiers came with him?" He asked her.

"Hmm. Oh, three. There were three others." She said.

He nodded seriously as he led her down the stairs. He gestured for a door guard to come over, and instructed him to get a Medica as quickly as possible.

"You stay here." He said as he sat her

down on the couch.

"Wait. What are you going to do?" She asked afraid for Alex.

He narrowed his eyes at her for a moment. "If the others are as dangerous as that one, we need to get them out of here."

She held onto his hand. "I don't want you to get hurt." She said.

"I'll tell them that we are closing for the night, promise them all another night with a lady at no charge. Hopefully, that will be all that needs to be done." He explained pulling his hand away from her and leaving her alone in the room.

Raucous shouts came from upstairs. The sounds of moving around. One by one the rooms emptied, and agitated, surprised, and loud men walked down the stairs. Several still dressing as they were led out the front door. Dale and Gerardo, the two soldiers that carried Alex in originally stumbled down the steps. They were both wavering the same way that Alex had been, they must have taken some of the Veruska. Neither of them comprehended what was going on, as they were ushered to through the door and into the night.

Rayden moved down the stairs buttoning

his pants. He looked at Marianna and scowled in confusion. He looked back up the stairs taking in the few other men that were moving down and then looked out the door searching. He was looking for Alex she knew. He looked back at her. She couldn't help but look ashamed. Alex and Rayden were best friends, and they had both been her friends. He frowned more deeply as he was pushed out the door along with several more men behind him. When the last man was guided out the door, the guards shut and locked it looking very uneasy.

Ladies began trickling out of bedrooms and down the stairs all talking in hushed tones. They all moved into the room with Marianna some taking seats while others standing. The rest of the guards moved down the steps along with Faisal. Several of them were covered in blood. She couldn't tell who was bleeding and who was wearing blood that wasn't their own. They moved around the room interspersing in with the ladies. The last time all the house members were in the same room together was the night of the storm.

Faisal stayed on the staircase a few steps

from the bottom, giving him a higher vantage point, where he loomed over everyone else. His posture was threatening and his expression serious. The room fell silent as everyone became aware of his presence. He looked around the room taking in every single person. His eyes rested on Marianna for longer than it had on any of the others.

"Things are changing here. As of this moment, we're out of the business of Breeders, you are all Vassal Ladies now." He said.

The room erupted in noise. Cries of protest and shock, mixed in with hushed conversations from both ladies and guards who were all surprised by the announcement as well.

Faisal raised his hands up causing the room to quiet.

"No lady is to bed a man without a guard present. Each lady will have at least two assigned guards, one to stay with her during the day, and one at night."

More hushed whispers moved through the room.

"But sir, there's not enough of us for that." One of the guards said near the door.

"There will be."   He proclaimed.

Everybody looked around at one another nervously.

"If anything happens to one of your assigned charges, I will hold you responsible."   He said looking around at each of the guards who each nodded respectfully.

"The guards will also be responsible for ensuring your ladies cooperation, I give you all full authority to discipline as needed."

Nervous conversations rose up.   Ladies and guards all were equally nervous.   Faisal was changing the way that everything was done, and nobody liked it.

"If I find that any guard takes advantage of his new authority, he will become a Vassal Lady used by the effeminate men, indefinitely."

The room fell silent as a nervous energy moved through everyone.

"If any of you fuck each other, I will find out, and I will find who is responsible for instigating the relationship. Whoever is found culpable; man, woman, or both, will spend the next month on The Horse."

Several loud gasps and a few whimpering cries moved through the room.

The horse was one of Faisal's more barbaric torture devices that he usually only resorted to using after extreme or repetitive acts of disobedience.   She didn't know that he would use it on the guards.   What other forms of punishment would he use on them? She understood a little bit more about why even the guards feared him.

"All previous rules are to remain in place and will be enforced. Nobody will be..."   He cut off as there was a knock on the door. Many of the house members jumped at the unexpected sound.   They were all on edge by Faisal's announcements.

One of the guards standing at the door pulled it open a little to look at who was out there and then pulled it open.   He let in the Medica and the guard who had gotten her. The guard was carrying a gurney.   People parted to let them through and up the staircase.   Nervous conversations started up again as Faisal waved Marianna to follow him up the stairs behind the Medica.

When they got to her room where the injured guard was Marianna saw that he was even grayer than he had been just minutes before.   The guard who was ordered to help him was covered in blood and looked queasy.   He looked up as they entered the room with a look of relief as the Medica knelt beside him.   She leaned down listening to the man's chest for several long moments.   She nodded and gestured to the guard who retrieved her, to set a large bag that he was holding on the floor next to her.

She opened the bag pulled out a bottle of water, unstopped the bottle and poured it over her hands and then over the guard's neck.

"You hold his arms down," she said pointing at the blood covered guard.   "You hold his head back like this."   She said to the guard who had retrieved her as she tilted the man's head back showing the gaping wound that continued to ooze blood.

"I need you too, come over here, sit right there."   She said to Marianna and then pointed to the spot on the other side of the man.

Marianna knelt across from the Medica. The woman poured water over Marianna's hands and then over the man's neck again looking closely as she pulled the wound open a bit.   She shook her head and then pulled out a long piece of thread with a sharp needle attached to it.

"Hold his neck like this, don't move or I might stab you." The woman instructed Marianna as she held the wound open revealing a spot where the blood was oozing from more than any other spot. Marianna did as she was told.

She and the Medica worked for a long time as the Medica carefully sewed the man's neck and Marianna followed all the woman's instructions helping her in every way that she was asked.

When the Medica had finished, she told the two guards who were holding the man down to put him on the gurney. She poured water over her hands again rinsing the blood off and then did the same for Marianna.

"I'll take him to the Medica. The hard part is done, now we wait and see if it was too late." She said standing up.

"Wait," Faisal said. Everyone looked at him. "I need you to look at a few others first."

She nodded. "Take him to the Medica, please. He doesn't need to remain here." She instructed the guards holding the gurney.

Faisal waved Marianna over. "You first."

He said tenderly.

"I'm alright." She assured.

"Now." He demanded as he walked her over to sit on the bed and moved her hair to show the Medica her head. His breathing sped up as his hand that was holding onto her arm tightened. He was furious and barely containing himself.

Marianna could see blood glopped onto her hair making it even more red than her natural auburn color.

"What happened?" The woman asked.

"My head hit the wall, I think. I'm not sure, I didn't know it was bleeding until after everything happened." Marianna said.

"Are you dizzy or nauseous?" The woman asked as she wiped something wet against her head. She winced in pain but held still.

"No. I'm alright." She reassured.

"Tell me the truth. This is a pretty serious head wound. Are you feeling dizzy? Do you have a headache?" The woman said fervently.

"No really. I feel fine. It barely even hurts."

"Good. Get me my bag." She said to

Faisal.

He nodded and did as he was told without hesitation, which surprised Marianna and apparently the guards too by the way they looked at him and then each other with shocked expressions. Nobody told Faisal what to do.

The woman pulled several things from her bag. "This may sting." She said to Marianna as she poured something on her head. She hissed and jerked away, as whatever the woman put on her head burned.

"This is going to hurt, but you need to stay still. Can you do that for me?"

Marianna nodded and then instantly regretted the movement as the pain in her head was more present.

Faisal sat next to her and grabbed both of her hands nodding to the woman. He interlaced his fingers with hers.

"Don't move." The woman said as a sharp burning pain moved through her head as the woman stitched her.

Every time the needle pushed through her flesh she winced but held as still as she could. Faisal squeezed her hands trying to help her relax. After what probably felt like longer than it actually was, the woman was done. Marianna's head throbbed as the woman poured some of the water onto her head. The coolness of the water felt nice.

The woman rinsed her own hands again as she stood back up.

"Thank you," Marianna said.

The woman smiled kindly at her and Marianna recognized her.

"I know you. Kania right?" Marianna said.

The woman nodded slowly and then tilted her head and studied Marianna's face.

"You helped me before. I was in the Medica for several weeks when I was a child, and you took care of me."

Kania smiled. "Were you sick?"

"No. I was being whipped, and it almost killed me. That's what you said actually." Marianna said.

"Oh," Kania said with a sad look in her eyes. She frowned and looked at Marianna again. "Oh." She said in recognition. "You were almost killed." She said with emphasis.

"I'd never seen somebody with so many overlapping lashes, and you were so young. This isn't the first time that I've had to stitch

your head." She said somberly. The
guards and Faisal all looked at her with
piteous expressions.

"How are you doing?" Kania asked
looking around, frowning at the chains on
the wall, and then looking at the guards
looking down at each of their swords,
looking more and more mournful as she did.

"I'm alright," Marianna said smiling.

Kania looked at her skeptically. She
looked at Faisal who was still holding
Marianna's hands but was staring back at
Kania. His body was tensed and his face
severe. He looked dangerous. Like a
coiled snake ready to strike. Kania took a
step back.

"Right. Well, I'm glad." She said
hastily. "Is there anyone else that I need to
look at before I go?" She asked. It was
clear that she wanted to get out as quickly as
she could.

Faisal nodded.

"There's one more I need you to look at,"
Faisal said standing up and guiding
Marianna to follow.

"You should probably stay here and get
some rest, take it easy for a while," Kania
said.

"She goes where I go," Faisal said sharply.

Kania slunk away from him warily. "She should be careful, and not do too much too quickly. Sometimes when the head is injured the severity of the injury can be delayed."

Faisal set his jaw as he squeezed Marianna's hand. He looked down at her with concern and then shook his head.

"She comes with me. If anything happens, you will tend to it." He said sternly as he walked out the room pulling Marianna along with him.

Kania grabbed her bag and followed.

They walked to the other end of the house.

"Just do what you must, to keep him alive," Faisal said coldly as he opened the door.

Alex was lying on a table at the other end of the room. His legs were spread apart, and his lower legs dangled below the knee off the edge of the table, shackled at the ankles. His wrists were shackled under the table behind his back in a way that made his arms bend at an awkward angle.

Marianna looked around the room and was shocked by what she saw. Three of Faisal's infamous Horses sat lined up against the back wall. Opposite from them were three different devises that she had never seen before. They were triangle shaped pieces of wood suspended in the air from chains attached to the ceiling. The blunted pointed end of the triangle was on top. Two chains with shackles sat on the floor below each of them. Multiple ropes and chains hung from the ceiling and walls at differing heights.

And hanging along one entire wall was a mix of terrifying tools and weapons: saws, pliers, forceps, and spikes; knives, pins, wires, and rings; hammers, corkscrews, and tongs; all mixed in with geared or hinged contraptions that Marianna couldn't identify.

"Oh, great spirit's," Kania whispered.

Marianna turned to see the Medica stepping away in terror until she reached the wall behind her and could go no further. Faisal turned to look at the woman, and she whimpered in fear.

"Come on." He ordered.

She hesitantly stepped into the room making a wide berth around him. She looked at Marianna mournfully and then looked back at Faisal terror-stricken.

She approached Alex trembling. His

breathing was labored with a wheezing whistle coming with every breath. He groggily turned his head to look at Kania, and then looked back at Marianna and Faisal and closed his eyes tightly groaning. The side of his face that Faisal had slammed against the floor was swollen and red. A line of blood trickled from his cheek like a tear.

He looked back to Kania who was leaning over him to listen to his chest she frowned and then looked back up to Faisal. She chewed on her lip and stared at him like she wanted to ask him something but was afraid to.

"Speak." He said noticing her questioning look.

"What...happened to him?" She asked hesitantly visibly swallowing.

Faisal looked down at Marianna for a moment squeezing her hand tightly and then looked back up at Kania stoically. "He fucked up." He said coldly.

She glanced at Marianna and then back to Faisal with understanding on her face. She nodded. "Right. But what happened? What kind of injuries has he received?" She asked, a little bit more confidently.

"He lost his fight with my guards, and then he got my boot in his ribs." He said through clenched teeth. He was breathing heavily and shaking with rage. Marianna could tell that he was trying his hardest to control his anger.

Kania visibly swallowed again and nodded. She was so terrified that she was unable to look at Faisal anymore.

She leaned back down to listen to Alex's chest again. She lifted his shirt up as far as she could revealing thick purple bruises that had formed where clear indentations in his ribcage could be seen. She listened to his chest again, listening first to the injured side and then the uninjured side. His breathing was still loud and labored. She stood back up and pressed gently on his side on top of one of the bruises. He shouted and arched his back as far as the shackles allowed.

"You need to relax. I need you to stop moving so that I can examine you." She said to Alex in a calm, sure tone.

Faisal dropped Marianna's hand and swiftly stepped over to Alex. He shoved him down, making his back slam onto the table. He held him down by the shoulders. Alex gasped, and Kania stumbled back in surprise.   She stood back trembling.

Marianna stepped around, and she could see all of Faisal's muscles in his arms and neck tense as he held Alex down.   The dangerous expression had returned to his face.   He wanted to hurt Alex or kill him, but he was holding back.   How had he contained his rage so well?   She was getting better about it, but it was so much harder for her to contain hers.

Alex took in a deep shuddering breath and looked back up at Kania who looked like she wanted to run out of the room.

"He's still.   Tend to him."   Faisal demanded.

Kania nervously nodded as she slowly stepped back up to Alex.   She felt at his side again with a trembling hand.   He groaned and yelled as she pushed around, but he didn't budge with Faisal holding him down. After she finished on his chest, she moved to his face and pressed against his cheek and jaw.   He tried to turn his head away, but there was only so far, he could go so she was able to examine fairly quickly.

"He's got at least six broken ribs.   I don't think anything is broken in his face, but I can't be certain with all the swelling.   He has no breath sounds on that side, so I think one of the broken ribs has punctured his lung. He has good breath sounds on the other side, so I think he will survive as long as he doesn't get sick, and if he keeps from doing anything strenuous for at least the next month. There's nothing that I can do for him. If he were in the Medica, I would just make him rest, and keep him fed and hydrated." She explained.

She babbled with confidence in what she said, but with a speed that made it obvious that she wanted to get out of there as soon as she could.

Faisal released his hold and stood back up. "Good. I don't need you anymore. You can go."

She made one last sorrowful glance at Marianna, looked around the room and shuddered and then raced out of the room without looking back.

"Well since you're not dying, you get to spend some quality time with me," Faisal said with a depraved smile that made the hairs on the back of Marianna's neck stand up.

Alex stared back at him defiantly. Faisal's smile widened.

Alex looked at Marianna.   She felt bad that he had been hurt so badly.   And that Faisal was so angry at him, because of her. She tried to tell Faisal that she was alright, but he didn't believe her.

What would he do to Alex?

She remembered back to the first day that she met Faisal when he told her that he didn't want to hurt her as long as she did as she was told.   He had kept his word on that. On that day he had told her that he didn't allow the men to hurt the ladies and since she had witnessed the punishment the disobedient ladies received from him, what would he do to a soldier who hurt one of his ladies?   And especially a soldier who hurt her?

Faisal walked towards her, grabbed her hand and pulled her out the door.   She watched Alex as the door shut, sadly watching her.

As they walked down the stairs, the people who remained, watched them with looks of revulsion.   Marianna was confused until she looked down to find herself covered in blood from helping with the guard.   Faisal's hands were also bloody from holding hers, and his whole demeanor felt malevolent.

What did they think had happened? In a small amount of time Faisal had forced all the patrons to leave the house, new house rules had been established, one of the guards was carried out covered in blood on a gurney, a Medica ran from the house, and then she and Faisal walked down the stairs soaked with blood. They had every reason to be terrified.

He led her into the bathing room where she washed her hands and arms off over a tub, as he cleaned his hands in the sink. When she poured water over her head, the pain rushed back to her causing her to squeal. He jumped and spun around looking ready to fight. When he saw that she wasn't being attacked he relaxed and stepped over to her.

"Sorry. The water hurts. But I'm alright." She said, not wanting to worry him any more than he already was.

He grabbed the cup and gently poured the water over her head. "You shouldn't be hurt at all." He said seriously.

"I don't think he meant to hurt me." She said trying to defend Alex. She didn't want to be the reason that he got punished.

"But he did, and he nearly killed Philip. Things shouldn't have gotten so out of hand. You're the third lady to be hurt since moving in." He said.

She cocked her head to the side. "Others have gotten hurt?"

"How do you manage to keep yourself so effectively cut off from what's going on around you? You know the chaos after the storm allowed you to blossom and form a reputation with the others. If you don't work on keeping that, by showing interest in what's happening to those you live with, you will lose that. Part of blending in is caring about what happens to others, even if you are just pretending."

She nodded. "I'll work on it."

"And I'll work on fixing the mess that the storm, cleanup, and move have all created. I have been too complacent with everyone. The other houses that have still been fully operational have been run by lazy Heads of House's, letting rules lapse. That is why these men think it's alright to harm my ladies; because they get away with it at the other houses. That is going to stop." He finished washing her hair, and she climbed out of the tub.

He draped a towel over her shoulders and kissed her on the neck, and the wrapped her in an embrace from behind her.   She relaxed as he held her and wrapped her arms around his.   She yawned.

"Let's get to bed, it's been a long night, and you need your rest."   He said.

"So early?   I'm tired, but I'm sure that you're not.   You don't have to go to bed yet."   She said as she dried herself off.

"I can't leave you alone.   This is the second time that I almost lost you.   I can't let that happen again."   He said seriously.

"I'm alright.   Really I am.   It was just a bump on the head.   I wouldn't have died from that."   She said smiling trying to make him feel better.

He shook his head.   "He cut Philip's throat.   That could have just as easily been you."   He said through gritted teeth.

"No.   That's not what happened.   Philip was down.   He had the sword pressed against him, but I don't think he wanted to actually hurt him with it.   Philip coughed while the blade was against his throat and it cut him.   Alex didn't do it on purpose. And he didn't mean to hurt me either.   He just pushed me so that he could shackle me.

He just wanted to get out of here. He didn't want to do anything with me, and I was trying to make him. He just panicked." She explained.

His expression made her think that she was possibly convincing him until suddenly he grew angry by what she had said. He narrowed his eyes at her suspiciously which made her nervous.

What had she done to upset him?

"Do you know him?" He asked bluntly watching her closely for her response.

She nodded, knowing better than to try and be untruthful with him. He narrowed his eyes even more. "How?"

"I used to know him. Before. Before I came here. We lived in the same town. We were friends. And then after we were brought to the camp, we stayed friends. But I haven't seen them in a long time."

"Them?" He questioned with more suspicion. She closed her eyes in frustration.

"Yes. Him and Rayden. He was here too. He's the one who left the room last when the guards came back in." She said.

He remained quiet for a moment thinking about what she said, and then he cocked his head.   "They were alone with you?"

Her heart raced.   She had no reason to be afraid.   But she was.   She nodded.

"What did you do when you were all alone?"

"We just talked."   She said.

He nodded thoughtfully.

"What did you talk about?"

She told him everything that she could remember about the drugging, and the village, and how she had killed Clive.   He listened intently.   He chewed on his bottom lip in the way he always did when he was trying to decide something.   Her fear increased.

"Tomorrow, you're going to fuck him." He said watching her for her reaction.

She frowned.   "What?   Why?"

He smiled eerily.   "He seems to be struggling with morality.   He fought so hard to avoid you fucking him, because of how guilty it would have made him feel.   It will be the first part of his punishment."

CHAPTER TWENTY-ONE

Alex

After waking, eating, and bathing, there was nothing else left to delay what Marianna had to do.   She had never felt so guilty about her work.   She was one of the only ladies in the house who enjoyed her job most days, and even when she had to do something distasteful, she still never felt like what she did was wrong.   But with Alex it was different.   He was her friend, and he was seriously injured.   And it was because of her.

Faisal's mood, when they woke up together, had shifted from a boiling rage from the night before to a vengeful anticipation.   She had recognized the mood in him before, when Crystal, the woman that he broke in her presence, hurt him.   She had seen him in similar moods with other ladies that he broke, but not to the extent that she saw with Crystal. But he was different. Instead of a calm coordinated punishment that she had watched with Crystal, he was on a warpath. And the war he was raging was directed at Alex.

Despite what he had said the previous night about not letting her be away from him, he left her to get ready on her own. He didn't speak to her, or anyone that she had seen. His silence was out of character and unnerving. What she did know from his unseemly mood and silence was that she did not want to disobey him in any way.

She made her way up the stairs to the room she knew Alex was in. The room filled with Faisal's toys of torture. She had known that he enjoyed hurting others, he had told her so, but she had never known how demented he was while he was dishing out punishments. The Horse that he treasured so much was the worst she had seen him use, and it was savage. She couldn't even imagine what he used all his other tools and devises for.

She had expected guards to be assigned to the door, but as she thought about it, she knew why there weren't any. Alex was shackled to a table with multiple broken ribs and a collapsed lung. He wasn't going anywhere, and if he had somehow managed to escape, he was no threat.

She reached out to open the door and found that her hand was shaking. She hadn't been so afraid in years. She didn't want to hurt Alex. She opened the door and stepped into the room.

Faisal was standing over Alex poking him in the side where he had been kicked. Alex was arching his back and groaning. He had a cloth in his mouth muffling the sound.

Marianna didn't know that Faisal had made it into the room already, although she was sure that he would have made an appearance to ensure that she was doing her job and to watch how it affected Alex.

Faisal looked up as she closed the door behind her and nodded. She walked to stand opposite of him next to Alex who looked at her with pleading eyes; one of which was swollen shut. She frowned and looked back up to Faisal, who was watching her with narrowed eyes.

He looked down at her dress and smiled. But the smile had no joy. He stepped around the table grabbing her by her hips and pulling her up against him kissing her suddenly.   It was harsh, lacking any compassion.   When he pulled away from her, she stared at him disturbed by the perverseness of it.

He had immediately looked at Alex after releasing her to watch his reaction.   Alex had turned his head to the side to look away. Annoyance was in Faisal's expression.   He stepped away from her and grabbed Alex's head and turned it to face him.   He leaned down to say something, but Alex lifted his head and tried to bite Faisal's nose.   Faisal jerked back before Alex could make contact and let go of his head.

He smiled cruelly as he walked to his wall of tools and pulled one down.   It was a curved, hinged, metal device with four spikes two protruding off the one side close to the hinge, and the other two on the opposite side on the far ends away from the hinge.

He opened it at the hinge and wrapped it around Alex's throat.   The two spikes near the hinge sat under his chin, and the other spikes sat on top of his collarbones.   Faisal attached the metal ends to the table with a screw tightening it until each of the spikes pressed into Alex's skin leaving indentations but not breaking it.

The device made it impossible for Alex to turn his head to either side without stabbing himself with a spike.

Alex looked at Marianna with pained eyes. She looked away feeling ashamed that it was because of her that he was even in the position that he was.

Faisal stepped to a large lever on the edge of the table and cranked it several times. The table which held Alex tilted so that Alex's head was higher than his feet. His body shifted putting more awkward weight on his arms and legs that were still shackled to the underside of the table. He groaned with each crank of the table. The shift in weight from the movement of the table caused one of the spikes to pierce his skin under his chin causing a trail of blood to trickle down his neck and soak into his already blood-stained shirt.

Marianna felt so bad for him. She wished there was something that she could do to help him, but she knew that there wasn't. She was powerless, and he was a prisoner. She had been in that position with Faisal deciding her fate as well.

She turned to look at Faisal. He was watching her with no expression on his face. He grabbed her wrist and pulled her towards him so that they were standing just in front of Alex.

He leaned over her kissing her on the neck and then biting down painfully. She yelped and tried to pull away in surprise, but he wrapped his arms around her keeping her close to him. He kissed her neck more and then dug his nails into her hip. She gasped at the unexpected pain. He leaned away from her to watch her with a sadistic look in his eyes. She tried to pull away from him again, but he held her tight.

He leaned down kissing her on the mouth and then the neck while untying her dress.

"What are you doing? Stop it." She begged.

He pulled away glancing beyond her at Alex and then smiling as he looked back at her, it was a vicious predatory look. She pushed at him with a sudden panic.

He grabbed her dress with both hands and tugged at it tearing it down the front of her. She screamed and pushed at him as he leaned in and sucked on her breast and then squeezed it painfully.

"Stop.   Please.   You're hurting me."

He pushed her dress off her wrapping one arm around her back and his other hand around her head pulling her into a kiss. The pain in her head exploded as he put pressure on her head wound.   She gasped and then screamed as tears ran down her face.

He wrapped his arm around the back of her knees while keeping his other at her back.   He swiftly swept her legs out from under her and dropped her to the floor. The sudden movement gave her a sense of vertigo.   He forced her legs apart, painfully far, and knelt between them.

She tried to sit up, but he pushed her back down causing her head to hit the stone floor and send starbursts of pain through her already injured head.   When her vision came back to her, he was unbuttoning his pants.   She tried to crawl away from him on her back, but he held her from the shoulder so that she couldn't move away.

"Why are you doing this?   Please stop." She cried.

The look he gave her was cold and spiteful.

He forced himself inside her making her scream in revulsion. He was cruel and violent as she pointlessly fought him. Nothing she did deterred him from his act.

He leaned down and kissed her harshly, and then wrapped his hands around her throat and squeezed. She flailed in a terrified panic. She tried to pry his hands off her, but his grip was so strong that she couldn't even get her fingers under his hands. He sat up watching her as he thrust inside of her and squeezed her throat making her gasp for a hissing breath.

Tears flowed from her eyes. He leaned in and kissed her again as he squeezed harder making it impossible for her to breathe at all. He finished inside her, which he had never done before and then collapsed on top of her breathing heavily.

He released the grip on her throat just as suddenly as he had grabbed it. She coughed and gagged as the air moved painfully through her throat. He pushed himself partially off her looking at her vindictively. He climbed off her buttoning his pants as he stood up.

She lay there coughing and gasping for air. She rolled onto her side and pulled her legs

up to hug them.   She cried pitifully feeling
hurt, betrayed, and confused by his sudden,
brutal attack.   She was wet and sticky from
him finishing inside her.   Why had he done
that?   He had more control over his body
than any man she was ever with.   It was his
job, his specialty.

Everything he did, he did for a reason.
But she couldn't understand his reason
behind what he had just done to her.

She sat up still painfully gasping for air.
Her head was throbbing.   She reached back
to touch her wound confirming what she
thought.   When her head hit the floor some
of her stitches tore.   She was bleeding again.
As she looked at the blood on her hand, she
saw how badly she was shaking.

She looked up.   Alex was watching her.
He looked disgusted, and angry, and sad all
at the same time.   She felt ashamed.   She
wrapped her arms around herself.   Faisal
stepped up to the table next to Alex looking
at her with narrowed eyes.   The coldness in
him was palpable.   She could feel herself
trembling as she looked at him.

He stepped over to her grabbing her by
the arm and making her stand up.   She
crossed her legs and wrapped her arms

around herself.   She could feel what he left inside of her drip down her leg making her shudder.

He wrapped his arm around her back. He reached down between her legs and rubbed around and scooped up what was dripping down her leg.

He watched Alex who was seething with hatred.

He moved his hand cupping it as he walked to Alex and rubbed his hand all over Alex's mouth and then pushed his fingers into his mouth and rubbed them around the inside of his cheeks.   She watched with confusion as Alex looked revolted and spat and Faisal smiled with loathsome satisfaction.

He unscrewed the contraption that he had around Alex's neck and put it back in its place on his wall.   He walked along the wall letting his hand brush against different tools leaving them swinging on their hooks.

He stopped at the other end of the room and turned to look between Alex and Marianna chewing on his lip the way he always did when he was trying to make a decision.   Her heart pounded even harder. She didn't want to be any part of his decision.

She looked at Alex who had lifted his head away from the table to watch Faisal.   He looked terrified but still defiant.   His defiance might be a good trait to have as a soldier, but it would only make things worse for him with Faisal.

Faisal grabbed a pair of scissors from the wall beside him and walked back over to Marianna.

"Fuck him."   He said pushing her towards the table.

Alex looked at her shaking his head.   She looked at Faisal as he lowered the table back down with the lever so that Alex was lying flat again.   He handed her the scissors.   She stared at him not sure what he wanted her to do.   Did he want her to hurt Alex?

He looked at her and nodded down at Alex.   "Well."   He said raising his eyebrow.

She frowned at him in confusion.   He huffed and rolled his eyes as he grabbed the scissors back from her.   He quickly sliced apart Alex's clothes.   A sense of relief washed over her when she saw that he didn't cut into Alex, and he wasn't expecting her to either.

She looked at how Alex was attached to

the table.   How could she fit on it with him? She looked at the deep purple bruises that wrapped around one whole side of his body where Faisal had kicked him and broke his ribs.   She lightly touched his swollen side. He hissed in pain.

"Oh sorry."   She said pulling her hand away.

She looked back at Faisal.   She wasn't sure how to proceed.   He was watching her with suspicious eyes.   She couldn't figure him out.

She circled the table to stand on Alex's other side.   She lightly touched the uninjured side of his chest as she walked around.   He watched her with pleading eyes.

She pushed aside the sliced pieces of his pants to reveal him.   She would have to get his body enticed if she was going to be able to do anything with him.   She ran her hand up his thigh as she circled the table so that she was standing between his legs where they hung off the edge.   She ran both her hands up his inner thighs as she leaned over and breathed a hot breath and gently stroked him, his body responded as he hardened.

"Anna.   Stop."   He whispered.

His eyes were closed. His breath was ragged but sped up as she touched him. So, she touched him more.

She climbed on top of the table awkwardly between his legs. She ran one hand up his chest as she straddled him and used her other hand to guide him inside her. He gasped and opened his eyes to look at her.

The way that she had to hold herself up to move him inside her was difficult, but she managed. He continued to protest, begging her to stop, but she ignored him, just focusing on doing what she had to do without falling off the table or putting any pressure on his broken ribs. She lifted herself off of him just as she could feel that he was on the verge of finishing.

She climbed off the table to finish him with her hand when Faisal grabbed her wrist to stop her. He stepped up so that his body was against her. He ran his hand up her back and kissed her lips gently at first and then more passionately. He moved her arms to wrap around him. He pushed her so that the back of her legs were against the lip of the table between Alex's legs.

He started unbuttoning his pants again. She leaned away from him as far as she could, but he was determined. His gentleness and passion had returned to him. He pushed her further down so that her back was lying on top of Alex. She could feel him throbbing against the middle of her back.

Faisal kissed from her stomach up her breasts to her neck and then her mouth as he gently pushed himself inside her. He was sensual with her touching and kissing her as he moved. She couldn't stop herself from moving with him, it was so pleasurable. It was revolting. She was enjoying the sensations from her body, but she could also feel her back slowly rubbing against Alex who was whimpering and shuddering.

Faisal sat up as he continued moving looking at her the way that he did when he was in ecstasy with her. It was a look that he only ever had with her. She wanted to pretend that Faisal hadn't just attacked her, but she couldn't. She couldn't figure out what he was doing.

He looked above her to where Alex would be and smiled. It was depraved. He thrust into her several more times finishing inside her again, staring down Alex the whole time. His vile smile never left his face.

He pulled himself out of her, grabbing her hand and pulling her off Alex.   She looked at Alex who appeared to be just as disgusted by what happened as she felt.

"You're a fucking monster," Alex said.

Faisal smiled broader.   Marianna wrapped her arms around herself again. She felt repulsive and embarrassed.

"Do I give you nightmares then?"   Faisal said.

Alex just glared at him.

"Give it time.   I will."   Faisal said.

"What time?   You can't hold me.   I'm a soldier in this camp, and you have no authority to keep me here.   The men that brought me to this fucking place will know that I never left.   They will see to it that I am released.   And when they find out what you have done, the Captain'll get rid of you." Alex said confidently.

But Faisal just shook his head the entire time he spoke.   "Your friends paid for you to spend the week.   Your leave time had already been approved by your commanding officer.   So, you won't be missed for a while.

"And as for what I did to you.   You almost killed my guard, attacked my lady,

431

and all you got were a couple of broken ribs. I was well within my rights. And you got off lucky."

"I'll tell them about this room. What you did here. You're disgusting. When the Captain finds out what you have going on in here, he's going to shut this place down and stop you for good." Alex said.

Faisal laughed. "You think that man has any sway on what happens to me? He may have the title, but I run this place."

Marianna wished that it was just boasting, but from what she had seen, she believed that he might be right. She found herself nodding.

"And what will you say happened to you. You were fucked by a Vassal Lady. That's what we were paid for. And as for this room. It's my understanding that you were brought here by your friends because of your constant dangerous insubordination, which you proved when you attacked my people. I'm just using this room to break you of your bad habits. I'm an expert at breaking people."

Alex looked at Marianna as Faisal said the last part. Faisal smiled again, and she hugged herself tighter.

"Did you like my puppet? I move her strings, and she dances for me. And what a lovely dance we shared." Faisal said stepping around Marianna's back and wrapping his arms around her. She felt ashamed.

Alex looked at her with a pained expression.

"I'm sorry." He said to her.

She frowned at him. What was he sorry for? He wouldn't have done anything if it wasn't for her.

She shook her head, and Faisal hugged her tighter. She could feel all his muscles tensing. She looked back up at him, and he stared back at her with the same dangerous look on his face as before. She didn't understand. Her breath caught as she watched him watch her. She wanted to get away from him. She was afraid he was going to hurt her again, but she didn't know why.

She didn't know what to do. She thought about kissing him to calm him down, but she doubted that it would work on him in his current state. She didn't want to say anything because she wasn't sure what it was that was making him so angry with her in the first place, so she could possibly say something that would just make him even more angry with her.   She didn't want to take her eyes off him because she was afraid that he would get angry about that.   She was terrified of him.

He turned his head to look at Alex, and so she followed his gaze.   He was glaring at Faisal with a murderous expression. Marianna had no doubt that if he had the capability at that moment, Alex would kill Faisal.   And at that moment, with how scared she was of him, she wasn't sure how it would make her feel if he did.   She hated feeling that way.

A knock on the door broke the tension in the room just slightly.   Faisal unwrapped his arms from her and grabbed her wrist dragging her to the door with him.   He opened the door just enough to see who was on the other side.   A guard was standing there with Rayden, Gerardo, Dale, and three more armed soldiers.

"Sir there's more of them downstairs. They wouldn't leave unless I brought them to you."   The guard said defensively.

"I'll be out in a moment," Faisal said as he pushed the door to close it.

"Not in a moment. Now!" Gerardo demanded as he pushed on the door.

Faisal put his foot in front of the door to keep it from opening, but Gerardo put his entire body against the door and pushed so hard that Faisal was forced to move his foot. The door slammed open as Gerardo fell in just past Marianna.

He pushed himself off the floor looking at Marianna's naked body and then into the room. His eyes widened as he saw Alex.

"What the fuck is going on here?" Gerardo yelled.

CHAPTER TWENTY-TWO

Faisal's resolve

Faisal's rage was barely contained as the six soldiers pushed their way into the room. He moved away from the door turning his body to face all the soldiers as they poured in. If there had been fewer soldiers or more guards, Faisal wouldn't have hesitated to strike them down for entering his house and then his room without invitation.

Despite it being an everyday occurrence for soldiers to frequent the house, they were never allowed in without paying first and never without Faisal knowing about their presence.   She could remember on two separate occasions when men tried to make their way into the house without permission and the justified recourse that Faisal and the guards had taken to protect the ladies.   Both times the uninvited men were sent to the Medica to recover from their wounds.

Faisal masked his anger well. Fury was bubbling in him based on his tense posture and the way his glare lingered on each of the men as if he was plotting ways to hurt each one of them as he looked at them. He managed to unset his jaw and even force a smirk on his face in an attempt to look calmer.

Each of the soldiers had their own expressions when taking in the sights of the room.

Two of the men she didn't recognize were fixated on the multitudes of tools used for torture hanging throughout the room. One looked horrified, his face contorting into a look of disgust. He looked like he could be on the verge of getting sick. The other one looked fascinated, which immediately made Marianna's hairs on her neck stand up. He was just as dangerous as Faisal, but he wasn't as good at hiding it as Faisal was, or Marianna had just learned how to recognize it because of her longtime spent with Faisal. She wasn't sure.

The third man that she didn't recognize just stared at her. His eyes would glance at her body for a moment, and then he would quickly look back up at her face with a look of sorrow, but then his eyes would move back towards her body.

Rayden kept looking back and forth between Alex and Marianna with a growing look of remorse.   His whole body was tense.   He wanted so badly to do something, but he held himself back.

Dale and Gerardo had both drawn their weapons and were fixated on Faisal.   He was able to appear completely calm as he looked between the two of them with a smirk.

"Is somebody going to explain what the fuck is going on here?"   Gerardo finally commanded.

Faisal's smirk twitched.

"Get me off this thing.   Please.   Get me out of here."   Alex pleaded.

Rayden moved over to him as well as one of the other soldiers, and each looked around the bottom of the table where the shackles were that attached Alex's wrists and ankles to the underside.   Rayden grabbed one of the shackles and did something causing clanking noises but then stood back up.

"It needs a key."   He said looking at

Faisal who nodded with a smug look of satisfaction.

He was no longer off guard and raging. He was calm and scheming. It was clear to Marianna that he thought that he had the upper hand. He was surrounded by armed, angry, dangerous soldiers, and he was the one in control of the room. And as she looked around at each of the men, she realized that he was. He had no weapon in his hand, but he was master.

She marveled at the whole thing. How had he managed to influence everyone? His reputation would be part of it, but it wasn't the only thing. It was just him. He had an air about himself that demanded obedience and the soldiers were all trained to follow the one in charge. They recognized his dominance and reacted to it, and he reveled in it.

"Do you have the key?" Gerardo pressed.

Faisal looked at him with an arrogance that she rarely saw in the man. He was in control, and he knew it. Gerardo puffed his chest up and gritted his teeth, as they glared at each other.

It occurred to her that Faisal was

displaying the look of arrogance intentionally.   He wanted to provoke Gerardo, and it was working.

"I do."   Faisal answered calmly.

His relaxed demeanor enticed Gerardo even more.

"Are you going to let him up, or are we going to have to make you?"   Gerardo asked lifting his sword higher.

Faisal's smile broadened, and Gerardo scowled.

"I wasn't planning on it.   It's not the time to release him yet."   Faisal said haughtily. Two of the soldiers unsheathed their swords at his comment.   He just glanced at them contemptuously.

"Are you serious?   This isn't what we paid you for."   Dale said staring regretfully at Alex.

Faisal raised one eyebrow.   "Isn't it?"

"What is wrong with you?   You really think this is what we wanted?"   Gerardo said gesturing to Alex.   He looked over at him with a disturbed expression, his hand tightened on the hilt of his sword as his agitation became more evident.   He looked back at Faisal glowering.

Faisal laughed.   Which caused several in

the room to jump, including Marianna. It was joyless and frightening.

"You paid me to ensure he got fucked. And he was, in more than one way." Faisal said sneering as he looked at Marianna.

Everyone turned to look at her, each of their eyes taking in her naked body. She crossed her legs and wrapped her arms around her chest feeling embarrassed under all their scrutiny. Rayden met her eyes, and she could see shame reflecting back on her. She turned her head away hugging herself tighter.

As she looked away, she looked at Alex. He looked nauseated. He was disgusted by what happened. He glanced at her and then closed his eyes and turned away from her. He didn't even want to look at her. She was ashamed and disgusted with herself.

She looked back at Faisal who was watching her with narrowed suspicious eyes, all hints of humor were gone. He was no longer having fun. Her heart sped up instantly as a sudden panic struck her. She didn't want him to hurt her again.

"I'll pay you again, double, just let him out of here," Rayden begged.

She looked back up to Rayden who was piteously watching Alex.

"No," Faisal said sternly.

Everybody looked at him. He somehow looked larger as if he was looming over all of them even though several of the men were at least as tall as he was. But it was more than his stature that looked bigger, it was his presence. It put all the soldiers on guard as the two holding swords raised them higher, and the four unarmed men unsheathed their swords.

Faisal smiled coldly.

He moved confidently towards Gerardo who looked to be the most willing to use his weapon against Faisal. He stepped so that the point of Gerardo's sword was pressed against his chest and glared at the man.

"You think you are going to use that on me, in my house?" He said in a booming voice.

Gerardo narrowed his eyes but made no movement. The other men in the room remained still as well. They were all intimidated by him.

"He's not going anywhere," Faisal said with a calm seriousness.

"You can't keep him here," Dale said with

a shrill voice.

"Your friend over there violently attacked one of my men.   He cut his throat, nearly killing him.   My lady was seriously injured by him when he threw her against the wall and then shackled her."   He said pointing at Marianna.

Rayden looked at her with confusion. She absently touched the back of her head and pulled her hand back to look at it.   It was covered in thick, sticky blood.   Would she have to get it stitched again?   She looked back up at Rayden who stared at her hand in shock.   He looked back to Alex who was also looking at her, but he had an expression of guilt.   Rayden frowned.

"He made his decision, and now he has to live with it."

"You can't hold him here.   Not like that. We have a police force to handle those kinds of things."   Dale argued.

Faisal smiled.   "You're right we do.   And I run it.   Where do you think the men came from who serve in that police force? They're not soldiers.   They're mine.   All of them.   So, tell me how I have stepped beyond my rights."

"You beat the shit out of him.   Look at

him.   You have no more right to do that than we do."   Dale countered.

"He got his wounds while my men and I took him down after he attacked my people. And then attempted to fight with us.   I have already set up a time to meet with the Captain.   I have the means and the space to hold him until the Captain decides what will be done with him.   As you can see, he's not going anywhere.   Do you have any way to ensure he will make it to his hearing if I release him to you?"   Faisal said calmly.

"You beat the shit out of him.   There's no way he could get away from all of us in that condition."   Dale said as he looked at Alex studying his wounds with a frown.

"Can you guarantee that?   Because if anything happened to him while he is in your care, if he disappeared for any reason before the Captain can decide his fate, you would all be held responsible.   Do you want to pay for his crimes?"

They all looked around nervously at each other.   And Faisal smirked.   It was only for a second and barely even noticeable, and if Marianna hadn't been looking at him at that moment, she wouldn't have seen it.   He was playing them.   He knew just what buttons to push.　As she looked at each of the soldiers, she recognized that he had swayed them.　All of them except Rayden.　He still looked resigned to help Alex.

"I know him better than anyone," Rayden said looking first at Alex and then to Marianna nodding at her.

She smiled at him, and as she did, she saw Faisal tense at the edge of her vision.　That was when it occurred to her why Faisal was acting the way that he was towards her.

He was jealous.

From the moment he became aware that she knew Alex and Rayden from her past he had been acting angry and suspicious towards her.　She was his. And he did not want to share her in any way.

Rayden noticed Faisal's shift in demeanor as well.　He took a wary step towards Faisal.　His grip tightened on his sword hilt, but he didn't raise it any further.

"He won't try to escape.　I know he won't.　He wouldn't do anything to put us in jeopardy."　Rayden said confidently.　A couple of the men were nodding, but they were still scared of getting in trouble because of him.

"There are other ways that he could

disappear," Faisal said darkly.

Although he didn't say it out loud, his intention was clear.   If they took Alex away, he would make sure that he never made it to his hearing with the Captain.   None of the soldiers doubted his ability to do so.

"You can't do that," Rayden said in a high pitch tone.

Faisal glared confidently, seemingly complacent about the sword that was still pointing at his chest.   "Do what?"   He said smiling smugly but with a dangerous air.

Rayden just shook his head.

"When's the meeting?"   Dale asked as he sheathed his sword.   Everybody else sheathed their weapons as well except for Rayden and Gerardo.

"In three days at noon.   At the Captain's." Faisal said.

"We can meet you there.   We can speak on his behalf, and ensure that his condition hasn't changed from today."   Dale said confidently.

He was warning Faisal without saying it out loud that they would report any changes to Alex's condition to the Captain. It was clear that he thought that the Captain still had some sway over what happened to

Faisal.   Marianna wasn't sure if he did or not.

Faisal just nodded as if untroubled by the veiled threat.

"You can put that away now," Faisal said contemptuously to Gerardo, as he lifted the tip of the sword from his chest and moved it to the side.

Gerardo glared at him for a long moment. He was struggling with his desire to attack Faisal and his duty to not attack a man with such high standing within the camp, without cause.   He took in a deep breath clenching his teeth and sheathed his sword.

Faisal smiled and nodded.   He had bested them all without ever needing to touch a weapon.   He always had the advantage, and he knew it.

"We'll see you at the Captain's place," Dale said nodding encouragingly towards Alex who looked just as defeated as the other soldiers in the room.   He nodded.

Rayden looked sadly at Alex.   "I'm sorry. We'll do everything that we can to help you."

Alex nodded.   "Thanks."

"Now all of you get out of my house," Faisal said sternly.

The soldiers all nodded and walked towards the door. Rayden and Gerardo both set their jaws as they watched Faisal with contempt, but continued with the others.

"Oh. And one last thing before you leave. If you ever try to raid my house again, you will be dealt with immediately. Test my resolve and see what happens."

Each of the soldiers left the room glaring at Faisal as they left. Faisal shut the door behind them. He stood silently with his head tilted towards the door. He was listening to make sure the soldiers were leaving. There were subtle sounds of them descending the stairs. In a few moments, the hallway outside the room silenced.

Faisal whipped around to face Alex. His demeanor changed instantly from calm and collected to enraged.

"Don't you think for one second that you have been saved from my wrath? You will pay for damaging my things."

He stalked over shoving a cloth into Alex's mouth so far that Alex gagged. He made a fist and jammed his knuckles into Alex's broken ribs rubbing back and forth forcefully. Alex screamed, but the sound of

448

it was muffled.

"I'll see you in three days.   I hope you enjoy my hospitality."   Faisal said walking away leaving Alex writhing in pain with the cloth still in his mouth.

He grabbed Marianna's wrist and tugged her toward him, pulling her out the door.

CHAPTER TWENTY-THREE

Changes

Faisal took her to their bedroom and ordered her to stay in there. She did as she was told not wanting to do anything that could make him direct his anger towards her. He left her alone until long after the sun went down when he joined her in bed. He said nothing to her, but she sensed that his agitation had been muted in the hours they had been apart.

When they woke up the next morning, he busily got himself ready. He was determined about something. She got dressed as well, feeling relieved when he didn't protest. She was afraid he was going to make her stay in the bedroom again.

"Today everything changes," Faisal said. He didn't look at her as he spoke. She wasn't sure if that made her uncomfortable or not.   The thought of change scared her. She had gotten used to the way things were, and her experience taught her that change was rarely a good thing for her.

She thought about asking him what he meant, but she was afraid of what his answer could be.

He grabbed her hand and forcefully pulled her towards him.   She shrieked and pulled her arm away fearfully backing up.   He moved slowly towards her with his hands out in front of him.   He gently wrapped his hands around her waist and pulled her closer to him.   He looked her in the eyes.

"I broke my promise to you."   He said softly, as he stroked her cheek with the back of his hand.

She looked away chewing on her lip.   He moved his hand down her cheek and lifted her chin to look at him again.   He released her waist with his other hand and grabbed her hand.   He interlaced his fingers with hers, pulling her hand up to kiss it gently.

"I let you get hurt......I hurt you."   He said, his face growing more serious.

She cried.   She didn't want to, but she couldn't stop herself.

He wrapped his arms around her pulling her into him, hugging her tightly.   She cried into his chest as he held her.

"I lose myself sometimes too."   He said.

She leaned away from him to look at him. He wiped her tears from her cheek and continued gently stroking with the back of his hand.

"When he hurt you, I was furious."   He said.   His face was grave as he studied her.

"And then you defended him, which I couldn't understand.   Even when you told me about knowing one another in the past, it confused me."   He looked uncomfortable admitting his confusion.

He planned for every possible outcome, and he read people so well that he was very good at anticipating what they would do or say.   So, he didn't handle it well when he was caught off guard.

"Why would you attempt to minimize what he did to you?   Maybe because of your head, maybe you weren't thinking clearly." He continued.

He sounded like he was rambling which was out of character for him.

"You stepped into that room, and you looked at him with pity.   But you looked at me with contempt. I've seen the look directed at me before, but never from you." His expression turned to stone as he stared at her.

"When I saw that look from you, I snapped. If you were going to see me that way, then I was going to give you a real reason to. I wanted to hurt you. But not just physically, that would be too easy on you. I wanted to hurt you in every way that I could. I could see the terror in your eyes. And I could see the pain and betrayal, but it didn't give me the satisfaction that I was looking for. Not like it does from others. It made it worse. I can't stand having you look at me in that way." He said grabbing both of her arms and shaking her.

He had never shown her so much emotion before. He was distraught. Or at least, he was distraught compared to his normal cool, controlled state. She wanted to comfort him, tell him that everything was alright, but she would be lying, and he would know that. It wasn't alright. She didn't want to be afraid of him in the way that she was, but she couldn't help it. He had attacked her in such a brutal way, that she couldn't just forgive him.

"I almost killed you."   He whispered.

She mechanically grabbed her throat.   He grabbed her hand and pulled it away as he ran his fingers across the bruises on her neck.

"I wanted to kill you."   He said shaking his head.

He put his hand on her shoulder.

"If it meant that you would stop looking at me like that.   The intensity of my physical pleasure gave me a moment of clarity.   I couldn't lose you."   He pulled her back in to hug her, kissing her on the top of her head causing her to wince as it put pressure on her injury.

He pushed her away squeezing her arms for a moment looking frustrated.   Her heart sped up as she feared what he would do. He looked into her eyes and then looked down towards the floor with disappointment.   He let go of her arms and walked towards the door.

He stopped for a second as he reached for the door handle.   He turned back to look at her.

"I will fix it.   Somehow.   We must fix this.   I can't lose you.   Don't let me lose you."

Even after everything that happened, she

didn't want to lose him either. She shook her head. He relaxed and smiled. He waved her over and left the room.

They descended the stairs to a surprising sight. The extra guards that Faisal had promised had arrived. The entire downstairs was loud with excited or nervous conversations.

There was a palpable uncomfortable feeling in the air. The old guard kept themselves separated from the new guards. Each group talked amongst themselves. There was an uneasy sense in the air as they connected with one another. The ladies were also separated. They all conversed in a single room away from all the men except for the three guards that were assigned to stay in the room.

Where had all the guards come from? Faisal had the ability to get whatever he wanted. It was astonishing.

Faisal gathered several of the senior guards. Trevino and Jon who were both in charge of a shift of guards, and Leonardo and Milo who had been with Faisal since the house was first established. He trusted them more than any other guards in the house.

He instructed the four senior guards to gather all new and old guards and follow him into the dining room. They obeyed immediately.

As they entered the dining room, Faisal gestured at the chairs and pointed at each person that he wanted to join him at the table. He had the four senior guards sit, as well as several more of the old guard. But he also had a few of the new guards interspersed among them at the table. He had Marianna sit across from him. The rest of the guards were left standing gathered around them. The room was so crowded it made Marianna uncomfortable.

"Sarafina," Faisal shouted.

Even though the woman couldn't have been in earshot, she entered the room hurriedly. She made her way past standing guards and stopped next to Faisal. She bowed her head down as was customary and waited for her orders.

"Get some of the ladies together and get us all some food," Faisal said.

"Yes sir," Sarafina said rushing out of the room.

It wasn't long before Marianna could smell food cooking. Her stomach growled as she remembered that she hadn't eaten anything since the previous morning.

"The structure of how things are done around here has to change.   The ladies are at too much risk and now that I am assigning them all to be Vassal ladies they will need even more protection.   There will be even more people moving in and out of the house, and so the way I have you all assigned will change as well.

"As many of the ladies are used to being Breeders, they may need more encouragement to perform their jobs as needed.   Any indiscretion will need to be dealt with at the moment, not later as has been done in the past.   So, because of this, I will be giving you all authority to ensure their participation.

"Once the house is back up and running there will be no time that it will be closed for business.   There have been requests for years to have ladies available at all hours to accommodate men who work non-traditional shifts.   There has been an entire demographic of men that we have been ignoring, this is to be remedied.   The ladies will be working the same shifts as the guards.

"There will be one guard assigned to each lady at all times. You will be working in assigned shifts as you have already been doing, but you will each have more guards working under you so I will promote two more to take charge. I would like for you two to take the lead." He said looking at Leonardo and Milo.

Both nodded. They both were proud of themselves and happy to have been picked. Faisal nodded.

"Good. You too will both be directly under Jon and Trevino. They will train you to know what is expected of you."

Jon and Trevino both nodded.

Marianna cocked her mouth to the side. If Leonardo and Milo were going to be taking the lead, then they should be given their own people to work over, instead of splitting the duty with Jon and Trevino. Otherwise, Jon and Trevino who were used to being in charge would continue to do as they had always done, and Leonardo and Milo would end up with all the jobs that Jon and Trevino wouldn't want to do themselves. They would be better utilized on their own.

Faisal watched her and lifted his eyebrow

at her. "Do you have a suggestion?" He said sounding intrigued.

She nodded.

"Please." He said smiling kindly at her. "I'd love to hear your thoughts."

The old guards were just as interested in what she had to say. They had all been around after the storm and had learned to listen to her ideas and trust her suggestions. She had a mind for planning and utilizing people in ways that benefited everyone, and the old guards knew it.

The new guards didn't know. Many of them watched her with surprise or curiosity. While some held some contempt towards her that Faisal would even consider what she had to say.

Faisal was watching the way that each of the newcomers regarded her. He watched them all as she spoke.

"Everything is changing right?" She asked.

Faisal nodded.

"Well, then I think that something that has already been a problem needs to change as well."

Jon and Trevino both wore expressions of worry. She didn't want to make it seem like they weren't doing their jobs effectively, because they were both very good at their jobs.

"We need more shifts. The two that we have now aren't as good as they could be. There tends to be a lapse in security during the shift changes; not because the guards aren't doing their jobs, but because there are a lot of distractions happening at that time." She said trying to reassure Jon and Trevino that she wasn't questioning their ability to control their charges or their men's ability to do their jobs.

"I agree," Faisal said casually watching the new guards, but Marianna knew what he was really doing.

He was reading them. He was learning who to trust, who to not worry about, and who to be wary of.

"If we had four separate shifts every twelve hours there would always be an overlap so that shift changes wouldn't have as much of an effect. It would also give everybody ample time to take breaks to eat or go to the bathroom without worrying about leaving their post." She explained.

Faisal nodded again. She watched some of the new guards to gauge their reactions.

Some of them paid as close attention to her as the old guards did, while some of the others still doubted her. Faisal was watching those guards more extensively.

"Since Leonardo and Milo have already been promoted they could take the lead over the two new shifts. Each shift leader can have equal numbers of guards working under them. The guards assigned to the shift will listen directly to their shift leader, and all shift leaders will listen directly to you. That way there is more of a chain of command. And it will free you up from dealing with some of the more mundane problems so your energy can be better spent running the house and tending to the more serious problems." She said.

Faisal smiled and looked at her.

"That's how we'll do it then." He said.

Several of the new guards were uncomfortable with his agreeing so freely with her suggestions. Leonardo, Milo, Jon, and Trevino were all nodding contently. They liked her ideas.

"Just one difference in your plan." He said sounding serious. She frowned at him.

"The shift leaders will answer directly to you." He said smiling again.

She stared at him dumbfounded.   As did many of the guards, both new and old.

"You are now..."   He stopped to think tilting his head to the side.   "You are the Head Mistress.   You report directly to me. You are no longer a Vassal lady."   He said happily.

She continued staring at him not sure what to say.   Her eyes welled up with tears of joy.   She took several deep breaths to calm herself and keep from openly crying.

"I want you to also choose four ladies to be Head Ladies.   They will lead the four shifts that the ladies will be working.   The Head Ladies will work directly under you as well.   They will work on the same level as shift leaders directing the ladies under them to do their assigned jobs."

She nodded.

He looked around at the guards who wore expressions ranging from agreement, to shock, to open disdain.

At that moment Sarafina entered the room along with several of the other ladies.   She placed a plate in front of Faisal first and then Jon and Trevino.   She was about to hand her fourth plate to one of the other guards when Faisal gestured for her to place it in front of

Marianna.   Sarafina frowned for a moment and then immediately obeyed.

"Tell all of the ladies to come in here for a moment while the others bring in the rest of the food," Faisal ordered Sarafina.

She nodded and left the room.

The outskirts of the room filled even more as the ladies all trickled in squeezing between standing guards.

"I want it to be understood.   There will be a new chain of command in this house.   I am still Head of House and expect to be obeyed by all.   Is that understood?"

"Yes sir."   Everybody in the room said in unison.

"The chain of command goes as follows: me, then Marianna, the shift leaders, and Head Ladies, then the guards, then the Vassal ladies."   He said closely watching every one of them.

"Yes sir."   Everybody said.

Several of the ladies looked at Marianna with looks of confusion, while others whispered to each other or to some of the guards to get more understanding.

Faisal nodded.

For the next span of time, everybody ate, breaking up into small conversations.

Faisal instructed all the ladies to also join in the meal.   So, everybody was eating in the large room that seemed tiny with so many people jammed within it.   Nobody complained though.   The old house members knew better, and the new ones wanted to make a good first impression.

"I need you to know something," Faisal said to her after finishing his food.

Most of the conversations stopped or quieted as he spoke.

"Hmm."

"I didn't give you the job to placate you. I know that it will take more than that to fix what I've done."   He said.

She looked at him.   She was stunned that he would openly admit to wronging her in front of everyone.   He was truly remorseful for what he did.   She didn't know that he had the capacity to feel remorse, but was clear that he felt it.

The room silenced.   Everyone wanted to hear what he had to say, and they all were curious about what he was talking about. The old guards and ladies were especially intrigued as they were probably also surprised by Faisal's veiled admission.

She was sure that they also needed to

understand his decision to put her in such a prominent position. It was well known that Marianna was Faisal's favorite lady. He claimed her as his own. But he still worked her. She was still a Vassal lady.

He hadn't exaggerated when he said that he was changing everything.

"You are the smartest, most resourceful person that I have ever known. You have a natural ability to lead others, and you are capable of recognizing and utilizing others strengths in ways that make everything flow seamlessly.

"It would be foolish of me to not use your strengths to make our house's new ventures successful. If things work out as I am certain they will, this house is about to get exponentially busier. You are the best person for the job." He said confidently.

Several of the old guards including the four shift leaders were nodding along as he spoke. Some of the ladies also agreed. Some of the new guards took notice as they regarded her with a new level of respect.

It was amazing to be regarded with such high honor. She smiled broadly.

"Oh, another change that needs to be addressed. Because this house will be open

at all hours, nobody will be sleeping here."
Faisal said.

Everybody looked at him with confusion, including Marianna.

He smiled. "I have purchased two additional houses. One directly across the street, and a smaller house down the road."

Surprised gasps moved through the crowd, but nobody spoke.

"The ladies who are off duty will sleep at the house across the street. You will each have an assigned room that will be yours alone."

The ladies all stared at him in stunned silence.

"As long as you all do your assigned jobs, your time away from work will be your own."

Another round of gasps and shocked squeals moved among the ladies. Several of the ladies cried.

"Don't take advantage of my generosity." He said sternly.

The ladies all shook their heads. "No sir."

"Well let's get everybody assigned to a shift and trained. I want this house open for business in one week."

Marianna stared at Faisal in awe. He surprised her so much, and she could plainly see that she was not alone in her shock.

The room steadily emptied everybody talking in excited even joyful conversations. She smiled.

Faisal remained sitting at the table just watching her coyly.

"What?" She asked finally.

He stood up and rounded the table grabbing her hand making her stand up beside him.

"Come with me." He said with an excitement in his voice.

He led her past everybody and out the front door.

"What...Where are we going?" She asked genuinely confused.

He wrapped his arm around her waist leading her down the road.

"Don't you want to know what the second house is for?" He asked playfully.

She turned to look at him and frowned. "What is the second house for?"

"It's our house."

She scoffed smiling. "Our house?"

He stopped in front of a much smaller house than what she was used to working in, but still an enormous house.

It had a large fountain with carved fish. Water splashed around each of the fish's tails making it look like they were swimming. It was amazing. As he led her towards the house, she could see live fish swimming in the fountain as well. She chuckled.

He stopped her in front of the door. He turned to look at her. He chewed on his lip his face growing more serious.

"I know it can never change what I did to you. But it's a way for me to show you how sorry I am." He said grabbing her face and kissing her. She kissed him back melting into him.

He pulled away. "I'm a difficult man to love, I know that. But I think you do."

She nodded. He sighed in relief and kissed her again.

"I can't promise that I won't snap again, just as you can't promise me that you won't either. We are both volatile, but together we buffer each other's dark natures. Can you ever forgive me?" He asked desperately.

She leaned up grabbing his face and kissed him. He wrapped his arms around her lifting her up as he embraced her.

He set her back down. And looked at her seriously again.

"I could make you be here with me. But I'm not going to force you to stay with me. If you don't want to be here for any reason, you have space at the other house with the ladies. If you choose to stay with them, the job that you were given today, will not change. As I told you before, I chose you because you are the best person for the job. And you will have the same freedom outside of your work as everybody else regardless of your decision.

"If you choose to stay with me, you agree to be mine. I am a possessive man. I can't share your affections with anyone else. Not anyone at the house, and not your old friends. If you choose to stay, you choose me." He explained.

She nodded. "I do. I choose you. I choose to stay."

He smiled broadly lifting her up again and spinning her around.

He opened the door and carried her into their new home where they spent the rest of the day and night breaking it in.

CHAPTER TWENTY-FOUR

Proposal

The next day Marianna woke up with a million ideas running through her head about how things should be done at the house. But she wasn't sure how much Faisal would let her do.

He rolled onto his side to look at her. He looked more relaxed than he had been in months. He lightly ran his fingers up her side tickling her a little. She giggled, and he smiled. He lifted his eyebrow as he looked at her.

"What's going through that head of yours?" He asked pushing her hair back behind her ear and then twirling one lock of long auburn hair around his finger. He only ever played with her hair when he was truly happy.

"Just some ideas about the changes at the house."   She said shrugging her shoulder as much as she could while she was propped up on her side.

He smirked.

"Like what.   I'd love to hear all of your ideas."   He said sitting up and putting his back on the headboard.

He put his pillow behind his back and lounged back.   He gestured for her to lay her head down in his lap, she obliged smiling as he ran his fingers through her hair.

"I have a bunch of them."   She said.

"I have no doubt that you do."   He said chuckling.   "Tell me."

"Well, I think that the ladies that I pick to be Head Ladies shouldn't have to work as Vassal Ladies, or at least not as much as the ladies under them."   She said looking at him to gauge his reaction.

He just nodded.   "I assume you are going to have other things taking up their time."

"Yes.   A lot.   If they are going to be in charge of a group of ladies, then they will be responsible for everything that their ladies do or don't do.   They should be just as responsible as the guards are for ensuring that the ladies perform their duties appropriately, and guide them or train them to do even better than they have been.   I also think that they should be the ones responsible for pairing their ladies with the appropriate men."   She said.

He cocked his eyebrow at her.   "The appropriate men?"

She nodded.   "Yeah.   Everybody has their own tastes and preferences, if we pair the men with ladies that meet those desires, then the men would be more easily satisfied. And would be more likely to be repeat patrons."

"Hmm."   He said nodding.

She continued.   "I think that the ladies need to focus on pleasing the men in more than one way.   Our house should be known for fulfilling all the men's desires.   We already have a reputation for having the most compliant ladies, now we should be known for having the most intuitive ladies, who can pleasure a man in ways he didn't even know he wanted.   Especially since we are moving away from Breeders and going to all Vassal Ladies, and our house will always be open, we will need to draw as many customers in as we can."

He smiled broadly.   "I knew that you would be perfect for the job.   You see things differently than I do.   I would never have thought of that.   What other ideas do you have?"

"What exactly will my position entail? What liberties or power do I have?"   She asked nervously.

She didn't want to push too much, but she needed to know what she would be allowed to do.

"You can make decisions, deliver or assign punishments to both ladies and guards, change shifts if someone isn't getting along or is causing issues, assign duties to Shift Leaders or Head Ladies, set responsibilities for guards and ladies, and so much more. Any major changes you will need to discuss with me, but otherwise, I give you full power to do whatever you must to keep our house running efficiently.   You are my second in command.   You have all of the same powers as I have."   He said watching her as he did when he was trying to read someone.

She was speechless.   She had not expected him to give her so much power and responsibility.   He kept telling her that he chose her because she was perfect for the job, but what if he was wrong.   What if what she did just made everything worse?   But even as she thought it, she didn't believe it.   She would do everything that she had to, to make things work better and be better for everyone.

"So, any substantial changes that you think we should instill?   Now would be the best time to impart anything new while everything is still in flux.   Once we get back into running things, major changes will take much more adjustment."   He asked.

He said we, not I.   He was serious about everything.

She nodded.   "I think we need to focus on making the ladies happy."   She said confidently.

He chewed on his lip for a moment as he watched her.

Had she gone too far?   What would he do if she had?

He nodded.   "How?   That is not something that I know how to accomplish.   I maintain order and control.   I break the ladies to make them do what they must.   Happiness is never a concern that I have for them."

He surprised her more and more. He was admitting his weaknesses to her. She was the only one that he was ever honest with, but he still tried to convey a sense of control and strength towards her, but that was changing.

"I think they need some regular time off." She said.

He frowned. "I'm giving them that. I said that when they are not working their time is their own."

She nodded. "I know. And that is a great start. But when we work for twelve hours a day, that doesn't really leave a lot of free time. Not if they are going to get any sleep.

"I think they should get a day off."

He cocked his head to the side. "When?"

"Every week." She said.

His eyes widened. "An entire day every week?" He said flabbergasted.

"Yes. And the guards too." She said.

He shook his head chewing on his lip even more. "You're asking a lot of me."

"I know. But you asked what I think we should do to make them happy, and this is it. I think the house would run much better if the ladies were happy. Also, if they have some personal time to do what they want, then they will be much more tolerant of doing their job with more enthusiasm. That enthusiasm will make the reputation for the house even better. Imagine how many men would want to come, if our ladies not only satisfy their desires, but they actually want to do it." She explained.

He nodded. "I don't have to imagine it. That's what made me fall for you in the first place. You weren't just fucking me because I made you, or because it was your job, you were doing it because you wanted to. You wanted me. It is intoxicating." He said closing his eyes.

She could feel him hardening beneath her head, and she laughed.

He opened his eyes and smiled playfully.

"Alright, they all get one day off a week where they are free to do whatever they want." He said as he adjusted himself.

"Is there anything else to make them happy?" He asked as he resumed running his fingers through her hair.

"If they are going to have personal time away from the house, it means that they will be doing things that require money. So, they should get paid." She said.

She couldn't believe how forward she was with her requests, she had already gotten him to agree to something huge, and now she was asking for something even more significant.

The expression on his face was unexpected. He looked guilty. "They do get paid." He said.

She frowned. "What?"

"I have to pay them. Captain's orders say that all adults must be paid for the work that they do. I can deduct living expenses for any housing or food that I provide, but they are still entitled to some pay."

"You've never paid me." She said confused.

"No. When you were first brought to me, you were a prisoner. You are not the first prisoner that has been assigned to me, not even the first murderer.

"Usually when someone is brought to the house as a form of punishment for their crimes they are considered my property until they are well established in their position. Once they are established, usually within about two years, I no longer own them they are my employees, sort of. They still can't leave their jobs, and they must do as I order, just as all of them do, but beyond that, they don't belong to me.   Since they are considered employees, I must pay them.

"But with you it was different.   Because of the nature of your crime, and how dangerous you were when you were first brought to me, you were given to me indefinitely.   You are my property, not my employee." He explained.

"Oh."   She said feeling disappointed.

Faisal watched her with care.

"Does that bother you?"   He asked with genuine curiosity.

"I'm never going to be able to get past what I did.   All because of something that happened in the heat of madness, when I was barely more than a child."   She said.

"Hmm."   He said.   He studied her face while chewing on his lip.

"Since I have promoted you, I could pay you.   Would you like that?"   He asked.

She looked at him in disbelief and nodded.

"Hmm."   He said cocking his mouth to the side again.

"I could..."   He stopped and chewed on his lip some more.   "I could do even better. But it would mean you would have to do something." He said looking nervous.

She frowned feeling uneasy.   His tone worried her.   He either didn't want to do what he was talking about, or he was afraid that she wouldn't agree to it.

"What?"   She finally asked as his nervous silence was making her uneasy.

"If you married me, then everything that I have will be yours." His voice shook as he spoke.

"Marry you?"   She whispered.

He bit his lip again and nodded.   He looked terrified his whole body was tense.

"I didn't know we were allowed to get married."   She said.

"I'm not conscripted to be here, and since you were granted to me, you're not anymore either."

"Oh."   She said.

He frowned at her.   "So will you?"

"Will I what?"   She asked.

His frown deepened.   "Marry me. Would you want to marry me?"

"Oh.   Yes.   I will.   I mean I want to. Yes."   She said.

He smiled as his whole body relaxed.

"Good.   Good."   He said nodding his head as he breathed a sigh of relief.

"When we have our meeting about the

prisoner with the Captain, we will make it official."   He said.

She widened her eyes.   "So soon?"

He frowned.   "You want to wait?"   He was genuinely perplexed.

"No."   She said shaking her head.   "I'm just surprised.   Doesn't it take time to prepare things?   I'm not sure how it works exactly, but in some of the books that I've read, it can take people a year before they actually get married."   She explained.

He smiled.   "Well, that's because they are planning a wedding.   We aren't going to be having one of those.   Who would we invite, the guards and ladies?   Besides, I already got everything prepared.   I've been thinking about this for a while, I just didn't know when to ask you."   He said sheepishly.

"You have?"   She asked smiling.

She had assumed that he had only asked her because of how much everything was changing, as he had said major changes took some adjustment, and so it was the best time for such a change.

"I want you to be mine.   Not in the way that I own you, I already have that, but that's not what I mean.   I want you to willingly be mine.   I've wanted that from you for a long time." He said as he stroked her cheek adoringly.

"I was certain that I had destroyed my chance. I thought that you would hate me." He said as he looked at her throat and gritted his teeth.

She shook her head. "I don't hate you."

He lightly touched her tracing along the bruises that he gave her. He looked so serious.

"Can I ask you something?" She said.

"Hmm." He said taking his eyes off her throat to look in her eyes.

She hesitated. She didn't want to think about when he attacked her, but she had to know.

"What is it?" He asked looking concerned.

"Why did you finish inside of me?" She said feeling the same sense of revulsion that she had before.

He nodded slowly as he chewed on his lip. She idly thought about how badly chapped they would be after they finished talking.

"I was going to kill you. In my rage, I had decided that I wanted you dead. And so, it wouldn't matter what I did. Afterward, since I had already done it once, I

figured it wouldn't matter if I did it again."
He explained apathetically.

"What if I get pregnant?"   She asked.

Just the thought of being around a child
again sent her into a moment of panic.   Her
heart sped up, and her breathing became
heavier.   She closed her eyes to try and calm
herself.

He cupped her cheek and turned her head
towards him.   She opened her eyes.   His
look of concern had returned.

"We'll figure it out."

She nodded, but the panic didn't diminish.

"We will. Together, we will figure it out."
He insisted.

He studied her face.   "Are you sure that
you don't hate me?"   He asked.

She nodded her head.

"I don't.   I should.   I hate what you did.
But I don't hate you.   I do want to marry
you.   I want to be yours.   And I want you
to be mine."

He smiled and nodded.   He wrapped his
hand around her back and lifted her so that
she was sitting up.   He leaned in and kissed
her sweetly.

"I love you so much."   He said.

She smiled.   "I love you too."

CHAPTER TWENTY-FIVE

Trial

When Faisal told everybody about Marianna's idea about ladies and guards all getting one day off a week, they were ecstatic.   Many of them went out of their way to thank her.   And several of them, even some of the new guards, told her how happy they were that she was going to be in charge of them.   They said that they trusted her, and knew that she had all their best interests at heart.

The next couple of days moved by in a blur.   Everybody was so busy training, moving into the ladies' house, and preparing the main house, that Marianna couldn't think of anything else.

After eating and getting dressed for going out, it was time to go to the Captain's quarters. Faisal and four of his trusted guards went upstairs to get Alex.

When they walked him downstairs, Marianna was surprised to see how bad he looked. The one side of his face was still swollen and purple, but the rest of him was pale and sickly looking. He looked miserable. And every step that he took pained him. His short gasps of breath as he descended the stairs looked excruciating. In the brief time that it took for him to reach the bottom, he was already winded.

He watched her with pleading eyes. She wished there was something that she could do to help him or ease his suffering in some way, but there was nothing.

They loaded into two separate carriages, Faisal and Marianna in one, and the four guards and Alex in the other.

The ride to the Captain's quarters was much shorter than Marianna had thought it would be. But as she thought about it, it was less surprising. The last time she had been there was the day that she killed Clive, and was sentenced to be a Vassal Lady. That day she had been carried by two guards from the Captain's quarters to Faisal's house, so a horse-drawn carriage would be much faster.

As they entered the building, memories of her infamous day came flooding back to her mind.   She braced herself for the influx of emotions that accompanied those memories, but was surprised to find that she was barely bothered by the thought of that day.   The crushing emotions that had for so long been connected to that fateful day had muted. She wasn't sure if the change was due to the passing of time, increased self-control, or her efforts with Faisal to reduce her triggers for her bouts of craziness, but she was thrilled to be liberated from the unsolicited reaction that had plagued her for years.

They moved through the Captain's quarters to a large room filled with chairs. Several people were sitting interspersed throughout the room.   Faisal explained that they were in the antechamber to the seat of judgment that the Captain held.   He said that it was a type of court used to sentence criminals.

He explained that because the growing population and the settling of the camp into more of an actual community, the crime rate had increased.   Faisal had recognized the increase in crime and offered the Captain the opportunity to employ Faisal's ever-growing number of guards to be used as a police force.   And because his police force had been so effective, the Captain had to hold court two full days a week to deal with the arrests and deal out punishments.

The group of them sat together in the corner of the room near the door that they entered through.   Nobody spoke, but she saw Alex glancing at her several times while they waited.   Two other small groups were called back before them.   One of the groups returned with all the people that went back, but the other was missing two of its members.   Where had they gone?

A couple of minutes after the second group left they were called back.   Faisal led the group, followed by the guards who held on tightly to Alex, and then Marianna.

The room that they entered was much larger than Marianna had expected.   It too was filled with chairs that all faced a large table where the Captain was seated.   Two armed soldiers were posted on each side of the table, blocking any possible access to the Captain.   And two soldiers were posted at each of the four doors that led out of the room. They all took seats sitting in the front row directly in front of him.

As Marianna looked at the man, she thought that she would recognize him, but she didn't. He didn't look at all familiar to her. Was her memory faulty? Or was the Captain a different person than the one she had met when she was a child?

"You all come before me today to bear witness about crimes committed by the Conscripted soldier, Sergeant Alex Cunningham. Do any of you contest the need for you to be at this hearing?" The Captain said in the clearest and official tone that she had ever heard from somebody.

"No sir." Faisal and the guards said in unison.

The Captain looked at her and raised his eyebrows.

"Oh. Uh, no sir." She said realizing that he wanted her to speak as well.

She assumed that she was only present because Faisal didn't want to leave her at the house for so long without him being there.

The Captain nodded once, and then looked at Alex. "You are the man in question?" He asked.

Alex nodded slowly. "Yes sir." He said solemnly.

"Very well.   The crimes that will be presented to me are as follows: One count of attempted murder, one count of breach of peace, one count of riotousness, and one count of property damage.   Is there anything that I have missed?"   He said looking directly at Faisal.

Faisal shook his head.   "No sir."

Marianna understood each of the charges except for the property damage.   Was it from all the blood?   That was the only thing she could think of.

"Is it also true that you have another matter of business with me?   A writ of marriage?"   The Captain asked.

"Yes sir.   That is correct."   Faisal said respectfully.

"Are you to be the wife?"   The Captain asked looking at her.

She nodded.   "Yes sir."   She said trying to keep the same level of regard that Faisal was maintaining.

Alex turned his head to look at her.   He looked mortified.

Each of his four guards looked at Faisal with shocked expressions on their faces.

"Very well.   We will address that also. As the accuser, explain the details of wrongdoing."   The Captain said to Faisal.

"The soldier in question was brought to my establishment four days ago by some of his comrades.   They had paid for a weeks' worth of services from one of my ladies as a gift for the soldier.   He apparently had a habit of disobedience, which was causing a lot of tension and problems within his squad.   So, his comrades paid extra to ensure that the services that they had paid for, would be rendered.

"As my lady attempted to entice him, he attacked her, injuring her and chaining her to the wall.   He then attacked the guard who was assigned to protect my lady.   He managed to get the guards weapon, and sliced his throat, nearly killing him.   When some of my other guards on duty heard the commotion and came to aid, he attacked them as well.   A scuffle broke out as the guards had to wrestle him to the floor injuring him, and several of my guards in the process.

"Once he was subdued, I found a place in the house to keep him detained.   I wanted to make sure he was kept away from anybody else in the house, to remove the risk of him hurting more people.   I sent for a

Medica to first tend to the nearly fatal wound that he caused my guard, then the serious head wound that he inflicted upon my lady, and then finally to tend to the wounds the accused soldier succumbed to." Faisal said.

His eloquent explanation was so precise and to the point that it sounded rehearsed. But Marianna had spent most of her days with him, and he didn't appear to be preparing the statement that he just made.

"Very well stated." The Captain said with a tone that made it clear how impressed he was with Faisal's explanation.

"As the accused, you will have the opportunity to defend yourself. Do you refute anything that you have been accused of?" The Captain asked Alex.

Alex looked torn. And Marianna understood why. Everything that Faisal had said was true, although not in the way that he presented it. Faisal's account didn't give the reason behind why Alex did what he did. It had all the cut and dry facts, but none of the motivation.

"I did do the things that he described, but it was never my intention to hurt anybody," Alex said in a shaking voice.

He took several deep, ragged breaths and groaned as he did.   "I was just trying....to get out of there."   He said desperately between more difficult breaths.   "I didn't mean to hurt you....I'm sorry.....I was just trying to stop you."   Alex said looking at Marianna as he leaned back so that the side of his chest that had been kicked stretched out.   He wheezed.

"I know."   She said quietly.

She felt responsible for the severity of his injuries.

"Sir....the whole thing just got way out of hand."   Alex finished.

The Captain sat for several moments narrowing his eyes as he looked between Faisal, Marianna, and Alex.

"You were the lady that he injured?"   He asked speculatively.

"Yes sir."   She responded.

He looked at Faisal suspiciously.   "It was my understanding that the lady injured, was the same one whose proprietorship was granted to you, because of how unstable she was."   The Captain said.

"Yes sir.   She is the same lady."   Faisal said.

He swallowed heavily.   He was nervous

about something, but probably not enough for anybody else to pick up on it.   She knew him well enough to know when he was uneasy even when he wasn't obvious about it.

"She is your property?"   The Captain asked.

"She is."   He replied.

"The same property that he is accused of damaging?"   The Captain asked, looking at Marianna as he said it.

She was the property.   Even though she knew she was not free, even though she knew that she belonged to Faisal, to know that she was actually considered damaged property, disgusted her.

She closed her eyes and took in several deep breaths to keep herself from becoming openly emotional.   When she opened her eyes again, she saw that the Captain was still watching her.   He regarded her with a look of understanding.

Out of the corner of her eye, she could see Alex looking at her.   The pity in his expression made her want to cry, but she refused to let herself.

"And she is the one you intend to marry?" The Captain asked.

"She is," Faisal answered.

His anxiety was growing enough that it would most likely be recognized by the others in the room.   That was unusual. Faisal rarely allowed anybody to see him afraid.   What was he so worried about?

"I see."   The Captain said looking between the three of them again.

"If she is your property she has no legal rights as a person, which means she cannot enter into a legal contract.   She can either be your property, or she can be your wife.   She cannot be both.   So, what will it be?   Do you maintain your claim of ownership over her?   Or do you release her, and in so doing, declare that she is no longer too mentally unstable to be indentured to you?"   The Captain asked.

Faisal chewed on his lip breathing heavily as he considered what the Captain asked. He looked at her for several long moments and then looked back up at the Captain.   He took a deep breath, "if you allow it, I would like to..."   He looked back at her chewing on his lip some more.

"Well?"   The Captain urged.

"I willingly release my ownership of her. If you deem it acceptable."   He said with a heavy breath.

His four trusted guards looked at him with stunned expressions.   They each looked at her.   The surprise that they all wore let Marianna know just how monumental his decision was.   As she looked back up at the Captain, she saw that he also noticed the guards' reactions.   He was nodding.

"You understand that if I uphold this request if she proves to still be dangerous, you will be held liable for any crime that she commits?"   The Captain said seriously.

Faisal took in a heavy breath as he gritted his teeth.

"I understand."   He said looking threateningly down at her.   His look said, 'don't make me regret this.'

"Very well.   I grant your request to release your ownership of her."   The Captain said.   "You must be someone exceptional."   He said with a hint of awe, as he looked at her.

"She is," Faisal said.

All four guards and Alex were nodding as well.

"You've gone from a conscripted servant to a prisoner, to property, to free woman."

The Captain said with a tone of amazement.

The way he laid it out so frankly made her understand the weight of what just happened.   She was free.   She didn't belong to anyone anymore.   She didn't even know what that meant.   All she had ever known was servitude.

"So that's one bit of business taken care of. On to the more pressing issue.

"Alex Cunningham, you stand accused of multiple crimes.   Crimes that you do not deny committing.   Any evidence or witness testimony, will not be used to determine guilt or innocence, but the severity and maliciousness of the crimes, and in so doing provide me insight to allocate your punishment justly."   The Captain said.

Alex bowed his head nodding.   "I understand."

"I have already listened to the testimony from the guard that you attacked.   He is recovering very well in the Medica."   The Captain said.

"Oh, thank the Great Spirits," Alex whispered, as he breathed a sigh of relief, and then groaned as the pain of what he did must have struck him.

Faisal frowned.   He looked worried

again, but quickly wiped the proof of it from his expression.   She wasn't even sure if the Captain would have noticed it.

"I have also heard some testimony that has proposed another possible issue that must be addressed."   The Captain said looking at one of the soldiers guarding him and nodding.

The soldier nodded back and walked over to a door on the side of the room and opened it.   Rayden, Dale, Gerardo, and several more soldiers stepped into the room.

Faisal's body tensed more and more as each soldier stepped into the room, but he kept his face calm.

"So, I will now take testimony from each of you.   Due to the nature of the charges and evidence, I will be questioning each of you separately."

The anxious look on Faisal's face was no longer masked.

"Alex Cunningham, I will speak with you first.   I will speak to you next."   He said looking at Faisal.

"I will speak to each of the soldiers that witnessed any part of the events before and following the accused attack."

"And now that you are no longer

considered property, your testimony will hold as much weight as his."   The Captain said looking at Marianna kindly and then looking to Faisal with an almost arrogant expression.   Faisal set his jaw but kept his face respectful and composed.

"I will take your testimony last."   The Captain said looking back to Marianna and smiling.

"I order all who have anything to do with these proceedings to wait in the antechamber until I call upon you.

"Nobody is to leave the building, and you are not permitted to speak about this case while waiting.   Any attempt to do either will result in immediate punishment, and any testimony that you give will be rejected. Go.   Now."

Faisal was the first to stand up.   He turned to walk out of the room, followed by his guards.

"Wait."   The Captain said.

Faisal stopped and turned to face him.

"You four.   Are you here to testify?"   The Captain asked looking at each of the guards that Faisal had brought.

"No sir."   They all said.

"We came to make sure he doesn't do

anything." One of the guards said pointing to Alex.

"My men will take care of that. If you are not testifying than you can leave that way. Peter will show you where you can wait for the others." The Captain said pointing at one of the side doors.

They all hesitated and looked at Faisal. His face looked serious, but he nodded, giving them permission to leave.

Faisal turned back around and left the room carrying himself with a portrayed sense of confidence. Marianna watched as one of the soldiers followed the guards as they exited through the side door. She then followed behind Faisal, and the soldiers followed behind her. When they got back out into the antechamber, they found several soldiers posted at each door and more throughout the room. There was at least one soldier for each person.

Nobody spoke, but Rayden and his squad, blatantly stared down Faisal, as if they were trying to intimidate him. Marianna was certain that he was not intimidated at all, but he was growing more and more irritated as the time went by, although he still managed to keep it masked.

After what felt like hours Alex stepped
into the room followed closely by a soldier.
He moved carefully in obvious pain as he sat
among the group of soldiers.   The
camaraderie between the men was palpable
and enviable.   Marianna had never had that
kind of connection with anyone in her life.
They were like family.   They were trained to
fight and die for one another, and each of
them would willingly do so.

Several more minutes went by with an
uncomfortable silence as they all waited.
Eventually, a man stepped out the door.
"Faisal Hollens, the Captain requests your
presence."

Marianna laughed out loud, and then
covered her mouth apologetically.
Everybody in the room looked at her
questioningly.

"Sorry."   She said sheepishly.

"Why was that funny?"   The man who
came to retrieve Faisal asked, with an air of
suspicion.

"I've lived under you in the house for five
years.   I've been your prisoner, your
property, and your lady, and in all that time,
I never knew your surname."   She said
looking at Faisal.

"I'm sorry; it was just funny to me."   She said to the man.

She chuckled again to herself.

He nodded in understanding.   All his suspicion was gone.   He looked to Faisal and gestured for him to follow.   Faisal stood up and followed him without a word or hesitation.

CHAPTER TWENTY-SIX

Always Friends

Moments after the door closed behind them Rayden moved to sit next to Marianna.

"Are you alright?" He asked with obvious concern.

She frowned at him and nodded. "I'm fine."

He sighed in relief. "Me and the guys are trying to convince the Captain to get you away from that fucking psycho."

She frowned deeper. "What are you talking about?"

"After we saw what he did to Alex, and that horrifying room, that man needs to be stopped. I mean he has always had a terrifying reputation, but I thought that most of that was over exaggerated. You know, to make him seem like a bad-ass. Not anymore though.   Great Spirits that man is scary." He said.   His eyes widening as he spoke.

Everybody was afraid of Faisal.   And the more time she spent with him, and the more things that she learned about him, the more she understood why.   She feared him as well.   It would be foolish not to.

But she didn't want to be away from him. She didn't know any other life than the one she built with him.   He understood her, accepted her, and knew how to calm her. He taught her, relied on her, and loved her.

If she was no longer with him what kind of life could she have?

If she left him what would he do?   He almost killed her when he thought that she was revolted by him.   What would he do to her if she willingly left him?

What would he do to those who took her away from him?   When Alex accidentally hurt her, Faisal broke his ribs.   He was too dangerous for her to leave.

She shook her head in a panic at the thought of what Faisal could be truly capable of.   She didn't want to be the cause of somebody else being killed; because of his rage.

She looked back up to find Rayden watching her. He was worried about her and confused.

"You don't want to get away from him? Look at what he did to Alex." He said with seriousness, as he pointed at Alex

She did look at Alex and found that he was leaning awkwardly in the chair taking in ragged, shallow breaths. The color in his face looked off. It had a yellow hue to it, making him look sickly. She hated seeing him in such a state. Even though it had been years since she called him her friend, he didn't deserve what he was going through. And she still cared for him He didn't mean to hurt anybody. As he said to the Captain, things just got out of hand.

"What he did to her was much worse than what he did to me." Alex wheezed as he lifted his head up to look at them.

She didn't want to think about Faisal attacking her. She absently touched her neck. Rayden frowned and looked at the bruises on her throat.

"He just snapped. He didn't want to hurt me." She said staring blankly at Rayden.

He frowned at her in confusion and looked very angry. "Fuck me. You're actually defending the bastard?"

"Anna, what he did to you was disgusting," Alex said looking mortified.

"He is vile.   There is no defense for what he did."   He gasped.

"But he's going to get away with it."   He growled in frustration.

"What?"   Rayden asked exasperatedly.

Alex shook his head.   He closed his eyes and shifted his body slowly groaning as he did.

"I told the Captain everything that he did. Every disgusting thing.   But she was his property.   She wasn't legally considered a person.   And so there can be no legal repercussions to what he did to her.   He is allowed to damage his own property as much as he wants."   Alex slowly explained between agonized breaths.

"Fuck," Rayden said.

"Should we be talking about this?   The Captain said that we weren't supposed to be talking about anything."   Marianna said looking nervously at the soldiers posted throughout the room.

Rayden laughed.   "They are all with us." He said with a tone of pride.   "So, he kicked your ribs in, huh?"   Rayden asked Alex.

Alex opened one eye to look at him for a moment and then closed it again. "I blame you for this whole thing." He said.

Marianna could tell that he wasn't serious about blaming Rayden, but it was clear that Rayden felt guilty.

"How do you know how he got hurt?" She asked trying to remember if it was ever mentioned before.

"I talked to the Medica who went to that house," Rayden said as if it should have been obvious.

"Oh." She said.

"She's the one who told me about Alex being chained up in that horrifying room. The way she talked about that place, it was like she was describing a nightmare that she had. I thought that she must have been taking some of that Veruska, and had been hallucinating. She had to have been, right? I mean things like that shouldn't be real." Rayden explained. He shivered as he said the last bit.

"That was a fucked-up place," Gerardo said.

"You have no idea," Alex said solemnly.

Everybody turned to look at him with looks ranging from disgust to sadness, to guilt.

"And you live there," Dale said looking at her in shock. "Does he actually use that shit on all of you?"

She didn't know for sure who he had used it on. She didn't even know that the room existed until she saw Alex in it. They had just recently moved into the house, so it was possible that his room was as new as the house itself, but she didn't think so.

There was a room in the old house that Faisal spent a lot of time in, which nobody was allowed to go into or talk about. Marianna had never seen the inside of that room. She had known about Faisal's prized Horse contraption that he liked to use on disobedient ladies, and apparently guards as she just found out. And just the sheer number and variety of tools and weapons that he had hanging on the wall in that room, made it unlikely that he had just started the collection.

"Oh shit," Dale said studying her face.

Her silence must have made him assume the worst, which she knew was possible for others in the house.

"He is one sick bastard," Gerardo said. All the soldiers nodded in agreement.

"I am so sorry that you've had to live with that monster," Rayden said mournfully.

"It's worse than that.   She's going to marry him."   Alex said still not opening his eyes.

The disappointment and disgust that he felt about it were clear in his tone.

Rayden widened his eyes and stared at her.   "What?"   He looked just as mortified as Alex had.

"Can that even be done?"   Dale asked frowning.

"It can now.   She no longer belongs to him.   The Captain just declared it today. She's not conscripted anymore either.   And the asshole has never been conscripted.   So, yeah, it's possible."   Alex said.

"Wow."   Gerardo and Dale both said at the same time.

"You're not going to do it though, right? I mean you can't."   Rayden asked her imploringly.

She shrugged feeling embarrassed.

"He no longer owns you.   He can't make you marry him.   He can't make you stay with him.   Not anymore.   You could leave that house today if you wanted.   Shit, you could leave this town if you wanted."

Rayden said.

The thought of leaving camp hadn't realistically entered her mind in years. What would she do if she left?   What could she do?   What would Faisal do if she left? He would go on a rampage.

"I can't leave him."   She said averting her gaze.

She didn't want to see the disgust on any of their faces that she knew they would be wearing.

"Yes, you can.   He can't make you stay. He has no power over you anymore." Rayden said more insistently.

"Yes, he does.   You don't know what he's capable of.   I do.   If I left him..."   She shook her head and absently rubbed her throat again.   She looked back up.   "I can't leave him."

The pity worn on everybody's faces made her want to hide or scream, she couldn't decide which.

"We wouldn't let him do anything to you," Rayden said confidently.

She scoffed at his presumption that they could somehow protect her.   "How could you stop him?   You don't know what kind of power he has, or the resources.   And I'm not just worried about what he would do to me." She said imagining Faisal's room of torture filled to capacity with people. She shook her head again. "No, I have to stay with him."

"You're worried about us?" Gerardo asked laughing. All the other soldiers in the room laughed as well. "You don't have to worry about us. How many of his men did it take to bring down our buddy Alex over there?" He asked tilting his head at him.

Alex smirked but kept his eyes closed.

"Five," Marianna said smiling.

"That's it? Your skills are slipping man." Gerardo said shaking his head in disgrace.

Alex turned his head and opened his un-swollen eye to look at him. "I was trying not to kill anybody; asshole." He said jokingly.

Marianna chuckled.

"Why? It'd be no great loss if you got rid of a few of his goons. Running around here thinking they're better than us. When everybody knows that they are all a bunch of imposter's." Gerardo said contemptuously.

"Yeah, and now the Captain's hired them to police this place. I thought they were full of themselves before." Rayden said laughing.

"That was the worst mistake he could have made.   Give them any semblance of actual power, and they get stupid with it." Dale said.

"Yeah, look at what happened with that asshole Faisal.   He thinks he runs this place. And he's got people believing it too." Rayden said nodding at Marianna.

"Don't discount him too quickly.   He is a seriously dangerous man to fuck with.   I don't know how he's managed it, but he has a lot of pull with the officers and nobility here.   And you should have seen how the Captain spoke in there when he was around. The reverence that he showed, I didn't think the Captain even had the ability to be so respectful.   I've never seen him act that way around anybody.   It was eerie.

"And he's weaseled his way into so much of what runs this place, that unless he publicly kills someone or something major like that, I don't think he has to fear any real repercussions for anything that he does.

"I'm proof of what he can get away with if somebody screws with him," Alex said with a defeated look.   "I'm fucked."   He leaned his head back and closed his eyes again, breathing raggedly.

Rayden was shaking his head. "We don't know that."

"Yes, I do. The Captain already said that we're not here to determine guilt or innocence. He's already decided that I'm guilty. He's just figuring out how bad he's going to punish me." Alex said shifting his body and groaning as he did it.

"Shit. Why'd you have to flip the fuck out?" Gerardo said throwing his hands up exasperated. "You couldn't just take the lay. You had to act all noble."

Alex shook his head. "It wasn't like that. And I wasn't exactly thinking straight. I can thank you assholes for that."

"Yeah, well we can thank you, for keeping any of us from getting laid. Leave it to you to fuck up so bad, that you shut down the entire whore house. And just as I was getting busy too." Gerardo said.

"Yeah. I had two guys bust into my room yelling, beat it. And I'm like, what kind of horse shit is this? The whole reason that I came here was so that I don't have to beat it."

Alex laughed out and then grabbed his side groaning. The other soldiers all laughed as well.

"Ah...shit. I can't laugh like that. Uh...gah. This shit hurts." Alex said trying to stop himself from laughing.

"You know what else hurts? Realizing that the only action I'm getting is if I fuck myself." Gerardo said.

"Aww. You didn't get to hear her ask, is it in yet? Well, at least you know your ego will stay intact." Dale said with a pouty face.

Alex broke out into pained laughter again. "Ouch...Shit. Stop it."

"Serves you right you bastard. Unlike you, I have no problem getting it on with a whore. I was primed and ready to go until you had to fuck it up." Gerardo said chuckling to himself.

He looked up surprised that Marianna was sitting there. It was like he had forgotten she was in the room. "Oh, sorry."

She shrugged and shook her head. "Why?"

"You know, the whole whore thing," Gerardo said.

"What he means to say, is that he is a fucking idiot who doesn't think before he speaks," Dale said smacking Gerardo on the

513

back of his head.

Gerardo pushed him away as he moved his hand to cover where he was smacked.

Rayden just shook his head smiling as he watched the encounter.

"So, what are you going to do?" Rayden asked her.

"What do you mean?" She asked.

"Are you going to let us get you away from that monster?" His expression got serious again.

She shook her head. "I can't. I just can't."

"Why not? You have no reason to stay with him. We can help you get out of here so that he can't hurt you. You really don't have to worry about him doing anything to us. Trust me; we can handle ourselves against him and his hired help.

"You don't have to even say anything to him. You can just leave with us from here, today. If he tries to stop you here, then he will give the Captain no choice but to punish him." Rayden said.

She didn't know what to do. Everything about her life was driven by Faisal. Could she just leave him?

When she agreed to marry him, it wasn't

out of fear. She wanted to marry him. Yes, he terrified her, but he also made her happy. She loved spending time with him.

But he almost killed her just days before, because of the way that she looked at him. She didn't actually do or say anything to provoke him. He just perceived what emotion he thought she felt towards him, and brutally attacked her because of it. If she left him, and he managed to get to her, she knew that what he did to her before would be nothing compared to what he would do to her. He would be ruthless.

Rayden frowned shaking his head. "You're going to stay with him." He whispered.

"What good would it do anybody if I left him? He would know that all of you had something to do with it. And you say that you're not worried about what he can do to you, but I am.

"He has so many ways to destroy people in every way. It's his job to break us and to keep us broken. And he is an expert at knowing exactly what to do to stifle anybody that gets in the way of what he wants. In some way, he will manage to destroy you all.

"And what about the other people at the

house?   When he's with me, I make him
happy.   I calm him down and keep his
cruelty at bay.   I was just able to convince
him to give the ladies one day off a week,
and the guards too.   I know you don't like
them, but some of them aren't that bad.
And they have all been given the freedom to
do whatever they want when they are not
working.   That has never been done before.

"If I leave him, I leave them too.   And he
will take his anger out on everybody around
him.   He will hurt anybody who ever
showed me kindness or caring, just to be
vindictive.   I can't do that to them.   Not
now.   Not when things are actually starting
to change.   Life is becoming bearable, I can't
take that away from them."   She said
desperately.

She realized as she spoke just how much
she really did care about her housemates.
She felt pride for the first time when they
told her how happy they were that she
would be in charge of them.   It wasn't
because she was given a position of power.
It was because of the validation that she got
from them.   They trusted her, they wanted
her to lead them, and she wanted to watch
the house grow and succeed.   She wanted to

see the ladies happy.

Rayden stared at her silently.   His face was grave and his eyes looked remorseful.

"But what about you?"   Alex asked turning his head to look at her.

She stared at him not sure what to say.

"You've always been like that.   You worry about how something will affect everyone else, except you.   In your whole argument that you just gave there, you never even considered how that decision will affect you."   He said shifting his body to face her better.

"I'll be alright."   She said trying to sound confident.

"Really?"   He asked with a heavy amount of doubt in his tone.   "I saw what he did to you.   Remember?"   Alex said setting his jaw.

"He snapped.   That was the first time he ever did anything like that to me."   She assured.

"He snapped huh?   Because that seemed pretty calculated to me."   He said.

She shook her head.   "It couldn't have been.   When he saw me look at him with revulsion, he said he just lost it."   She argued.

Alex was shaking his head. "No. He didn't just suddenly attack you in a heated rage. He sat me up to watch. He locked my head in place so that I couldn't look away. He put you in the most observable position that he could. And then he attacked you. It's obvious that he planned the whole thing."

She didn't know what to say. Everything that he described was true. She had never considered the possibility that Faisal did what he did purposely. She believed him when he told her that he had snapped.

"He planned it." She whispered.

She shook her head over and over again staring blankly. "Why? Why did he want to do that to me?"

And then it occurred to her. She focused on Alex. "It was because of you."

Alex frowned and stared back at her. "What? Me?"

"He found out that I knew you. That we were friends. He's very possessive of me." She said. And as she thought about it more she knew that she was right.

"I defended you. I explained that you didn't mean to hurt me, or the guard. He was suspicious of that. He asked me if I knew you. He thought I was trying to hide it from him. I wasn't, it just didn't come up yet, but I know that he thought that I was.

"He said that when I entered that room, I showed you pity, but I showed him revulsion. He hurt me because I cared about what happened to you. I cared that you were hurt.

"I hated seeing you attached to that table. I hated seeing how badly you were hurt by him. I hated that you were hurt because of me. He was punishing me for caring about you. He attacked me in front of you, to hurt both of us." She said, feeling numb.

It made much more sense than the fabricated story that he told her, and she tried to convince herself to be true.

"That bastard," Rayden said balling his hands into fists. "You can't stay with him." He insisted.

She looked at him. Any sign of his usual jovial nature was gone. She could see the dangerous, well-trained soldier. He was intimidating.

She closed her eyes, trying to stop the rush of emotions that she was feeling. She was angry, upset, and betrayed. She was foolish, naive, and stupid. Her stomach

turned as she thought about everything.
She wanted to scream.   She wanted to cry.
But neither would actually help.   She knew
the truth of what Faisal had done to her, but
it didn't change how dangerous he was, it
just validated it.

She opened her eyes again.   "I can't leave
him.   He'll never let me go.   He'd never
stop looking for me.   I would never feel
safe."

"And you'd feel safe staying with him?"
Rayden asked shocked.

She shrugged.   "I don't think I will ever
feel safe.   Not really.   No matter what I do.
But at least if I am with him, I might be able
to keep him calm and keep him from hurting
me.   That was the only time that he has ever
done anything like that to me.   He promised
me that he would never hurt me again."
She said.

But he had promised that before, and it
didn't stop him.

"As long as I don't give him another
reason, I should be fine."

Alex was shaking his head.   "No.   You
won't be.   I saw him.   He may hold off for a
while; convince you to trust him again.
Nobody has a room like that unless they get

satisfaction out of torturing people.   It was clear that he enjoyed what he was doing to you.   That thrill he got, he will want it again.

"You might do something to set him off, or talk too nicely to the wrong person, or he'll just get bored one day.   And you'll suffer for it.   And next time, he might not stop. He'll kill you.   If you stay with him, eventually, he will kill you."   Alex said watching her closely for her reaction.   "And I think you know that."

She was nodding despite her internal protests that Faisal wouldn't kill her, she knew that not only was he capable of it, but he had already come close to it.

"I know.   He wanted to kill me that day. He told me that he did.   And it wasn't the first time that he wanted to kill me.   The Captain had already given him the choice to let me live or die.   He told me how exciting it was to hold my life in his hands."   She grabbed her throat again and chuckled at the irony that he literally had her life in his hands.

"He chose to let me live because he said that I was just like him."   She said.

Rayden and Alex were both shaking their

heads.

"That's horse shit.   You are nothing like him.   Nothing."   Alex said.

"I am.   I do the same thing that he does. He breaks ladies.   And I break men.   I get the same thrill when I conquer an unwilling man, as he does with the ladies.   It's like a game for me."   She said feeling disgusted with herself.

Alex looked at her with a nauseated look. He bore witness and had fallen victim to her game to conquer.

"No.   It's still horse shit.   You are doing your job in the best way that you can. You've got to find a way to live with what you must do every day.   Just because you've found a way to make it fun for yourself, doesn't mean you are anything like that piece of shit."   Rayden said reassuringly.

She wanted to believe him, but she didn't. She wrapped her arms around herself as she looked away from him, not wanting to see his encouraging face.

"He's right.   We do the same. Sometimes we have to do things that are fucked up.   We may not like everything, but we have to follow orders.   So, we shoot the shit. Joke around, dare each other to do something to make fools of ourselves, make bets to see who will do the most fucked up shit." Gerardo said encouragingly. "What you do is no different."

She smiled at him. He didn't know her, and he knew almost nothing about her. And yet it didn't matter, he was still trying to make her feel better.

"Do you use any of the shit in that room on anybody?" Dale asked seriously as he watched her closely.

She frowned shaking her head. "No. Never."

"Do you want to?" He asked with a little bit less seriousness.

"No. Great Spirits, no." She said, shivering at the thought.

He shrugged one shoulder. "See? Nothing like him."

She smiled at him too. He was right.

The door made a noise, and Rayden jumped up and quickly sat back down where he had been before. A couple of seconds later the door opened, and Faisal stepped back into the antechamber. She couldn't read his mood as he sat back down next to her. She did note how much shorter his time in the courtroom had been than Alex's. What had that meant?

The uncomfortable silence fell back through the room. The group of soldiers went back to staring Faisal down. Each of their expressions was more serious and intimidating. Was the change because of what had been discussed?

Not long after Faisal re-entered the room, the same man that had called him back opened the door.

He called each one of the soldiers into the room to speak with the Captain alone. Each of their testimonies were differing lengths. There was no way to gauge what anybody had spoke about, but every person who exited the courtroom looked more morose and they could not stop looking at Alex with pity. It was clear to Marianna that they were worried that the worst would happen to him.

Rayden was the final soldier to be called into the courtroom. He was in longer than anybody else other than Alex. When he stepped back into the room, he seemed to have difficulty looking at Alex. That seemed to be even scarier than the other men staring at him with pity.

The door guard stepped back into the room just moments after releasing Rayden to sit.

"Your turn." He said looking at her.

Her heart sped up, and her stomach flipped. She was so nervous. She didn't know what to expect. She wanted to look back at somebody for encouragement, but she stopped herself. She was so torn by how she felt towards Faisal, that she didn't want to rely on him for anything. And she didn't want to give away that she had been talking to the soldiers. She was sure that if she even glanced at them, especially if she looked to them instead of Faisal, he would know that something was wrong. She couldn't risk it, so she carried on into the room.

CHAPTER TWENTY-SEVEN

Listening to lies knowing the truth

As she was seated directly in front of the Captain, Marianna thought that he looked more relaxed somehow.

"What is your name, young lady?" The Captain asked.

"Marianna." She said. "Sir." She wasn't sure if it was necessary, but she figured that it wouldn't hurt for her to show him respect.

"Is that your actual name, or the one he gave you?" He asked knowingly.

"It's my real name." She answered.

He lifted his eyebrows in surprise.

"Faisal said that it was a pretty name, so he would let me keep it. Sir."

He nodded.

"So, Marianna, how's it feel to be a free

woman?" He asked with a smile.

She shrugged. "I don't know. I've never been free before. I don't even know what it means." She said honestly.

"It means that you don't have to live under anybody else's rule any longer. You are free to make your own decisions, and to choose your own loyalties." He said.

She nodded in understanding. She thought that he was trying to tell her more than what he had actually said. He meant that she could be loyal to Faisal or to the soldiers. Or that was what she thought that he meant, but until she was sure she didn't want to give any indication about her suspicion.

"So, I have heard a lot of testimonies about this case. All of them were close to the same story but altered just enough so that the intentions and responsibilities behind the crime is skewed. I will ask you specific questions, and I want you to answer them fully and truthfully. Do you understand?"

"Yes sir." She said nodding.

"Good. If I catch you trying to lie to me for any reason, I will have to discredit anything else that you have told me as possibly false. And you will be punished

for wasting my time.   Is that clear?"   The
magnitude of his words made his intentions
evident.

"Yes sir.   I understand."   She said
swallowing hard.

Her nervousness returned to her.

"Did Alex Cunningham hurt you?"   He
asked without pause.

"Yes, but I don't think he meant to."   She
said.

"It is my job to determine his intentions.
Just answer my questions."

"Alright."

"Did you see Alex Cunningham cut a
man's throat?"

"It was an accident, Alex was holding the
sword towards him..."

"Answer my question.   Did you see Alex
Cunningham cut the guards throat?"   He
said interrupting her.

"No."   She said feeling frustrated.

He tilted his head in question.   "I saw the
guard.   His throat was cut.   Are you saying
that somebody else cut it?"

She shook her head.   "No.   He coughed,
and the blade cut him.   Like I was saying it
was an accident."   She said defensively.

"What is your relationship with Alex

Cunningham?"   He asked quickly changing direction with his questions.

She swallowed hard.   "He was a friend of mine when I was still on the other side of the camp."

"So, you are acquainted with him?"

"Yes."

"So, you don't want your friend to be in trouble?"

"What?"   She asked.

He was trying to find a reason to discredit her.

"Until that day, I hadn't seen him in over five years.   I don't know him, not anymore. It wouldn't affect me one way or the other if he got in trouble.   I just don't want him to be in trouble for something that he didn't do."   She assured.

He narrowed his eyes, but a smirk passed on his lips for a moment.   She had gotten used to watching tiny changes in emotions since Faisal was so good at concealing his. The Captain was amused, but she didn't know what about.

"How did you end up in Faisal's possession?"

She frowned.   Shouldn't he know the answer to that?

529

"Um.   I was sent there as a punishment."

"What were you being punished for?"

"Murder.   I murdered one of the young ones that I was in charge of."   She said matter-of-factly.

His eyes widened in surprise and then narrowed again in recognition.

"No.   You can't be her.   Can you?   That girl was completely insane."   He said looking at her with more scrutiny.

She nodded.   "I was at the time yes.   I've learned to control myself since then."   She said.

"You look different."   He said eying her.

She refrained from rolling her eyes.   She didn't know why it irritated her so much. Normally she wanted to get men looking at her the way he just did, but it made her feel minimized.

"I was a child then.   I've grown up."

"Yes, you have."   He said looking at her again.   "So, it's been five years since then? I'm surprised to learn that you're still alive." He said with awe.

"I was given the chance to kill myself, but I chose not to.   And Faisal was given the chance to get rid of me if he wanted, but he found a use for me."   She said frankly.

"Yes.   Apparently, he found a personal use for you."   He said with one eyebrow raised.

"He has a personal use for all of the ladies."   She said.

"I'm sure he does."   The Captain's face grew more serious at her comment.

"Tell me of the room that Alex Cunningham was detained in.   And everything that occurred within it."

She described her experience and the room in as much detail as she could remember. She explained Faisal's attack towards her, she explained what they did on top of Alex, and she explained everything that happened and was said when the soldiers entered the room.   She finished by describing Faisal gagging Alex and rubbing his knuckles across his broken ribs.   She tried to only tell the facts of what happened, without describing or displaying any emotions.

The concern and disgust on the Captain's face increased as she spoke.   He remained silent for a long time after she finished.   He was in deep contemplation.

She recognized the differences in tone, posture, and even word use between the meeting in front of the Captain that Faisal was present for, and the one with just her. Alex was right when he said that the Captain held Faisal in high regard. Her explanation painted Faisal in a much darker light.

"What do you know about the laws here?" He asked.

She frowned at him not expecting the question, and not sure how to answer.

She shrugged. "I don't know anything about them. Except that murder is illegal." She said chuckling at herself.

He cocked his head to the side and regarded her curiously. He smirked again, but this time he left it on his face.

"As we are the military branch of the Atheran Kingdom, we fall under all of the same laws. There is a law for example that states that a person can be considered the property of somebody else. Like you were." He said.

"Alright." She said.

"If the owner injures or even kills the person that has been deemed their property, a crime has not been committed, because there is nothing illegal about destroying one's own property. Do you understand that?" He said.

She nodded. "I understand."

"So, your accusations against Faisal are not punishable." He stated watching her closely for something.

She nodded her head again.

"They weren't accusations. You wanted me to tell you everything that happened, and I did. I don't expect anything to be done about it."

He nodded watching her for a long time. She wasn't sure what he was looking for, but she was sure that he was looking for something.

"As property, the weight of your testimony would be lower than anybody else's. There is a legal hierarchy in place here. On the top is the nobility, below them the free citizens, then the officers, then the conscripted citizens, then the prisoners, and then finally the owned. Do you know what that means?" He asked doubtfully.

He seemed to think that he was describing something that was far beyond her understanding, but she followed him easily.

"Are you an officer or nobility?" She asked.

He looked at her questioningly.
"Officer." He said with curiosity.

"So, does that mean that Faisal has more

legal standing than you do?"

He looked annoyed but answered, "It does."

"Am I on the same level as Faisal now?" She asked.

He nodded. "Yes, you are." He said with growing enthusiasm.

"So, my testimony here, now, has as much weight as his does." She said.

He smiled and nodded at her. He was trying to get her to know that, but she couldn't figure out why.

"Is that why you got him to ask you to grant my freedom before we testified?"

He nodded once.

"He couldn't get in trouble for hurting me. And he knows that I'm sure. Could he get in trouble for hurting Alex?" She asked.

He bobbed his head from side to side. "Yes and no. If he would have attacked the soldier without cause, then yes absolutely, but because he was defending his people, no."

She cocked her mouth to the side.

"Can the weight of my testimony help Alex?" She asked thinking about how Alex, Rayden, and the other soldiers talked about the Captain.

They spoke of him as if he was one of them.

The Captain nodded one time again. He smiled at her. He was pleased.

"If I find that your depiction of events lines up with other testimony and evidence more than his does than your testimony will be used to determine punishment, rather than his."

He wanted to help Alex. And she was glad of it. She had thought when the Captain first questioned her that he was siding with Faisal. But he was ascertaining who her allegiances were with.

"Since I no longer belong to him, if he..." She touched her throat and frowned. "Can he still do whatever he wants to me?"

The pity on his face made her want to turn away, but she needed to know.

"No. He can't. You are not his property, and you are not conscripted to him either. You now have the same legal rights as he does." He insisted. "But that can change." He said with emphasis.

She frowned at him. "What do you mean?"

"What do you know about marriage laws?" He asked.

"I didn't even know anybody could get married here." She explained.

He looked at her speculatively.

"Surely you have seen a married couple at some point during your time here."

She shrugged.

"Only some of the nobility. I don't work with people who would want to talk about their wives."

He nodded exaggeratedly.

"That's true. Well, it's more common than you would think. And not just for the nobility. It's even being considered for those who are conscripted to be here now."

"Well that's good I guess. It gives people something to look forward to."

He nodded.

"Did you know that when you are married, legally you cannot testify against your spouse? And that the testimony of one becomes the testimony of both, giving more weight to the couples' testimony, than to an individual."

"No." She said barely louder than a whisper.

The Captain narrowed his eyes and watched her.

"When was marriage proposed to you?"

"Two days ago. After everything happened." She said slowly as she put the pieces together. Her mouth fell open, and she closed her eyes, as the truth struck her like a physical blow.

"What is it?" He asked causing her to open her eyes to look at him again.

"He did it to me again. He made me believe that it was spontaneous. But he planned the whole thing. Just like when he hurt me." She said to herself more than the Captain.

She touched her throat absently.

"It's just another way to manipulate things to benefit himself."

She felt like she was going to be sick. He had played her. Again. And she so willingly believed him. He knew just what to do and say to get what he wanted from her.

"He seems to be very good at that." He said.

She nodded. "He's an expert." She said setting her jaw.

She wanted to cry, but she wasn't going to give him that kind of power over her.

"I can't offer you retribution for anything that he has done to you, but I can offer you security.　You are now a free woman.　It is your choice, what you do from this point on. If you would like me to get you away from him safely, I will provide you with a squad of soldiers, who can escort you to the nearest town.　I will give you enough money to last you the month, after which you would be on your own to live your life as you see fit." He said with more care than she even knew was possible to be directed at her.

　She considered it.　She could be free from the house, free from Faisal, and free from her past.　But she would be alone, with no skills, and no job.

　"I appreciate your offer.　But I don't want to leave.　As crazy as it sounds, this is my home, and I think I know how I can build a real life for myself here."　She said.

　"That's commendable.　But if you stay here, I cannot offer you security from him." He insisted.

　"I understand.　Can I ask you something?"　She said.

　"Anything.　I can't assure that I will answer, but please ask."　He said.

　His curiosity was piqued.

　"You knew about the request for marriage when we first got here."　She said.

.

"I did."   He said looking at her with even more interest.

"In order to allow the contract to be valid, I couldn't be his possession, right?"   She said.

He nodded.

"So, you got him to ask you to release me, which I'm assuming is the only way that I could legally be freed.   Otherwise, you would have just done it."

He smiled and nodded again.

"Faisal would have assumed that you would have either granted the writ of marriage before the trial started, which would have given his testimony twice the weight.   Or you would have granted it after the trial, which would have given my testimony the least amount of weight. Either way, he would have a stronger testimony than everybody else.

"So, you granted my freedom, before my testimony, but you didn't grant the marriage yet.   By doing that, you gave my testimony the same weight as his, but didn't give our testimony more weight as a couple.   You're playing his own game against him, aren't you?"   She said smiling.

He stared at her in awe, chuckling a bit.

"You are a brilliant woman."

She smiled more broadly.

"Yes, you are correct. I also wanted to make sure you understood that as a free woman, you do not have to follow through with the marriage if you do not wish to." He said.

She nodded and thought about it for a moment.

"I still wish to marry him." She said with confidence.

The surprise on his face was almost comical. He was not expecting her to still make that choice.

"Are you certain. He cannot coerce you. If you tell me now, I will make sure he knows that he is to leave you alone. I can't assure your safety, but I can swear to him that if anything were to happen to you, he would be the prime suspect." He explained.

"Again, I really do appreciate your consideration for me. I've never experienced anything like it before. But I am certain about the marriage. Faisal had said that if we were married, that everything of his, would be ours. Is that true?" She asked.

"It is." He said speculatively.

"Then I definitely want to marry him still. If that is true then I will have the same resources as him. I can use those resources to gain the same kinds of influences that he has.

"With nothing at all to my name, no resources, and no freedom, I've been able to convince him to give the ladies and guards one day off a week. They have been given separate living quarters from where they work. They have the freedom to do as they wish when they are not working. I think he did all those things because of my influence on him.

"What kinds of things can I help change if I used that influence with all of his resources, on a bigger scale? Things are changing in this camp. I can see that. I would love to be a part of what makes it change for the better. I would love to be a part of what makes life more livable for everybody here." She explained with enthusiasm.

The way he looked at her was almost reverent. "You are one of a kind. You really got him to instill all those changes in the house?"

"Yes. He also made me Head Mistress. I

have the same power as he does within the house." She said.

"Really?" He said his mouth gaping. "How did you convince him to do that?"

"I don't know. He said after he saw the way that I so easily took control of everything, after the storm's destruction, he knew that I would be able to handle the job." She explained.

He looked at her with confusion, and then a new recognition. "That was you? You were the one who orchestrated the rescues and the cleanup for the whole camp? Your quick thinking and superb planning saved hundreds of lives."

She snickered. "You heard about me?"

He lifted his eyebrows. "Yes. We had a running joke about it." He said rubbing his chin.

She smiled. "What was it?"

He looked at her uncomfortably and licked his lips. "Just how funny it was that it took a whore to finally get the job done." He said.

She laughed as she thought about what he meant. Her laughter calmed his discomfort.

"I understand why everybody likes you so much. I have no doubt that you will be very influential in whatever you decide to do."

"Thank you." She said smiling brightly.

"No. Thank you. I've never met somebody so genuine. I spend most of my days here and in my other jobs, sorting through lies and manipulations. It can get exhausting. You haven't lied to me a single time today, have you?" He asked with his tone of reverence returning.

"No." She answered without hesitation.

"Hmm. One of a kind. Don't change that about yourself. Stay genuine."

She smiled. "I'll try."

"Right, we should get back to business. Is there anything else that you can think of that I may need to know before I make my final decision?" He asked.

"Just that Alex really didn't mean to hurt anybody. He wasn't in his right mind, and he just reacted. Everything got way out of control really fast." She implored.

"What do you mean, he wasn't in his right mind?" He asked suspiciously.

"When he was brought to the house, he was barely conscious. His friends gave him something so that he wouldn't fight them."

He ground his teeth. "Veruska. They all

failed to mention that."   He said sounding frustrated.

She nodded.

"I'll have to deal with that problem before it gets completely out of control."   He said with annoyance.

"Well thank you again for your honesty. It's refreshing.   I hate listening to all the lies when I already know the truth."   He said.

"Me too."   She said thinking about how much of her life was built on Faisal's lies and manipulations.

"Bring everybody back in."   He said looking at the man who had let her into the courtroom.

"I don't think you need to marry him to influence the changes that you want."   He said to her with certainty, as the man opened the door.

Everybody filed into the room, Faisal in front and then followed closely by Alex, Rayden and the rest of the soldiers. Everybody found a place to sit in front of the Captain, whose posture and bearing had returned to one of respect and dignity.   She hadn't known how relaxed he had been with her.

Faisal took a seat on one side of her and

Alex on the other. Faisal didn't like the arrangement. He glared at Alex for a moment, but Alex just smiled defiantly back at him.

Rayden and the rest of the soldiers each took spots on either side of them and in the row of seats behind them.

"I have listened to all testimony that is necessary for me to make a decision on the charges against the soldier Sergeant Alex Cunningham." The Captain said without pomp.

The smile on Alex's face was gone in an instant. He looked terrified, and Faisal looked arrogant and presumptuous. She was just nervous for Alex and hoped that Faisal's presumption was wrong.

"But before I announce my decision, there is something that needs to be addressed. The evidence that I have seen and the testimony that I have heard has brought several things to my attention. The first is that you Faisal, have been taking too many liberties when it comes to training and punishing your guards and ladies." The Captain said.

Faisal's back stiffened as his expression hardened.

"This special room of yours that I have heard about in great detail is deplorable. It is sickening to know that you would use such a place on people. As you are a private citizen, and you own the building, I cannot require you to dismantle the room. But because it is a place of business, and the ladies and guards conscripted to you are your employees, you are bound by the same laws regarding punishment as anybody else.

"There are established methods of punishment that are allowed. Public lashings are the only allowable physical punishments that are permitted any longer. Those lashings can only be assigned by me. And I only assign them when all other non-physical forms of punishment have failed.

"You are the reason for that law." The Captain said looking at Marianna.

She frowned at him. "Me?" She asked in confusion.

"Yes. I decided the day that you were brought to me following your crime. When I saw how numerous and severe your layers of beatings and lashings were, I realized how dangerous it was to continue the way we were going. You were driven to insanity and murder because you grew so desperate. I couldn't allow that to happen again.

"So, after years of fighting the politicians, my request was finally granted. Just recently in fact. You were present at that ruling. I know that because you fought against my proposition." The Captain said to Faisal whose face was stone.

Marianna remembered one of the political favors that he promised when negotiating for the house. He had agreed to drop his dispute regarding that law change. She smiled. The Captain looked back at her and nodded ever so slightly.

"Physical punishments are no longer allowed to be assigned by the employer or supervisor of conscripted individuals, except under extreme extenuating circumstances. All disagreements are to be brought to me for final ruling. I believe it was you who suggested that. You wanted to ensure that I understood the burden of such a law being in place." The Captain said to Faisal.

Faisal smiled sarcastically.

"So, you see, it was because of your influence that a good change was able to happen in this place." He said to Marianna.

She smiled.

Faisal looked down at her questioningly. She just smiled at him as well.

"So, do what you will with that room, but if you find it necessary to set up a physical punishment for one of your employees, you must bring them to me. The first offense for your disregard of the law is a hefty fine. Any offense after that and you will be imprisoned. I will be sending some of my people to regularly inspect your establishment to make sure that this law is maintained. Is that understood?" The Captain asked.

Faisal looked annoyed, but he nodded. "Yes sir."

"Good. The second thing that has been brought to my attention is the use of Veruska by this squad. Is it true that you acquired and used the drug Veruska on a fellow soldier?" The Captain asked looking at each of the soldiers.

Several of them averted their gaze.

"Yes sir." They all answered intermittently.

"I know that each and every one of you knows the law regarding that drug. I am assigning each of you to watch duty along the border for the next three months. I am also revoking a year's worth of leave time from all of you. And your pay will be docked by half for the next year. If I learn that any of you is involved in any way with Veruska again, you will be placed on border watch duty indefinitely. Do I make myself clear?" He said with an obvious intensity behind his threat.

"Yes sir." All the soldiers answered simultaneously.

"Is it true that you were under the influence of Veruska when you committed your crimes?" He asked Alex.

"Yes sir," Alex answered without hesitation.

The Captain nodded. "Very well. I find you guilty of riotousness and breach of peace. The evidence and testimony provided do not support the charges of attempted murder or damage of property so both of those charges will be dropped. You are sentenced to the same watch duty as your squad for the next three months."

The room erupted in cheers from the soldiers. Marianna couldn't help but smile as well. Faisal looked irritated but didn't say anything.

Rayden wrapped Alex in a tight embrace

causing him to shout out in pain.   Rayden
released him with an apologetic look on his
face.   Alex groaned as he sat back in his
chair, but despite his pain he still wore a
relieved smile.

"Is it still your intention to marry this
young woman."   The Captain asked Faisal
after the room calmed back down.

"It is," Faisal said.

"It is my duty to inform you that as a free
woman, you cannot be forced, coerced, or
threatened into a contract."   He said to her
with weight behind his words.

Faisal's hands balled up.   He looked
confused.   As if he didn't know why the
Captain would have told her.

"Do you wish to marry him?"

She looked at Faisal as he looked at her.
The look on his face was one she had only
ever seen a handful of times.   He was afraid,
terrified even.   His eyes were pleading.

Was it just an act?   He had made her
believe so many lies that she couldn't be
certain.   He had told her once that he didn't
feel like other people all seemed to.   He
assumed that she was just like him, but he
was wrong.   Did he know that as well?
Perhaps he wanted to believe that she was so

that he wouldn't be alone.

She studied his face. She had never seen him look so desperate. Would he be able to mimic that emotion? She was sure that he would. But as she thought about it, she didn't think that he would willingly let so many other people see him so vulnerable.

"Miss. I need a response." The Captain said.

The fear and desperation in Faisal's expression increased. He chewed on his lip as he frowned at her.

She took a deep breath and looked back at the Captain. "I do." She said confidently.

The relief on Faisal's expression that she saw at the edge of her vision made her feel queasy. He sighed and smiled.

Alex and Rayden both leaned forward to look at her with obvious expressions of bewilderment. She turned to look at them and smiled encouragingly. She wanted to let them know that she was alright, but the sorrow on each of their faces told her that they didn't think that she was. The other soldiers were either looking at her with shock over her decision or shaking their heads with looks of disappointment.

"Very well." The Captain said with no

expression.

"Do you stand witness to this bond?" He asked looking at Rayden.

Rayden shook his head slowly staring at Marianna with a look of disgust. "No. I can't."

The room fell silent.

"Alright." The Captain said with a tone that said that he was not expecting that answer.

"You then." He said looking at Gerardo who immediately shook his head with a serious expression on his face.

"No sir. I will not." He said.

The Captain frowned. "Who here will stand witness to this union?"

All the soldiers were shaking their heads in disapproval. Faisal looked around at all of them. He looked furious.

"Will nobody stand witness?" The Captain asked perplexed.

"The guards will," Marianna said calmly. "They will witness our marriage."

"Anna? Why are you doing this? Get away from him." Alex asked despairingly.

She smiled kindly at him. She reached down and grabbed Faisal's hand and interlaced her fingers with his. "I want to do this." She insisted. "I'll be alright."

"You better be." He said seriously as he looked at Faisal with a determined ferocity.

His look was dangerous, and his intention was clear. He meant to threaten Faisal without words. All the soldiers looked at Faisal with the same amount of menace.

"She will be," Faisal said tenderly as he squeezed her hand.

She looked at him and saw that he was speaking to her, not Alex. He nodded and pulled her hand up to kiss it lightly.

She smiled at him.

"I promise."

Her smile disappeared. She didn't trust his promises anymore. He frowned at her. The sadness in his eyes was clear. He glanced around at everybody in the room as he chewed on his lip.

"I'm sorry that I hurt you." He said lightly touching the bruises on her throat.

She looked away feeling embarrassed. Even though everybody knew what had happened. And she had openly talked about it to the Captain, she still felt ashamed.

He touched her chin and moved her head to look at him again.

"What I did to you is unforgivable. I

know that.   I can never make it right.   I
betrayed you.   I used your love for me as a
way to hurt you.   It was wrong.   And I will
spend every moment of every day trying to
make it up to you.   I love you."   He said.

He spoke loud enough for everybody to
hear him.   And she knew that he did that
for a reason.   He was making his apology
and affirmation public.   Was he doing it
because he was trying to show her how
much he meant what he was saying, or was
he doing it as a way to manipulate her into
believing him again?

Would she ever be able to trust him again?
Would she ever stop wondering if he was
manipulating her?   If she ever did stop
wondering she would be a fool.   He might
be genuine with what he was saying, but he
could never really be trusted entirely.

But she could live with that.   At least she
knew before marriage that he couldn't be
trusted so that she wouldn't be shocked
when he did something else to her.   Because
he would do something else to betray her.
He would break his promise in some way.
But she knew what to expect now.

"I love you too."   She said finally.

His whole body relaxed and the relief on

his face was clear.

She looked back up to the Captain who regarded her with curiosity.

"The guards that came with us.   They will bear witness."   She said.

He nodded and gestured to the soldier standing at the side door.   The man left the room and came back in a bit later with the four guards following behind.

They stopped on the edge of the room.

"Please step forward."   The Captain said to them moving his hand to indicate that they step in front of him.   They each looked at one another in confusion but did as told.

"You have been asked to bear witness to the legal binding of Faisal Hollens to Miss Marianna."   The Captain said.

One of the guards turned to look at them with a look of surprise and nervousness. They would agree to witness the marriage even if they didn't agree with it. Otherwise, they would fall victim to Faisal's wrath. She felt bad for putting them on the spot.

"Do you willingly bear witness to their marriage?"   The Captain asked.

Two of them nodded, and the other two said, "yes sir."

He nodded at each of them and then

looked back up to Faisal and Marianna. And in an unceremonious tone, he said, "I declare you husband and wife."